34134 00203095 2

D0296826

Western Isles Libraries
Leabharlainn nan Eilean Siar

Please return this item by the due date.
Items can be renewed online or by phone.

www.cne-siar.gov.uk/library   01851 822744

22 JUL 2017

24 MAR 2018

-6 JUN 2018

23 AUG 2018

25 JUL 2019

WITHDRAWN

EISLER

F90801221

SPECIAL MESSAGE TO READERS

This book is published under the auspices of

THE ULVERSCROFT FOUNDATION

(registered charity No. 264873 UK)

Established in 1972 to provide funds for research, diagnosis and treatment of eye diseases. Examples of contributions made are: —

A Children's Assessment Unit at
Moorfield's Hospital, London.

•

Twin operating theatres at the
Western Ophthalmic Hospital, London.

•

A Chair of Ophthalmology at the
Royal Australian College of Ophthalmologists.

•

The Ulverscroft Children's Eye Unit at the
Great Ormond Street Hospital For Sick Children,
London.

You can help further the work of the Foundation by making a donation or leaving a legacy. Every contribution, no matter how small, is received with gratitude. Please write for details to:

**THE ULVERSCROFT FOUNDATION,
The Green, Bradgate Road, Anstey,
Leicester LE7 7FU, England.
Telephone: (0116) 236 4325**

**In Australia write to:
THE ULVERSCROFT FOUNDATION,
c/o The Royal Australian and New Zealand
College of Ophthalmologists,
94-98 Chalmers Street, Surry Hills,
N.S.W. 2010, Australia**

Barry Eisler spent three years in a covert position with the CIA's Directorate of Operations. During his time with the Agency, he was trained in small arms, long arms, hand-to-hand combat, improvised explosive devices, small water craft, surveillance, counter-surveillance, counter-terrorism, and agent recruitment and management. After leaving the CIA he went to live and work in Japan — where he earnt his black belt in judo from the Kodokan International Judo Centre in Tokyo. He has also written the critically acclaimed John Rain thrillers *Choke Point* and *One Last Kill*. He now lives in California.

THE LAST ASSASSIN

When John Rain learns that his former lover, Midori, has been raising their child in New York, he senses an opportunity for reconciliation and a chance to get out of the killing game. But Midori is being watched by Rain's enemies, and his appearance puts mother and child in danger. To save them, Rain is forced to use the same deadly talents he had hoped to leave behind. With the help of Tatsu, his friendly nemesis in the Japanese FBI, and Dox, the ex-marine sniper, Rain races against time to flush out his enemies and eliminate them once and for all. But to finish the job, he'll need one more ally: Israeli intelligence agent Delilah, a woman who represents an altogether different kind of threat . . .

Books by Barry Eisler
Published by The House of Ulverscroft:

CHOKE POINT
ONE LAST KILL

BARRY EISLER

THE LAST ASSASSIN

Complete and Unabridged

WESTERN ISLES
LIBRARIES
P90801221
WITHDRAWN

CHARNWOOD
Leicester

First published in Great Britain in 2007 by
Michael Joseph
Penguin Books Limited, London

First Charnwood Edition
published 2007
by arrangement with
Penguin Books Limited, London

The moral right of the author has been asserted

This is a work of fiction. Names, characters, places, and incidents either are the product of the author's imagination or are used fictitiously, and any resemblance to actual persons, living or dead, businesses, companies, events, or locales is entirely coincidental.

Copyright © 2006 by Barry Eisler
All rights reserved

British Library CIP Data

Eisler, Barry
    The last assassin.—Large print ed.—
Charnwood library series
    1. Rain, John (Fictitious character)—Fiction
    2. Intelligence officers—Fiction
    3. Suspense fiction 4. Large type books
    I. Title
    813.6 [F]

    ISBN 978–1–84782–002–0

Published by
F. A. Thorpe (Publishing)
Anstey, Leicestershire

Set by Words & Graphics Ltd.
Anstey, Leicestershire
Printed and bound in Great Britain by
T. J. International Ltd., Padstow, Cornwall

This book is printed on acid-free paper

For my brother and sister, Alan and Judith

1

I've never liked doing a job in a new place. You don't know how to get in and out undetected, you don't know what tools you'll need to access the target, you don't know where you'll stick out and where you'll be able to fade into the background or disappear in a crowd.

To compensate, I start by studying the area from afar, move in only when I've learned as much as possible, and always arrive early enough to become familiar with the local terrain before it's time to act. Tactics like these have kept me alive, and even reasonably prosperous, during more than a quarter century of doing the thing I've always been best at.

But this time the preparation was reflex, not necessity. I wasn't on a job, for one thing; I was done with the life. Or almost done. There was one last thing, a big one, but I didn't want to face that just yet. Barcelona was supposed to be an interlude: pleasure, not business, and it was disturbing that some part of my mind seemed not to understand the difference.

Still, in alien circumstances, we tend to cling to habit, and so I found myself defaulting to my usual approach. I should have known better. Barcelona was unfamiliar, but the real territory I was trying to navigate isn't marked on any map.

I flew JAL from Tokyo via Amsterdam and arrived at Barcelona El Prat on a mild winter evening with nothing more than the plain carry-on bag in my hand and the cheap business suit on my back. On my feet were a pair of plain brown leather loafers, purchased in a mass market Aoyama men's store; on my nose, nonprescription steel-framed eye-glasses, calculated to obscure my features; in my pocket, a guidebook in Japanese. For my first days in the city, I would be an anonymous salaryman, recently divorced, his children grown and out of the house, seeking distraction through travel slightly more intrepid than last year's jaunt to Hawaii or Saipan. When Delilah arrived I would morph into something else.

The staff at Le Meridien hotel on Las Ramblas spoke their delightfully Catalan-accented English slowly, as my own halting, heavily Japanese-accented attempts indicated I would need. I certainly looked the part. My face is courtesy mostly of my Japanese father, and what vestiges my American mother contributed to the mix were diminished by surgery many years ago. The act came easily, too. I've had a lifetime to practice playing roles: no drama school training, true, but if you've lasted as long as I have in a business as literally cutthroat as mine, you learn a thing or two.

I was tired. Jet lag had been a nonissue in my thirties, a nuisance in my forties, and now it was more noticeable than ever. I went straight to my room, ate a room service meal, took a hot bath, and slept fitfully through the night.

I got up at dawn. I'd never been to Barcelona before, and wanted to see the city at first light, not yet on its feet, not yet wearing its makeup. I showered quickly and went out just as the sun was cresting the horizon. I scanned the street as I moved past the lobby window, then checked ambush positions from in front of the hotel. Everything looked fine.

I walked out to Las Ramblas, my breath fogging just slightly in the morning-chilled sea air, and paused. Ten meters down, three men in sanitation overalls and rubber boots were rolling up a dripping hose; the cobblestones were still slick from their work. I stood silently and didn't let them notice me. They finished with the hose, got in a truck, and drove off. When the sound of the engine had faded, it was followed only by silence, and I smiled, pleased to have the city to myself for a while.

I strolled east into the Barri Gòtic, the gothic quarter. I sensed I had arrived during a tenuous interlude between the departure of the night's last revelers and the morning's first arrivals, and I paused, enjoying the feeling that I was privy to some secret transition. I wandered for a long time, listening to my footfalls on the narrow stone streets, enjoying the aroma of fresh bread and ground coffee, watching as the area's residents gradually emerged from behind the centuries-old façades of scarred but stalwart dwellings to start another day.

After a breakfast of croissants and coffee *cortado*, I paid a visit to Ganivetería Roca, a famous cutlery store I'd read about while preparing for the trip. There, among the pewter razors and steel scissors and related items, I selected a Benchmade folder with a three-inch blade. I'd gotten used to carrying a knife in the last year or so, and no longer felt comfortable without something sharp close at hand.

Now properly outfitted, I started my customary systematic exploration of the city. I wouldn't feel at ease here until I had learned how best to blend, or how to escape, should my attempts at blending fail. So I went everywhere, that day and for the five days and nights after, at all times, by all means of transit. I absorbed the layout of the streets and alleys; the location of police stations and security cameras; the rhythms and rituals of pedestrians and tourists and shopkeepers.

But there were so many distractions: the mingled smell of tapas and shawarma among the winding alleyways of El Raval; the sounds of music and laughter echoing in the public squares of Gràcia; the feel of the sea breeze on my face and in my hair on the peaks of Montjuic and Tibidabo. I liked that the locals took for granted morning mass in six-hundred-year-old cathedrals. I liked the contrasts: gothic and modernista; mountains and sea; historical weight and exuberant esprit.

And the distractions weren't limited to the city itself. I was also suddenly aware of parents with infants. They were everywhere: walking their babies in strollers, holding them in their arms, gazing at their small faces with crippling devotion. Tatsu, my sometime nemesis and current friend in the Keisatsucho, the Japanese FBI, had warned me this would be the case, and, as in so many other matters, he had been right.

What Tatsu hadn't prepared me for, what he couldn't, were the thousand other ways his news about Midori had left me ambivalent, confused, almost in shock. I had nearly canceled with Delilah, but then decided not to. I owed her an explanation, for one thing. I still wanted to see her, wanted it a lot, for another.

I never could have predicted the affection I'd developed for Delilah, or that she seemed to have developed for me. Certainly our initial encounters were inauspicious. First there was Macau, where we learned we were working the same target. Then Bangkok and Hong Kong, where she was supposed to be working me. And yet the inherent mistrust born of working for competing intelligence organizations — Delilah, for the Mossad, and I, freelance at the time for the CIA — had paradoxically provided a stable foundation. Each of us recognized in the other a professional, an operator with an agenda, someone for whom business imperatives would always trump personal desire. All of that became the basis for respect, even mutual understanding, and ultimately provided the context for the indulgence of undeniable personal chemistry. The sex couldn't lead anywhere, we both knew it. So why not enjoy what we had, whatever it was, for as long as it lasted?

But it did last, and it deepened. We spent a month together in Rio, after which Delilah had defied her paymasters when they ordered her to set me up. Defy, hell, she had very nearly betrayed them. She had warned me what was coming, and then worked with me to straighten

5

things out. There must have been something between us, something worthwhile, if we had managed to avoid so many potentially lethal obstacles, and Barcelona was going to be the time and place to figure out what.

On the day Delilah was due to arrive, I checked out of Le Meridien and did some shopping in preparation for my transition from anonymous salaryman to the more cosmopolitan persona I think of as the real me. I bought pants, shirts, and a navy cashmere blazer at Aramis in Eixample; underwear, socks, and a few accessories at Furest on the Plaça de Catalunya; shoes at Casas in La Ribera; and a leather carrying bag to put it all in at Loewe, on the ground floor of the magnificent Casa Lleó Morera building on the Passeig de Gràcia. I paid cash for everything. When I was done, I found a restroom and changed into some of the new clothes, then caught a cab to the Hotel La Florida, where Delilah had made a reservation.

The ride from the city center took about twenty minutes, much of it up the winding road to the top of Mount Tibidabo. I had already reconnoitered the hotel and environs, of course, during my exploration of the city, but the approach was every bit as impressive the second time around. In the late afternoon sunlight, as the cab zigged and zagged its way up the steep mountain road, the city and all its possibilities appeared below me, then disappeared, then came tantalizingly back. And then vanished once again.

When the cab reached the entrance to the

hotel, seven stories of taupe-painted plaster and balconied windows overlooking Barcelona and the Mediterranean beyond, a bellhop opened the door and welcomed me. I paid the driver, looked around, and got out. I had no particular reason to think Delilah or her people wanted me dead — if I had, I never would have agreed to meet her here — but still, I stood for a moment as the cab drove away, checking likely ambush positions. There weren't many. Exclusive properties like La Florida aren't welcoming to people who seem to be waiting around without a good reason. The hotels assume the lurker is a paparazzo waiting to shoot a celebrity with a camera, not a killer possessed of rather more lethal means and intent, but the result is the same: inhospitable terrain, which today would work in my favor.

The bellhop stood by, holding my bag with quiet professionalism. The grounds were impressive, and he must have been accustomed to guests pausing to enjoy the moment of their arrival. When I was satisfied, I nodded and followed him inside.

The lobby was bright yet intimate, all limestone and walnut and glass. There was only one small sitting area, currently unoccupied. It seemed I had no company. My alertness stayed high, but the tension I felt dropped a notch.

A pretty woman in a chic business suit came over with a glass of sparkling water and inquired after my journey. I told her it had been fine.

'And your name, sir?' she asked, in lightly Catalan-accented English.

'Ken,' I replied, giving her the name I had told Delilah I would be traveling under. 'John Ken.'

'Of course, Mr Ken, we've been expecting you. Your other party has already checked in.' She nodded to a young man behind the counter, who came around and handed her a key. 'We have you in room three-oh-nine — my favorite in the hotel, if I may say so, because of the views. I think you'll enjoy it.'

'I'm sure I will.'

'May I have someone assist with your bag?'

'That's all right. I'd like to wander around a little before going to the room. See a bit of the hotel. It's beautiful.'

'Thank you, sir. Please let us know if there's anything else you need.'

I nodded my thanks and moved off. For a little while, I 'wandered' around the first floor, checking everything — eclectic gift shop, low-key bar, comfortable lounge, spacious stairwells, abundant elevators — and found nothing out of place.

I took the stairs to the third floor, paused outside 309, and listened for a moment. The room within was quiet. I placed my bag and empty glass on the ground, took off my jacket, crouched, and loudly slipped the key into the lock. Nothing. I held the jacket in front of the door and opened it a crack. Still nothing. If there was a shooter in there, he was disciplined. I shot my head over and back. I saw only a short hallway and part of a room beyond. I detected no movement.

I stood up, eased the Benchmade from my

front pocket, and silently thumbed it open. 'Hello?' I called out, stepping inside.

No answer. No sound. I let the door close. It clicked audibly behind me.

'Hello?' I called out again.

Nothing.

'That's weird . . . must be the wrong room,' I muttered, loudly enough to be heard. I opened the door and let it close. To anyone hiding inside, it would sound as though I had left.

Still nothing.

I padded down the hallway, toe-heel, pausing after each step to listen. My newly purchased soft-soled Camper shoes were silent on the polished wood floor.

At the end of the hallway, I could see the entire room but for the bathroom. The closet door was open. Probably that was Delilah, knowing I would approach tactically and wanting to make it easier for me, but I wasn't sure yet.

There was a note on the bed, conspicuous in the middle of the flawless white quilt. I ignored it. If this had been my setup, I would have put the note on the bed and then nailed the target from the balcony or bathroom while he went to read it.

The glass doors to the balcony were closed, the curtains open, and I could see no one was out there. Probably Delilah again, lowering my blood pressure.

All that remained was the bathroom, and I started to relax a little. The worst part about clearing a room, especially if you have only a knife and the other guy might have a gun, is traversing the 'fatal funnel,' where the enemy has the dominant position and a clear field of fire. In this case, narrowing down the ambush points to just the bathroom reduced my vulnerability considerably.

I walked to the side of the open bathroom door. I paused and listened. All quiet. I waved the jacket in front of the door to see if it would draw fire — nothing — then burst inside. The bathroom was empty.

I let out a long breath and walked past the glass-enclosed shower to the window. The views, as promised, were stunning: the city and the sea to one side; the snowcapped peaks of the Pyrenees to the other. I looked out for a few minutes, unwinding.

I went back to the door and looked through the peep-hole. All clear. I retrieved my bag and the glass, brought them into the room, and picked up the note from the bed. It said: *I'm at the indoor pool. Come join me. — D.*

Hard to argue with that. I checked the room for weapons first, then paused for a moment, just breathing, until I felt calmer. I pocketed the note, threw my jacket over a chair, and headed out. A minute later, I entered an expansive glass-and-stone solarium with vaulted ceilings and a sparkling, stainless-steel-bottomed swimming pool.

Delilah was on her back on one of the red upholstered lounge chairs surrounding the pool. She wore a one-piece cobalt-blue bathing suit that showed off her curves perfectly. Her blond hair was tied back, and oversized sunglasses concealed her features. She looked every inch the movie star.

I glanced around. No one set off my radar. It troubled me for a moment that even now, with all we had been through, all we had shared, I still felt I had to be careful. I wondered whether I'd ever be able to completely relax with her, or with anyone. Maybe I could hope for something like that with Midori. After all, isn't that why medieval kings married off their sons and daughters, to seal blood alliances and make murder unthinkable? Wasn't it the idea that children trump everything, even the most deep-seated resentments and rivalries, that they trump even hate?

I walked closer and paused, just a few feet behind her. I wanted to see whether she might sense my presence. Delilah's antennae were as sensitive as any I've known, but on the other hand there aren't many people who can move as quietly as I can.

I waited a few seconds. She didn't notice me.

'Hey,' I said softly.

She sat up and turned toward me, then pulled off the sunglasses and broke into a gorgeous smile.

'Hey,' she said.

'I've been standing here awhile. I thought you'd notice.'

Her smile lingered. 'Maybe I was just indulging you. I know you like to feel stealthy.'

She stood up and gave me a long, tight hug. I caught a hint of the perfume she wore, a scent I've encountered nowhere else and that I will

11

always equate with her.

There were people around, but we were suddenly kissing passionately. It was always like this when we'd been apart for a while, and sometimes even when we hadn't been. There was just something about the two of us that wouldn't let us keep our hands off each other. I don't know what it was, but sometimes it was overpowering.

I had to sit down on the lounge chair before the condition she had caused attracted further attention. She laughed, knowing exactly why I had broken the embrace, and sat down next to me, her hand on my leg.

'How long have you been here?' she asked.

'I just arrived a few minutes ago.'

'Not the hotel. The city. Barcelona.'

I paused, then admitted, 'A few days.'

She shook her head. 'What a waste. I could have gotten here earlier, you know. But I knew you'd want to have a look around alone first.'

'Guess I'm getting predictable.'

'I understand. I'm just worried I'll have nothing new to show you.'

I looked into her blue eyes. 'I want you to show me everything.'

Her hand moved on my leg, playful, insistent. 'All right. Shall we start with the room?'

We hurried, but getting back to the room seemed to take a lot longer than my trip to the pool a few minutes earlier. We made it, though, and I had her out of that bathing suit before the door had closed behind us.

I kicked off my shoes and we moved into the

room, kissing again, Delilah pulling off my shirt and pants. I paused at the foot of the bed to get out of my boxers. Delilah scrambled up and reached suddenly under one of the pillows. Even though I'd checked there already, I tensed, but then saw it was only a condom. It was a measure of her own abandon that she hadn't reached more slowly — she knew my habits, and what could set me off — but also of mine, that I hadn't spotted the move in time to have done anything about it.

She lay back and I moved up on top of her, advancing between her open legs. She kissed me again and was rolling the condom onto me even as I moved inside her. For a second I thought of Midori and was glad we were being smart this time. We hadn't been, in Phuket.

We made love hard and fast. We didn't talk, talk was beside the point, it was just moans and breathing and finally a pair of sharp groans that were probably heard in the adjacent room.

As we lay side by side after, catching our breath, I realized that, for a few minutes, my nearly constant security awareness had been temporarily eclipsed by blind lust, and then by its afterglow. On the one hand, it was liberating, hell, it was life affirming to realize I could have a moment like that. But at the same time, it was worrisome. I hadn't told Delilah yet what I'd learned about Midori. I didn't know how to tell her, or when. What I did know was that I had never needed my skills as much as I would need them for what I planned to do next.

2

We spent the rest of the afternoon and evening
dozing, making love again, then dozing some
more. I remember thinking at some point it was
good Barceloneans eat so late, or we would have
missed our chance for dinner.

We finally managed to shower and get dressed,
and then had a hotel car take us to Torre d'Alta
Mar, a restaurant perched seventy-five meters
above the sea atop the Torre de Sant Sebastián,
one of three towers that serve the city's cable car
system. Delilah had made the reservation, and
once again she had chosen well. The 360-degree
views were jaw-dropping; the food, even more
so: partridge and lobster and filet mignon, all
flavored with Catalan specialties like Ganxet
beans, Guijuelo ham, and Idiazábal cheese. We
killed two bottles of cava from a local winery
called Rimarts. I'd never heard of the place, but
they knew what they were doing.

I didn't bring up anything about Midori. It
seemed too early. We'd only just gotten together,
and the meal and atmosphere were so perfect, I
didn't want to spoil any of it. Also, after all those
hours of lovemaking, I was just too confused, not
only about what I was going to do, but even
about what I wanted.

So we stayed with familiar subjects instead,
mostly work and travel. She told me she was
still on administrative leave, pending her

14

organization's completion of an inquiry into what had happened in Hong Kong, where Delilah had defied orders and helped me. They'd lost a good man there, and there were people who thought Delilah was to blame. I knew better, of course, but it wasn't as though she could call on me as a character witness.

'I don't mind,' she said. 'I'm happy to have the time off.'

I nodded. 'I was wondering how you managed to get away for this.'

She raised her glass. 'I'd say it worked out well.'

We touched glasses and drank. I said, 'How do you expect it's going to turn out?'

'I'm not even thinking about it.'

I knew her better than that and smiled sympathetically. Delilah didn't like to take shit from her supposed superiors, or from anyone.

After a moment, she shrugged. 'I'm a little worried. Not so much about whether I'm going to be reinstated or reprimanded or whatever. It's more . . . I just hate the way they use me and then judge me for doing the jobs they send me on. You'd think Al-Jib dead would trump everything else, but no.'

Al-Jib had been a terrorist, part of the A. Q. Khan network, who'd been trying to buy nuclear matériel so he could assemble a bomb. Delilah had killed him in Hong Kong, a target of opportunity, and right now that victory was probably the only thing holding the line against her organizational detractors.

'Well, they've got their priorities,' I said.

'Yeah, their little tsk tsk meetings, that's the priority. I swear, sometimes I feel like I should just tell them to go to hell.'

'I've dealt with that type, too,' I said, reaching over and taking her hand. 'Don't let them get you down.'

She smiled and squeezed my hand. 'I haven't even thought about it since I saw you. Not until we started talking about it, anyway.'

'Well, you'll have to see me more often, then,' I said, before I could think better of it.

She squeezed again and said, 'I'd like that.'

I didn't answer.

We finished after midnight and walked northwest into La Ribera. It was a weeknight, but even so El Born, one of the most ancient streets in the city and the heart of La Ribera, was hopping, with crowds spilling out from the bars lining the street and from the surrounding clubs and restaurants. We managed to get a table at a bar called La Palma. It was a beautiful old place, unpretentious, with wine barrels in the corners and sausages hanging from the ceiling. I ordered us each a shot of a 1958 Highland Park, one of the finest single malts on earth — ridiculous at 150 Euros the measure, but life is so short.

Afterward we strolled more. Delilah hooked an arm through mine and snuggled close in the chill night air. It felt so natural it almost worried me. I wondered what it would feel like to be this way all the time. Then I thought of Midori again.

We drifted south, into the Barri Gòtic, where the maze of stone streets narrowed and the crowds thinned. Soon the echoes of our footfalls, the shadowed walls of dark cathedrals and shuttered apartments, were our only companions.

A few blocks west of Via Laietana, I heard loud voices speaking in English, and as we turned a corner I saw four young men coming in our direction. From the clothes and accents, I guessed working-class British, probably football hooligans; from the volume and aggressive tone, I guessed drunk. My immediate sense was that they had struck out with the local girls in La Ribera, hadn't found any prostitutes to their liking along Las Ramblas, and were now heading back to La Ribera for another pass. My alertness ticked up a notch. I felt Delilah's hand on my arm stiffen just slightly. She was telling me she had noted the potential problem, too.

The street was narrow, almost an alley, and there wasn't much room to let them go by. I steered us to the left so I would have the inside position.

They saw us and stopped shouting. Not a good sign. Then they slowed. That was worse. And then one of them peeled off and started crowding our side of the street, with the others drifting along with him. That was unwelcome indeed.

I eased out the Benchmade and held it hidden against my open palm with my thumb. I didn't want anyone to know there was a knife in play until I decided to formally introduce them to it.

I had hoped simply to pass them, maybe absorbing a predictable shoulder check en route. But they had fanned out widely enough so that going past wasn't an option. Well, I could go through just as easily. I envisioned dropping the nearest one with *osoto-gari*, a basic but powerful judo throw, which I expected would provide an attitude adjustment sufficient for the remaining three. And if Delilah had fallen in behind me, I would have done just that. But she was close beside me, and therefore in my way. I felt her slowing, and I had to slow, too.

A paranoid notion tried to grip me: Delilah could have set this up. But I knew instantly it wasn't that. The four of them were too young, for one thing. Their vibe was too hot, too aggressive. For professionals, violence is a job. For these guys, it felt like an opportunity.

Besides, Delilah hadn't been leading me as we walked. I would have noted that, as I had noted its absence.

We all stopped and faced one another. *Here we go*, I thought.

'Lovely evening, isn't it, ladies?' said the one who had originally started drifting onto our side of the street. He was looking at me, smirking.

'You must be the leader,' I responded, my voice low and calm.

'What's that?' he said, his brow furrowing.

'You moved first, and your friends followed you. And now you're talking first. I figure that means you're the leader. Am I wrong?' I glanced behind us just to ensure no one was closing in from the other direction — all clear — then back at the other three. 'Is it one of you? Come on, who is it?'

The interview wasn't going the way they had

hoped. I wasn't cringing. I wasn't blustering. If the idiots had any sense, they would have realized that now I was interviewing them.

'Oh, it's me, all right,' the first one said, trying to recover some initiative.

I nodded as though impressed. 'That's brave of you to say.'

'Why?'

I smiled at him. The smile was in no way pleasant.

'Because now I know to kill you first,' I said.

He glanced at his friends as though reassuring himself of their continued presence, then back at me. I felt him starting to reconsider.

But one of his friends was too stupid or drunk or both to notice the position they were in. 'He's calling you a wanker, man. You going to take that?'

Fuck. 'I'm not calling anyone a wanker,' I said, my voice still calm and steady. 'I'm just saying neither of us wants to spoil the other's evening. La Ribera's like an outdoor party right now. Isn't that where you're going?'

The last question was calculated: not a command, just a reminder, a mere suggestion that could be taken with no loss of face. And I could tell from the guy's eyes that he wanted to take it. Good.

He glanced at his friends again. Unfortunately, they didn't give him what he was hoping for. He looked back at me, and I saw he had decided. Decided wrongly.

He started to move in, his arm coming up, probably for a finger jab to my chest or some other classic and stupid next-step-on-the-road-to-violence. He didn't know that I don't believe in steps. I like to get where I'm going by the shortest route possible.

But before I could move in and drop him, Delilah stepped between us. She had been so quiet, and the guy had been so focused on me, that it took him a moment to adjust. He paused and started to say something. But he never had a chance to get it out.

Delilah snapped a rising front kick directly into his balls. He made a half-grunting, half-retching sound and doubled over. Delilah moved close and stomped his instep. He grunted again and tried to shuffle back. As his forward leg straightened, Delilah swiveled and thrust a sidekick into the side of his knee. There was a sickening snap and he spilled to the ground with a shriek. I saw her measuring the distance. Then she stepped in and kicked him full-on soccer style, directly in the face. Blood shot from his nose, and he shrieked again, like a field mouse being torn apart by a falcon.

Delilah stopped and looked at the other three. There was no particular challenge in her expression, just a question: *Who wants to go next?*

They all looked wide-eyed from her to their twisting, wailing compatriot, then back again. Finally one of them stammered, 'Why, why'd you have to do that?'

If I had been feeling more talkative or even just kindly inclined, I would have explained that it was called a 'finishing move.' The idea is that, when your attackers are just bullies, not real operators, you do something so nasty, so gratuitously damaging, to one of them that the collective mindset of the rest veers from *Let's kick some ass!* to something more like *Thank God it wasn't me!* And while they're thus momentarily paralyzed with schadenfreude, you get to walk away unmolested.

All they needed now was a task to focus their scattered attention. 'You'd better get your friend to a hospital,' I suggested evenly, knowing that would help. I touched Delilah's elbow and we moved off.

We changed cabs twice on the way to the hotel. No sense making it easy for anyone to inquire about who we were or where we might have been going. We just kept our heads down and our mouths shut.

Back at La Florida, I let us into the room and locked the door behind us. The bed had been neatly turned down, the lights lowered, and the serene atmosphere was slightly surreal after what had just happened in the street. Delilah pulled off her shoes and examined them. One of them must have had blood on it, because she took it into the bathroom. I heard water run, then stop. A moment later she returned and put the shoes down together by the window. Then she sat on the bed and looked at me, her cheeks still hot and flushed.

'Sorry about that,' she said.

I shrugged. 'Makes me glad that time in Phuket was at least half-consensual. I guess I'd be limping right now if it hadn't been.'

We both laughed at that, harder than the comment really warranted, and I realized we were still giddy. The aftermath of violence is usually like that. I wondered if she recognized the signs, as I did.

When our laughter subsided, I said, 'I wouldn't have stopped to engage them, though. I would have just gone right through them, before they had a chance to get themselves worked up.'

She nodded. 'I realized afterward that's what you were thinking. But I don't have your upper-body strength. I have to play it differently. Plus, you have to admit, I can bring a certain element of surprise to the equation that you can't.'

'That's true. I guess we'll have to get used to each other.' I wasn't sure about the way that sounded, so I added, 'To the way we do things.' No, that wasn't right either. 'So we can . . . handle situations like that better.'

Her eyes softened and she smiled just slightly, and I felt she was seeing right through me. 'You think we should get used to each other?' she asked, ignoring my stupid qualifications.

I looked at her. I didn't know what to say.

'I don't think it's a bad idea,' she said, still smiling gently. 'I've been thinking about it myself.'

'You have?'

'Sure. Haven't you?'

I sat down on the bed next to her. My heart started kicking harder.

'Yeah, I've been thinking about it.'

She put her hand on my thigh and squeezed. 'Good.'

I had to tell her. And if I didn't tell her now, later it would seem like deceit.

'But just recently, right after the last time we talked, I got some . . . news.'

The pressure from her hand lessened. 'Yes?'

'Remember when we were talking at the Peninsula in Hong Kong?' I asked. My words were coming out fast, but I couldn't slow them down. 'The night you told me about Dov. I told you there was a woman, a civilian I'd screwed things up with.'

'I remember.'

'Well, it looks like, the last time I was with her, which was before I met you, we didn't . . . we weren't that careful. So it seems . . . '

'Oh, *merde* . . . '

'So it seems there's a child. A boy.'

There was a long pause. I sat there, my heart still kicking, wondering which way this was going to go.

Delilah said, 'She contacted you?'

I shook my head. 'I have a friend in Japanese intelligence. He got hold of some surveillance photos of the woman and the child, taken by my enemies. These people don't know how to find me, so they're hoping I'll reappear in the woman's life. They're watching her for that.'

'Is she in danger?'

'No. I don't think so.'

'What's her name?'

I paused, but I didn't want it to seem as if I was holding anything back. 'Midori.'

'Pretty name.'

'Yeah.'

'These people . . . they're hoping you'll hear about the child? And that hearing will make you go to Midori?'

'It looks like that, yes.'

'What are you going to do?'

'I don't know.'

'I think you do. Otherwise, you wouldn't have brought it up.'

I rubbed my temples and thought. 'I'm not even sure the child is mine. But I have to know. You can understand that, can't you?'

There was another long pause. Her hand was still on my thigh, but it felt like an afterthought now.

After a moment, she said, 'I can. But from what you've said, right now, Midori and the boy aren't in any danger. If you go to them, you might put them in danger, and yourself, too.' She paused, then added, 'But you know that.'

'Yeah.'

She took her hand off my leg. 'Well, it's not as though I was expecting us to figure out our crazy situation in just a few days together. It was going to take time no matter what. So you should do what you have to.'

I looked at her. 'I'm sorry.'

She shook her head. 'It's not your fault.' Then she laughed. 'Things are never easy for us, are they?'

'Should I not have told you? We don't have much time together, and I didn't want to ruin it.'

'You didn't ruin anything. I'm glad you told

24

me. It was respectful.'

'What do we do now?'

'We enjoy the time we have together. Like always.'

But I didn't want it to be like always. I wanted it to be more than that, and so, I was beginning to understand, did she.

I wanted to tell her all that. But I didn't. I just said, 'Thank you.'

She shook her head and smiled. 'I'm going to take a bath. You want to join me?'

I looked at her, still wanting to say more, still not knowing how.

'A bath would be good,' I said.

★ ★ ★

Later, Delilah lay next to Rain in the dark. Pale light from a half-moon shone through one of the windows, and she watched him sleep in that almost spookily silent way of his. Most people would be wired all night after a run-in like the one they'd had earlier — she was — but Rain had dropped off almost immediately after they got in bed.

He could be so gentle with her when it was just the two of them that it was hard to remember what he was capable of. But she'd seen his other side before, first on Macau, then in Hong Kong, and she'd felt it surface again tonight in the Barri Gòtic. She wouldn't have told him, but she'd interceded with those drunken Brits in part because she was afraid of what Rain might do if she didn't. She'd noticed

25

him palm something from his front pocket during the confrontation, and assumed it was a knife. She'd hurt that guy badly tonight, it was true. But she was pretty sure Rain would have killed him.

Before going to bed, they'd made love again in the bath. She was glad of that, and took it as a good sign. They had a new situation to deal with, true, as it seemed they always did, but it didn't affect their fundamental chemistry. She hoped it wasn't the situations that were fueling the chemistry. She'd had affairs like that, where it was the illicitness, or the danger, or some similar thrill that kept the thing going. She didn't want that with Rain. She wanted something more stable. Something . . .

She smiled. The word that had come to her, and that she didn't want to say, was *lasting*.

She'd been aware of these feelings before meeting him here, but she hadn't fully acknowledged them. She'd been afraid to. But now that she was faced with the prospect of losing him, of another woman who'd thrown a trump card down on the table, she couldn't hide from her hopes, either.

She realized she was thinking in Hebrew, and that was strange. French was her default setting for matters of the heart. The one exception was Dov, and she realized with a pang that somewhere along the line Rain must have come to occupy a similar place in her consciousness, the place where she kept her first language, her first love, perhaps her first self.

She watched him. It was good with this man

lying next to her, it really was. It wasn't what she had with Dov, but how could it be? She had known Dov before she was formed, when she was guileless, even defenseless. When she was just a girl, in fact. That girl was long gone, so how could she expect a love like hers?

But there were elements of what she had with Rain that she hadn't had with Dov, or with anyone. She and Rain were of the same world. Each understood the other's habits and didn't judge the other's past. They recognized and accepted the weight they each carried from the things they'd done. Both knew that weight irrevocably separated them from civilian society, and at the same time brought them together like some secret sign.

On top of all of which, she couldn't deny, was some astonishing personal chemistry, and the sex that went along with it.

But she didn't think it was love, exactly. It was more like ... the possibility of love. She wondered for a moment what the difference was, or whether she would ever even know the difference, but she didn't want to think about that now.

She doubted he was seeing things clearly, and that concerned her. His tradecraft was superb, but as far as she knew he'd never before had to use it when he was this emotionally involved. He could screw up. He could get killed. And for what?

He was taking a risk in going to see Midori and the child. He'd acknowledged as much. And a man like Rain would never take a risk like that unless there was something serious he was hoping to gain from it.

She considered for a moment. What do men do when they're facing a hard decision? They defer it by trying to collect more data. Maybe that's all he was up to. But it hurt to know there was even a decision to make.

She tried always to be realistic, to keep her hopes in check. She knew she had no future in her organization. They used her for the things she was good at, but would never trust her with real power. And she'd long ago accepted that, after the things she'd done, she could never have a normal life. She could never have a family. She could never let someone get that close.

Except . . . Rain had been getting that close. Which was why what he'd told her tonight hurt. Worse than hurt. It ached in a place she couldn't describe, a place she hadn't even known was part of her.

Their reservation was for a week, but she didn't know now how long he was going to stay. She realized this could be their last time together. Even their last night.

Maybe the child wasn't his. That was possible; he'd said so. Or the woman would otherwise reject him. Or something else would happen to make this turn out the way she wanted it to.

She watched him sleep, and was surprised at how possessive she suddenly felt. And threatened. And angry.

She wasn't helpless, of course. There were things she could do to create the right outcome.

She'd gotten a little more information from

Rain in the bath. Not much — just that he was going to New York. But combined with the name he'd mentioned, and a few other details she remembered from Hong Kong, it ought to be enough. She'd be looking for a Japanese female, first name Midori, who emigrated to the U.S. from Japan in the last three years, was currently residing in New York, and who gave birth to a boy, probably in New York, in the last eighteen months. Her organization had found people before with a lot less to go on than that.

She lay there for a long time, struggling with warring impulses: hope and fear, sympathy and anger, temptation and guilt. Eventually, just before moonlight gave way to sun, she slept.

3

Delilah and I spent the rest of the week in Barcelona. My 'situation,' as I thought of it, wasn't on my mind as much as I would have expected, and its absence seemed linked to Delilah's presence, because I found myself thinking of it mostly when she was off doing something else and I was left alone. At those times I would be gripped by a vertiginous combination of excitement and dread, and I was always glad when we were together again.

Of course the news had been a surprise to her, but beyond that I couldn't tell. I didn't know what I was expecting, exactly — that she would be angry with me? Argumentative? Sullen? But she wasn't. We would get up early and stay out late and make love before napping every afternoon and we didn't discuss it again.

The only clue I had to how she might really be feeling was that she was less moody than she had been in Rio. Rio had been the first extended time we'd spent together, and it had taken me a while to get used to her periodic pouts and petulance there. But in the end I'd come to appreciate that side of her because it felt real. It told me she was comfortable with me, she wasn't acting. And now I wondered if the more consistent good cheer on display in Barcelona was deliberate, a form of overcompensation intended to obscure whatever was really going on inside her.

The morning I left, she came with me to the airport. I shouldered my bag outside security and tried to think of something to say. She looked at me, but I couldn't read her expression.

'I hope you're going to be careful,' she said, breaking the silence.

That wasn't really like her. I shrugged. 'That's not a hard promise for me to make.'

'I'm more concerned with whether you'll be able to keep it.'

'I'll keep it.'

She nodded. 'You going to call me?'

That was even less like her. 'Of course,' I said, but the truth was, my mind was already half elsewhere.

I kissed her good-bye and got into the security line. When I turned back a minute later, she was gone.

Once I was past immigration, I used a prepaid card to call my partner, Dox, from a pay phone. The burly ex-Marine sniper had provided me with his new, sterile cell-phone number via our secure electronic bulletin board. He was stateside at the moment, visiting his parents, and to contact Midori securely I would need his help.

The call snaked its way under the Atlantic and rang on his mobile somewhere on the other side. Then the irrepressible baritone rang out: 'Dox here.'

I couldn't help smiling. When he wasn't in stealth mode, Dox was the loudest sniper I'd ever known. One of the loudest people, even. But he'd also proven himself a trustworthy friend. And, apart from certain stylistic differences that sometimes drove me to distraction, a damn capable one.

'It's me,' I told him.

'Who's 'me'? I swear, if this is another one of those 'switch to our cellular service and we'll send you a free set of steak knives . . . ''

'Dox, keep it together. It's me, John.'

He laughed. 'Don't worry, partner, no one else even knows this number, so I knew it was you. Just wanted to see if I could get you to talk a little on an open line. I see you're loosening up some, and that's all to the good.'

'Yeah, well, I guess I owe that to you.'

He laughed again. 'You don't have to thank me, I know how you feel. What's on your mind? Didn't expect to hear from you so soon.'

'I've got a . . . situation I could use your help with. If you're interested.'

'This one business, or personal?'

'This one is personal. But it pays.'

'Son, if you have a personal situation you need help with, I'm not going to take your money for it. We're partners. I'll just help you, like I know you'd help me.'

I was so used to thinking in terms of me against the world that I was momentarily speechless at how much I could depend on this man.

'Thank you,' I managed to say.

'It's nothing, man. Tell me what you need.'

'How soon can you be in New York?'

'Shit, I can be there tomorrow if you need me.'

'No, take the weekend with your folks. I've got a few things to do first anyway. How about if we

32

plan to meet on Monday?'

'Monday it is.'

'And maybe you won't take money for this, but I'm not letting you go out of pocket. You tell me what you spend on travel, okay?'

'Sure, I'll just take my customary suite at the Peninsula and you can settle it directly with them.'

'That's fine. Although somewhere downtown might be more convenient.'

'Shit, man, I'm joking. Not about the Peninsula — that's an outstanding institution. About letting you pay. You shipped me your share of the proceeds from the Hong Kong operation, remember? That ought to cover my current expenses, and then some.'

In Hong Kong, Dox had walked away from a five-million-dollar payday to save my life. Afterward I'd given him the fee I'd collected for the op as a small way of saying thank you. He hadn't wanted to take it, but had finally agreed.

'All right, I'm not going to argue with you,' I said.

'Good. You can buy the beer, though. Or that fancy whiskey you like.'

I smiled. 'I'll call you Monday.'

4

I wasn't pressed for time, so I flew indirectly, which is always safer. I cleared customs at Dulles, outside Washington. The Watanabe identity I had created to get me to Brazil three years earlier was still functional, and it took me through customs without a hitch. From there, it was just a short flight to New York.

Despite my oblique approach, when I arrived at JFK, I scanned the crowd outside the arrivals area, then followed a circuitous route through the airport that would draw out any surveillance and render it visible. Arrival areas are natural choke points, typically with lots of waiting people who unintentionally offer good concealment for an ambusher, and I always go to a higher level of alertness, and engage in appropriate counter-measures, at this point when I'm traveling.

When I was confident I was alone, I went outside. I emerged to a cold and rainy New York afternoon. The sky was lead gray, and it looked like the rain might turn to wet snow any minute.

I hadn't been here in several years. My childhood was divided between Tokyo and upstate New York, and Manhattan was the first big American metropolitan center I ever saw or spent significant time in. Since then, I've been back on business any number of times, but never business like this.

The cab line wasn't long. When it was my

turn, I got in and told the driver to take me to the Ritz Carlton Battery Park. I'd made a reservation from Barcelona, but hadn't wanted to mention that over the phone when I was talking to Dox. Maybe I was loosening up a little, as he'd suggested. But some habits die hard.

I watched through the fogging windows as we drove. The cab's wipers beat relentlessly, thump-thump, thump-thump, and I heard thunder in the distance. We crossed into Manhattan, and what pedestrians there were all had their heads down in the hoods of raincoats and under the canopies of umbrellas, their shoulders hunched as though by the weight of some ominous circumstance.

I thought I was going to be excited when I arrived here, but I wasn't. Instead I felt scared.

When you live your life in danger, you're afraid a lot of the time. But you develop a system for dealing with it. You favor certain tools, you refine your tactics, and with success you come to trust both. You learn to focus more on the approach than on the destination, and that keeps the fear at bay. Gearing up calms you down.

So as we pulled up to the hotel, I tried to focus on how I would get to Midori, the kind of thing I'm comfortable with, and not on what I would do afterward, about which I had no idea.

I checked in and headed to my room on the twelfth floor. I liked what I saw: spacious layout, high ceilings, and a wall-to-wall window overlooking the Statue of Liberty and New York Harbor. Somehow the location felt right:

Manhattan, yes, but at a safe distance, literally the water's edge, not the tangled inland terrain where I might easily find myself confused or lost or worse. I unpacked, showered, and called housekeeping to have my laundry picked up. Then I grabbed a hotel umbrella and headed out to do a few evening errands.

I walked north on West Street, the rain beating steadily against the umbrella. A few financial district commuters hurried past me, but the area was otherwise dark and deserted. At Vesey, I walked up a gray riser of stairs and cut east along an elevated walkway. Water dripped from the corrugated roof into puddles on the concrete. On the left, through chain mesh fencing, clusters of construction equipment lay dormant in dust and darkness. I moved to the right and paused for a moment before the metal wall like a visitor in front of a hospital curtain, then looked down through a gap. Below me, frozen in the glow of sodium arc lamps as unflinching as those of any coroner's examination room, was the enormous hole where the towers had burned. At first glance, it was just a large construction site, much like any other. And yet the air was undeniably heavy with the enormity of what had produced this amputated place and the contorted walk-ways around and above it. The debris had been cleared, the equipment positioned, the lights turned on . . . and then, it seemed, some odd rigor had taken hold. The dead had been carted away but the land had yet to be resettled, and so the area felt sad and pernicious, a purgatory, an inbetween. I looked around and noticed other people who had similarly paused to observe the strange urban absence, and realized the mood of the site was infectious. I moved on.

I kept walking until I reached Tribeca, where the lights and laughter from restaurants and clubs pulled me from the pall that had gripped me farther south. I started to think operationally. The first item I needed was a mobile phone. Ordinarily I eschew mobiles. I've never liked the idea of carrying something that's quietly tracking and in fact broadcasting my location — especially after revelations about the NSA's post-9/11 eavesdropping program — and I prefer to rely on electronic bulletin boards and, when necessary, random pay phones. But now I needed something I could use to communicate quickly with Dox. Well, a prepaid mobile ought to be secure enough for the short time I'd be using it.

I would have preferred to purchase a unit without identifying myself, but governments all over the world, including Uncle Sam, are cracking down on the anonymous purchase of prepaid cell phones because terrorists seem to like them. Still, using the Watanabe ID, I was able to pick up a pair of slim Nokias with five hundred prepaid minutes apiece at a Cingular store in Chinatown, along with two sets of wireless earpieces.

Next on my shopping list was a folding knife. I'd left the Benchmade behind in Barcelona because to get it on the plane I would have had to check a bag, which I prefer not to do. Finding a replacement in New York, however, was tricky. The local laws governing concealed knives are so stringent that I couldn't find a store that sold anything other than the small Swiss Army variety. I had just about decided to rig up a kitchen knife in a shoulder harness when I came across the right kind of street vendor, a bald black man of indeterminate age with a megawatt smile and secrets in his eyes, who sold me a Strider folder with a four-inch recurve blade.

Next I stopped in an army/navy store and found a gray windbreaker that would be so anonymous in the city as to make me invisible. I also grabbed a plain black umbrella and dumped the blue logo-sporting Ritz Carlton model in a cluttered corner of the store. A navy baseball cap and a navy shoulder pack completed the ensemble, and, thus properly provisioned, I continued north. I adopted a steady gait, not too fast, not too slow, someone with business in whatever neighborhood I was moving through, a reason for being there, but nothing important enough to hurry over.

Tatsu had gotten me Midori's address, an apartment on Christopher Street in the West Village. His position, high up in the Keisatsucho, had its advantages when it came to acquiring information, even if the quid pro quo was an occasional off-the-books 'favor.' Tatsu's ends were noble, but he certainly believed they justified a wide range of means.

The last time I had seen Midori was in Tokyo, more than two years earlier. She had tracked me down to confront me over what had happened to her father, and I admitted what I had done. And somehow, in the midst of it all, her grief and rage and confusion, we had still fallen into bed one last time. I've thought about that night a lot since then. I've replayed it, dissected it, mined it for meaning. But it always ends the same way: Midori, leaning in close from above me, shuddering as she came and whispering *I hate you* through her tears.

Well, we were going to find out how profound that sentiment really was. And how permanent.

I headed up Sixth Avenue all the way to Christopher, where I made a left. Of course I had already familiarized myself with these routes using various Internet maps, but there's never a substitute for direct experience with the local terrain. There it was, on the other side of the street, a seventeen-story building, prewar, from the look of it, with a doorman in a long coat standing under a green awning out front. In this light and these clothes, and with the umbrella held low against the weather, I wasn't worried about being spotted, and I slowed. I looked at the building and imagined where I might set up if I were the one waiting here for myself. There weren't a lot of great spots. There was no parking on this section of the street, so vehicle surveillance was out. And the restaurants and gay bars Christopher Street is known for were too far from the apartment to be useful.

There was the doorman, of course. It wasn't impossible that someone had gotten to him, bribed him to keep an eye out for the Asian man in some file photo. I filed him for later consideration.

I kept walking. The bars at the end of the

street had some people in front of them, mostly smokers, but no one who was in a position to watch Midori's building or who otherwise felt wrong to me. I noted that several of the places offered live music, and wondered if Midori had chosen the neighborhood in part because of its proximity to her nightly gigs. Probably she had. I thought about taking a look inside, just to see if anyone caused a radar ping, but as always there was a cost-benefit equation at work and this time it argued against being too thorough. Anyone who was here to watch Midori would have to do so from close by her apartment, not from within one of the neighborhood watering holes. And if there were anyone relevant in one of these places, he could as easily spot me as I could spot him. Indoors, I wouldn't have the windbreaker and umbrella to hide behind.

I zigzagged my way south. It was hard to say what it meant that I hadn't spotted anyone tonight. It could be they were focusing more on her public performances, or that she was out at the moment and they knew it. I'd have to know more before I could safely close in.

I stopped at a SoHo bistro for a quick dinner and moved on. According to her website, Midori had a four-night appearance coming up at a jazz club called Zinc Bar on the corner of Houston and La Guardia. The club took me a minute to find, even though I knew the address. It was hidden below street level at the bottom of a steep set of stairs, and the gold letters announcing its existence were only visible when you were directly in front of the place.

I walked down, went through the red curtains, paid the five-dollar cover, and moved inside.

It took a moment for my eyes to adjust to the dark, but when they had I was pleased to see that the place was exactly what I was hoping for. The room was a long rectangle with a bar to one side and tables along the other. The stage was set up at the far end. If someone were here watching Midori, Dox would have no trouble spotting him.

I hadn't planned to stay, but I liked the guy who was playing, a guitarist and vocalist named Ansel Matthews, so I ordered an eighteen-year-old Macallan, then sat listening and musing in the semidarkness. I pictured Midori playing in this very room just a few nights hence, and my heart kicked faster.

I spent the next three days walking ceaselessly through lower Manhattan, getting comfortable with the rhythms of its neighborhoods, reacquainting myself with the layout of the streets. The city felt remarkably safe these days. A few times, very late at night, I passed some rough-looking individuals, but my vibe was different without Delilah by my side, and the natives here had no trouble reading it and steering clear as a result.

On one of these excursions, on a garbage-strewn, graffiti-covered street on the Lower East Side at close to two in the morning, I passed an unmarked door just as a well-dressed couple was leaving it. I realized there was a bar or club inside, and, on uncharacteristic impulse, I pressed the buzzer on the building's façade. A moment later there was the sound of a lock releasing, and I pulled the door open. It was pitch-dark beyond, and it took me a moment to realize I was looking at a curtain. I moved past it and encountered another. I parted this one as well, and found myself standing at the far end of a quietly spectacular bar.

It was a single room, with a brick wall on one side and plaster and some sort of hammered metal on the other. There were about eight booths, lit mostly by candlelight, with a small wood and metal bar in between them. Soft music I couldn't identify but immediately liked played in the background, mingling with quiet laughter and conversation. The bartender, a pretty woman in her mid-twenties, asked if I had a reservation. I admitted I didn't, but she told me it was fine, I could have a seat at the bar anyway.

The place, I learned, was called Milk & Honey. The bartender, who introduced herself as Christi, asked me what I did, and I found I didn't want to lie to her. I told her I'd rather hear about the bar, and she and a colleague, Chad, explained that Milk & Honey existed to provide the best cocktails in Manhattan and the right atmosphere in which to enjoy them. They squeezed their own juice and prepared their own tinctures and even carved their own ice — it was that kind of place. I enjoyed myself so much that I wound up staying for three of their stunning mixes — including a caipirinha made with Pot Still rum and infused with muddled concord grapes. All were prepared with a level of care and enthusiasm I had never seen outside Japan.

42

I imagined taking Midori here, with no reason or circumstance other than our desire to be together. We'd never had that before, I realized. Initially, I'd used her for information about her father. Then I'd gone on the run with her, protecting her from the people who'd hired me to kill him. Finally, when she was safe, she'd hunted me down to confront me over her suspicions about who I was and what I had done. All of it had been so intense, we'd never had a chance to just relax, to see what it was between us.

What it was between us? I thought. *You killed her father.*

Jesus. What the hell was I thinking? I was never going to be able to take her here, here or anywhere else. This was crazy, it was never going to work.

I wanted to get out, get the next plane to anywhere and forget that Midori lived here, forget everything. What I had with Delilah was good. I was an idiot for doing anything to risk it.

But I had to see the child. I had to know.

The problem was, it wasn't just Delilah I was risking. It was much more than that, and I knew it.

But I couldn't think of the stakes now. I couldn't fully face them.

5

I called Dox Monday evening as we had discussed. He had already arrived and checked in at 60 Thompson in SoHo, and at his suggestion we met at a place called The Ear Inn, on Spring between Washington and Greenwich. It was about a half-hour walk from the Ritz and the weather was cold and crisp, so I strolled north along the river, then cut east to the restaurant. I went inside and liked what I saw: a dark, unpretentious room of wood and brick with a palpable sense of history. There was a long bar and a dozen wooden tables scattered throughout.

I looked around and there was Dox, big as a line-backer and still as the Buddha, sitting at a corner table with a view of the entrance. When he saw me, he got up, strode over, and gave me one of his bear hugs. Other than the momentary inability to breathe it induced, it felt good, I had to admit, and I found myself hugging him awkwardly back.

'Good to see you, man,' he said, slinging an arm around my shoulders. 'And in the Big Apple, of all places.'

I scanned the room and saw an odd but somehow natural mix of what I classified as teamsters and hipsters. No one was posturing, no one was using a cell phone, no one was paying us any attention. People were just enjoying themselves. No one set off my radar.

'It's good to see you, too,' I told him. 'No goatee today?'

He grinned and rubbed his chin. 'You heard Delilah, partner. When she told me in Hong Kong I had good bones, my facial hair was gone forever.'

I laughed. We walked back to his table so we could watch the room and talk more privately.

'You just fly in today?' I asked.

'Nah, I drove in. Been away a lot and wanted to spend a few days seeing the country go by. Plus there's so much security in airports these days. I hate to choose between death by paperwork on the one hand and disarmament on the other just to travel a little, you know what I mean?'

'You mean they wouldn't let you bring a rifle on the plane with you? There's no justice, Dox.'

He laughed. 'Well, there's always a work-around. Got my trusty M40A1 in the trunk, just in case. Like they say in the ads, don't leave home without it.'

We ordered burgers and Guinness stouts. While we ate, I briefed him on everything: Midori, and my role in her father's death; my last night with her in Tokyo; Tatsu's revelation about the baby; what was going on with Delilah. Everything.

'Damn, man, my first impulse is to congratulate you,' he said, when I was done. 'But you seem so ambivalent I don't know what to say.'

'How would you react?'

'Well, that's a fair question. I've had a few

scares along the way, but they all seemed to resolve themselves before I really had a chance to panic.'

'So you were on the verge of panic at the prospect, and you're giving me a hard time for being ambivalent at the reality?'

He smiled. 'Not a hard time. Just trying to be sensitive to what you're going through. Underneath this rugged exterior I'm actually a caring and compassionate man.'

'I don't know what I'm going through.'

'Well, what do you want to do?'

'I need to see her. And the baby. But with Yamaoto's people watching her . . . it's complicated.'

'What's with you and this Yamaoto again?'

'He's a politician with his fingers in everything in Japan — construction kickbacks, bribery, prostitution, narcotics, extortion, you name it. Close ties to the yakuza. In fact, he *is* yakuza. They take orders from him, not the other way around. The politics is just a hobby he can use to indulge his right-wing convictions and convince himself that all the crime is really for a noble purpose.'

He scratched his head. 'And you met Midori through him?'

'Sort of. He was the one who hired me to take out her father, although at the time I didn't even know I was on his payroll. I met Midori by a coincidence after that, and when I learned Yamaoto was gunning for her, too, I stopped him. Midori and I . . . for a while we were on the run together. It was . . . I don't know, it was just one of those crazy things that happen.'

He nodded. 'Yeah, I've had a few of those.'

'Anyway, apparently Yamaoto is still unhappy about the damage I did to him when we locked horns. It's become a grudge.'

'He's in Japan but he's got people here?'

'He's getting help from the triads. The Chinese mob has a bigger presence in New York than the yakuza.'

'Haven't those triad boys been moving into Japan, too?'

'Yeah. There's a long-running struggle in Tokyo between the yakuza and the triads there. They both want the drug and prostitution trades for themselves. Yamaoto must be ceding something to the triads in Tokyo in return for their watching Midori in New York.'

'All right, I get it. And you want me to help you identify the surveillance so you can circumvent it.'

'Exactly.'

'Well, hell, this isn't even much of a favor. When you first called, I figured it was because you wanted to send someone on a Valhalla vacation.'

'If that's all it were, I could take care of it myself.'

'Yeah, I expect you could.' He took a swallow of beer. 'You know, the surveillance doesn't really bother me. I reckon we can spot the gaps easily enough and slip you through one of them.'

'Okay, good.'

'But, have you thought about . . . you know.'

'No, what?'

He finished his beer and signaled the waitress to bring us a couple more. 'I mean, she knows you killed her old man. I expect that's a hard thing for a person to get over. It sure would be for me.'

'Well, what am I supposed to do? Just pretend I don't know there's a child?'

'No, I guess you can't do that, either. It's a complicated situation, I'll give you that.'

The waitress brought our beers and moved off.

'They've been watching her since when?' Dox asked.

'Since they learned about the baby. About a year. That's what convinced them I'd come back to her.'

He looked at me, half amused, half concerned. 'Well, looks like they might have been on to something there.'

I shrugged.

'You thought about calling her first?' he asked. 'Or sending an e-mail?'

I shook my head. 'I don't think it's a good idea.'

'You worried they're monitoring her electronically?'

'No, Tatsu told me they're not. But I don't know how she'll react to hearing from me. It's better if I do it in person.'

He nodded and drained a third from the mug. 'Well, she's a jazz pianist, right? Her schedule's public. If you wanted to get to her, that's where you'd most likely start.'

'Right. So we can expect surveillance at her

performances. But the photos Tatsu acquired weren't taken at a performance. She was at an outdoor café somewhere, with the baby. Daytime.'

'If it was daytime, my guess is they followed her from where she lives.'

'Agreed.'

'You know, sending a foot soldier to take in a public jazz performance from time to time is one thing. But if they're giving Yamaoto enough local manpower to watch Midori's apartment, too, that's a pretty big favor he must be doing them in return.'

'Told you he's got a grudge.'

'I swear, man, you've got an uncanny knack for getting people pissed at you. You ever considered charm school?'

'Yeah, it's on my to-do list.'

He paused as though considering. 'One thing we might not have thought of. Has her building got a doorman? Those boys aren't paid the best wages in the world, and . . . '

'Yeah, I've thought about that, too. There is a doorman, and it's possible someone got to him. But I think the odds of that are low. If Yamaoto had the doorman in his employ, why would he need to bother with the Chinese? We know they're costing him more than a bribed doorman.'

He nodded. 'Well, what does all this mean for you and Delilah?'

I hesitated. 'I don't know.'

'Guess you couldn't ask for her help on this one, under the circumstances.'

'Very funny.'

'If she dumps you for me, you won't be bitter, will you? She's bound to get tired of your Hamlet routine, and I can tell she's secretly in love with me.'

I looked at him, but he didn't flinch. Dox always liked to push things.

'I'll find a way to adjust,' I said.

He laughed. 'All right, I'll remember you said that. Now, what's the plan?'

'We start with the public performances. They're the easiest approach. It's where they'll be expecting me, so we'll know to expect them.'

'And who are we looking for, exactly?'

'My guess would be a lone Chinese man, age eighteen to thirty. At any given performance, you'll find only a relatively small percentage of Asians. Among them, a smaller percentage of males in the right age range. Among those, if you see a guy by himself, he's the one we want.'

'What about you?'

'I'm the one they're looking for, so I can't go in. But you can. We'll get you an escort from one of the services so you'll have a date and won't stand out.'

He grinned. 'I'm liking the sound of this more and more.'

'I'll wait outside. If we see our man, we'll follow him after the performance to learn more about who we're dealing with and what kind of coverage they're employing. We'll get you a digital camera, something that works well in low light. If you can take his picture, we can send it to Tatsu. He might be able to match it to something in a database.'

'He'll be able to recognize a lowly foot soldier?'

I shrugged. 'What Tatsu doesn't know, he always knows where to ask.'

'What about commo?'

'I don't have the gear we were using in Hong Kong, but we ought to be able to manage with cell phones and wireless earpieces. Here.' I pulled out one set of the equipment I had picked up and slid it across the table to him. 'That's a prepaid unit. Sterile, for now. I've got one like it. Just to be on the safe side, let's stay off your personal phone.'

'Yeah, I've learned my lesson there. Still, I'll have to insist on one thing.'

'What?'

'I get to choose the escort.'

'Absolutely. But I think she ought to be female this time. It'll be lower profile.'

We both laughed, remembering Dox's accidental come-on to a *katoey*, or lady-boy, in Bangkok. I planned to harass him about it as long as there was breath in my lungs.

'Yeah, poor Tiara,' he said. 'I reckon she's pining for me still. She was a near miss. 'Near miss,' you get it?'

I closed my eyes as though in pain and nodded. 'I get it,' I said.

He chuckled. 'All right, where's the first performance?'

'Zinc Bar. Just a few blocks from here. She's there four nights in a row starting tomorrow, two sets every night. I've already checked the place out and it'll work for us. We'll show up for the second set tomorrow, at midnight. I want to see what happens when she's done for the evening.'

'Sounds good.'

'Make sure you spend time learning the area first. The streets, the alleys, everything.'

'Yes, Mom.'

I looked at him, but there was just no arguing with that irrepressible grin.

We spent another hour going over the plan. When we were done, Dox went off to find an escort, and I went back to the hotel, alone.

6

At midnight the following evening, I sat in a
second-floor window seat at a place called Pegu
Club, a bar at the corner of Houston and
Wooster, kitty-corner to Zinc. I nursed the
eponymous cocktail, an admittedly tasty gin-
based infusion, snacked on some of their light
fare, and read a copy of *The Economist* so I
wouldn't look like a guy on a stakeout.

At twelve-thirty, I saw Dox emerge from the
stairway. He had the Nokia out. Mine vibrated a
moment later. I was already wearing the earpiece
and pressed the receive button after the first
buzz.

'Yeah,' I said.

'He's here,' he said. 'Just like you thought.
Chinese guy, maybe twenty or so, hundred forty,
hundred and fifty pounds. All by himself, hardly
drinking, just watching the stage. Hard-looking
kid. Hasn't tapped his foot once since the music
started.'

I could hear the band playing from inside. The
piano especially. I tried not to think about it.

'Just the one?' I asked.

'Yeah. He's alone.'

'You get his picture?'

'Three or four of them. This little Panasonic
you picked up works nicely in the dark.'

'Has he noticed you?'

'I'm in stealth mode, partner, he doesn't even

know I'm here. Plus I'm accompanied by the lovely and charming Miss Jasmine, who I met via the Internet earlier today.'

'All right, go back inside,' I said. 'Be ready to follow him out when he leaves. I want to see where he's going, whether he stays with Midori, whether there's a handoff to anyone else.'

'Roger that.' He closed the cell phone, nodded subtly in my direction, and went back inside.

Forty-five minutes later, I saw patrons leaving Zinc and realized the set was over. My phone buzzed.

'Yeah.'

'Here he comes,' Dox said. His normally booming voice was coming through just loud enough for me to hear but not, presumably, for Miss Jasmine or anyone else. 'You should see him on the stairs right now.'

'Midori's still in there?'

'Still in here, talking to a few people. Nice-looking woman, if you don't mind my saying. I love that long black Asian hair. And a hell of a piano player.'

The Chinese kid came out, walked a few yards west on Houston, and stopped to light a cigarette.

'I see him,' I said. 'Looks like he's going to enjoy a little tobacco break.'

'Someone ought to tell him that stuff'll kill you.'

Sure enough, the Chinese kid leaned back against the building behind him and stood there, smoking. I smiled. It seemed to me that the primary beneficiary of Mayor Bloomberg's indoor smoking ban, aside from the hearts and lungs of all New Yorkers, was anyone running foot surveillance and needing an excuse to hang around outside a restaurant.

'Yeah, he's not leaving,' I said. 'And as long as Midori's still in there, I don't think he's going anywhere. Stay put and let me know when she's coming out.'

'Roger that.'

I closed the phone and watched for a few minutes more. If someone else were going to pick up Midori from here, this would be the time for the Chinese kid to make a call. But he didn't take out a phone. I didn't know what Yamaoto was paying the triad for the surveillance, but it looked like he was only getting solo coverage for his money. Well, that suited me.

I paid the bill, walked downstairs, and headed out of the bar. From street level I didn't have as clear a view of Zinc, so I crossed to the north side of Houston and started strolling west. I called Dox.

'How're we doing?' I asked.

'Looks like she's getting ready to go. Saying good night to the proprietor right now.'

I passed a group of people smoking outside a bar and paused nearby, just someone polite enough to leave the bar for a cell phone call.

'Here she comes,' Dox said.

I swallowed and watched Zinc's entrance. A moment later, Midori emerged from the stairwell. She paused at the curb and looked my way. I felt my heart accelerate. But she wasn't scanning the sidewalk; she was watching the street, looking for a cab. And anyway I was keeping the smokers between us. She wouldn't have seen me.

She was wearing a waist-length black leather jacket. Her hair was as long and luxuriant as Dox had noted and as I remembered. I wished I could have been closer. I wanted to see more.

I couldn't help frowning at her innocence, though. She hadn't even looked both ways as she came out of the club, let alone checked the surveillance hot spots. If she had, she would have made the Chinese kid in a heartbeat. He was standing exactly where you'd expect.

She flagged down a cab and got in. The kid made no attempt to follow. He remained for a minute, finished his cigarette, then started heading toward my position. I went into the bar and watched from behind the glass door as he passed. It was darker inside the bar than it was on the streetlight-illuminated sidewalk without, and with the light reflecting on the glass outside I knew he wouldn't be able to see me even if he were to look. But I got a good look at him.

When he was safely past, I slipped out of the bar and fell in behind him. I knew Dox would be trailing me, per the plan.

I hung well back in case the kid turned, but he never did. He just continued southeast into Chinatown. I watched him go into a seedy-looking noodle place on Mulberry, across from Columbus Park. I crossed the street and walked past from the park side. I saw him sit at a table across from an older, heavyset Chinese man with a bald head and a boxer's nose.

I couldn't hear what the kid and the bald guy were saying, and even if I could it was probably in Chinese. But from their postures I sensed they didn't much care for each other. The kid sat slumped in his chair almost sullenly. At one point, he must have said something disrespectful, because the bald guy stood up and cuffed the kid across the head, twice. The shots didn't look too hard: more something intended to humiliate and establish dominance. After that the kid sat up straighter and the bald guy sat back down.

Dox walked past the restaurant, and I knew he was taking more pictures. The flash was off and they'd be grainy, but Tatsu had people who could enhance them. Dox returned to his position behind me and we watched for a few minutes more, but there wasn't much else to learn. I noted the name and address of the place, then we linked up outside the park and headed over to a twenty-four-hour diner, where we compared notes and planned the next night.

When we were done, Dox said, 'Assuming that's all for the night, I'd like to go back to the diner where I left the alluring Miss Jasmine. She's hot for me, I can tell.'

'Plus her meter is running,' I suggested.

He laughed. 'Yeah, and she's got the kind of meter I like to feed. See you tomorrow, amigo.'

While Dox was off getting my money's worth, I went to an Internet café to upload the photos and other information to Tatsu.

When the message and upload were done, I called Tatsu to give him a heads-up to check our bulletin board. He didn't sound good when I

57

spoke to him. His normally quiet but assured voice was raspy and he sounded like he was making an effort to talk. When I asked, he told me it was the flu.

Yeah, we were both getting older. I wanted to be done with this soon.

7

The next morning, I went to another Internet café and checked the bulletin board. There was a message waiting: the Chinese kid's name was Eddie Wong. He was a *ma jai*, a foot soldier with a New York branch of United Bamboo, the Taiwanese triad, and the noodle place on Mulberry was their headquarters. Wong was only twenty-two, but he had an extensive criminal record in his hometown of Taipei, mostly drug smuggling but also extortion. He was known to carry a Balisong, the Filipino butterfly knife, and apparently was quick to use it.

The bald guy I'd seen him talking to was Waiyee Chan, the local gang's *dai dai lo*, or leader. If the gang leader was meeting directly with a mere soldier, Tatsu suggested, the matter must be important to the leader personally. United Bamboo had been at war with the yakuza in Tokyo, but currently there was an uneasy accommodation there. Tatsu speculated that the lull was the result of United Bamboo's assistance to Yamaoto in New York in exchange for some quid pro quo in Japan, just as Dox and I had speculated earlier. He was trying to find out more.

That night, Dox and I set up as we had the previous evening. This time, when Dox called me to confirm that Wong was at Zinc again, I got up and headed to the West Village.

I was more heavily disguised than before. I had a wig sprouting from under the baseball cap, horn-rimmed glasses, and two layers of thick fleece under the windbreaker that added the appearance of twenty-five or thirty pounds. I reconnoitered the area on foot, my posture, gait, and presence maximally unobtrusive. I checked the spots I would have used to watch the apartment. I even checked the local watering holes in case Wong had a partner who was waiting in the area to pick Midori up after her performance at Zinc. Everything was clear. I parked myself in a jazz joint called 55 Club a block from her building and waited.

A half-hour later my phone buzzed. I went outside to answer it.

'Set's over,' Dox said. 'Midori just got in a cab.'

'And our friend?'

'He's staying put for the moment. Just like last night.'

'Has he used a phone?'

'No.'

'All right. Sounds like we're in business.'

'You know, I've been thinking. Just because he didn't go there last night doesn't mean he's going to do the same tonight. What if . . . '

'Look, if he hasn't followed her yet, he's not going to. Not tonight, anyway. And I've checked all the possible spots around her apartment. It's clear. This is my chance.'

'Yeah, but . . . '

'I'll be fine.'

'I'm not saying you won't. But why don't I just

swing by and have a look anyway. Can't hurt to have me around.'

'I appreciate that. But I'd rather . . . do this alone. You know?'

There was a pause. Then he sighed and said, 'It's your party, man.'

Part of me was trying to speak up, to tell me he was right, it couldn't hurt. But things felt under control. Midori would either invite me inside or send me packing. All I needed was a minute either way.

'I'll call you after,' I told him. 'I'll let you know.'

'All right. Be careful, partner.'

I closed the phone and turned it off. This was apt to be delicate and I didn't want any interruptions.

I walked partway down the street and pulled off the baseball cap and wig. I started to pocket the wig, but then imagined Midori seeing it protruding from one of my pockets and decided to toss it instead. It would have made her too suspicious, and at this point it had served its purpose. I stuffed the baseball cap in one of the windbreaker's pockets. I waited. A few minutes later, a cab approached from down the street. I started walking toward it.

The cab stopped in front of Midori's building. The door opened. I paused ten feet away on the sidewalk.

Midori got out. She thanked the driver and closed the door. The cab pulled away.

Midori looked up and saw me. She froze.

I tried to say something, but nothing came

61

out. A long moment went by.

Finally I said, 'Midori.'

She watched me. I wanted to look around, to check my surroundings. I fought the urge. She had always hated that kind of awareness. It made her distrust me.

'Why are you here?' she asked.

'You know why.'

'How did you . . . ' she started to say, then stopped. She'd probably decided it didn't really matter. Or that she didn't want to know.

'Can I come up?'

She was silent.

'Just for a minute,' I heard myself saying.

After a moment, she nodded. We went inside. Although I hadn't seen any cameras, I assumed they would have some sort of remote security in the lobby and I kept my head down. Midori said, 'Hello, Ken,' to the doorman, and we got in the elevator. She didn't look at me on the ride up. We didn't speak.

We got out on the seventeenth floor and walked down the corridor. She unlocked a door and we stepped into a nicely furnished living room. Dark wood floors, Gabbeh rugs, black-and-white photos of leafless winter trees. Comfortable-looking upholstered chair and couch. Some sort of indoor infant swing set was parked in a corner, surrounded by brightly colored toys. We took off our jackets and shoes and moved inside. I peeled off the double fleece, too. I didn't need it now and it was warm in the apartment.

A pretty brown-skinned woman emerged from

behind the door to what I assumed was a bedroom. She glanced at me, then looked at Midori.

'Everything okay, Digne?' Midori asked.

The woman nodded. 'The little angel is sleeping. I give him a big bottle before he goes to sleep.'

Her accent was Latina. I guessed El Salvador.

Midori nodded. 'Thank you. I'll see you tomorrow night?'

'Of course.' The woman picked up a coat from the couch, slipped on her shoes, and paused at the door. She smiled and said, '*Oyasumi nasai*,' with a passable Japanese accent. Good night.

Midori smiled back and said, '*Buenas noches*.'

The woman closed the door behind her.

We stood there. I heard a clock ticking on the wall.

'How . . . how old is he?' I asked, after a moment.

'Fifteen months.'

That would be about right. Almost exactly two years since our last night in Tokyo.

'I heard you call him Koichiro,' I said, remembering my conversation with Tatsu.

She nodded.

'It's a good name.'

She nodded again.

I tried to think of something that wouldn't sound banal. Nothing would come.

'You're happy?' I asked.

Still just a nod.

'Damn it, Midori, will you at least say something to me?'

'Your minute is up.'

I glanced away, then back to her. 'You don't really mean that.'

'Maybe you forgot. You killed my father.'

I imagined myself saying, *Come on, haven't we been over all that?* I decided it would be the wrong approach.

'Then why did you have the baby?' I asked.

She looked at me, her expression frozen in neutral. 'When I learned I was pregnant,' she said, 'I realized I wanted a baby. The fact that it was your baby was incidental.'

She was being so hurtful, it occurred to me that maybe it was deliberate. That she was protecting herself from something she was afraid of.

'Look, I can imagine how you feel . . . ' I started to say.

'No, you can't.'

'I've told you, I'm sorry for what happened with your father. But you know I did everything I could to make things right afterward. To carry out his wishes.'

I thought about adding, *And remember, he was dying of lung cancer anyway. At least the way I did it, he didn't suffer.*

But I had a feeling she might take that as a rationalization. And maybe it was.

'Well, you didn't do enough,' she said.

'This is punishment, then,' I said.

There was a long pause. She said, 'I don't want you in his life. Or mine.'

There it was. The very thing, the very words I'd been afraid of. Hanging in the air between us.

'What are you going to tell him?' I asked. 'That his father is dead?'

It would be a sensible enough lie. But the thought of it horrified me. Because I realized if she said it, in many ways that mattered it would actually be so.

'I haven't figured it all out,' she said.

'Well, maybe you should. Maybe you should think about what something like that would cost him.'

She laughed harshly, I supposed at my impertinence.

'Can I ask you a question?' she asked.

I nodded.

'When was the last time you killed someone?'

I tried to think of how to answer. A long moment went by.

She laughed again. 'Don't you see right there that something's wrong? How many people have to think about a question like that?'

I felt myself flush. 'You want to know the last time I killed someone? It was about a month ago. And the guy I killed was one of the worst bomb makers in the world. You know what killing him did? It saved who knows how many lives.'

'I imagine that's what all killers tell themselves.'

The anger I'd been trying to contain suddenly burst through. 'And that's what I imagine all yuppie jazz pianists tell themselves, because it makes them feel so fucking superior.'

She glared at me. *Good*, I thought. *I needed that*.

'Maybe you're right,' I said. 'Maybe my problem is rationalization. But yours is denial. You think you can live a squeaky-clean life like this one without someone else getting his hands dirty? Do you really want Koichiro to grow up in a world where no one's out there trying to cull the same kinds of people who leveled the towers just two miles south of here?'

We were silent for a moment, glaring at each other, breathing hard.

'But you're still killing people,' she said.

I closed my eyes. 'Look, I've been trying to change. To do something good. And a lot of that . . . a lot of that is because of you. And your father.'

There was another pause. She said, 'Maybe you're right, maybe what you're doing keeps children like Koichiro safe in their beds at night. But that's not what I'm talking about. I'm talking about you. The life you lead and the things you do, it would put Koichiro himself at risk. Can't you see that?'

I almost sagged under the weight of her words. After all, hadn't I needed to find the gaps in Yamaoto's surveillance just to achieve this single clumsy visit?

'I know you care about me,' she went on. 'And that, even though you haven't met him, you care about Koichiro. Why would you want to put us in danger?'

I closed my eyes and exhaled. I had no argument. She was right. I wondered what the

66

hell I'd been thinking, why I had come here.

A long, silent moment spun out.

'All right,' I said, nodding. 'Okay.'

She looked at me. I saw sympathy in her eyes and it hurt.

'Thank you,' she said.

I nodded again. 'Could I just see . . . my son?'

'I don't think . . . '

I looked at her. 'Please. Don't turn me away without that.'

After a long moment, she gestured toward the door Digne had come through earlier. She turned and I followed her.

It was a small bedroom in the corner of the building, with curtained windows on two of its walls. I saw a crib, a changing table, a rocking chair. A lamp shaped like a bunny had been turned to a low, comforting setting.

We walked over to the crib. I put my hands on the edge and looked down into it.

On the mattress, covered in a blue fleece blanket, was a little person with a dark head of hair. His eyes were shut and he had a tiny nose and I could see his chest rising and falling as he slept.

For the first time, I understood that all of this was real. This child was mine. I was his father.

I felt tears trying to surface and blinked them down. I couldn't remember the last time I'd cried and I wasn't going to start tonight, in front of Midori.

'Could I . . . would it be all right if . . . ' I started to say.

Midori looked at me, then nodded. She

reached into the crib and carefully lifted out Koichiro, still wrapped in his blue blanket. She kissed him softly on the forehead, then looked at me again. Her eyes were wide and honest and I saw that she was afraid. But she was doing this anyway. Fuck, I had to blink again.

She eased the baby into my arms and stayed close, watching. The boy let out a long sigh in his sleep and turned toward me as though searching for warmth. I looked at him and suddenly the tears were flowing down my cheeks and I couldn't stop them. I couldn't even wipe them away. All I could do was blink to clear my eyes and look at that little face until I had to blink again.

I don't know how long we stood like that. At some point Midori put her hand on my shoulder and I became aware of an ache in my jaw from the way I had been clenching it. I handed Koichiro back to her and wiped my face while she got him settled again in his crib.

We went back into the living room. Midori closed the door behind us.

I looked up at the ceiling and deliberately breathed in and out, in and out, trying to steady myself. A hundred jumbled thoughts were pinballing through my brain.

'What if . . . ' I started to say, then thought better of it.

'What?'

I looked at her. 'What if I could get out of the life? Really out of it.'

She sighed. 'I don't believe you can.'

'But what if I could.'

A long moment went by. Finally she said, 'I guess we'd have to see then.'

I wanted her to say more, but I was afraid to ask.

There was a pad of paper and a pen on the coffee table next to the couch. I walked over and wrote down my cell phone number.

'Here,' I said. 'If you ever need help, with anything, call me.'

She took the piece of paper. 'Is this a phone number?'

'Yeah. Cell phone. If I don't answer, leave a voice mail. I check it all the time.'

'Wow, a number where I can actually call you,' she said, with a small smile. 'I guess that's progress.'

I smiled back. 'Told you I could change.'

'We'll see.'

I reached out and touched her shoulder.

'Thank you,' I said.

She nodded.

I was still touching her shoulder. I realized she hadn't objected.

I moved closer, and she didn't step back.

I wrapped my arms around her and squeezed. Then, after a moment, she was squeezing me, too.

We stood like that for a while, just holding each other. I kissed her forehead, then her cheek. Then her forehead again. She smelled good, she smelled the way I remembered.

She whispered, 'Jun, don't.'

She was the only one who called me by the diminutive of Junichi, my Japanese given name.

It felt good to hear her say it.

I kissed her eyelids. Again she said, 'Don't.'

I didn't care. I didn't care about anything. I kissed her softly on the lips. She didn't kiss me back, but she didn't move away, either. I could hear her breathing.

She put a hand on my chest. I thought she was going to push me away, but she left it there. It felt warm through my shirt.

I kissed her again. This time she made a sound that was somewhere between a whimper and a reproach and suddenly seized the sides of my head with both hands. Then she was kissing me back, kissing me hard.

I put my hands on her and she pressed against me. But when I started to lift her shirt out of her jeans, she twisted away.

'Jun, stop. We have to stop.'

I nodded, breathing hard. 'Yeah,' I said.

'You need to go. Please.'

I blinked and shook my head. 'Will you call me?' I asked.

'Will you get out of the life?'

'I'll try.'

'Then you call me. When you're out.'

I couldn't ask for more than that. I walked to the door and pulled on my shoes, the fleeces, and the jacket. I nodded to her. She nodded back. Neither of us spoke.

I got the baseball cap on in the elevator and moved through the lobby with my head down. I stepped outside and checked the hot spots. All clear. I headed east. The chill air hit my face but I was barely aware of it. I felt exhausted, empty. I should have known I wasn't in the right condition to protect myself. I should have known what was going to happen next.

★ ★ ★

Midori stood and watched the door for a long time after Rain left. He was gone as suddenly as he had appeared, but his presence lingered everywhere and changed everything, from the feel of her lips and tongue to the contours of the apartment to her thoughts of the future.

How many times had she told herself she hated him, for what he did to her father, for the lies he told her afterward, for everything he was? And yet, not two minutes earlier, she had been kissing him with such abandon that she was still light-headed from it. How the hell had she summoned the will to send him away? She wished for a moment she hadn't, and the thought made her feel ashamed.

She sat on the couch, closed her eyes, and put her head in her hands. That thing he had said about what she was going to tell Koichiro about his father had stung. She had considered the issue many times, of course, but could never come up with a comfortable answer. It was easier to just defer things, to tell herself she would figure it out as Koichiro got older, but now she wasn't sure.

When she had first learned she was pregnant, she felt her body had betrayed her, as though she was a woman carrying the child of a soldier who had raped her in war. She had made an appointment at a clinic, determined to end the pregnancy immediately and never think of it again. But that same night, as she lay in bed staring at the ceiling, one hand half-consciously rubbing her belly, she thought maybe it was better not to act so hastily. It was still early. Why not sleep on it for a few nights, make up her mind more deliberately? The option to abort would still be there. It wasn't going away.

But those few nights turned into many. She thought ceaselessly about her circumstances. She loved living in New York, loved doing gigs here, loved the freedom of life away from Japan. And meeting men was easy enough. She saw the way they gazed at her while she played, many of them repeat customers, and she was aware of the nervous timbre of their voices when they approached her to thank her after a performance. She went out with a few, but none of them had interested her long-term.

At some point, she had come to understand that, in her late thirties, the chance for marriage and a family had probably passed. But that was okay. She concentrated on all the good things in her life and told herself that a husband and the rest would have interfered. But on those long sleepless nights after she learned she was pregnant, she realized she had been making a virtue of a necessity. Because her circumstances had seemed unchangeable, she had been motivated to accept them. But everything was different now.

She believed in fate, and this felt like fate to her. Yes, she knew she could choose to abort as

72

she could choose to have the baby, so how could either alternative be fate, really? But she didn't care about the logic so much. It was her intuition she listened to. And her intuition told her to have the baby.

But she felt no desire to try to contact Rain. It wasn't only because of her father. It was because of what Rain was. Then, when the baby was born, her conviction that she should never tell him only deepened. From the moment the doctor brought that tiny child from her agonized, exhausted body and she heard him cry and held him hot and slick in her arms, she knew she had to keep him from the danger Rain represented.

And now that she had Koichiro, she couldn't imagine anything other than the two of them together. Her previous life, good as it was, seemed almost a dream, and the thought that she had nearly gone through with an abortion was enough to make her feel sick, as though she had once in a moment of weakness contemplated murdering her child. She would never have thought it possible, but she defined herself as this little boy's mother more than she had defined herself as anything else before.

She stood up, went into the bedroom, and watched Koichiro sleep. She realized that all her internal protests about her feelings for Rain had been window dressing, a flimsy façade that had crumbled at his first appearance. She felt a pang of guilt, as though her own feelings for this man were a betrayal of her father. But would her father have wanted her to die leaving him no grandchildren? And would he have wanted his grandchild to grow up not knowing his father? Surely Koichiro's paternity was of small significance in comparison with these larger issues. And it was true that Rain had tried to finish her father's efforts to expose corruption in the government, that this was his way of trying to rectify, even to atone for what he had done. She felt that in some inexplicable way, her father would have appreciated what Rain had done afterward. That he might even have . . . forgiven him.

She leaned over and kissed Koichiro's forehead, then stood looking at him again. Seeing Rain holding their baby, and for the first time seeing him cry, had softened something inside her, she knew. She didn't know what she wanted, or what she would do if Rain came back. She no longer felt sure of anything. Except for this sweet child. She would do anything to protect him. Anything in the world.

8

I turned left on the sidewalk at Waverly, devoid of plan or purpose. I just wanted to walk, to keep moving.

I couldn't get the image of Koichiro's face out of my mind. He was so small, so innocent in his sleep. So helpless.

Midori had been right to keep me away. The thought that my presence could put my little son in danger horrified me.

But you can change, I told myself. *Maybe you already have. There's a way out. All you have to do is find it. For Koichiro.*

I walked. Of course I could do it. Wasn't this what I'd been looking for? What Tatsu had always told me I needed? What was it he'd said in Tokyo the last time I saw him: *You know as well as I do that you need a connection, you need something to pull you off the nihilistic path you've been treading.*

Well, maybe this was it, just as he'd contended.

I could still smell Midori, still taste her on my lips. She'd been upset when she first saw me, true, but she'd left the door open just now, no doubt about that. All I had to do was figure out the right way to walk through it. I thought of Koichiro again. God, this could really work out. It could.

When I was fifteen feet from the end of the

75

block, I heard footsteps from around the corner. I looked up and *pow*, before I could do anything about it, there was Eddie Wong, turning onto Waverly from Tenth right in front of me. And I'd thrown away that fucking wig. *Stupid. Stupid.*

If I'd been myself at that moment, I could have reacted more effectively. I would have turned my face away, retracted my antenna, passed without his even knowing.

But I wasn't myself. My body was back on the street, but my mind was still in Midori's apartment, digging out from under an avalanche of hope. Instead of looking away, for a second I stared straight at him, like a man unable to avert his eyes from the scene of a grisly accident.

He looked at me, too. And the recognition hardening on his face was undeniable. I realized he was seeing the same expression on mine.

No, I thought, *no, fuck no* . . .

Wong slowed down, his mind no doubt struggling to sort it all through. Whatever planning he had done had probably gone on the assumption that he would spot me surreptitiously, not that we would suddenly spot each other. His body was responding to his unconscious wish for more time, for a few more precious seconds to decide what to do.

I decided faster. It wasn't even a decision as such, more a reflex honed by a lifetime of killing. A reflex that had been delayed by my unaccustomed emotional state, but that now, as I recognized the threat to Midori and my child, snapped ferociously into place.

I went straight for him. As I closed the

76

distance, his right hand moved to his coat pocket, probably where he kept the Balisong he was reputed to carry.

There's value to favoring a certain weapon and to practicing with it regularly. But there's a potential downside, too: you can come to rely on it, and to try to reach for it, when you would have been better off doing something else. This is why cops are often killed by knifers with their guns half out of their holsters. The cop sees the knife coming, but is so dependent on his pistol that he fails to recognize he's not going to have time to deploy it before he's already being stabbed. If someone has the jump on you, the better tactic is to create distance or otherwise slow down the attack and then access your favored weapon so that you'll actually have a chance to use it. Otherwise, the gun in your holster might as well have been in a safe back home.

But apparently Wong didn't know all that. He reached for the Balisong, and while he was reaching for it, I reached him.

I stepped in and blasted him across the front and right side of the neck with my right forearm, in the same instant catching his right bicep with my left hand. The neck shot might shock his brachial plexus and interrupt the functioning of his right arm. The bicep grab was backup.

Wong grunted and straightened from the impact. I nailed him again with my forearm, and some of the rigidity flowed out of his body. Continuing to move in so I was facing him from his right side, I pushed his arm higher with the bicep grip and slipped my right hand to the back of his neck to arrest his backward movement. Then I yanked his head down and slammed my knee into his face. His head bounced and I kneed him in the face again. And again.

I felt his body go slack. I kicked his feet out from under him and swept him to his back. He hit the pavement hard. I raised my foot and stomped his exposed throat. His body jerked but he was already out and probably never even felt the blow that killed him.

The whole encounter had lasted less than ten seconds. I glanced around, fully tactical again. I heard footsteps coming from beyond the same corner Wong had rounded moments earlier, and coiled to kill again. But there was no need. It was Dox. I was so ready to go off on him that my body twitched from the effort of holding back.

He pulled up short at the sight of me standing over Wong's prone form. 'Holy shit,' he said.

I glanced around again. The street was deserted. A building opposite us was being renovated, and there was a dumpster in front of it.

'Give me a hand,' I said. 'Get him into that dumpster.'

'The dumpster? Why . . . '

'Goddamnit, just do it!'

Without another word, Dox grabbed one of Wong's wrists and hauled him up off his back. He stooped and swept the body up into a fireman's carry, then strode with it over to the dumpster. I went with him.

In front of the dumpster, I reached into

Wong's right jacket pocket. I felt something cold and smooth inside and pulled it out. Sure enough, it was a Balisong, with what looked like titanium handles.

'That what he was carrying?' Dox asked.

'Yeah,' I said, dropping the knife into my pocket. 'Let's get him in there.'

The top of the dumpster was about six feet up and mostly in shadow, thank God. The two of us managed to get Wong's shoulders up to the lip, then shoved him until his torso tipped inside. We lowered him by his ankles until he was hanging upside down with only the backs of his knees against the top, and then let go. He slid down and hit whatever debris was at the bottom with a low thud.

I looked around again. Still all quiet.

'Let's go,' I said. 'At this hour, I doubt anyone saw or heard anything. But I want to be sure. I'll come back in a little while.'

We started walking. 'Come back for what?' he asked.

'I can't leave the body here. It's too close to Midori's apartment, they'll know what happened.'

'Well, how are you going to move it?'

'I need to borrow your car.'

'I was afraid you were going to say that.'

'He's not bleeding much,' I said. 'I didn't stab him. I'll put something down under him, it'll be okay.'

'Yeah, but where are you going to . . . '

'I'll punch holes in him and sink him in the Hudson. But I need a way to get him there.'

79

We turned onto Sixth Avenue and were suddenly amid lights and people. The street felt normal. It was calming.

'What were you doing there, anyway?' I asked as we walked.

'The way you got off the phone, partner, I had a bad feeling. You just didn't seem like you were being your old careful self.'

'I didn't expect him there,' I said lamely. 'I thought he'd go back to the noodle shop, like he did last night.'

'He did. I watched him talk to his boss again. Looked like they had another fight. I guess the boss man told him to get his ass back out there in the cold and do what they were paying him to do, because out he went.'

'They were talking to each other the whole time, not looking at a video monitor, anything like that?'

'No, they were just talking to each other. Why, you think you got your picture taken?'

I shook my head. 'I wondered if maybe there was a hidden camera in the lobby. But even if there was, even if they had access to the feed, it doesn't sound like that's what brought Wong. Anyway, when he came upon me, I could tell he wasn't prepared.'

'There's an understatement. You know, when I saw where he was heading, I tried to call you, but I couldn't get through.'

'I turned the phone off.'

'Well, if anybody ever compiles a list of the high-water marks of human cleverness, I'm afraid that's unlikely to merit consideration.'

I didn't respond. I deserved the sarcasm, and worse. What the hell had I been thinking? I knew better. I'd always known better.

Maybe I'd been trying to behave the way Midori would want me to behave. More like a civilian. Maybe I was trying to show her, show us both, that I could do it.

The attempt had lasted for all of thirty seconds. And look what happened within that brief span.

'I'm sorry,' I said.

'That's okay. A situation like yours, it'd throw anyone off. Speaking of which, all I was going to say before was, Why go to all the trouble and risk of getting him in and out of the dumpster? I would have just left him on the ground next to it, covered him with his jacket, and pissed on him so he'd look and smell like a passed-out drunk.'

I stopped and looked at him. Why the hell hadn't I thought of that?

'You're right,' I said. 'I don't know what's wrong with me.'

'You've just got a lot on your mind, that's all.'

'And if we're using your car, who cares if he has urine all over him, anyway?'

Dox frowned. 'You know, now that I'm thinking about it, maybe the dumpster wasn't such a bad notion after all.'

We found a twenty-four-hour diner and went inside. We sat away from other people and ordered coffee. I was still too on edge to eat anything.

'Let me see what he was carrying,' Dox said.

I pulled out the knife and slid it to him under a napkin.

'Damn, son, that's a double-edge Cold Steel Arc Angel. That boy knew his hardware. You going to keep it?'

We'd been over this kind of thing in Bangkok, not with entirely satisfactory results. Dox was a trophy taker and I wasn't.

'I was going to get rid of it,' I said.

He made a face of exaggerated sadness. 'That strikes me as a shame.'

I rolled my eyes and extended a hand palm up in a 'help yourself' gesture. Dox gave me one of his irrepressible grins, rubbed the knife down with the napkin, and put it in his pocket.

'Don't forget to scrub it,' I told him. 'Alcohol, then bleach.'

'Yeah, yeah,' he said. 'Although I think your Mr Careful image might need a little polishing after tonight's outing.'

I let it go. I looked at my watch. It was just past three. The sun would be up in about three hours.

I realized that getting rid of Wong's body wouldn't buy me much time. Presumably his boss, Chan, knew where he was going tonight. Dox had seen them talking right before Wong headed to Midori's apartment. So Chan would assume that whatever happened to Wong had happened while he was watching the apartment. The place and timing in turn would implicate me. Chan would report this to Yamaoto. I didn't think Yamaoto would attack Midori and the baby directly, but he would probably do something to

82

increase the pressure on them, as a way of drawing me out. And if Midori had any hint that my sudden presence had brought Yamaoto and company back into her life, whatever hopes I harbored of being with her and with Koichiro would instantly be snuffed out.

There had to be a way out of this. There had to be.

I thought about what I knew. Chan was the gang's captain. Wong reported to Chan. It was a conservative assumption that Chan reported, directly or indirectly, to Yamaoto. That meant Chan was the link between Wong's disappearance and Yamaoto's more active involvement.

Meaning, if something were to happen to Chan, too, no one would know where or when Wong had gone missing. Hell, if I handled things right, no one would even know what had happened to Wong. In fact, they might just think . . .

'You know what?' I said, a plan starting to take shape. 'I'm going to need that Balisong after all.'

'Why?'

I wanted to tell him, but I knew if I did he'd want to help. And I'd put him at enough risk already.

'I'll fill you in later,' I said. 'But we don't have much time now. How soon can you get your car?'

He shrugged. 'I valet parked it at the hotel, and they put it in some local garage somewhere. So probably a half hour, forty-five minutes.'

'Good. Go get it, and stay mobile around East Houston. I'll call you shortly.'

He looked at me. 'What are you planning on doing, man?'

'Don't worry about it. I'll tell you after.'

'You're fixing to take out Mr Chan, aren't you?'

I sighed. 'Maybe.'

'Yeah, devious minds think alike. But that's not going to make things worse?'

'It could. But we know from having seen them together that there's some kind of bad blood between Wong and Chan. Other people must know about it, too — it wasn't as though they were doing a lot to hide it. And Wong's got a reputation for being quick to use that Balisong.'

Dox grinned. 'This one, you mean,' he said, taking it out of his pocket.

'Exactly. There's an opportunity for some strategic deception here, and I want to take advantage of it.'

'So the plan is to do Chan with Wong's knife, make it look like they had a fight. Then Wong's missing, people figure he's in hiding after what he did.'

'Exactly.'

'Crude, but effective. Are you sure you want to do this all by yourself, though? That'd be the second time tonight, and the first one didn't go all that well, if you don't mind my pointing it out.'

'Yeah, you've mentioned it. I appreciate your honesty.'

'It's one of my charm points, it's true.'

'I'm just going to take a look at that noodle place. At this hour, I don't even know if Chan

84

will still be there. Depending on what I find, we'll figure out what to do next.'

'Yeah, but . . . '

'Look, I need your car to move Wong's body regardless. So you get the car and while you're doing that, I'll just check out the restaurant.'

'You're not going to do anything without me?'

'Have I ever?'

He laughed. 'I lost sight of old Wong tonight for all of ten seconds. When I turned the corner, there he was, already dead. So no, you've never done anything without me.'

'The knife,' I reminded him.

He wrapped it in a napkin and slid it across the table.

'All right,' I said. 'Let's do it.'

9

Dox went to get his car and I caught a cab to the northern edge of Chinatown. The streets were quiet. I walked to Columbus Park and looked in the restaurant. What I saw there was classic good news/bad news. The good news was, Chan was there. The bad news was, he was playing cards with two other hard-looking Chinese men. Probably mid-level gang members.

I watched and waited, shivering in the cold. At a little before four o'clock, the men got up. Okay.

My phone buzzed. I took it out and opened it. 'Yeah.'

'Got the car and I'm in the neighborhood. What's your status?'

'Watching and waiting.'

'He in there?'

'Yeah, with two other guys. But I think they're getting ready to leave.'

'Why don't I swing by? I've got my rifle right here with me. From the park, I can reach out and touch all three.'

'No, I told you, a shooting's no good.'

'Look, man, you've got three guys to deal with there. You need some kind of backup, a plan B. You're parachuting without a reserve, partner.'

The men walked toward the door.

'They're coming out,' I said. 'So it's too late to stage something from the park, anyway. I'm going to stick with Chan. Just stay in the car, stay mobile.'

'But . . .'

I closed the phone and took out the knife. The three men reached the door.

There's a horrible intimacy to all forms of face-to-face killing. Firearms, impact weapons, bare hands . . . they all carry a cost. But a knife is the worst. Partly it's the blood. Partly it's the sounds a man makes when he's dying of knife wounds. Partly it's the almost sexual act of penetration. I know soldiers who've cut men's throats in war and who can no longer change their own engine oil as a result. It's the feel of it on their hands.

I would have done it another way if another way had existed. Christ, the thought of Dox dropping the three of them from a hundred yards out was practically seductive. But if I could just get close to Chan, alone . . .

The men came through the door. Chan turned and locked it, then pulled down a graffiti-covered corrugated metal gate and locked that, too. They all headed north on Mulberry. I paralleled them from inside the park.

At the corner of Bayard, the two men continued north. Chan went right.

I took a deep breath and let it out. *Okay.*

I emerged from the park and started closing in on Chan. I glanced left. The two men were moving away, their backs to me. I crossed Mulberry. Twenty feet. Ten.

The quickest, surest, and, from behind him, cleanest way would have been to cut his throat.

But I didn't want this to look military or otherwise professional. I wanted it to look like something a hotheaded gangbanger had done in the grip of resentment and rage.

Five feet. I moved noiselessly toe-heel on the sidewalk.

Chan stopped and started to reach into his coat pocket. I knew he hadn't heard me, so I doubted he was going for a weapon. More likely a smoke. Although at this point it made no difference either way.

I clapped my left hand over his mouth and pulled him back onto his heels. My right hand was already coming forward, the Balisong in a hammer grip. I plunged the blade in and out of his right side, again and again and again, hitting his liver probably five times in two seconds. I made sure to stay below his ribs and above his pelvis. A Balisong is at its best for slashing, not stabbing, and if I hit bone my hand might slip forward right over the blade. Then I came around under his zyphoid process and stabbed upward and to the left to lacerate his right ventricle.

I spun him around and slashed his face. He got his arms up but I didn't care, I was just trying to make the attack look personal. Then I pushed him away, and he spilled to the ground. The attack had been so sudden, and the pain likely so shocking, that he hadn't made a sound. From the wounds I had given him I knew he'd be unconscious from blood loss inside twenty seconds and dead in not much more than that. Even a paramedic team right around the corner couldn't save him now.

I continued around him, heading toward Bowery. I folded up the Balisong and dropped it in my coat pocket. It was covered in blood and so was I. Not a surprise and nothing I could do about it at the moment.

I ducked into an alley just west of Bowery, pulled out the phone, and called Dox. My hands were shaking.

He picked up instantly. 'What's going on?'

'Pick me up at Bayard and Bowery. Northwest corner.'

'Be there in less than a minute.'

'I'm a little messy.'

'Damn it, I knew you were going to do something by yourself. All right, I'll put some newspaper down.'

I looked at my clothes and thought, *Better be the Sunday fucking* Times.

'What are you driving?' I asked.

'Dodge Ram Quad Cab. Black.'

'Just slow down when you get to the corner. You won't see me at first.'

'Roger that. I'm turning on Bowery from Canal now. You should spot me in a second.'

I peeked out from the alley. There he was.

'I see you,' I said. 'I'm hanging up.'

I clicked off and walked out to Bowery. The passenger door opened and I reached it just as Dox was tossing a thick wool blanket onto the seat. We opened it enough to cover the seat and floor and I got in. Dox glanced at me and took off.

'Yeah, you are a mess,' he said. 'Good thing I

come prepared. That blanket there has seen its share of bodily fluids over the years, mine and a variety of lucky ladies', but not any blood before that I know of.'

'I'll get you one just like it. There's a Salvation Army place north of Delancey.'

He chuckled, cool as ever. 'Where to?'

'The dumpster. If it's clear, I'm going to get rid of Wong.'

'You leave the knife near Chan's body just now?'

'No. That would be too obvious. Besides, I've handled it too much. It's contaminated.'

'Guess that means I won't be keeping it.'

'You're damn right that's what it means.'

'All right, all right, just checking.'

We headed back into the Village. I had been cold before, but now I was sweating. There were no police, and Waverly was deserted. Dox pulled up in front of the dumpster. I climbed inside and managed to hold Wong up against the side long enough for Dox to reach down from above and take hold of one of his wrists. We hauled him out, laid him down in the back seat of the pickup, and drove off.

'What are you carrying these days?' I asked him.

'You mean knife-wise?'

'Yeah.'

'Shoot, partner, you know I've got more blades than a combine. I've still got that Fred Perrin La Griffe we acquired in Bangkok, and . . . '

'I mean what's your primary. Right now.'

'Right this very second that would be an Emerson CQC-12 Comrade. Hell of a knife. You could cut through a car door with it if you needed to. Here.'

He reached down, eased the blade out of his pocket, and handed it to me. I opened it. Yeah, this would do. And then some.

Bodies that have been thrown into rivers resurface because gases produced by putrefying bacteria can turn the digestive tract and other areas into balloons. If you don't want the body to float, you have to puncture the balloons so they can't fill. The problem is, it's not just the stomach you're worried about. The phenomenon can occur in the limbs, trunk, face, and other areas, too. Preventing it entirely is therefore a grisly task.

We found a suitably dark stretch along the Hudson River piers south of the Holland Tunnel. Dox pulled off the West Side Highway, cut the lights, and pulled in behind an empty playground. The river was right next to us.

We dragged Wong out and dumped him on the ground. Dox started to lift him.

'No,' I said. 'I'll take care of it. You drive out of here and swing past every five to ten minutes. When I'm done I'll be waiting.'

'Come on, man, let me give you a hand. It'll go quicker.'

'I don't want the car here. It'll draw attention. Besides, I've put you at enough risk as it is. I'll be fine. Just go.'

'All right. I'll be back in five, and five after that.'

I nodded. Dox drove off. I hauled Wong into a fireman's carry and lugged him to the end of the pier, my breath fogging in the chill air. The body felt heavy as hell and I realized how tired I was.

I set him down as close as possible to the edge, took out Dox's knife, and started doing what was necessary. There were going to be some stains on the planks when I was done, no doubt. But dead bodies, lacking a beating heart, bleed a lot less than live ones. Besides, it looked like the city was in for another spell of rain. That would clean things up. And who was going to pay any attention to a dark spot on a Hudson River dock anyway?

I worked. I tried to concentrate on the task at hand, but my mind kept offering up images from Midori's apartment. My son in my arms. Midori's expression as she handed him to me. I looked down at what I was doing and the contrast made me feel sick. The hope and wondrous sense of possibility I'd felt just hours earlier were receding with each stab of the knife.

Just finish this. Just get through.

The whole thing couldn't have taken longer than a minute, but it seemed like more. When I was done, I pocketed the knife and paused, kneeling, to catch my breath. I leaned my head back and breathed the cold air and tried not to think at all.

I heard a car coming south on the access road paralleling the highway. I looked over and saw the outline of police flashers eighty yards away. A spotlight was trained over the water.

Oh, shit. Without another thought, I rolled

Wong into the river and vaulted in after him.

I hung on to the edge of the pier with my fingertips, but even so I was dangling past my waist in freezing water. The cold hit my testicles like a blow and I struggled not to gasp.

I heard the car coming closer, closer. It seemed to be taking forever. Were they slowing? Looking for something? At something?

I looked down. Wong was already gone, sunk beneath the surface.

I listened but couldn't hear anything. Had they stopped? The spotlight lit up the pier and I was sure they had. I pictured two cops coming toward me with guns drawn. There was nothing I could do but hang there and wait.

Finally, the light moved on. I heard their tires moving past. I felt confused and couldn't tell how much time had gone by. I counted. One, one thousand. Two, one thousand. When I reached thirty, I pulled myself back onto the pier. I dragged myself forward a few feet and lay there, exhausted. I couldn't feel my legs. If anyone came now I was doomed.

But they were gone. After a minute, I sat up. I sucked wind and tried to massage some life back into my useless limbs. I was shivering and my teeth were chattering like an electric typewriter. I realized I was moaning.

I heard another car coming. This time I recognized the lights and grille of Dox's pickup. I stood awkwardly and started stumbling toward him.

He got out. The next thing I knew he had clapped an enormous arm across my back and was practically levitating me to the truck. He threw me into the passenger seat and a moment later we were back on the highway.

'What the hell happened?' he asked.

'C-Cops,' I said, through convulsively chattering teeth. 'Had to get in the water.'

'Ah, Jesus, we've got to warm you up. You're bluer than old Wong back there. Can you get those pants off?'

'Yeah.' I fumbled at the belt buckle but my fingers felt thick and useless.

Dox turned the heat on full blast and angled the vents onto me. He drove and eventually I managed to get all the wet clothes off. I rolled them up around my shoes and tossed the bundle into the back. My skin had goose bumps the size of ski moguls. The heat blasting onto my naked thighs was a godsend.

Dox glanced over. 'Son, you call that thing a penis? I don't know what fine ladies like Delilah and Midori find interesting in you, I really don't.'

'You know . . . '

'Yeah, yeah, I know, it was the cold water. That's what they all say.'

I might have laughed, but my teeth were still chattering too hard.

Dox, like any sensible-minded person who travels prepared for the worst, had a change of clothes in the truck. He also had water, food, a tent and sleeping bag, a medical kit, and about a thousand rounds of ammunition. The clothes were too big on me, but that would be a lot less noticeable than returning to the hotel naked.

We dumped everything I'd been wearing, the blanket, and the tainted knives in a variety of sewers and dumpsters around town. When we were done, I realized I was famished. We stopped at a diner and I wolfed down a tureen of chicken soup and a mountainous pastrami sandwich. All the twenty-four-hour places in New York were certainly handy if you had a job that kept you out at night.

By the time Dox dropped me off near the Ritz, the sun was coming up and I was flat-out exhausted. I told him I'd call him later in the day, after I'd slept and could think clearly.

I took the hottest shower I could stand to get the last traces of cold from my bones and the stench of blood and the Hudson from my skin. I fell into bed, and for a moment, I was outside Midori's apartment again, suffused with beguiling hope. I wasn't yet asleep, but it already felt like a dream.

10

I slept until later that morning, then went out to a pay phone and called Tatsu in Tokyo.

It took him four rings to answer. Ordinarily he got it on the first.

'*Hai*,' he said. He sounded tired. Well, it was night out there.

'*Ore da*,' I said in Japanese. It's me.

'Let me call you back from a different line.'

His voice was really raspy. Must have been a hell of a case of the flu he was fighting.

'Sure,' I said, and clicked off.

A moment later the phone rang. 'Sorry,' he said. 'I'm changing phones more frequently lately than I used to.'

'Not using scrambled?'

He laughed, then coughed. 'Only when we're trying to get the NSA's attention.'

I smiled. A scrambled digital signal attracts the NSA the way blood brings sharks. It's as useful as leaning close to whisper in someone's ear: anyone who sees you do it will immediately start listening intently. Better to just move the conversation somewhere else, where no one is looking.

'How did things go?' he asked. 'Were you able to meet her?'

'Yes.'

'And your son?'

'I saw him, too.'

'Just saw him?'

'No, it was more than that. I . . . ' I paused, the memory seeming to shift something inside my chest. 'I held him in my arms while he slept.'

'That's good,' he said, and I imagined him smiling.

'You okay?' I said. 'That flu sounds pretty bad.'

'I'm all right.'

'I've got a situation I need your help with. I'll put the information on the bulletin board.'

'I may not be able to access the bulletin board for a while. I'm in the hospital.'

I frowned and pressed my ear closer to the receiver. 'What's going on?'

'Nothing, I'll be out of here soon. Tell me about your situation. It sounds more pressing than mine.'

'You sure your phone is all right?'

'Positive.'

Okay. I told him everything.

When I was done, he said, 'What are you thinking?'

'You know what I'm thinking. I can't stop halfway. The only way to finish this is to keep going until it's done.'

'You mean . . . '

'Look, the Chinese are just contractors on this. They don't know me, they don't know what I'm capable of, so they'll believe the obvious explanation for what happened to their people — a junior guy with a history of violence lost his temper, killed his boss, and went into hiding. But Yamaoto is going to know better. And he'll have an incentive to try to persuade the Chinese that I was behind the deaths of two of their people, as a way of getting them personally involved. So all I've done by taking out the two Chinese is buy myself a little time. If I don't finish Yamaoto, too, it'll have been for nothing. Worse than nothing, because if the Chinese figure out what really happened, they could retaliate against Midori and my son. They know where they live, goddamnit. They've been watching them.'

There was a pause. Finally he said, 'I agree.'

'Of course you agree. This is exactly what you wanted. Don't think I don't know it.'

'I had no intention of putting your son in danger.'

'You showed me those photos to make the baby more real to me, to make it impossible for me to ignore. Otherwise you could have just told me.'

'Perhaps, but . . . '

'You're a manipulative bastard, Tatsu. You know it's true. But I don't have time to argue with you about it. I don't even have time to hate you. I need your help.'

'You want me to move them?'

I knew he could do it. He'd moved Midori to New York in the first place, to protect her from Yamaoto. But Yamaoto had found her anyway.

'I don't want you to do anything,' I said. 'If she gets wind of what's out there she'll never see me again. Just tell me how I can get to Yamaoto.'

'You can't just get to him. He's afraid of you, you know. Even obsessed. He goes out infrequently. Uses bodyguards. Travels in an armored car . . . '

'I've got access to a sniper. All I need to know is where and when.'

'That's exactly the information Yamaoto now guards most jealously.'

'What about his headquarters? His residence?'

'The very locations where he most expects trouble, and where he takes the most precautions.'

We were silent for a moment. I was so frustrated I was breathing hard.

'You know,' I said, 'I wish you would just arrest this guy. I really do.'

'We've been over this before. In addition to his other activities, Yamaoto is a powerful politician, well protected by his network of patronage and blackmail. Moving against him directly would do nothing but get me fired. Believe me, I wish I could.'

'Fine, then just tell me how to get to him.'

'I'm trying to. But if something happens to Yamaoto immediately following the deaths of the Chinese, it won't look good for you. It could cause a problem between you and the triads, which you just said you would rather avoid.'

'How, then?'

'You have to turn Yamaoto and the Chinese against each other. Make them suspect each other, rather than suspecting you.'

'I'm listening.'

There was a pause: It sounded like he was taking a drink of something. He coughed, then said, 'For the last ten years there has been a boom in the manufacture of methamphetamine in China and Taiwan. Chinese triads cooperate with the yakuza in smuggling the drugs into Japan.'

'Is this the quid pro quo Yamaoto has been offering them in exchange for watching Midori and the boy?'

'Not the smuggling itself. That's been going on for a long time. What's new, I've learned, is that Yamaoto has switched suppliers. Formerly he bought his product from Korean gangs. Now he has switched to United Bamboo, the triad based in Taiwan, in exchange for UB watching Midori in New York, where UB has a large operation. That's the quid pro quo.'

'Where's our opening, then?'

'The new arrangement is unstable. The players are unaccustomed to each other, and suspicious. The bad blood that is always festering and that lately has worsened between China and Japan has infected gang relations, too. Like the countries themselves, the gangs are always ready to think the worst of the other's motives. All they need is a little push, and they'll turn on each other.'

'What do you have in mind?'

'Up until now, Yamaoto and UB have been dealing in relatively small shipments of methamphetamine because they don't yet trust each other. But I have an informant who's told me of a particularly large shipment arriving later this week, the largest one yet. The parties are nervous because of the amount of product and cash involved. If something were to go wrong . . . '

I thought for a moment. I couldn't be sure the Chinese would buy into my hoped-for explanation for what had happened to Wong and Chan. And regardless of what they believed, if Yamaoto learned of Wong's disappearance and Chan's death, he would draw his own conclusions. If he suspected I'd been in touch with Midori and the baby, he might move against them as a way of flushing me out. I hated to leave them alone and defenseless. But the only way I could see to protect them was to go after Yamaoto.

'You trust your informant?' I asked.

'He's always been reliable. It's what's kept him out of prison.'

'How many principals?'

'Two yakuza making the pickup. An unknown number of Chinese handling the delivery. But my guess is at least two Chinese.'

So a total of at least four, maybe more. Too many to handle alone. This wasn't going to be easy.

I sighed. 'What is it with Yamaoto? Why is he so obsessed with me? I mean, I'm the one who was forced to leave Japan. Yeah, I won a couple of battles, but couldn't he look at himself as the winner of the war?'

'I don't think so. It's not just your beating him that rankles. He's also afraid of you. He knows what you can do.'

'I left the fucking country. Live and let live.'

'Remember, he killed your friend Harry, even if he didn't pull the trigger himself. He's a vain man, and would insist on avenging such a loss. He assumes you would do the same, and that he is in continual danger as a result.'

The words stung. Sure, he was just explaining why Yamaoto had it in for me. But he was also reminding me of a debt I'd failed to pay, knowing my shame about Harry would goad me. Tatsu had a way of imbuing his sentences with multiple meanings.

I'd always known, deep down, that eventually, I would have to finish things with Yamaoto. And now it wasn't just about the past. Yamaoto was keeping me from having something, whatever it might turn out to be, with Midori and my son here in New York, right now. Today. I'd been foolish, a coward even, to have waited so long to face up to reality. And now I would have to work on the fly, at an inherent disadvantage.

Well, there was nothing I could do about that now. Except to tell myself this would be it, the last battle, the last war.

'Where are you? What hospital?' I asked.

'Jikei.'

'It's too late to catch today's flights. I'll leave tomorrow and be there Saturday afternoon your time. You can brief me then.'

11

Delilah sat on the couch in her Paris apartment. She tried to concentrate on the book she was reading, but couldn't turn off her conflicted thoughts. She'd come back from Barcelona a week ago — a week! — and still hadn't heard from Rain. Things had always been open-ended before, true, but this time he had told her right at the airport that he would call. And especially after the things they'd said to each other, or nearly said, in Barcelona, what did it mean that he hadn't gotten in touch? Only one thing, she knew: he'd fixed things with his ex and lacked either the courage or the courtesy to tell Delilah. What was she supposed to do, call him, instead? What would she say? 'Hi, John, did you reconnect with your past love and your new family? Is there still any place in your life for me?' Please. She'd said too much already.

No, it hadn't been a great week, coming as it did in the middle of what was turning out to be an interminable administrative review. Her colleague Boaz had called her to see how she was doing, and when she pressed him he admitted he'd heard the news wasn't good. It seemed they were trying to decide between a formal reprimand, which would be merely humiliating, and yanking her from the field permanently, which she didn't know if she could bear at all. Boaz was a friend and he'd tried to leaven his honesty by telling her how many supporters she had, but what difference did that make? If they decided to hang her, she was going to hang.

Her mind's eye wasn't being kind to her. For work, she pictured conference rooms staffed by bald, paunchy men stroking their chins and clucking their tongues. For Rain, she envisioned a joyous reunion with Midori in the afternoon; tearful explanations and apologies in the evening; tender, intimate lovemaking all night, with a baby asleep in a crib nearby. Logically, she knew better, but this was a tough time for her and she couldn't control her imagination, only negotiate with it.

She had fed Boaz the pieces of information she had acquired from Rain. Boaz knew that under the circumstances the request couldn't be operational, but he helped her anyway. The computers returned a single name: Midori Kawamura, thirty-eight, Japanese national, residing in New York City, mother of Koichiro Kawamura, born in New York fifteen months earlier. Jazz pianist. Delilah had looked up the woman's website and the moment she saw the bio photo, she knew it was her. She didn't need an intel report for that.

The woman was beautiful, Delilah had to admit. She had that thick, shiny, perfectly straight Asian hair, and porcelain skin most women would kill for. And she was obviously talented. But she was a civilian. It didn't make sense.

Well, attractions could be strong enough to survive long separations. They could even survive much worse, as her own relationship with Rain demonstrated. It hurt to admit it, but maybe it was no more complicated than that. Rain was in love with the woman and wanted to be with her, that was all.

Or maybe he'd been telling the truth, maybe this was about the baby, not Midori. But the woman had never told him, he'd only found out from some thirdhand surveillance photos. Rain had said he'd screwed things up with her, but what did that mean? Screwed things up so badly that afterward the woman had tried to hide from him the existence of their child?

Among the collateral information Boaz had supplied was a report that the woman's father had died of a heart attack less than a month before Midori left for America. By itself, nothing more than happenstance. But Delilah knew Rain's specialty was 'natural causes,' that he'd even been planning on causing a heart attack for his target on Macau when he and Delilah had first run into each other.

Delilah had asked Boaz to check a little further, and had learned that the father, Yasuhiro Kawamura, had been a career bureaucrat with the Construction Ministry, which meant he would have been neck deep in all the corruption over there. A player, not a civilian.

She moved these pieces around in her mind, and a possible pattern started to form. Rain and Midori's father . . . It was a little hard to believe, but somehow she felt it was right. But did the woman know?

If her suspicions were correct, she might have

an important tool. But a dangerous one. She'd have to think about how she could use it, or whether she should use it at all.

Her mobile phone rang. She looked at it. No number appeared on the caller ID display.

She closed the book, severely irritated with herself at how much she was hoping, and opened the phone. '*Allo*,' she said.

'Hey,' Rain said. 'It's me.'

She paused, her heart beating hard, and said, 'How did things go?'

'They got . . . complicated.'

'How do you mean?'

'I can't really talk about it.'

'Why? I'm listening.'

'I just can't right now.'

'Oh, really?' She could hear the icicles in her own voice.

'Come on, Delilah, don't be this way.'

'What way is that?'

Damn it, what was it about him that made her sulk and pout like a schoolgirl? She hated it.

There was a pause, then he said, 'I'm sorry, Delilah.'

Her heart beat harder. 'Sorry for what?'

There was another pause. He said, 'I have to go to Tokyo for a few days to straighten some things out. I'll be in touch after that, okay?'

She almost said, *You mean like you were in touch after Barcelona?*

She bit it off and said instead, 'What's in Tokyo?'

Another pause. He said, 'I'll call you soon. Bye.' And hung up.

She stared at her phone for a moment, and it took all her self-control not to hurl it across the room.

Goddamn him! Tokyo? What was that about, going to meet the family? What? And what was that good-bye? Was it, *good-bye?*

He had just let her go, hadn't he? They'd been getting closer and closer, she'd been opening up more and more, but as soon as he'd gotten a better offer, he was gone. What did he think, he could just have her for fun whenever it was convenient and then discard her at a whim?

And all this after the risks she'd taken to help him in Hong Kong, too, which was exactly what had caused her current troubles in the first place. Damn him. Goddamn him.

She knew she wasn't taking this well, but at the moment she didn't care. She wasn't going to just sit alone on the other side of the world while the men in her organization tried to figure out what to do with her at work and the man in her heart tried to figure out what to do with her in his life.

She thought again about what could have made Midori try to hide the baby from Rain, about what Rain could have done that would have precipitated that. Then she thought, *The hell with it*.

She went to her laptop and made a reservation on the next afternoon's Air France flight to New York. If he was going to fuck with her, he was going to see that she could fuck with him right back.

12

Dox and I met for dinner that evening at a Japanese restaurant called Omen on Thompson in SoHo. It was a good place, quiet and dark and private, and the food was first-rate. Over sushi and beer, I explained the situation in Japan, the risks and the possible benefits.

When I was done, he said, 'There's something I want to ask you about.'

'Okay,' I said, thinking there was something serious.

'Well, in all the excitement, you never did tell me how things went last night before everything went haywire.'

I realized I should have known better. 'It went okay,' I said.

'Okay? What is okay?'

'You know . . . okay.'

'I'm talking about your lady.'

'Yeah, it was good, I guess.'

'Goddamn, man, what do I have to do, the old Rayovac to the nutsack to get you to talk?'

'It was good. She didn't throw me out. She let me see . . . my son.'

My son. I wondered if the words would ever feel familiar. Just saying them made me feel slightly dizzy, good and anxious and confused all at the same time.

'Well, how was that?'

'It was . . . good.'

He rolled his eyes. 'John Rain, Captain Eloquence. Did you at least . . . you know.'

I looked at him. 'Did I what?'

'You know . . . did you get any.'

'Oh, for Christ's sake . . . '

'You got some then.'

I shook my head in exasperation and said nothing.

He grinned. 'And here you were just in Barcelona with the lovely Miss Delilah. You slut.'

'I just called Delilah.'

'How was that?'

'I don't know. I told her things were complicated, that I needed a little time to sort them out. She got pretty sullen with me. She does that sometimes. But with the shit I'm up against, I just can't deal with it right now. I can't.'

'Well, making a woman like Delilah sullen, that's quite a privilege.'

'Look, let's talk about Japan, okay? Are you interested?'

''Course I am. You're in a tight spot, I ain't gonna let you down.'

I nodded. I was going to owe this man more than I could ever repay. At least it looked like he might walk away with a good payday this time.

'According to the informant,' I said, 'the shipment is unusually large. So we should be talking about an unusual amount of cash, too. Still, no guarantees.'

'Well, I never imagined myself squaring off against the Japanese and Chinese mobs, but I guess that's where the money is. Plus it's the kind of killing and thievery a man can feel good about after it's done. You know, it ain't like we're raping and pillaging a bunch of candy stripers.'

'No, you can bet these people won't be candy stripers,' I said. I wanted to add, *Don't get cocky*, but at the moment, I wasn't in a great position to dispense advice.

He took a swallow of beer, then leaned back and belched. 'Well, the potential upside is fine,' he said. 'You can count me in for that. But you're not doing this for the money, are you?'

'I'm not going to give it to charity afterward, if that's what you mean.'

'What I mean is, you're doing this to try to clean up the mess you made outside of Midori's apartment last night.'

'That's right.'

'So you can be with her and your boy.'

'Yes.'

'So you can get yourself a normal life.'

I nodded, uncomfortable, not sure what he was getting at.

'I've got a little joke I want to tell you,' he said. 'I think you might like it.'

I looked at him. 'Okay.'

'There's this hunter. He's in the woods with his rifle, and he sees a big, ugly-looking bear. Takes aim, shoots, and he misses. The bear walks over and says, 'Mister, I don't like the feeling of being hunted. I reckon I'm just gonna have to teach you a lesson.' So the bear bends the hunter over a log, pulls his pants down, and sodomizes that boy for all he's worth.'

'Okay . . . ' I said again.

'So a little later, the hunter is still prowling around, he sees the bear again. He takes aim, he shoots, and he misses again. The bear walks over and says, 'Damn, son, you sure are a slow learner. Okay, I guess we'll just have to repeat the lesson.' And he bones him a second time.'

I wondered where he was going with this.

'Well, sure enough, an hour later the hunter sees the bear again. And he tries to shoot him again, and he misses again. Well, this time, the bear comes over looking especially grave and sober. And he says, 'Mister, I want you to be honest with me. This isn't really about hunting, is it?''

At that, Dox burst into laughter. I looked at him, quietly marveling at his sense of humor.

After a moment, his guffaws subsided. 'You get it?' he asked.

'Yeah, but . . . '

'The hunter is you, partner. You keep telling yourself you're just trying to do the right thing, or be with your family, or get out of the life, or whatever. But it always comes down to killing with you. Always.'

For a guy who liked to play the hick, Dox had insight that could cut like a scalpel.

'It's like America,' he went on. 'I mean, look at us, we're always telling ourselves how peace-loving we are. 'We're a peace-loving people, we love peace.' I guess that's why we spend more on our military than the rest of the world combined, why we have over seven hundred overseas military bases in a hundred and thirty countries, and why we've been at war pretty much

111

continuously since we were just a bunch of colonies. Shoot, you think if a Martian visited Earth and tried to identify the most peace-loving culture, he'd pick the U.S. of A.? I'm not saying there's anything wrong with it, mind you. We're a warlike people, it's obvious, we're good at war and we like it. I just don't know why we can't admit it to ourselves. I bet sales of Prozac would go down if we could.'

'Maybe,' I said, absently.

'You see my point, though, right? You are what you are, just like that hunter. The rest is just excuses for what you want to do anyway.'

'I hope this doesn't mean you think you're the bear.'

He laughed. 'What I'm trying to say is, at some point, you should face up to your nature. I think you'd be more at peace with yourself if you would. Hell, look at me. Why do you think the ladies like me so much? I mean, aside from the generous nature of my natural endowments. It's because I'm comfortable in my own skin. Ladies like that kind of thing.'

I closed my eyes. 'If you see another way out of this situation, tell me, and I'll take it.'

'I don't know that there is another way, right now. But that ain't really the point, and you know it.'

I nodded. 'Look, I need to go. We've got to leave for Tokyo early in the morning and I haven't even made reservations yet and I'm running on fumes.'

'Shit, man, don't look so glum. Last night was a near thing, but you handled it. How many people you think could have come through like that? You're goddamn exceptional is what you are. And now you've got a good plan for fixing things and a good partner to help you. So snap out of this misery or I swear I'll kick your ass right here in this restaurant.'

'All right,' I said, giving him a wan smile. 'I'll think about what you said.'

He laughed again. 'You mean you'll try to find reasons to reject it. And you might find a few. But they won't last you. Because what I'm telling you is the truth.'

13

I left for Tokyo from JFK in the morning. I would have preferred an indirect route, but we didn't have a lot of time. For security, Dox was traveling separately, and we would link up again at Narita.

Before going through security, I found a restroom at the end of the departures area. It was more distant from the check-in lines and from security screening than any of the others I had passed and, I hoped, would therefore be frequented by fewer travelers. I used a length of duct tape to secure the Strider to the underside of one of the toilets. I figured there was at least a fifty-percent chance it would be found by a cleaning crew, but if I got lucky, it would be waiting when I got back after finishing my business with Yamaoto, and I would be saved the hassle of having to get a new one.

I arrived at Narita late in the afternoon of the following day. After taking steps to verify the absence of a local welcoming committee, I found Dox and we caught a Narita Express train to Tokyo Station. The big man seemed perfectly at ease in the Asian surroundings, and I remembered how much time he had spent in the region. As for me, my feelings were, as always, mixed at being back here. For a long time, Tokyo had been the closest thing I had to a place I might call home. But it's not as though I ever belonged here, either, or ever really would.

While Dox roamed the mazelike station, I stopped at the local Vodafone shop so Mr Watanabe could buy another pair of prepaid cell phones. I would have preferred not to put the additional stress on the Watanabe identity, but the mini-bazaars for black market phones that were running out of Shin-Okubo and Ueno when I lived in Tokyo had been cleaned up, and I didn't have time to go searching for wherever they might have been reconstituted. Anyway, the connection between Cingular in the States and Vodafone in Japan seemed manageably remote. I would have asked Dox to buy the phones, but I was determined to do everything I could to obscure his involvement.

When the phones were taken care of, I called Midori. She didn't pick up, but I left her a voice mail giving her the new mobile number. Even if she didn't need to reach me, or want to, I wanted to show her I could be there for her, and for Koichiro, even if only by phone. I didn't want her to think I was going to just disappear like a ghost, the way I had when she'd first left Tokyo.

We headed out. I wanted to see Tatsu right away, so Dox, who had spent enough time in Tokyo to know his way around, went to outfit himself with his customary personal cutlery while I headed to Jikei hospital. I caught the Yamanote line train to Shinbashi Station and walked the short distance from there. It was a cool but clear evening, and it felt good to be outside after the long trip from New York.

I circled the hospital, checking the hot spots,

115

and used a side entrance to go in. On my own I felt secure, but Tatsu was a known nexus of mine, with plenty of his own enemies, and in going to see him I might be walking into an ambush. Nothing set off my radar. I went to the information desk in the bustling reception area and told one of the women sitting there that I wanted to see Ishikura Tatsuhiko, a patient. The woman checked the computer and told me that Ishikura-san was in the hospital's Oncology Clinic.

The sounds around me faded out. A wave of cold stole across my face and neck and spread through my gut. The woman gave me directions but I just stared at her, not hearing. I asked her to repeat herself but then after I walked away I realized I couldn't remember most of what she had said. I followed signs, feeling lost in the winding, fluorescent-lit corridors.

I found the ward, but couldn't recall the room number the receptionist had told me. I asked a nurse and she escorted me down the hall. Outside one of the doors stood an athletic-looking crew-cut Japanese man in a gray suit. There was a bulge under his jacket and a communication device in one of his cauliflower ears. He looked at me as I approached and I made sure to let him see my hands.

We stopped outside the door. While the man patted me down, the nurse poked her head inside and said in Japanese, 'Excuse me, Ishikura-san, you have a visitor . . .'

'Ii yo,' a weak voice responded from inside. Okay.

The nurse gestured to the room. The bodyguard walked me in, staying just behind me.

Tatsu was propped up in bed, surrounded by the usual depressing hospital machinery, an IV line snaking into his arm and a tube up his nose. I'd seen him only a month before, but he was ten kilos lighter now and looked as many years older. Whatever he had, it was eating him alive, and I could instantly see that all the machinery and IV lines in the world were nothing but a sick joke by comparison.

A pretty young woman sat to the right of the bed, a sleeping infant in her arms. Tatsu's daughter, I realized. He had told me the last time I saw him that his first grandson had just been born.

I hesitated, feeling I was intruding, but Tatsu waved me in. '*Hisashiburi*,' he said weakly. It's been a while. He nodded to the bodyguard and the man left.

A number of lies came to my lips, but none made it farther than that. 'Damn, Tatsu,' I said, shaking my head, looking at him. 'Damn.'

He nodded weakly as if to say, *Yes, I know*, then gestured to the woman next to him. 'My daughter, Kaoru. And grandson, Arihiro.' His eyes were sunken but they lit up with his smile.

I bowed to the woman. 'It's good to meet you,' I said stiffly.

Because of the baby, she stayed in her seat, but bowed her head. 'I've heard a lot about you,' she said. 'You help my father in his work.'

I glanced at Tatsu. 'I try to.'

Tatsu said, 'Don't tell him what I say.'

The woman smiled. 'Only good things.'

I nodded. 'He's probably lying, then.'

Tatsu chuckled. The woman stood up, the child in one arm, her free hand on Tatsu's shoulder. 'I should get the baby home,' she said. 'Feed him and put him to bed.'

'Yes,' Tatsu said. 'Go. My friend here doesn't talk much, but he's good company.'

Tatsu turned toward the woman with a slight grimace, and she lowered the baby and held him there. Tatsu whispered something in the child's ear, and then, with another grimace, moved closer and kissed him softly on the cheek. He eased back onto the bed and let out a long breath.

'I'll see you tomorrow,' the woman said, her hand on his shoulder again.

Tatsu nodded. 'Yes. Bring the little one.'

The woman smiled and said, 'Of course.' She walked to the door and turned to me. 'Thank you,' she said. I wasn't sure for what. I bowed, and she was gone.

Tatsu looked at me and gestured to the chair. 'Let's talk, my friend. You didn't bring any good whiskey, did you?'

I sat down beside him. 'I thought you were off that stuff. Wife's orders.'

He looked at me with the trademark wry expression he reserved for moments of stupidity too monumental to bear comment, and for an instant he looked like himself again. 'Well, it doesn't matter very much now, does it?' he said.

'It's bad?'

The wry look gave way to a smile, as though

this was the most amusing conversation he had had in a long time. 'What do you think?' he said.

We were quiet for a moment. I asked, 'How long?'

He shrugged. 'A few weeks, maybe.'

Christ. 'They can't . . . '

'Gastric cancer. Stage four. It's already in the lymph nodes, the esophagus . . . that's why I've lost all this weight. I can't hold anything down.'

'The whiskey would have been a waste, then.'

He chuckled. 'I could have just smelled it.'

We were quiet again.

He said, 'I assume you're still interested in finishing Yamaoto?'

I didn't know what to say. He had so little time, it didn't seem fair to make him use it talking about this. But then I realized, *That's what he wants, maybe even what he needs.*

'I'm still interested.'

'Good. The delivery will be at Wajima harbor.'

'Wajima . . . '

'On the Noto Peninsula, Ishikawa prefecture. The Sea of Japan. The gangs avoid large ports because of better security in the major facilities. They prefer quiet places like Fushiki in Toyama, Minamata in Kumamoto, Hososhima in Miyazaki.'

'Or this time, Wajima.'

'Yes. Yamaoto's men have made reservations at an inn there called Notonosho. The area is known for a hot spring, Nebuta, and apparently these men like the waters. Their names are Kito and Sanada, but they might be traveling under something else.'

'What timing are we talking about?'

'They arrive the day after tomorrow. The delivery will be the night after that. My informant still doesn't know how many Chinese will be involved. But my guess is no more than three. Otherwise the two yakuza would feel uncomfortable.'

I was thinking the same thing, but I only nodded.

'Rain-san, forgive me, but you're not as young as you used to be. Can you . . . '

'Look who's talking,' I said.

He laughed.

'Don't worry,' I told him. 'I've got help.'

He raised his eyebrows. 'Anyone I know?'

I shook my head. 'What about you? I know you're a workaholic, Tatsu, but how are you able to . . . ?'

'During the day, I have a steady stream of visitors. The doctors hate it, but when they complain I say, 'So? A little work won't kill me.''

We laughed, then were quiet again.

'It has to look as though Yamaoto's men killed the Chinese and stole the drugs,' he said. There was an odd fervor in his eyes. 'This will put a great deal of pressure on Yamaoto. A great deal.'

Most men, lying on their presumable death-beds, would be focused on other matters. But not Tatsu. Fighting corruption was his life's work, and he would devote every last breath to it.

I put my hand on his shoulder. 'I'll take care of it.'

He nodded and seemed to settle in his bed.

120

'Good,' he said, patting my hand.

Without thinking, I turned my hand around and took his in mine.

He gritted his teeth for a moment and groaned, then whatever pain had caused the groan passed. He said, 'You have to hurry, Rain-san. Soon I won't be able to help you.'

I nodded.

He smiled. 'Why do you look so sad?'

I shook my head. 'You're an asshole.'

I thought he would laugh at that, but he didn't. Instead he squeezed my hand for a moment and then said, 'I've thought a lot about what you said, you know. About being a manipulative bastard. I don't have a lot I can do besides lie here and think.'

'You come to any conclusions?'

'That you're right. That I knew exactly what I was doing when I showed you those photographs. That the situation has turned out exactly as I had hoped. Except for one thing.'

'I forgot the whiskey?'

He squeezed again. This time he didn't let go. 'That I might have put your family in danger. If something were to happen to your son . . .'

Tatsu had lost his only son in an accident when the child was an infant. He had spoken of it to me only twice: first, when I had asked him years earlier, and again, on the night he told me that I, too, had become a father. The boy had died over three decades earlier, but the pain still showed in Tatsu's eyes. It always had, and I knew now there was only one thing that could deliver him from it. And that thing was coming far too soon.

'Nothing's going to happen to him,' I said. 'We're going to take care of this.'

He closed his eyes and mumbled something. It took me a moment to pick up what it was. *Onegai shimasu.* Please.

We sat like that for a few minutes more. His eyes remained closed and I realized he was sleeping.

I got up and moved to the door. I nodded to the bodyguard, then checked the corridor. All clear.

I used the stairs and a back exit, then ran a route to make sure I wasn't being followed. It was good to have something operational to focus on. It helped me to not think.

When I was satisfied I was alone, I called Dox. He had already checked into his hotel, the large and anonymous Shinagawa Prince. We agreed to meet at a Starbucks in Shinagawa Station in two hours, after I'd checked into the equally unremarkable Shinjuku Hilton.

I clicked off and headed toward the Yamanote. Tatsu's words echoed in my mind: *Soon I won't be able to help you.*

14

When I arrived in Shinagawa, I was initially bewildered. The area, once a seedy backwater reeking of meat processing, had been gentrified. South of the station, everything was brand-new: glass high-rises, sparkling esplanades, expensive-looking restaurants. Christ, there was even a Dean & DeLuca at the station entrance.

I found the Starbucks Dox had described, on a terrace inside the station, overlooking a passenger walkway. Dox was already up there, sitting by the railing, looking down at the crowds, doubtless enjoying the feeling of holding the high ground with an unobstructed field of fire. He spotted me and nodded once to let me know it was safe to approach.

I went to the counter and ordered a herbal tea. I was tired from the trip and the time change, but wanted to maximize my chances of a decent night's sleep.

I took the tea and joined Dox at the table. 'Figured you'd get here early,' he said. 'So to save time, I came early, too.'

Over the last year or so, he'd learned my habits, of course, and this was an opportunity to tweak me. I was getting used to it. 'That was thoughtful of you,' I said.

'I'm a thoughtful guy. In fact, I brought you a present. And, at the risk of disappointing you, I'll tell you now it ain't a kimono or dainty silk undergarments.'

He put a paper bag on the table and I looked inside. I saw a black folding knife and slid it out. I opened it under the table.

'That there is a Benchmade Presidio 520S,' he said. 'Three-and-a-half-inch blade and a combo edge. Thought you might like it.'

'I like it a lot,' I said, closing it and sliding it into my pocket. 'Thanks.'

He nodded. 'What did you hear from your friend?'

I briefed him on what I'd learned from Tatsu. When I was done, he said, 'If the meet is the night after tomorrow, we're going to have to scramble. Can your friend get us the equipment we're going to need?'

'No. To do this right, we're going to need some unusual stuff.'

He smiled. 'Well, I reckon we know where to go for the specialty items.'

I nodded. He was referring to Tomohisa Kanezaki, of course, a Japanese-American CIA officer based at the embassy in Tokyo. Dox and I had both worked with Kanezaki over the years. Some of the things he used us for were official; others were undertaken pursuant to a slightly more entrepreneurial initiative. At this point he was more a friend than an enemy, although you never want to get overly distracted by classifications like those. In the end, business is business.

'I'll call him,' I said. 'But I'm going to leave your involvement out of it. The less he knows, the better.'

'Agreed on that.'

124

'Let's be ready to roll at oh-six-hundred the day after tomorrow. Check-in at the inn where Yamaoto's men are staying is at two o'clock, and I want to get there before they do.'

'We're staying there, too?'

'I'm staying there. Already made a reservation. But you we're going to have to keep under wraps. There aren't many white faces in those parts, and we don't want to do anything to be remembered.'

'Am I going to be camping out? I don't mind, just want to know what to bring.'

'I'll rent a van. We'll need it operationally, but it'll also be a mobile home, if you follow me.'

'I follow you. All right, I'll do a little shopping tomorrow for gear. Looks like I'll be enjoying a last couple of nights of luxury here at the Prince and roughing it after that.'

I nodded. 'Let's figure out what we need, and I'll call Kanezaki.'

We went through everything, starting with what we wanted to accomplish and working backward from there. When we were done, Dox went back to the Prince and I found a pay phone in front of the station.

Kanezaki picked up on the first ring, a habit I knew he had acquired from Tatsu. '*Hai*,' he said curtly, also in imitation of the older man.

'Hey,' I said.

There was a pause. He said, 'What, are you living in Tokyo at this point?'

I smiled. Caller ID was exactly why I'd used a pay phone. I wanted to keep the cell phone sterile for as long as I could.

125

'I've got some business here,' I told him. 'Nothing that would displease you if you knew about it. I could use your help.'

'Okay.'

'Your phone secure?'

'Yes.'

'One tranquilizer rifle with a night vision scope and a minimum of ten darts; two suppressed pistols each with infrared laser and night sights, spare magazine, a hundred rounds of hollow point, and a right-side tactical thigh rig for carry; two pairs of night-vision goggles; one GPS vehicle tracking system with magnetic mounts.'

'That's it?'

I heard the sarcasm. 'Yeah.'

'Is this for Christmas? I don't know if I can get it all in a stocking . . . '

'I need it by tomorrow night.'

'John, come on.'

Kanezaki liked to play up the difficulty of whatever favor he was asked, as a way of extracting greater concessions in return. He might have been doing it now. Or my request might really have posed a problem. It didn't matter. I didn't have time to screw around.

'Can you do this?' I asked. 'If you can't, I'll figure something else out.'

'I'm not saying I can't do it . . . '

'Then what are you saying?'

'Look, don't get short with me. Checking out that kind of hardware isn't like borrowing a few yen from petty cash.'

'I imagine it's not.'

'If I can do this, you're going to owe me.'

'Owe you what?'

'A favor. A job.'

Your soul, I heard. My hopes for Midori and Koichiro seemed to recede in the distance, like the light going out on a television screen.

Well, I shouldn't have been surprised. I could have argued with him, but there were things more important than my soul in play at the moment.

'If that's the way you want to do it,' I said. My voice sounded far away.

'Is that a yes?'

I suddenly and badly wanted to tell him *Fuck you*. Tell him in person, in my own special way.

Instead I simply said, 'Yes.'

'Okay. How long are you going to need this stuff?'

'Seventy-two hours, if that.'

A pause. 'Is any of this going to come back to bite me on the ass?'

'Not if it goes well.'

He laughed. 'God, I feel so much better now.'

'Yeah, me too,' I said.

'Let me see what I can do. Call me tomorrow afternoon.'

'I'll post it on the bulletin board, too. Just to make sure you've got it all.'

'Good enough.'

I hung up and, out of habit, wiped down the phone.

I stopped by an Internet café and posted the shopping list on the bulletin board we used.

After that, there was nothing to do except try to sleep.

I went back to the hotel and took a molten bath. It cooked the tension out of my muscles, and afterward, as I lay in bed, my body was almost rubbery with relaxation. But my mind refused to shut down. I kept picturing Koichiro's face, and remembering the way he had nuzzled closer when I held him. I stared at the ceiling for a long time, and at some point I realized that, like Tatsu, I was whispering *Onegai shimasu*, over and over. Please. Please.

15

Delilah woke from a nap in her room at the Mercer Hotel in SoHo Friday night. She hadn't slept at all on the flight over, but had dropped off instantly at the hotel after checking in and unpacking. It was early morning back in Paris now, and her body felt ready to go.

She opened the curtains and looked out onto what the hotel called a 'courtyard view.' Actually, the view wasn't bad. There really was a courtyard, pretty in the light of a gibbous moon, and she would rather face a quiet courtyard than a noisy street.

She liked the hotel. It was a little on the hip side — aspiring-actor doormen in black turtlenecks, a condom provided along with the cotton swabs in the bathroom, that kind of thing — but this was SoHo, after all, and it felt right.

She showered, blow-dried her hair, and put on just a little makeup — mascara, blush, a hint of liner for drama, that's all. Then a few drops of her favorite perfume — something she'd had made just for her at Guerlain and which happened to be what she wore for Rain. She knew he liked it, and that knowledge would feel good in the back of her mind.

She walked into the bedroom, laid out the clothes she was thinking about, and looked them over: dark, snug jeans, definitely. Her favorite boots, mahogany brown with high heels, definitely. Now the top. Hmm, there was the vintage silk Chanel jacket she had picked up at Les 3 Marches de Catherine B on the Rue Guisarde; that was certainly gorgeous. But . . . no, maybe the glass-beaded detailing would be a bit *too* fabulous for a jazz bar in SoHo. So . . . yes, better to go with the Santa Eulalia bolero. It was a lush, chocolate brown that looked great with her hair and would work with the jeans, too. Rain had just bought it for her in Passeig de Gràcia in Barcelona . . . that would also feel good tonight. And underneath . . . yes, the Sabbia Rosa dark brown silk camisole and matching bra and thong panties; they were sexy even just lying there on the bed. Okay.

She was more used to dressing for men than for women, but when she'd put it all on and checked herself in the mirror, she felt she'd gotten it just right. The look was sexy, but in a quiet way, like something she would do more to please herself than out of concern for anyone else.

She grabbed the Jekel shearling coat she had brought and took the elevator down to the lobby. Some of the hipsters chatting there eyed her as she passed, probably wondering whether she was one of the celebrities the hotel was known for. She was used to that kind of reaction and ordinarily it barely registered, but this time it felt good. She kept moving without returning any of the looks.

According to Midori's website, tonight was the last of four consecutive shows at a nearby bar called Zinc. So there was a little over an hour to kill before the second set. Just enough time for a bite to eat. Delilah found a place called The Cupping Room, on West Broadway and Broome, which had exactly the kind of quiet, low-key atmosphere she wanted. She ordered a salad and marinated baby lamb chops and a glass of the house red. She thought while she ate, but arrived at no conclusions.

When she was done, she walked the few blocks to Zinc. She looked around inside but the second set hadn't started yet and Midori must have been somewhere in back. She half-expected to see Rain. She didn't know when he was leaving for Tokyo. Well, if he showed up, the hell with it, he could just sort out the situation himself. She had as much right to be here as he did.

The place was mostly full, but there was an open seat at the front of the room, near the stage, and she took it. Her heart was beating moderately hard and she realized she was nervous. It almost made her laugh. She'd handled assignments where if she'd slipped, or if anyone had otherwise caught on to her, she would have been killed without question. But here she was, with the stakes trivial by comparison, and she had an amateur's shakes. It was ridiculous. She ordered another red wine.

She felt men at some of the tables watching her, and knew a few of them would be trying to get up their courage to approach. It was like that whenever she went out by herself. Invariably one man would come forward. If she liked him, which was rare, she would have a companion. If she didn't like him, she would send him off and after that the others would all be afraid to try.

Out of the corner of her eye, she saw someone get up two tables down. *The one with the short dark hair and stubble in the beat-up leather jacket*, she predicted. She had noticed him on the way in, as she was scoping the room for any problems.

She was right. The man stood a respectful but not timorous distance from her table and said, 'Excuse me.'

Delilah looked at him and raised her eyebrows.

'You're probably waiting for someone,' he went on, with a smile, 'but if you're not, my friends and I would love to have you join us at our table. Are you a fan of Midori's?'

Actually, he was kind of cute. She liked the jacket and he had an appealing bad-boy smile. But not tonight.

'I'm just getting to know her,' Delilah said. 'And I am waiting for someone. But that was nice of you. Thanks.'

The man nodded. 'Well, if for some reason he loses his mind and doesn't show up, we're two tables down.'

Delilah said, 'Thank you.' This time the thanks was a dismissal. The man gave her another smile and left.

A moment later, Midori and two young men came out from the back. They were all wearing black, but on Midori, as opposed to some of the poseurs at the Mercer, it looked unpretentious. God, unpretentious was the least of it, alongside that black hair and white skin it looked fantastic. The words *she has a child with him* flashed across her mind, and she was surprised by the intensity of jealousy that accompanied the thought.

Midori sat at the piano; the men, at the bass guitar and drums. The lights went down and they started to play. Delilah didn't know jazz the way Rain did, but she recognized the piece they began with, Bill Evans's 'Detour Ahead.'

Sure, she thought. *But for whom?*

A waiter brought her the wine she had ordered. By the time she was halfway through it, some of her earlier jumpiness had started to smooth out. She realized why she was nervous: she wasn't pretending to be someone else. On assignment, she was always undercover. Cover, that was the perfect word. Something you could hide behind, something that would protect you. Something without which you would feel naked.

She'd come here with only a vague notion of what she wanted to do. Warn Midori off, scare her, say something or do something that would poison whatever was happening between her and Rain. But that was just crude reflex. Her ego wanted it so badly that it was blinding her to other possibilities.

Information, that was the thing. There was a lot she wanted to know. And she wasn't going to get it by being the hurt, angry, resentful woman she felt like. No. She would get it by putting all that aside tonight and being someone else. Someone Midori would feel comfortable with, even drawn to, someone she would talk to and open up with.

By the time the set ended and the applause was over an hour later, her nervousness was long gone. She knew who she was tonight, she knew what she wanted, she knew how she was going to get it.

Some of the patrons were lining up to exchange a word with Midori or her band. A few had bought CDs up front and were waiting to have them signed. Delilah watched. The woman was friendly and gracious with her fans, but Delilah could tell there was a professional façade she stood behind while chatting with them. The façade wasn't fake, exactly, the warmth was certainly real enough — but it wasn't the real woman, either. Delilah smiled slightly. Seeing the public display would make it that much easier to know when she had burrowed through to the private person beneath.

The guy in the leather jacket came over and said, 'Looks like whoever he was, he did lose his mind. You feel like a drink?'

Delilah smiled. She knew he'd been watching, and that he'd noticed she was still alone. She liked that he asked again. Someone with a little less confidence might have just sent a drink over at some point. She got that all the time and hated it. It was so lame, a way of trying to force an obligation on someone from a safe distance.

'Thanks for asking,' Delilah said. 'But I'm going to meet him now. I just want to talk to Midori first.'

'Okay . . . ' he said, that nice smile lingering, hoping for more.

Delilah smiled back to let him know she was flattered — he deserved that. But she also dipped her head to let him know the answer was final. He said a gracious good night and they were done.

When the line had dwindled, Delilah got up and walked over. She knew Midori had noticed her during the performance, and then afterward, and now the woman offered a smile, part welcome, part apology for having kept her waiting, part curiosity about who this attractive woman alone might be.

Delilah smiled back and said in a heavier than usual Parisian accent, 'I have to tell you, you play beautifully. I'm so glad I had to come to New York on the same night you were performing.'

Midori said, 'Thank you. Where are you from?'

'Paris.'

'You've heard of me in France? I'm flattered.'

Yes, that was the idea.

'I have friends all over the world who recommend music to me,' Delilah said. 'A girlfriend in Tokyo told me I would like you, so I went online and bought your CD *Another Time*. I love it. I come to Manhattan a few times a year, but this is the first time we've overlapped.'

There, a few more brushstrokes to fill in the canvas. Friends all over the world: cosmopolitan. Interested in music: sophisticated. Frequent trips abroad: wealth, status, an important job, perhaps? With that conjoining *we* at the end

135

subtly implying that Delilah's intriguing international existence might extend also to Midori.

And of course Delilah had as always researched all these points: the name of Midori's album, online availability, etc. She was even ready to talk about her friend in Tokyo, but Midori didn't follow up on that. Instead she asked, 'What brings you to Manhattan from Paris?'

'I'm a fashion scout for some of the boutiques there. I travel around and photograph native clothing styles, art . . . anything that inspires the Paris designers. The business meetings are usually in New York, Milan . . . '

The story was true, too. Delilah really did have relationships with some of the Paris designers, and they really did use her photos. A cover wasn't worth much if you didn't live it.

'Wow,' Midori said. 'That sounds like a fabulous job.'

'I can't complain. But it feels boring compared to what you do.'

Midori laughed. 'I don't know about that.'

'Really. I would kill to have a talent like yours.'

'Well, I guess I can't complain, either.'

'Where did you learn to play? And why jazz? Did you know when you were a child that . . . I'm sorry, you must get this all the time.'

Right. Gorgeous, sophisticated, intriguing women who were ten times more interested in talking about Midori than they were about themselves? Delilah doubted it.

Midori laughed again. 'Not really, no.'

'Well, I'd love to hear more. Look, I know it's

late, and you probably get this all the time, too, but . . . is there somewhere around here we could get a drink? I would really enjoy that. My name is Laure, by the way.'

Midori paused, then said, 'Sure, why not. Let me just call the nanny first, make sure she can stay a little longer.'

Delilah raised her eyebrows innocently. 'Oh, you have kids?'

Midori nodded. 'Baby boy. Hang on.' She pulled out a mobile phone and walked a little way off. After a moment, she came back. 'Okay, we're fine. How about L'Angolo, right next door? It's a neighborhood kind of place, if you like.'

'That sounds great.'

'Just give me a few minutes, then.'

Delilah nodded. Midori disappeared in back for a moment, then came out in a waist-length black leather jacket. They headed for the door. A few more patrons thanked Midori on the way out. She got hugs from the bassist and the drummer. The bartender waved and the bouncer gave her a European double kiss. She was obviously liked here, and at ease. It was her world.

They walked over to the bar Midori had in mind. Delilah unobtrusively checked their surroundings as they moved. She noted that Midori did not.

The bar was nice — a neighborhood place, as Midori had said. It was old and dark, with couches and other upholstered furniture arranged in clusters across an expanse of white tiled floor. The sounds of conversation and music were nicely balanced. You could talk here without shouting.

They sat at a table in one of the corners. Delilah took one end of a couch, her back to the wall; Midori, an overstuffed adjacent chair, her back to the window. Delilah paused for a moment to listen, then said, 'Good song. Oystein Sevag. Learned about him from a friend in Oslo.'

'So it's not just jazz, then?'

Delilah smiled. 'Oh, no. I like everything.' She picked up a menu. 'Well? What do you feel like?'

'Oh, I don't know. Probably just a glass of wine.'

'Should we see if they have a Beaujolais? The Nouveaux just came out, and there are some fun ones this year.'

'That sounds great.'

Delilah looked at the menu and was pleased to see that they had the Domaine Dupeuble, which she thought was among the best of the recent harvest. When the waitress came over, Delilah ordered a bottle. That might have been more than Midori had in mind, but she didn't object.

'How do you like New York?' Delilah asked. 'Your website says you're originally from Tokyo.'

'I love it. This is the second time I've lived here, and it feels like another home.'

'What brought you back?'

'Mostly a job opportunity.' The reply had been smooth enough, but Delilah thought Midori's features had clouded just for an instant as she recalled the circumstances of that move. Interesting.

138

The waitress brought the wine and moved off. Delilah picked up her glass. 'Cheers,' she said. 'It's very good to meet you.'

'Likewise,' Midori said. They touched glasses and drank.

Delilah knew to start slowly. The secret to seduction isn't really the target's attraction to the seducer. It's more how the seducer makes the target feel about himself. Or, in this case, herself. Yes, looks and appearance are important, but only as a foundation. What has to follow is the feeling of pleasure and flattery brought on by the notion that such an alluring creature could be so genuinely fascinated with *me*. Making someone feel important, worthwhile, the center of a universe to which he would ordinarily fear to aspire . . . that was a seduction.

So during their first, and then their second, glass of wine, Delilah asked mostly about Midori's jazz background. Delilah was a fan, after all, and the questions were natural enough. Where did you learn to play the piano? What's the connection to New York? What attracted you to jazz? Who are your influences? What does it feel like to compose a song?

Unlike most men, Midori wasn't entirely blinded by Delilah's attention. She asked lots of questions of her own. But Delilah always managed to turn the conversation back to Midori.

When they had poured out the last of the bottle, Delilah glanced at Midori's hand, as though noticing for the first time that she didn't have a ring. 'Are you married?' she asked.

Midori shook her head. 'No.'

'Forgive me. You had mentioned a baby, so . . .'

'Nothing to forgive. The father lives in Japan.'

Delilah thought it had the feeling of a rehearsed response. It was just deliberately vague enough to ward off further inquiries without causing discomfort.

'That must be hard,' Delilah said.

'No. It's actually for the best.'

Midori offered nothing further, and Delilah understood that, even buzzed from the wine and Delilah's evident interest, Midori wasn't inclined to talk about this.

Change tack. Try a revelation, a shared confidence.

'My mother raised me alone,' Delilah said, now entirely improvising. 'When I was a girl she wouldn't talk about my father.'

Midori leaned forward slightly. 'Why?'

'Well, I didn't find out until much later. My father left her pregnant with me for another woman.'

'Did you . . . are you in touch with him now?'

Hmm. Midori had just jumped about two conversational steps ahead of what Delilah had been expecting. Delilah's story had obviously tapped into something that was on Midori's mind.

'I've seen him,' Delilah said, holding back to see whether her story provoked enough curiosity to get Midori to ask more questions.

It did. Midori asked, 'How was that? I mean, if I'm not being too personal.'

Yes, this subject was definitely on the woman's mind. Interesting. Delilah shook her head and said, 'It was okay. He'd like to have a relationship now, but I don't know. I grew up without him and never missed him. At this point, I don't know that I need him in my life.'

Midori nodded. 'So you didn't miss him when you were a girl? You didn't wish . . . you know, that he and your mother had reconciled, that kind of thing?'

'No. I think it was better that they didn't. Some things shouldn't be forgiven.'

'Not even for the children?'

'No, of course for the children. But the question is, what's best for the children.'

Midori took a sip of wine. 'You're right. That is the question.'

There was a long pause. Delilah said, 'It sounds like this is something you've been thinking about.'

Midori nodded. 'Just recently, the father showed up unexpectedly and paid us a visit.'

Delilah felt her heart beat harder, but her face betrayed nothing.

'Really? How was that?'

Midori sighed. 'Confusing. I thought I'd made up my mind, but now . . . I don't know.' She took another sip of wine.

Delilah saw an opening. 'Well, if he's the father, why isn't he in your life?'

'It's a long story, actually, and not something I'm comfortable talking about.'

Okay, that wasn't the right approach. She would have to find another way. 'I'm sorry.'

141

'No, it's all right. It's just . . . you know, when he saw the baby, that's what really turned my head around. He cried. I'd never seen him cry before. He's not the crying type. And then, two minutes later, we were kissing like I couldn't believe. I don't know how I managed to ask him to go. If he'd pushed it a little harder . . . I don't know. I just don't know.'

Delilah's face went hot with jealousy and anger and she hoped she wasn't flushing. She had always assumed that, when he wasn't with her, Rain had other women. She certainly had her fill of other men. They didn't get to see each other frequently, and she didn't expect either of them to remain celibate during the other's absence. But a passionate kiss with an ex-lover, which sounded like the start of something much, much more? That was totally different. After all, he had said he was coming to New York to see his child, not to fuck his old girlfriend. And he would have, that was clear, he'd been trying to do just that but Midori had turned him away.

She let out a long breath and took a sip of wine. 'Sounds like you have a pretty strong connection.'

'I don't know what we have. Good chemistry, definitely. And we went through this really intense . . . experience together once. But now, for me, it's really about the baby. I worry about him growing up without his father. I worry about what I'm going to tell him.'

Delilah shrugged. 'Don't tell him anything. That's the way my mother handled it with me.'

'That's what I was planning on, more or less.

142

Now I don't know.'

Delilah's heart beat harder and she said, 'Well, when you saw him, where did you leave it?'

'I don't even know exactly. He lives in a different world than mine. I told him if he ever gets out of that world, he could call me then. But I don't think he can get out of it. He's been in it forever, and I actually think . . . ah, I don't know.'

'What?'

Midori took a sip of wine. 'I think he likes it. I mean, he says he wants to get out, but if he really wanted to, he could, couldn't he? And he's had good reasons. The baby being the most recent.'

Every piece of information Delilah had teased out so far had been disappointing, even painful to hear. Still, there was that one thing, the one she'd wondered about in Paris, that might trump all the rest. She had tried for it subtly a moment ago, but Midori had blocked that approach. Well, subtlety was only a tool. There were other tools available. She felt a flush of adrenaline in her torso as she prepared to strip away the cover she had been wearing and emerge from beneath it.

'Maybe he's reticent because he knows he can never completely get out,' Delilah said, looking at Midori intently. 'And if he tries to live like a civilian, with a civilian, he'll always be a danger to that person. And she'll always be a danger to him.'

Midori shook her head slightly as though to clear it. 'What?'

'You know, a man like Rain has a lot of enemies.'

Midori looked at her. A long, silent moment spun out.

'And even if he could get out of the life,' Delilah went on, 'his enemies won't.'

'I'm sorry. You . . . know him?'

Delilah nodded. 'I know him well.'

'You . . . oh, my God.'

'Listen. If you do care about him, if you care about yourself and your son, you'll know to stay the hell away from him.'

Midori's eyes narrowed and some of the color drained from her face. 'Listen to me, you bitch. I don't know who you are. But if you ever threaten my child again, I will hunt you down and I will fucking kill you.'

Delilah held up her hands, realizing she had dangerously misspoken. 'I'm not threatening anyone. I want you and your son safe. My point is just that Rain can be a danger to the people around him. Haven't you noticed that?'

There was a long pause. Midori said, 'So you're part of his world, is that right?'

'Yes.'

'And . . . you're involved, in some way?'

Delilah shrugged.

'So . . . Jun must have told you about the baby, told you he was coming to see us. And you came here, you met me tonight with this bullshit story, because you were jealous. Is that about right?'

'I came here tonight because I don't want to see anyone get hurt. You and Rain together is an accident waiting to happen. I saw you on the way over here, and forgive me, but you don't have a clue. You never once checked your surroundings, you didn't look at the vehicles around us, nothing. I told you I'm no threat, but what if I had been? What would you have done? You're going to live like that with Rain? And if he starts living that way, how long do you think he's going to last?'

Midori said nothing. Delilah knew that right now, the woman's thoughts would be swirling around inside her head like a whiteout blizzard. This was the moment.

'Besides,' Delilah said, 'what kind of future can you have with him after what he did to your father?'

Midori flinched as though she'd been slapped. She stared at Delilah for a moment, and the shock and hurt in her eyes were palpable. Then her expression hardened and she stood up.

'I'm sure there's nothing else we have to say to each other,' she said. She turned and walked out.

Delilah watched her go. She felt suddenly off balance. Maybe it had been the abruptness of the woman's departure. Maybe its dignity.

But that was it, then. Rain had killed Midori's father, and Midori knew it. The look in the woman's eyes when Delilah spoke had confirmed it as definitively as a signed affidavit.

That was exactly what Delilah had come here to learn. It suggested that Rain's attachment to the woman had something to do with guilt, which could be managed. And it suggested that no matter what else might attract Rain and Midori to each other, there was one fundamental thing that would always keep them apart.

All of which was good news. She finished her wine and signaled for the check.

Good news, she told herself again.

So why did she feel so horrible?

★ ★ ★

Midori paced back and forth in her living room. Digne had left. Koichiro was sleeping peacefully.

She felt violated. How could the woman have known about her father? Had she been involved in his murder? No, that didn't seem right, a blonde like her would stand out in Tokyo, and besides, Midori had a feeling the woman's acquaintance with Rain was more recent. But how, then? The only way she could think of was that Rain must have told her. My God, was that his idea of sharing intimacies? Was that their pillow talk?

She sat down and breathed deeply, in and out, trying to quell a rising feeling of nausea. The thought that she had been half-consciously looking for some way to forgive Rain suddenly shamed her. And here he was discussing the source of her shame with some new lover. How could he? *How could he?*

She tried to focus on her breathing, but she couldn't calm down. Why had the woman come here? To warn Midori off, that was clear. To tell her Rain would always be a danger to her and Koichiro. Tell her, hell, the woman had proven it. What had it been — forty-eight hours since Rain had shown up in Midori's life? And already his world was trailing after him like some foul wake.

And why would the woman have told her that she knew about her father? *To get me to react exactly like this*, Midori thought.

But that realization didn't change the fundamental fact that Rain had discussed the most intimate secret Midori could imagine, discussed it as though it was just some common problem he'd had with a woman from his past.

She hunched forward, her eyes squeezed shut, fistfuls of hair balled in her hands. She'd actually been hoping. She had. She realized that now.

Maybe she was jumping to conclusions. Maybe Rain didn't tell the woman. Maybe she found out some other way.

But that didn't matter. It didn't even matter what the woman wanted. What mattered was that she had been telling the truth. Rain was a danger. And he always would be.

She wanted him out of her life. Hers and Koichiro's. Forever.

16

The next morning, I used the Watanabe identity to rent a van at a place in Shinjuku. After that, I shopped for some supplemental items: warm, dark clothing; waterproof boots; two-way radios in case cell phone coverage was lacking by the Sea of Japan. I spent the balance of the day sleeping. Not an ideal way to adjust to the local time zone, but I needed the rest and Dox and I were going to be working at night, anyway. I woke up just as the sun was setting, and after the proper procedures to ensure I was alone, I went out to a pay phone to call Kanezaki.

'*Hai,*' he said, after the customary single ring.

'You get what I asked for?'

'It's all right here. Oplus-XT Gauged CO_2 rifle with AN/PVS-17 Mini night-vision scope, two SOCOM HK Mark 23s each with Trijicon night sights, AN/PEQ-6 infrared laser aiming module, Knight's Armament suppressor, spare mag, one hundred rounds of Federal Hydra-Shok, and Wilcox tactical thigh holster, two pairs of AN/PVS-7 night-vision goggles, Agency-designed GPS transmitter with magnetic mounts for surreptitious emplacement and accompanying monitor with mapping software. The only thing I couldn't do was the ten darts. Turns out we only had five on hand.'

'Shit,' I said, and started running through the plan to see how we could adjust.

'You were lucky we even had the rifle and the five darts. This kind of stuff is used mostly for rendering bad guys in Europe and the Middle East. The only reason we had any of it is because someone in the embassy must have realized there was some counterterror money left over in the budget and wanted to use it up.'

'What's in the darts?'

'Some commercial variation of liquid succinylcholine chloride. There's a small explosive charge that injects the drug on impact, so pulling the dart out won't help. Very fast-acting, depending on where you place the shot. The neck is best.'

'Is weight a factor?'

'No. These things are rated for anything up to a rhinoceros.'

'All right, five will have to do it.'

'This is some expensive equipment, you know. I'm going to be in major shit if any of it goes missing.'

'I can tell you you're not getting the darts back.'

'I'm not talking about the darts. Or the ammo.'

'Where do I pick it up?'

'Wherever you want,' he said, knowing I'd be more comfortable choosing the place.

I considered. I knew I was clean at the moment and didn't need time to run a route. And I didn't want to give Kanezaki time to set anything up. Not that he would — especially if he assumed I was on the hook now for a 'favor' — but it always pays to be careful.

'JR Harajuku Station platform,' I said. 'Thirty minutes from now.'

'Okay.'

Twenty minutes later, I stepped off the Yamanote onto the platform at Harajuku. Nothing pinged my radar. Crowds were moderate, and divided more or less equally between teenagers heading to nearby Takeshita-dori, the grunge/retro/hip-hop shopping strip, and smartly dressed adults heading to the bistros and boutiques of adjacent Omotesando-dori. That the two disparate groups and places existed side by side in parallel dimensions would never cease to please me. It was part of what made Tokyo tick.

Kanezaki arrived on time, stepping off a Shinjuku-bound train with a medium-sized blue duffel slung over his shoulder. He was wearing a dark suit and, but for something detectably western in his posture and gait, could have been just another young Japanese corporate samurai.

He saw me and headed over. I scanned the other people who had gotten off the train. I noted no problems.

He put the duffel down and we shook hands. The bug detector my late friend Harry had made for me slumbered in my pocket. Kanezaki was clean.

'How've you been?' he asked.

'All right,' I said, looking him over. 'You?'

'Fine.'

'How's the Global War on Terrorism?'

He smiled. 'These days we call it the Global Struggle Against Violent Extremism.'

I liked that he didn't get defensive. Not so long before, he would have taken my derisiveness personally. I wondered if his people knew how capable he was becoming. Probably not.

'Yeah, GWOT just wasn't a winning acronym,' I said. 'I'm sure it'll go better now that you've renamed it.'

He chuckled. 'You want to tell me what all the hardware's for? And who you're working with? Two of this, two of that, it's not like you.'

I looked at him. Yeah, he was capable. But maybe getting a little full of himself, too.

'You're charging me a 'favor' for this,' I said, my voice cold, 'and now you're asking for freebies?'

He looked taken aback. 'I only meant . . . '

'Look, are we doing this as an exchange of cooperation and goodwill, or as a sales transaction?'

'I was hoping it could be both.'

'It can't. Choose one. And live with it.'

He was quiet for a moment. Then he said, 'Let me think about it.'

I shrugged. We were quiet again.

'Have you been in touch with Tatsu?' I asked.

'For a while, but not just lately. He's busy, I'm busy . . . '

'He's in the hospital.'

He looked at me, and the concern I saw was genuine. 'No. Nothing serious?'

'Gastric cancer. If you want to see him, he's at Jikei. But you better do it soon.'

'Oh, shit.'

'Go see him. He thinks of you as a kind of

151

protégé, someone who can carry on his work. But he's too proud to say it.'

He nodded. 'Thanks for telling me.'

I shouldered the duffel. 'I'll be in touch.'

He held out his hand and, after a moment, I shook it.

'Be careful,' he said.

'Yeah,' I told him. 'I wouldn't want you to miss out on that favor.'

17

The drive to Wajima the next morning lasted about five hours. Japanese highways, burdened as they are by frequent and excessive tolls, tend also to be mercifully free of traffic. I used cash for the tolls, having declined the rental car company's offer to set me up with the latest in electronic collection technology. Electronic payment is too easy to track.

Along the way, we stopped at an abandoned building site to check out all the equipment. Dox had never used a CO_2 rifle before, and the reason I had wanted more darts was so he could train with it. With only five darts in our arsenal, though, I felt we could spare only one for practice.

'Make it count,' I told him, as he took a prone position eighty meters away from an aluminum can I'd propped up at the top of a fence.

There was the soft crack of suddenly discharging compressed gas, and an instant later an answering ping eighty meters downfield. I looked through the binoculars and the can was gone. I started to tell Dox, but he already knew. He looked up at me and smiled. 'Shit, eighty meters,' he said. 'I could hit 'em with a rock from this close.'

Before getting back in the van, I used a toothbrush to comb some white liquid shoe polish into my hair. The polish gave a nice salt-and-pepper effect, far more pronounced than what had lately been creeping in naturally at my temples and over my ears, and would add ten years to a witness's description. A pair of hopelessly unstylish thick-framed non-prescription eyeglasses that I had picked up before leaving Tokyo completed the effect.

We arrived at Wajima at a little after noon, and I called the inn to see if I could check in. As expected, they asked if I could come at two. That was fine. It suggested that Yamaoto's men weren't there yet, either.

Dox and I spent the next hour and a half driving around, familiarizing ourselves with Wajima. The area was still pretty in places, I thought, but like much of Japan it was under siege from development. The native deciduous trees, orange and red in the chill air, were everywhere being cut down and replaced with monoculture cedar by the region's logging interests. What remained looked like a patchwork of native flesh half covered with green bandages that did nothing to stanch the wounds beneath. Everything was paved — riverbeds, hillsides, even the coast. It seemed that only the sea itself was free from the metastasizing onslaught of development, but as we drove along the coast I saw that some council or interest group or bureaucracy was in the midst of partially enclosing Wajima harbor with a giant wall of concrete. I thought of what Dox had said, about Americans professing to love peace but always waging war. Japanese maintain a traditional reverence for nature, but here they were

154

entombing all traces of it in a concrete sarcophagus. At what point would this culture have to look in the mirror and admit that its traditional love of nature had become a living lie?

When we had seen as much as was useful from the van, we parked so I could have a look around on foot. Dox wanted to get out, too, but accepted that in sleepy Wajima, his white face and outsized frame would eclipse his ordinarily strong cloaking skills. He lay down in back while I set out underneath a cold sky darkening with rain clouds.

The town felt tired to me. I saw much gray hair and no children, although I imagined the latter must exist somewhere. The local economy seemed to be on a subsistence diet of foresting, fishing, and farming, supplemented by a trickle of tourists taking the waters and returning home with gifts of locally made lacquerware.

I walked down to the harbor, my shoulders hunched against a bitter sea breeze. The road in was hemmed on both sides with detritus from the fishing industry — torn nets, broken ballast, rusted-out crab traps. Much of it was covered in blue tarpaulins that blanketed the shapes beneath like trembling shrouds. Everywhere there were gulls, cooing and cawing. Beyond the debris, scores of small fishing boats rose and fell, creaking against their moorings, their tangled rigging skeletal against the scudded horizon. A crushed coffee cup skidded past my feet, impelled by the wind, and a cold mist started down from the sky and in from the water.

They might have been planning to meet here,

but I doubted it. The layout was too confusing, for one thing; people might be around, for another. I headed east along the coast. Giant concrete tetrapods lay at the water's edge like unexploded ordinance from a long forgotten war. The mist was getting heavier and the clouds darker, and I sensed we were in for a storm.

Past the tetrapods, I came to some sort of park that was being used as a staging ground for further construction. Trucks were parked here and there and I saw piles of cement and girders and similar materials. A wide grassy field gave way to dirt, and dirt gave way to open water. *Here*, I thought, *they're going to do it right here. It's perfect*. And perfect sniping ground, too. I used the camera we'd bought in New York to take pictures from various angles, then went back to the van so I could walk Dox through the terrain.

We finished going through the pictures just before two o'clock, and I drove us to the inn. It was a small, three-story structure separated from the sea by the narrow coastal road and a short embankment of grass. I parked in the lot behind the building. 'You going to be all right?' I asked Dox. 'I don't know when Yamaoto's people are going to arrive. It might be a while.'

'Partner, I once waited three days in the mud before my quarry came into view. Nailed him, too, from eight hundred yards out. The inside of a van feels like paradise by comparison. Got my sleeping bag, foam mattress, food, water, a plastic jug for number one and a bucket and plastic bags for number two. Plus reading material, including some high-quality Japanese pornography. Life couldn't be better.'

'Well, I'll be sure to knock before I come inside,' I told him, and he laughed.

I looked through the driver's and passenger's side windows. There were three other cars in the lot, possibly belonging to inn employees, possibly to guests who had checked in yesterday or earlier. They were all small, older model Toyotas and the like, and none had Tokyo plates. I had a feeling Yamaoto's men weren't here yet. Still, I would remember the cars so I could compare later.

'You might see them before I do,' I said. 'I expect they'll be parking back here, just like us.'

'Yeah, I'll sneak a look whenever I hear a car pull in. If I see anything promising, I'll call you on the cell phone.'

I got out and walked around to the front entrance. I stepped inside and was immediately transported by the warm smell of incense and tatami mats. A middle-aged woman in a blue kimono welcomed me with a bow. I took off my shoes and followed her in. She had me sit at a low table in the lobby while I — or I should say Mr Watanabe — filled out some check-in paperwork.

The procedure had an air of ritual about it, and I realized Yamaoto's men would probably have to pause here, too. I looked around for a good vantage point and was pleased to see a second-story sitting area open to the lobby below. It offered stellar views of the sea and, more important from my perspective, of where

157

Yamaoto's men would enter as I had.

The woman returned with a cup of barley tea. 'You're traveling alone, Watanabe-san?' she asked, no doubt hoping for an answer to her implicit question of 'Why?'

'Yes,' I told her. 'My wife passed away recently, and because we honeymooned in this area I wanted to return to it.'

'I'm saddened to hear of your loss,' she said, bowing her head. As I expected in the face of Watanabe's sad story, she asked no further questions, and I needed tell her no further lies. But I was confident that word would now circulate among the staff, and that consequently no one would find it at all remarkable that sad Watanabe-san might sit brooding for long hours alone on that second-floor balcony.

I dropped off my bag in my room on the third floor, a twelve-mat square with an alcove and a view of the sea that was impressive in spite of the tangle of high-tension wire in front of it. Then I went down to the lobby restaurant, sat so I had a view of the entrance, and ate a long, leisurely lunch of oysters from Anamizu Bay, sweet shrimp from the deep waters of the Sea of Japan, and locally caught winter yellowtail with sliced radish and red pepper. During my repast a few elderly couples checked in, but they obviously weren't the people Dox and I were waiting for.

Afterward, I repaired to the second-story balcony, where I waited as though absorbed in my memories. It was just getting dark outside when my cell phone buzzed. I glanced at the caller ID readout — Dox.

158

I pressed the receive button. 'Yeah.'

'Looks like our company has finally arrived,' Dox said.

'You sure?'

'Let's just say I've got a strong feeling. They're coming in now.'

'What do they look like?'

'Oh, don't worry, you're not going to miss them.'

'What do you mean?'

'Just watch, you'll see.'

I looked down into the lobby. I heard the front door open and close. The blue-kimonoed woman who had greeted me called out '*Irasshaimase*' — welcome — and hurried out from behind the check-in counter. A moment later, two gigantic men, obviously sumo wrestlers, appeared below me. I sat well back to conceal myself and from the angle I couldn't be sure, but I estimated each of them at north of a hundred and fifty kilos. It was like looking down on the heads and shoulders of a pair of bison.

'Holy shit,' I whispered.

'Guess you've seen 'em,' Dox said.

'Christ, we've only got four darts.'

'Yeah, as I think Roy Scheider put it in *Jaws*, 'We're gonna need a bigger boat.''

They said something to the woman, but I couldn't quite make out what. She escorted them inside.

It wasn't just their bulk that advertised their background. They had that slow sumo swagger, that air of royalty — almost of divinity — born of size and celebrity. They were used to being looked at, to being the objects of attention and awe, and they moved as though bearing the adoration as of right, with no obligation to repay it with anything more than impassive acceptance.

I moved farther back, out of their view. 'Did you see what they're driving?' I asked.

''Course I did. Big burgundy Cadillac, with the steering wheel on the left side.'

Sounded like a yakuza ride. It had to be them.

'You get the license plate?'

'Yeah.' He gave it to me, and I wrote it down. 'Hang on,' I said. 'I'll call you back.'

'Roger that.'

I called Tatsu. The phone rang a few times, then his weak voice said, '*Hai.*'

'How are you holding up?' I asked.

'I'm still here.'

I had the sudden sick knowledge that one day soon I would call him and he wouldn't answer, he wouldn't still be here at all.

I pushed that aside and said, 'I think our guys have arrived, but I need to be sure. Kito and Sanada . . . are they sumo wrestlers?'

'I don't know. But I can find out.'

'All right. Here's the license number of the car they're driving. Tokyo plate.'

I read it out to him. He told me he would call me back.

I stole another peek down at the lobby. The men had finished signing in, and the woman in blue was walking them to the elevator, presumably to show them their rooms.

Fifteen minutes later, Tatsu called back. 'It's them,' he said. 'Both former sumo wrestlers, their careers cut short by injuries. The car is registered to Kito.'

'Okay. Let me get back to business. I'll call you again soon.'

'Good.'

I hung up and called Dox.

'You were right,' I told him. 'They're the ones we've been waiting for. Former sumo wrestlers.'

' "Former?" They look pretty current to me.'

'I know what you mean.'

'Were they any good?'

'How the hell should I know?'

'Just wondering if we could handle 'em if we had to.'

' "Handle" them? There must be seven or eight hundred pounds between the two of them. We're going to handle them with long-range weapons, that's how we're going to handle them. And only because we can't call in an air strike.'

'All right, just trying to contingency plan, that's all.'

'If we have to tangle with these guys up close, I advise prayer.'

'You stick with the prayer. I prefer to rely on something sharp if it comes to that.'

'I hope it's a harpoon. I doubt anything else could reach a vital organ.'

'Well, how about if . . . '

'Look, it's not that I don't want to sit around figuring out how to kill a sumo,' I said, 'but if it's clear now, maybe you could duck out and put the transmitter in place on their car. I'll stay here and warn you if anyone's coming.'

'Roger that.'

Two minutes later he called me back. 'It's done. Anywhere they go, we can tail 'em from a distance and we'll know where they stop. And if they walk, we can just follow the sounds of the earth shaking beneath their feet.'

'Right,' I said. I pictured the four darts we had. Kanezaki had said they were good for anything up to a rhino. I hoped he meant it literally. Otherwise, we were going to be in trouble.

18

The next thirty hours were mostly watching and waiting. The inn's *kaiseki* — Japanese haute cuisine — was excellent, and its *onsen* hot spring baths were wonderful. I availed myself of both lest my reticence be remarked on, and felt a little bad amid the luxurious surroundings about having to leave Dox in the van. Twice on our second day at the inn I drove us out to more remote areas so he could stretch and get some air. He was never anything other than cheerful and I thought some distant Marine gods must be proud.

The clouds of the previous day coalesced into a storm that broke just after midnight. I sat in the alcove of my room, the lights off, my gaze alternating between the GPS monitor, which indicated the Cadillac hadn't moved, and the dark sea without. At a little after two, my cell phone buzzed. It was Dox.

'Our friends are getting in the car,' he said. 'Wonder who they could be going to meet at this hour and in this weather.'

'We're going to find out,' I said. I got up, pulled on the waterproof pants and jacket I had bought for this very occasion, and headed for the door.

The lobby of the inn was deserted. I was prepared with a story, of course, about wanting to walk in the rain, but that would have been thin and I was glad not to have to employ it.

We followed the Cadillac from a half-kilometer back. Dox, in a black nylon-lined fleece, monitored the transmitter from the passenger seat. The Cadillac showed up as a blinking red light on the mapping software and we had no trouble tracking it. So far, so good.

We passed no cars on the coastal road. After a few minutes, the red light started moving around erratically — figure eights and zigzags.

'They're looking for problems,' Dox observed.

I nodded. 'That's why we're hanging back.'

After another few minutes, the red light turned right, into the park I had reconnoitered earlier, then stopped.

'What did I tell you,' I said, smiling.

He chuckled. 'Like I said, devious minds think alike.'

I cut the lights and we drove the rest of the way with the night-vision goggles on. Everything showed up fine. A hundred meters past the park, we pulled off the road and stopped. The rain played a drumbeat on the van's steel top while we geared up inside.

'Remember, the neck,' I said, wrapping tape around my pant legs to make sure the material from the left wouldn't make noise rubbing against the right. 'The farther away from the neck you hit, the longer it's going to take the tranquilizer to kick in. And I don't want to have to dance in the dark with two half-drugged, pissed-off sumo wrestlers.'

'You sure? I'd pay good money to see it.'

In the green glow of the night-vision

equipment I saw he was grinning below his goggles. 'Start with one dart each,' I said. 'See if that does the trick. We'll only need them down for a minute, but with the size of these guys I don't know. So if the first shot doesn't work right away, hit them again. Don't take chances. If we wind up having to shoot them, it's not going to look like they ripped off the Chinese. And that's the whole point here.'

'Roger that.'

I double-checked the HK to make sure a round was chambered. 'You ready?'

'Never readier, son.'

'Let's go.'

I had already made sure to shut off the interior dome light, and the van stayed dark as we exited. We closed the doors softly, but the rain was really coming down now and I doubted anyone would have heard regardless.

We crept along the sodden ground to the Cadillac, heads and guns tracking left and right as we moved. Everything was illuminated beautifully in the goggles. The car was empty. We paused alongside it and looked down the gently sloping ground to the water.

There they were, ten meters away, standing at the edge of the surf like a pair of boulders overlooking the sea. They were wearing trench coats and held umbrellas that looked like little parasols hovering above their bulk.

'Man,' Dox whispered. 'If you stuck bulbs in their mouths, you'd have yourself a pair of damn lighthouses.'

One of the sumos had a phone to his ear but I

couldn't hear him over the steady downpour. The other guy was looking at a small LCD monitor, and I realized they were using their own GPS equipment to link up with the boat that was bringing in their shipment. A black cargo bag was on the ground between them, presumably payment for the drugs.

I took off the goggles for a moment and let my eyes adjust. I wanted an idea of how well anyone could see unaided in the darkness. Not well at all, I was pleased to note. There was some ambient light from distant streetlights and the moon behind the rain clouds — enough for the Chinese and sumos to make the exchange, I thought, but not enough to make out individual faces. As long as we took care not to silhouette ourselves against the reflected light from the town we wouldn't be seen until it was too late.

I put the goggles back on. A moment later there was a flash from somewhere on the water. The sumo with the phone took out a flashlight and blinked back. I signaled to Dox and he nodded, then moved off to settle into sniping position.

There was another series of flashes from sea, closer this time, and responses from the sumo. After a few minutes I heard the thrum of an engine through the steady beat of the rain, and then an inflatable catamaran came cutting through the waves.

My heart started hammering. *Here we go*, I thought.

I took out the cell phone and called Dox. The screens on both our units were taped to prevent

166

light from giving us away. 'You in position?' I whispered.

'Roger that. I'm fifty yards behind you, prone on higher ground. Perfect position and a clear field of fire.'

'You see the boat?'

'I see it. Looks like two . . . no, wait, make that three Chinamen on board.'

'All right. Wait until they're off the boat, or as many of them as look like they're going to get off, then drop the sumos. I'll take it from there.'

'Roger that.'

I clicked off and put the phone away.

The boat came closer. As it reached the shoreline, I could make out individual faces. No one was sporting any night-vision equipment. Apparently, they didn't think they'd need it.

One of the Chinese cut the engine and raised it out of the water. Another jumped into the surf and waded in, pulling the boat behind him by a rope. When the boat was grounded, the other two Chinese got out, too. Each of them carried a large waterproof duffel bag. They went back to the boat twice more. When they were done, there were six duffels lined up next to the boat.

The Chinese who had jumped out first gestured to the sumos. The other two stood off to the side, watching the sumos warily. One of the giant men picked up the cargo bag and came closer, his buddy following from behind, no doubt to provide cover if something went wrong. As indeed it soon would.

I eased out from behind the Cadillac and moved silently toward the water.

The Chinese unzipped one of the bags, presumably to show the lead sumo the product inside.

I reached the surf ten meters down from them and went in up to my knees. The water was cold but I barely felt it. I started moving in from their flank, crouching low, the HK out at chin level in a two-handed grip. I moved deliberately, trading speed for stealth, wanting to get as close as possible. If I failed to drop them all instantly, whoever I missed might return fire on whatever muzzle flash escaped my suppressor, and I was less than enthusiastic about the prospect of panicked triad members spraying bullets in my uncovered general direction from a stone's throw away.

There was a soft crack from somewhere behind us. The rear sumo cried out and slapped a hand to his neck with a loud *thwack*.

Everyone froze and looked at him.

I crept in closer. Four meters now.

If the lead sumo hadn't turned, too, I expected the Chinese would have dropped him then and there. But his hands were out and he seemed as surprised as they were.

The rear sumo took an unsteady step forward. The lead Chinese yelled something, a warning, presumably, and backed away.

Three meters.

The lead sumo started to turn back to the Chinese, his hand going to his jacket.

There was another soft crack. Instead of reaching into his jacket, the sumo cried out and grabbed his neck.

The CO_2 cartridges produced no muzzle flash. And in the dark and rain, it was impossible to tell where the sounds of fire had come from, or even what they were.

The sumos were both staggering now. The Chinese were all watching with the internationally approved expression for *What the fuck?* frozen on their faces.

The first sumo sank to his knees. The other stumbled into him and tripped. The Chinese scattered, and the falling sumo landed on his partner like a tree felled by a logger. The ground shook with the impact, and, as one, the Chinese cried out and pulled out machine pistols. They pointed them first at the sumo pile, then, their higher brains perhaps getting a word in edgewise, started looking around wildly, their eyes wide in the dark.

I put the infrared laser on the head of the man farthest from me. I saw the dot clearly in the night-vision goggles. Without the goggles, I knew, the dot was invisible. I took a deep breath, exhaled, and rolled my trigger finger in.

Pfffttt. The .45 round caught him in the side of the head and he flopped soundlessly forward onto the ground.

Pfffttt. The second guy went down the same way.

The third guy looked at his fallen comrades. Then, possibly realizing what had happened, he started to wheel around toward me.

Too late. I shot him in the head, too, and he collapsed beside the others.

I scanned the beach. A few meters away the

sumos were still piled one on top of the other, both facedown. I realized with a start that the guy on the bottom might be suffocating. His face was in the mud, and large as he was, that was a hell of a load bearing down on him from above. If he suffocated, this wasn't going to look the way we needed it to look. I signaled to Dox to come in, and started wading ashore.

I walked up from behind and prodded them each with a wet boot. No response. Okay, they were out. I secured the HK in the holster and felt under their jackets. The lead guy had reached for something at one point, so I knew they were carrying. There it was, a pistol in his unending waistband. I pulled it out and flung it into the surf, then, in spite of all the folds of flesh, managed to repeat the operation for the other guy.

I grabbed the top guy's wrist. I pulled hard but it was like trying to uproot a tree.

Shit, the bottom guy was definitely eating mud. I pulled hard again. Again he didn't budge.

A moment later, Dox reached my position. 'Nice shooting,' he said. 'One shot, one kill. Or in this case three shots, three kills.'

'Give me a hand with this guy,' I said, still trying to pull the sumo by the wrist. 'I think he's smothering the one underneath him.'

'Ah, shit.' Dox dropped the tranquilizer rifle and grabbed the sumo by the arm. We managed to pull him partly off his partner, but not enough. I squatted down and lifted the bottom guy's head off the ground. His eyes were shut and his face was covered with mud. I couldn't

170

tell if he was breathing.

'If that boy needs resuscitating, you can count me out,' Dox said from behind me.

I put my ear near the sumo's mouth but couldn't hear anything. 'He's still getting crushed. We've got to move the one on top. Roll him or something.'

'Shit, man, I'd rather try moving that Cadillac back there.'

'I'm serious, goddamnit. We can't have one of these guys dead from suffocation. It won't fit.'

Dox moved up alongside me and we both grabbed the back of the top guy's coat. The material was slippery with rain and mud and it was hard to get a solid grip. I thought, *Worst case, if he's dead, we grab one of the machine pistols and shoot him. Then it'll look like he died in a gunfight with the Chinese and his partner got away with the money and drugs. Not as good as three dead triads and two missing yakuza, but not a total loss, either.*

I looked at Dox. 'One, two, three!'

We pulled. The inert mass of the sumo pulled back. The inert mass won.

'Now there's a quality garment for you,' Dox said. 'For a second there, about four hundred pounds were suspended by nothing but raincoat.'

'Again. One, two . . . '

With a berserker yell, the sumo rolled over and seized my wrist in one massive paw. Whether he'd been playing possum or had come to suddenly, I didn't know. I yelled, 'Fuck!' and tried to jerk away, but I might as well have been a child.

171

Dox reacted instantly. He took a long step back and cleared leather. 'Don't shoot!' I yelled. 'Not with the same guns that did the Chinese!'

The sumo's face was glistening with dripping mud and water. His eyes were wild, his teeth bared. He snarled and started reeling me in by the wrist.

I dropped down on my ass and planted both boots against the side of his face. I strained backward, and the combined strength of my back and quadriceps broke his grip.

I rolled away from him and came to my feet at the same instant he did. He bellowed something unintelligible and charged me. I dodged and yelled to Dox, 'Tranq gun!'

The sumo charged again. This time I barely managed to slip by him. His speed and coordination were off because of the tranquilizer, but I didn't know how much longer that was going to last.

The sumo stopped and faced me, his breath rumbling in and out of his chest. He was starting to think, I could tell. He was going to slow it down this time, and he wasn't going to miss.

There was a soft crack off to the side. The sumo grabbed his stomach and grunted. Then he looked up at me, his eyes blazing.

'I told you, neck shots!' I yelled, and pulled out the HK.

'I'm doing the best I can here!' I heard Dox yell from somewhere on my right.

'*Ugoku na! Samonaito utsuzo!*' I yelled in Japanese. Don't move, or I'll shoot! I hoped the threat would give him pause. If I really had to shoot him, it would ruin everything. But if I didn't, he was going to break me like a matchstick.

Then I realized: the sumo had heard us speaking English, and now Japanese. That wasn't something I wanted remembered. But maybe I could obscure it.

'*Wau ai ni!*' I yelled at him, using pretty much the only Chinese I know. '*Wau ai ni! Ni ai wau ma?*'

My shouting seemed only to make the sumo angrier. He dropped one hand to the ground like a linebacker in a three-point stance. His breathing was locomotive loud. I wondered for a crazy second, *Maybe the guy speaks Chinese?*

I feinted left, then right, thinking, *Come on, come on, the shit is supposed to be fast-acting . . .*

The sumo tracked me with rage-filled eyes. Then he shook his head as though to clear it. I breathed silent words of gratitude.

The sumo took an unsteady step toward me, then another. I circled toward the surf. There was less light in the sky over the water, and he would have a harder time silhouetting me there.

He kept coming, but he was on autopilot now, his arms stretched out in front of him as though he was sleepwalking. I moved off to the side and watched him. He took two steps. Three. Another.

Oh, shit, he was going to make it to the water.

'*Oi! Kochi da! Kochi da!*' I yelled. Hey! Over here! Over here! Then some Chinese again, to obscure things: '*Wau ai ni! Wau ai ni!*'

as at the edge of the water now. I yelled
in.

He started to turn toward me. I let out a sigh
of relief.

He tottered for a second, swaying first toward
shore, then toward sea.

Dox moved up next to me and shouldered the
rifle. We watched in mute fascination.

Shore, sea.

I realized Dox and I were leaning backward as
though to influence him with body English. Dox
whispered, 'Come on, come on . . . '

The sumo pitched forward and hit the surf
with a crash that sent a geyser up around him.
'Shit, here we go again,' Dox said, and we
charged in after him.

For a guy who weighed just south of a quarter
ton, the sumo floated pretty well. We got ahold of
the lapels of his jacket and somehow managed to
turn him on his back and drag him up onto the
muddy beach far enough so that his face was out
of the water.

We moved a few feet away from him and stood
sucking wind. After a moment, Dox laughed.
'Well, that was a mad minute if I ever had one,'
he said.

I laughed, too. Yeah, it had been a close one.

'Hey, man,' he said, 'what the fuck were you
yelling at him in Chinese?'

'I don't want them telling anyone their
attackers were using English and Japanese. If it
gets back to Yamaoto, it sounds too much like
me. I was trying to obscure things.'

'Yeah, but '*Wau ai ni*'? 'I love you'? You're

telling that boy you love him, no wonder he tried to kill us!'

We laughed again. 'It's the only Chinese I know,' I said.

'Well, it is a useful phrase, in my experience. Sometime you'll have to tell me the story behind how you learned it.'

'All right,' I said, still catching my breath. 'Let's . . .'

The ground shook underneath us. I looked up and there was the second sumo, barreling down on us like a freight train along the surf.

Dox swung the rifle off his shoulder. Everything seemed to be moving in slow motion.

I yelled, 'For Christ's sake, neck shot!'

Dox dropped to one knee and brought the rifle around. But there wasn't enough time. The sumo blasted into him like a cannonball and the dart went skidding along the mud without its small charge going off. Dox flew through the air and hit the ground hard. The sumo turned on him.

Without thinking, I took two steps in and leaped onto the sumo's back. I slammed in *hadakajime*, the sleeper hold I'd employed thousands of times in my decades of judo at Tokyo's Kodokan. Properly placed, the strangle cuts off the flow of blood to the brain and induces unconsciousness in seconds. But proper placement against a guy whose neck could have stood in for a telephone pole wasn't really an option. I could tell the hold wasn't putting the sumo out. If anything, it was making him angrier. He snarled and reached back for me but

175

I hunkered down away from his desperate grasp. Then he started spinning in circles, trying to fling me off. I hung on for dear life. He went faster and gave my arms a mighty northward shove. His neck and head were slippery with mud and I lost my grip and flew off him. I hit the ground and rolled away, primally terrified he was going to body slam me.

He stood for a moment, looking left and right, and I realized that in the dark and perhaps still groggy from the drug, he had momentarily lost track of me. I looked over and saw the yellow tail of the dart Dox had fired sticking out of the mud. I started inching toward it.

Dox groaned and the sumo spun toward the sound. I grabbed the dart and came to my feet.

Dox groaned again. The sumo grunted angrily and started stalking toward him. I saw that he was only a few feet away. I charged in, praying he was so focused on finding Dox that he wouldn't hear me.

At the last second he did, but it was too late. He started to turn and I leaped onto his back with *hadakajime* again — the critical difference being that, this time, instead of bracing one hand against the back of his head, I stabbed him in the side of the neck with the dart. The charge went off with a pop and a flash. He howled and started trying to spin me off again. But this time even as he got started he was already sinking to one knee, then the other. I realized the tranquilizer was working, and eased off slightly on his neck.

He dropped onto all fours. I dismounted

warily and stepped away.

Then he straightened and started to come up again. I thought, *You can't be fucking serious.* I drew the HK and aimed.

The sumo wobbled, then fell on his side and lay still.

I ran over to Dox. The night-vision goggles had been knocked clean off his face by the force of the impact. 'You all right?' I asked, squatting down next to him.

'Goddamn,' he grunted, rolling from side to side. 'Goddamn.' He let out a marvelously inventive string of expletives.

'Well, you're moving,' I said. 'Can't be that bad.'

He sat up with a loud groan. 'Son of a bitch knocked the wind out of me. Thank God there was nothing behind me but air or I'd be a goddamned pancake right now. Hoo-ah, it's good to be alive.'

I helped him to his feet. We found the goggles and he pulled them on. The sumo was out cold.

'Yeah, I'm glad he didn't just suffocate before,' Dox said, rubbing his ribs. 'That would have been a tragedy.'

'I thought you were a sniper! For Christ's sake, you shot one of them in the stomach, the other in the mud!'

'Hey, big talker, when was the last time you tried to drop four hundred pounds of pissed-off primate doing the forty-yard dash with you in the way?'

'About ten fucking seconds ago!'

'Yeah, well, if you hadn't been so busy

dancing, you might have noticed I barely had time to bring the damn rifle up, let alone aim it!'

We stared at each other angrily. Then Dox snorted. I did, too, and then we were laughing so hard that for a few seconds we couldn't speak. That's just the way it is. When the danger's past, hilarity likes to fill the void.

'Tell me one thing,' Dox said, moving the goggles so he could wipe his eyes. 'I couldn't be sure without the goggles on, but did I see you jump onto that man-mountain's back or what?'

I was still laughing. 'Yeah, I did. I just . . . '

He started slapping his thigh. 'Goddamnit, partner, that was no shit, straight up, the stupidest thing I've ever seen a man do in my life. I mean, if that boy had figured out all he had to do was flop down on his back, I'd be scraping you up with a spatula right now.'

'I guess I shouldn't have tried to choke him.'

'Yeah, no shit you shouldn't have tried to choke him. You should have just climbed up his body and levered him over by the head. A little guy did it to me once, and I'm lucky I'm here to tell you about it.'

We laughed more. When it subsided, Dox said, 'Thank you, man. I won't forget it.'

'Forget it? I'm worried you're going to keep reminding me of it.'

'Oh, you can count on that.'

'All right, come on, before they wake up again.'

'Partner, if they show any signs of wakefulness whatsoever, I'm going to empty my HK into both of them, reload, and do it again.'

'I know. So let's just finish up and get out of here. Can you carry those bags?'

'Yeah, I'm just sore. I don't think anything's busted.'

While Dox loaded the bags into the van, I retrieved the transmitter from under the Cadillac. Then I went back to the Chinese. They were all lying facedown. I turned them over on their backs and shot them each in the torso. I wanted it to look as though the sumos had ambushed them and then finished them off with the head shots I had started with.

I went back to the sumos. I could see they were breathing. With some trepidation I placed the HK in each one's hand and fired a few shots into the water. I was probably being more thorough than necessary, but I wanted gunshot residue on their hands. They still had the tranquilizer darts stuck in their necks and belly. I pulled them out and pocketed them.

Dox was already waiting in the van with the engine running. I got in and we left.

While I drove, Dox checked the cargo bag. 'Damn, partner, I ain't gonna count it now, but there is a whole lot of cash here.'

'Good,' I said, smiling. I wanted him to get a big payday out of this. He deserved it.

We found a deserted stretch of coast, parked, and waded in. We started emptying the duffels into the water and in no time were standing amid a small sandbar made of hundreds of thousands of pills. We kicked them around under the surf to make sure the salt water had plenty of access to dissolve them. 'Going to be some

179

mighty jumpy fish in here,' Dox observed when we were done.

We drove back to the inn. I didn't want to stay, but if I left in the middle of the night it would have looked suspicious.

I parked in the same spot I'd been in before and shut off the engine. We stowed the goggles and the tranquilizer rifle, but kept the HKs close at hand.

'You think those boys will come back here?' Dox asked.

I considered. 'They might stop by, just to pick up their stuff and begin their new lives as fugitives. But they've got no way of connecting anything to us. They couldn't have made out our faces in the dark, and anyway, they never saw me inside the inn.'

We were quiet for a moment. Dox said, 'Engine's still warm, though. Ticking a little, you hear it?'

I nodded. 'That's a good point. All right, let's give it a little while to cool down. Better to know if they come back and notice.'

He patted the HK. 'And to be awake and armed.'

We sat quietly in the dark for about an hour. I was tired, and I knew Dox was, too. After the adrenaline rush of combat, there's a powerful parasympathetic backlash, and the body craves rest so badly that you can fall into a kind of stupor. That's why Napoleon knew the best time to counterattack was immediately after the battle, when the other side was still drugged with victory.

180

Gradually the engine's ticking slowed, then stopped. The little wisps of steam that had been coming off the hood disappeared.

'All right, I better get in,' I said. 'The staff will be up soon, and I don't want to be seen. Sorry you've got to spend another night in the van.'

He patted the cargo bag and grinned. 'I'd say it's worth it.'

Yeah, so far it had been. But it wasn't over yet.

19

Delilah sipped a cappuccino at Chez Prune on the Canal Saint-Martin, one of her favorite cafés in Paris. Ordinarily, a solitary hour here people-watching or with a book or just looking out on the water relaxed her body and emptied her mind, but today the effect was lacking.

The few days she'd spent in Manhattan after seeing Midori had been much the same. She'd visited the Neue Galerie and the galleries in Chelsea and shopped in the boutiques in the meat-packing district and run for miles in Central Park, but none of it had been any good. She was glad to finally abandon it and just come home, and now here she was and this didn't feel right, either.

The thing that was bothering her was the recognition that she probably hadn't needed to go to New York at all. At the time, she'd been frustrated and jealous and angry, and all of that had clouded her judgment. But now, having confirmed that Rain had killed Midori's father, and that the woman knew it, her perspective had changed. People didn't get over things like that, not even for the sake of a child. Midori might have felt 'confused' at the moment, and maybe whatever passion she had once shared with Rain had temporarily reignited when her former lover suddenly reappeared in her life. But shacking up with your father's murderer would be a betrayal of blood. It would violate everything Delilah understood of human nature, or at least human nature as it continually manifested itself in the violent little corner of the world from which Delilah derived.

Yes, she probably would have been better off just letting Rain and Midori realize on their own that what Rain had done would forever poison the ground they stood on. Probably over time they would have worked out some accommodation for the sake of the child, but that was to be expected and in itself wasn't undesirable. People had children from previous relationships all the time. They divorced and remarried but of course were still involved with their offspring. Why would Rain be different? And why would she want to deny him the opportunity?

So what had she gained by visiting the woman? Just some knowledge, really, but nothing that would change the route things were going to take anyway. And the knowledge came at potentially high cost: if Midori mentioned Delilah's stunt to Rain, he was going to be understandably upset. She didn't know where things would go at that point.

She was worried, too. The woman said Rain cried when he held his child. That was exactly the kind of thing Delilah had been afraid of when Rain left Barcelona. Afraid that it would cause him to gravitate toward Midori, yes, but also that he wouldn't be himself, that these new emotions would impede his ability to protect himself. She wondered what he was up to in Tokyo. Whatever it was, she doubted it was smart or well thought out.

But there was something else bothering her beyond all this. When she really thought about it, she had to admit that what she'd done was run an op on the man she professed to care about so deeply. At the first sign of trouble, her first doubts and fear, she'd defaulted to the professional tools and tactics that in their proper context divided the world into operators and assets, assassins and targets. Ironic, too, because Rain had gotten through to her precisely by bypassing her operator's persona and somehow accessing the person beneath it.

If she couldn't keep her professional and personal lives separate, if she brought the same mindset to bear in both, she was going to lose herself. She knew men like that in her organization, men who thought they were superior because they used their training to solidify their power bases and manipulate their colleagues and hide mistresses from their wives. She thought they were burnouts and found them pathetic. And now she was appalled to see that she shared with them some common indecency.

Well, the only thing she could do was stay aware of the problem, stay watchful, and never, ever give in to the temptation again. No matter what it cost her.

She almost wanted to laugh. She was still so angry at him, and yet now she felt she'd wronged him, too, almost betrayed him.

She didn't know how she would make it up to him, but she would try. If he ever gave her the chance.

20

Yamaoto Toshi was asleep in his Moto Azabu apartment when his mobile phone rang. He glanced at the bedside alarm clock, which read 5:30 A.M. A call at this hour could only mean bad news, and he immediately thought of the delivery that had been scheduled to take place in Wajima just a few hours earlier.

He sat up, switched on a light, and cleared his throat. He looked at the caller ID display on his phone. It was Kuromachi, Kuro, the man who was handling the Chinese. Yamaoto's foreboding that something had gone wrong in Wajima increased.

He opened the phone and placed it to his ear. '*Hai*.'

'Yamaoto-san, forgive me for calling at this hour,' Kuro said in Japanese. 'We've had a problem with tonight's delivery, and I thought you should know right away.'

'What is it?'

'The Chinese sent three men ashore on a catamaran to deliver the shipment and collect payment. When the men failed to return, another launch was sent to find out what had happened. The second crew found the three men shot to death. The money and the shipment are gone. So are Kito and Sanada.'

Yamaoto wiped a hand over his face and thought, *Komatta*. Shit.

185

'Kito and Sanada are reliable men, sir,' Kuro continued after a moment. 'I'm certain . . . '

'For the moment,' Yamaoto said, cutting him off, 'it doesn't matter what we're certain of. It's what the Chinese think that matters. You heard this from them?'

'Yes, sir. From the pilot of the boat. He called just five minutes ago.'

Kuro had spent several childhood years in China when his father's employer had sent the man there to work in a fan factory, and as a result Kuro spoke excellent Chinese and was the perfect conduit to United Bamboo. Yamaoto had been happy having Kuro run that operation and the man had been doing well, but there were times when the boss had to become personally involved, if only to convey the appearance of proper concern to the other side. Kuro would understand that.

'You have men looking for Kito and Sanada?' Yamaoto asked.

'Yes, sir.'

'Make that a priority. All your resources. Find those men and find out what happened.'

'Yes, sir.'

Yamaoto clicked off. He sat for a few minutes, thinking. What the hell had happened? Kito and Sanada were indeed reliable. Even if they weren't, they would know stealing from Yamaoto would mean at best a paranoid life as a fugitive, and more likely a swift death.

Still, with the amount of drugs and cash involved, the temptation would have been substantial. And if they were innocent, why didn't they come to him?

The moment he posed the question to himself, he knew the answer. The Chinese would want blood. Whether his men were guilty or innocent, Yamaoto was almost certainly going to have to sacrifice them if he wanted to prevent a war. Kito and Sanada would understand that. They would know their deaths now represented the quickest and surest way of resolving the matter.

He got up, used the bathroom, and pulled on a robe. He went to his study and took a codebook out of his wall safe. Inside was the mobile number for the man called Big Liu, the head of United Bamboo in Taiwan. Yamaoto input the number and waited.

A moment later, a deep, gravelly voice came through on the other end. '*Weiwei*.' Hello.

'Hello, this is Yamaoto Toshi,' Yamaoto replied slowly. Big Liu's English wasn't good but it was their only common language.

There was a pause. Then Big Liu said, 'We have big problem. Fucking big.'

'I know. I just received a phone call from one of my men.'

'This . . . very bad.'

'Yes. We're looking for the missing men right now. We will do everything we can to find them.' Not *my* missing men. *The* missing men. Better to imply some distance. The subtlety might be lost on Big Liu, but it couldn't hurt, either.

'You find missing men,' Big Liu said, 'you give to me. And you pay missing money. And you pay interest for dead men. Then I think, 'Okay, this was bad men problem. Not Yamaoto problem. Yamaoto and Big Liu, still friend.''

Yamaoto understood the implication without Big Liu having to spell it out: *Protect your men, and I will hold you responsible for what they did.*

And that would mean only one thing: war.

Yamaoto thought for a moment. If he pushed back too hard, things could easily spiral out of control. If he gave in too easily, Big Liu would ask for more. The trick was to find the right middle ground, something that would satisfy Big Liu without seeming weak, something that would preserve Yamaoto's room to maneuver depending on what happened next.

'I understand your concerns,' Yamaoto said slowly, 'as I'm sure you understand mine. I know that neither of us is the kind of man to give in to immediate suspicions or otherwise leap to conclusions. We don't want things to get out of control.'

He paused to let Big Liu internally translate the words into Chinese, then said, 'I think the main thing now is to find the missing men. I'd like to keep you informed of that effort. Would it be all right if I called you several times a day, just to make sure you know what's going on?'

Under the circumstances, the two of them would have to be stupid not to talk frequently. This sort of polite conversation was an effort for both of them, Yamaoto knew, but they were going to need a good deal more of it if they hoped to prevent suspicion and anger from festering. But by phrasing the thought the way

188

he had, Yamaoto had made it seem that he was both offering a concession and requesting permission. There was no nourishment in any of it, but Big Liu might like the taste enough to bite.

Big Liu said, 'Can give only forty-eight hours for this. Not because distrust Yamaoto. Because . . . very angry men in Big Liu group. Men now saying, 'Blood! Revenge!' Can't control angry men so long.'

It was more or less what Yamaoto had been expecting, although he'd been hoping for longer. The 'it's not that I don't trust you, it's my constituents' approach was something Yamaoto himself used all the time. And in this case, in all likelihood, there was a lot of truth to it. Yamaoto had to find Kito and Sanada before things got worse.

'I understand,' he said. 'I'll call you later today with an update.'

'You find missing men,' Big Liu said, 'you no kill. Give alive. Want to . . . talk with them.'

This gambit wasn't unexpected, either. Yamaoto expected Big Liu to push until he encountered resistance. Now was the time to offer it.

'I can't promise that,' Yamaoto said. 'First, because anything could happen when I find them. And second, because I'm already going to have problems from my people just for doing what needs to be done. If Big Liu asks for too much, my people will become angry, even though I will tell them not to be.'

There was a pause while Big Liu absorbed

Yamaoto's own version of the 'constituency' defense. Like Liu's from a moment earlier, it had the benefit of being largely true. If Yamaoto offered up two of his men to be tortured to death by the Chinese, he would face rebellion, no matter what the cause.

'Okay,' Big Liu said. 'You handle men. Call soon.'

'Yes,' Yamaoto said, and hung up.

He paused for a moment and thought. Could Big Liu have staged this? If so, he would get to keep the drugs and take the money . . .

But almost as soon as he considered the possibility, he rejected it. The gain wouldn't have been worth the loss of Yamaoto as a buyer, and Big Liu had worked hard to win Yamaoto's business. On top of that, Big Liu had lost three men. That in itself was a considerable expense.

He called Kuro. The man answered promptly. '*Hai.*'

'Do the Chinese have people in Tokyo who would recognize Kito and Sanada?' Yamaoto asked.

'Yes, sir, there are several we work with.'

'Good. Make sure at least one of them is immediately available for the next forty-eight hours. We'll need him for when we find Kito and Sanada.'

There was a pause, no doubt while Kuro considered what this request meant for the two sumos. 'I understand completely, sir,' he said.

There was no need to tell Kuro not to mention this part of the conversation to any of Yamaoto's men. Yamaoto would deal with that himself. Afterward.

21

Dox and I got back to Tokyo that afternoon. I called Tatsu on the way to let him know I would be coming by to brief him. Dox, who had remained alert and armed the rest of the night in case the sumos returned, slept for almost the entire trip. He had counted the money — or a portion of it, anyway, because there was a hell of a lot — and estimated that it was about a half-billion yen. Over four million U.S. Not a bad night's work.

It was strange to have so much cash, but even stranger was how little it seemed to mean at the moment. Not so long ago, it would have been the answer to my dreams. Independence, freedom from the life. But independence wasn't what I was after anymore, or at least not the way it had been. And the freedom I wanted involved the freedom just to see that child I had held in my arms. Money wasn't going to be enough for that. Hell, the way I was going about things, I didn't know what would be.

Just see this through, I thought. *You're in it now, you have to finish it. It'll be your last, and you'll figure the rest out after.*

We bought a dozen smaller bags and divided up the cash. Some of it we shipped to certain overseas mail drops we employed, some of it we parked in train station lockers, some of it we hid in our hotels. There was just too much to risk keeping it in the same place. When we were done dealing with the money, I went to see Tatsu.

I approached and entered the hospital in the same cautious manner I had used before. There were no problems. The bodyguard I had seen last time was outside Tatsu's door again. He nodded in recognition when he saw me and let me inside.

This time, Tatsu was alone, sleeping. I stood watching him for a moment. Absent the dynamism that still shone from his wakeful eyes to obscure it, the devastation the disease had wreaked upon his body was painfully apparent. He looked wasted and weak, with nothing but a lone bodyguard to defend him against a lifetime's supply of enemies.

He sighed and cleared his throat, then opened his eyes. If he was surprised to see me standing there, he gave no indication of it.

'Checking to make sure I'm still here?' he asked, with a wry smile.

'Just wondering what your wife ever saw in you.'

He chuckled. 'For that, you have to look under the sheets.'

That wasn't like him. I laughed and said, 'I'll take your word for it,' and he laughed, too.

I sat in the chair next to the bed and leaned close so I could keep my voice down. 'There's something I have to tell you,' I said.

'Yes?'

'Next time I go after two of Yamaoto's men, if you know they're hundred-and-fifty-kilo sumo wrestlers, don't be afraid to mention it. It might be relevant.'

He laughed. 'Some things get past even me.'

'Yeah, you're slipping. But it went well anyway.'

'Yes, I've already heard.'

Tatsu. He might have been down, but he was far from out. I raised my eyebrows and he went on.

'My informant tells me the two men who went to pick up the shipment in Wajima last night haven't checked in.'

'Really.'

Tatsu briefed me on what seemed to have gone down in Wajima. His information was accurate, and I told him so.

'The Chinese are livid,' he went on. 'They're squeezing Yamaoto hard.'

'Yamaoto's response?'

'Stalling for time. He told the Chinese he's looking everywhere for his two men and will find a way to straighten this out.'

'Are the Chinese going to buy that?'

'Not for long.'

I nodded. 'What do you think Yamaoto's going to do?'

Tatsu shrugged. 'Kill Kito and Sanada. Either they'll come in trying to explain or Yamaoto will find them. He doesn't have much choice.'

'You think he'll be able to find them? They're going to know what's coming.'

'They might come in. They could be stupid, and they're certainly feeling desperate. But even if they don't, Yamaoto will know all their acquaintances, all the places they might try to hide. And from what you've told me, they're not exactly inconspicuous men.'

He stopped, and I could tell the talking was tiring him out. He pulled an oxygen cannula up from his chest and adjusted it under his nose. 'I hate this fucking thing,' he grumbled.

I helped him with the oxygen. 'So everything we're trying to get going here,' I said, 'Yamaoto could bring it to a halt if he gets to the sumos.'

He looked at me, but said nothing. I knew what he was doing. He wanted it to come from me, so I would feel that I wasn't being manipulated, that I was making my own decisions. Which is, of course, the most artful manipulation of all.

But none of that changed the basic facts. 'Of course, if the yakuza were to come under attack in the meantime . . . ' I said.

Tatsu nodded. 'Yamaoto would look foolish and weak. He would have no choice but to hit back. Positions on both sides would harden after that.'

'What if he suspected he was being set up, though?'

'He probably already does. But what can he do? As things get worse, there will be a few cool heads on both sides, certainly. There always are. But cool heads rarely prevail in the midst of ongoing bloodshed. Especially when the bloodshed is accompanied by the kind of nationalistic antagonism that has lately worsened in China and Japan. Think of it. Chinese upstarts, killing yakuza with impunity on the yakuza's own turf?

194

It would be intolerable to Yamaoto's rank and file. After that, the reaction will no longer require a catalyst. It will have taken on a life of its own. Yamaoto won't be able to stop it.'

'All right. But how does this get me to *him?*'

'If you start taking out Yamaoto's lieutenants, you will force him to assume greater day-to-day control over his operations. This would bring him into the open.'

'Won't he just appoint new lieutenants?'

Tatsu gave me his trademark look of long-suffering patience in the face of impossibly slow minds. 'This isn't General Electric, Rain-san. Men like Yamaoto don't have strong succession plans. They're afraid it would make it more likely that someone would succeed them.'

'But eventually . . . '

'Yes, eventually Yamaoto would fill the positions, but in the midst of a war with the Chinese he would have to do things himself. And if Yamaoto were to die during the course of that war, who's to say who actually killed him? Perhaps the Chinese. Perhaps disaffected or grasping elements of Yamaoto's own organization. There would be suspicion all around, but none of it directed at you. United Bamboo would have no reason to link the deaths of the two Chinese in New York with Yamaoto's death in Japan. Neither would anyone else. This could be your last job. You'd be free afterward.'

I thought for a moment. 'If it really does look like a war is starting, wouldn't that make Yamaoto more careful? If we drive him underground, the situation gets harder for us, not easier.'

'If Yamaoto goes underground in the face of Chinese provocations, he'll risk being overthrown from within. Beyond that, someone has to manage his operations if they become disrupted. There are too many players who would like to take over for themselves.'

Tatsu coughed. He pointed to the counter next to the bed and said, 'Hand me that water, will you?'

I gave it to him and he sipped from it through a straw for a minute, then handed it back to me with a nod of thanks.

'The main thing is this,' he said. 'Right now, Yamaoto is physically secure because nothing is moving around him. If you want to create opportunities, you have to create movement. In shoring up other positions on the playing board, he would necessarily be weakening his own.'

I nodded, seeing inside his shrunken body the thriving spirit of manipulation I had always resented and admired.

As if reading my thoughts, he said, 'I want all this for myself, Rain-san. I'm not afraid of dying, only of dying with my work left undone. But I also want it for you. I want you to have the chance for a life with your family.'

'When this is over.'

He nodded, conceding my point. 'When this is over.'

22

I ran a route to make sure I hadn't picked anyone up while visiting Tatsu, then called Dox. We found a coffeehouse and I briefed him on what I had discussed with Tatsu.

When I was done, he said, 'Well, it sounds sensible to me.'

Dox was one of the few people I knew who without any self-consciousness might describe a plan to take a man's life as sensible and leave it at that.

'You know we're not going to make any more money out of this,' I said. 'Not that we need any.'

'Hey, I wouldn't be the rich man I am today if it weren't for you.'

'Spend too much time with me, and you might not live to enjoy that money.'

'I'm willing to take that chance.'

I nodded. 'All right. If we wanted to create the appearance of a Chinese sniper at large in Japan, what kind of ammunition would we be talking about?'

'Shit, man, these days just about everybody's using NATO 7.62. Got your Russian Dragonov, British L96, Canadian C3A1, your various U.S. and NATO configurations, of course. The Chinese Type 79 and Type 85 are basically just copies of the Dragonov. They all use 7.62.'

'So there's nothing specifically identifiable as Chinese?'

'Ah, you're talking about those rounds painted with a red PRC flag with yellow stars in the corner and a little 'Made in China' insignia? There aren't too many of those, no.'

I ignored the sarcasm. 'All right, if we tried to be too specific it might look obvious, anyway. Sounds like something chambered in 7.62 ought to be close enough for government work.'

'Well, I'm partial to the HK PSG/1 I employed in our little Hong Kong adventure. That's 7.62 and has a twenty-round magazine, too. Get me another one of those, and I can cause all kinds of mayhem from damn near a thousand yards out. Or the dreaded M40A3, that's a fine weapon, too. Trigger pull like snapping a glass rod.'

'We'll see what Kanezaki can do.'

'You ask him for a sniper rifle, he's going to know who's using it. He accused us of forming a damn union after what we did in Hong Kong last year, remember?'

Shit, I hadn't thought of that. Dox and I had partnered on that op to take out a French/Arab arms merchant named Belghazi, and Kanezaki had provided the hardware. Yeah, asking him for another sniper rifle, I might as well have just handed him Dox's business card.

Dox saw my discomfort and laughed. 'I ain't objecting, man, just saying. Half the jobs I've done in the last three years I've done for him. I don't mind if he knows I'm involved in this one. He knows if he ever crosses me he'll spend the rest of a short and anxious life glancing up at the rooftops around him, wondering if that prickling

198

he feels on the back of his neck is me smiling at him from behind a scoped rifle.'

I nodded. 'All right. But I want to handle him a certain way.'

'You just tell me the plan, partner, and I'll follow your lead.'

I smiled, thinking, *Poor Kanezaki.*

23

Yamaoto called Big Liu twice that day. There was nothing to report, but it was important to keep the channels open, to let Big Liu know that Yamaoto was on top of things, that he was concerned.

Yamaoto's men had been to every one of Kito's and Sanada's known associates. Someone had even flown to Fukuoka, Kito's hometown in Kyushu, to interview the man's parents. But the sumos seemed to have become invisible. Yamaoto was beginning to grow concerned. Maybe they really had stolen the money and drugs and were embarked on some long-planned escape route.

He was at his desk, getting ready to call Big Liu for another uncomfortable 'no news' discussion, when his mobile phone rang. Kuro's name appeared on the caller ID.

Yamaoto opened the phone. '*Hai.*'

'They're here,' Kuro said. 'They came in.'

Yamaoto leaned forward, relief flooding through him. 'Where?'

'My place in Shinjuku.'

'I'll be there in twenty minutes. Don't let them leave.'

'Understood.'

Yamaoto hung up. He called his driver and had the man bring around the armored Mercedes S-Class that he'd taken to traveling in after his last encounter with John Rain.

Twenty minutes later, he walked into a popular 'Fashion Health' massage place Kuro ran in Shinjuku. Kuro had a way of managing these kinds of establishments. The man was a good earner. Reliable.

The doorman recognized Yamaoto and welcomed him with an obsequious bow. Yamaoto ignored the women lounging on red velour couches in the subdued light and headed straight through a door into the back office.

There they were, occupying opposite ends of a gray leather couch, heads hanging and hands twisting in their laps as though they were the world's largest errant schoolboys. It was a wonder the furniture could support their combined bulk. Kuro was off to the side, seated behind a metal desk. Yamaoto knew he kept a gun back there, highly illegal in Japan, and that if Kito and Sanada had tried to leave, Kuro would have used it.

The men looked up when Yamaoto entered. They both shot to their feet and bowed deeply. '*Moushiwake gozaimasen, kumicho!*' they cried in unison. We humbly beg your forgiveness, boss!

Yamaoto stood silently, looking from one to the other. Eventually they straightened and met his eyes.

'What the hell happened in Wajima?' he asked. 'And where the hell have you been?'

The men looked at each other, then back at Yamaoto. They were plainly terrified.

Kito spoke first. 'We . . . we're not sure, *Kumicho*.'

Sanada added, 'We arrived on schedule. The

Chinese signaled from off the coast and came ashore. We walked over to do the exchange, then . . . something happened.'

Yamaoto said, 'What?'

Kito said, 'We think someone shot us with a drug. Each of us felt a . . . a slap in the neck. Then we were waking up in the mud. It was dark, but we saw two men. We tried to fight them, but we were groggy and they shot us again. When we woke up the second time, the Chinese were dead and the shipment and payment were gone. *Kumicho,* we swear to you this is the truth!'

Sanada stuck his chin high and gestured to his neck. '*Kumicho,* look, you can see the marks! They shot us with tranquilizers or something.'

Yamaoto looked at Sanada's massive neck. The skin was indeed discolored in two places, and there were red marks in the center of the discolorations, like the result of a hornet's sting. But what did that mean? They could have made the marks themselves.

'And here,' Kito said, lifting his shirt and exposing a planet-sized belly. He had an identical mark there.

'You didn't get a good look at the men?' Yamaoto asked.

'No, *kumicho,*' Kito said. 'It was dark.'

'Nothing that could help us identify them? Did you hear them talking?'

The men looked at each other. Sanada said, 'I think I did, I remember hearing yelling, but I was confused from the drug.'

'Was it Chinese? Japanese?'

'I think Japanese, but also there were parts I couldn't understand. Maybe some English. At one point . . .'

'What?'

'At one point, I thought one of them was yelling 'I love you' in Chinese. But I . . . I'm just not sure, *kumicho*.'

Yamaoto wondered if the man was becoming unhinged. Or perhaps they had indeed been drugged. 'Did you tell anyone beforehand about the meeting in Wajima?' he asked.

'No, *kumicho*!' Kito exclaimed. 'Not a soul!'

Yamaoto looked from one to the other as though having trouble believing their story. As indeed he was. 'Why did you wait to come in?'

The men looked at each other, then back to Yamaoto. Sanada said, '*Kumicho*, we're . . . we're afraid. We know how this looks. But we were set up. We swear to you.'

Kito added, 'In our fear, we lost our heads. But then we decided, we must leave this matter to our *oyabun*. He will do whatever is truly best.'

Kito's reference to Yamaoto as their *oyabun*, their father, was clever. The term invoked the traditional relationship between the yakuza boss and his underlings, and so was designed by implication to cast Kito and Sanada as Yamaoto's *kobun*, his children. And surely no wise and compassionate father could harm his own child.

Yamaoto began pacing the room as though in frustration. He walked past Kuro's desk, admiring as he always did the beautiful Kamakura era *daisho* sword set the man kept on a stand beside it. The *daitou,* or long katana, was displayed on top, blade up, the folded steel polished to a mirror finish, with the shorter *wakizashi* below. The black lacquer *saya* scabbards, each adorned with a pair of golden Tokugawa family crests, were on separate stands alongside the blades. The set was of museum quality, and Kuro claimed a dealer had once offered him twenty million yen for it, an offer Kuro refused even to consider. He allowed no one but Yamaoto to touch it, both out of deference to his boss's rank and in recognition of his extensive martial arts background, which included not only unarmed arts like judo, but also *battoujutsu,* combat sword cutting.

Yamaoto paused before the sword stand and turned to face the two men. 'You 'lost your heads'?' he said, his voice rising. 'I pay you to think! You say I'm your *oyabun,* and yet at the first sign of trouble you insult me with your doubt!'

The men dropped their heads in shame and Yamaoto went on, shouting now. 'Do you have any idea of the trouble you've caused with your incompetence? You say you were set up, and maybe you were. But whose responsibility is it to prevent such things?'

The men, heads still bowed, said in unison, 'Our responsibility, *kumicho.*'

Despite his outward anger, Yamaoto was calm within. He had already decided how to resolve this, and there was no longer anything to be angry about. But if he showed his inward calm to these men, they would understand what was to happen. Better that they should believe him angry, which would indicate he was still undecided. That would keep them focused on how they could manage his anger and try to lessen the penalty for the situation they had placed him in.

What he needed to do now was shame them just a little more. They would welcome that, believing if Yamaoto were inclined to punish them with shame, he might be willing to forgo something more severe. More important, it might also cause them to bow lower, perhaps even to assume *chinsha*, the most apologetic bow of all, where the offender drops to his knees, his palms wide in front of him and his forehead to the ground.

'Yes, your responsibility!' Yamaoto exploded. 'Yours! But now I'm left with the burden of cleaning it up! All because you failed to do what I entrusted you with! And then you compounded your mistake with this shameful lack of confidence in your *oyabun!*'

As one, the men cried out, '*Moushiwake gozaimasen!*' and dropped down into *chinsha*.

Yamaoto grasped the hilt of Kuro's *daitou* and snatched it clear of the stand. In an instant he had reached the two prostrate men, his fingers naturally and automatically tightening around the hilt in a two-handed grip as he moved. Barely slowing, he pivoted to his right, hips leading the way, elbows and wrists following like the trailing edge of a whip, creating the optimal combination of chopping and cutting that had been drilled into him in long hours of *battoujutsu* training.

Kito started to come up, perhaps sensing in some primitive way that something was amiss, but too late. The sword sliced through his massive neck and was blurring skyward again even before the man's cleanly severed head had fallen to the floor. Blood sprayed onto Sanada's face, but before the startled man could react the sword had completed its second lightning arc and his head, too, was on its way to the ground.

Yamaoto stepped to the side, away from the spray. Without thinking, he wiped down the blade on one of the men's wide backs, reversed the sword in his hand, and prepared to resheath it in a scabbard he suddenly remembered wasn't there. He walked over and handed it hilt first to Kuro, who took it with trembling hands without even rising from his seat.

Yamaoto looked for a moment at the fallen men. Their bodies had remained in *chinsha*, the heads on the floor beside them. Blood pumped vigorously from their severed necks. *Lost your heads, indeed*, he thought.

He turned to Kuro. 'I assume you have ample cleaning supplies in this establishment?' he asked.

Kuro, his skin pasty white, nodded wordlessly.

'Good. Have someone bring them and take care of this mess. And call the Taiwanese who can identify these men. Have him come here immediately.'

24

A half-hour later, two of Kuro's people escorted a nervous looking Taiwanese man into Kuro's office. Kuro's staff had already mopped up the remarkable quantities of blood the sumos had lost and laid out the enormous bodies on plastic tarps. The next step would be to take them to a food preparation establishment friendly with Yamaoto's organization, an establishment with heavy equipment used in more ordinary circumstances for grinding fish into fishcake.

The Taiwanese saw the bodies and flinched. When he looked over at Kuro's desk and noticed the actual heads propped up there, he turned and tried to flee. Kuro's men blocked the door.

'Do you recognize these men?' Yamaoto asked in English. The man struggled for another moment, to no avail. He turned and looked at Yamaoto, his eyes wide, but didn't answer.

'Do you recognize these men!' Yamaoto shouted, but still the man was mute.

Kuro repeated the question in Chinese. After a moment, the man stammered, 'Y-Yes. I recognize.'

Yamaoto nodded to Kuro. Kuro took out his mobile phone and input Big Liu's number. He handed the phone to the Taiwanese.

For someone who had been reluctant to speak a moment earlier, the man was suddenly garrulous. He let loose a torrent of agitated

Chinese, his eyes darting from the heads to the bodies to Yamaoto and back again.

After about a minute, he returned the phone to Kuro with a trembling hand. Kuro gave it to Yamaoto, who raised the unit to his ear and said in English, 'This is Yamaoto Toshi.'

'Okay, very good,' Big Liu said. 'You kill bad men. Big Liu happy. But still missing money. And Big Liu men still dead.'

'Yes,' Yamaoto said. 'And we should talk about all of that.'

'Okay, talk.'

Yamaoto didn't like to be issued commands, but decided it was better to attribute the construction to a faulty command of English and let it go for now.

'I killed those men because there was no other way to avert a war,' he said. 'But I don't believe they were responsible for what happened at Wajima. They claimed there were two men there who shot them with tranquilizers. And if they really were the perpetrators, they never would have come in. They would have had escape plans in place and they would have used them. So there is a leak in one or both of our organizations, or worse, a collaborator. We need to discuss this and try to figure out who.'

'Tran . . . tran . . . ' Big Liu said, and Yamaoto realized the man hadn't followed anything after the word tranquilizer. He handed the phone to Kuro and said, 'Translate what I just told him.'

Kuro complied, then gave the phone back. Yamaoto said, 'You see? We really should talk about this face-to-face. May I suggest my associate Mr Kuro's club in Minami Aoyama in Tokyo? Whispers, you may remember it's called. I think it would provide the right setting.'

Whispers was Kuro's most lucrative and high-class establishment, staffed by stunning women from all over the world. It was the very club where they had sealed the current supply arrangement, and Big Liu had been so overwhelmed by the beauty of the hostesses that he had stayed in Tokyo two extra days and taken a different blonde back to his hotel every night. Yamaoto sensed that the allure of another all-expenses-paid trip to the club would be enough to bring Big Liu around.

'Big Liu still missing money,' the man said, holding out. 'And Big Liu's men still dead.'

'My men are dead now, too,' Yamaoto said, 'although I suspect they were as blameless as yours. Blood has been repaid with blood. As for the money, I'm certain we can reach an accommodation. We're reasonable men, after all. Won't you be my guest in Tokyo for a few days?'

There, pushback on Big Liu's attempts to squeeze Yamaoto for the missing money and restitution, but without an actual no. And a sweetener that Big Liu could tell himself was a concession: confirmation that all aspects of Big Liu's trip, including, doubtless, another stay in a suite at the worldclass Grand Hyatt in Roppongi Hills, suitable for afterhours entertainment by multiple blonde Whispers hostesses, would be complimentary.

'When?' Big Liu asked.

Yamaoto smiled. 'Whenever would be convenient for you. But I would propose that sooner is better.'

'Saturday,' Big Liu said, after a moment. 'Busy before then.'

Yamaoto shrugged. Maybe Big Liu really was busy for the next three days. Maybe he was just trying not to seem too eager, to maintain the appearance of control. Yamaoto didn't particularly care. The main thing was that he was coming. If they sat down together, Yamaoto was confident they could work out what had happened, then settle this in a reasonable way.

'Saturday, then,' Yamaoto said. 'I'll arrange a suite for you at the Grand Hyatt.'

'Good,' Big Liu responded, and Yamaoto could feel his eagerness. 'Thank you. Yamaoto good man. Good friend.'

Yamaoto detested these sorts of false protestations of friendship between business partners who would as happily kill each other if that's where the profit lay, but sometimes they were called for. 'Yes, and so is Big Liu,' he said. 'I'll leave it to Mr Kuro to sort out the details, and will look forward to seeing you on Saturday.'

Yamaoto clicked off and handed the phone back to Kuro. And suddenly, for the first time since the sumos had told him their story, his mind flashed on a possible explanation: *John Rain*.

He paused to consider, but then dismissed the thought. How would Rain get access to the particulars of the Wajima meeting? The man was formidable, but he wasn't supernatural. The

210

more likely explanation was the simpler one: a turncoat, either in Yamaoto's organization or Big Liu's, working with people outside, and motivated by nothing more complicated than greed.

Besides, Rain was still in hiding. There had been no sign of him in New York, where Big Liu's people were watching Midori and her child and where Yamaoto expected Rain would resurface if he resurfaced at all.

Now that he thought of it, though, he realized Chan in New York was overdue to call him. Ordinarily the man checked in at least once a week to update him on the New York surveillance operation, but now Yamaoto realized he hadn't heard from Chan in, what . . . eight days? Nine?

Chan had been late once before, but Yamaoto had told Big Liu about it and there hadn't been a problem since. He imagined Chan didn't like reporting to a Japanese, but that's what he was getting paid for, and Yamaoto was irritated that the man was being lazy and disrespectful again.

If Big Liu had still been on the phone, Yamaoto would have mentioned it to him. But there had been more pressing things on his mind just then. Well, it wasn't a material thing, just an annoyance. If Chan had anything to report, presumably he would have done so. Yamaoto would mention it to Big Liu when they met on Saturday. They'd straighten it out then.

He heard Kuro saying, '*Kumicho*,' and realized the man had been trying to get his attention.

'Yes,' Yamaoto said, looking at him.

'Shall I . . . shall I have them taken away?'

Kito and Sanada. It was a shame he had needed to dispatch them. Most likely they were guilty only of incompetence, not of betrayal. They had come to him hoping for mercy, and look what he had been forced to do instead.

'Yes, take care of it,' he said to Kuro, with a dismissive wave.

He walked out to the club entrance and signaled to his bodyguard, who was waiting inside. The man went out and checked the street, then returned and escorted Yamaoto to the Mercedes, waiting with its back door open just in front of the entrance.

On the ride home, Yamaoto thought about what he was going to do next. One thing he knew for sure. Whoever was behind what happened in Wajima wasn't going to go quickly, like Kito and Sanada. No. This one would suffer before he died.

25

We met Kanezaki that night at a coffeehouse in Roppongi. We watched from the van to make sure he was alone, then followed him in. Dox carried the duffel bag with the gear Kanezaki had lent us.

Kanezaki had his back to the wall and saw us when we came in. If he was surprised to see us together, he didn't show it. Good for him.

We sat down. Kanezaki smiled and said, 'Yeah, I had a feeling.'

Dox grinned. 'How've you been, Tom?'

'Not bad. You?'

'Ah, you know. Staying busy. Keeping the world safe for democracy, that kind of thing.'

'I'm afraid to ask what that's been entailing.'

'Hell, you know most of it.'

'And what I don't know isn't going to hurt me, is that right?'

'Look,' I said, 'we just wanted to return your toys. Thanks for lending them to us.'

He raised his eyebrows. 'That's it?'

I looked at Dox, then back to Kanezaki. 'Yeah. That's it.'

Dox slid the duffel over to Kanezaki's chair.

We were all quiet for a moment. I knew Kanezaki had been hoping for information, his life's blood, and that he would be frustrated at not getting it. I waited for his next move.

'How do you like Japan?' Kanezaki asked, with a nod at Dox.

'It's all right. I like the ladies a lot. I keep asking my friend here to take me to see some geishas, but he won't do it. You know where I could find some?'

I thought Dox might be laying on the country bumpkin routine just a bit thick, but it seemed to have the desired effect. Probably despairing of getting anything via a more circuitous route, Kanezaki said, 'I hear they have geishas in the countryside. On the Sea of Japan.'

'Sea of Japan?' Dox asked. 'Sounds far just for a little entertainment.'

Kanezaki looked at Dox, then at me. 'All right. Are you guys going to tell me what the hell you pulled in Wajima?'

I looked at Dox. 'Do you know anything about Wajima?'

Dox knitted his brow. 'Wajima, Wajima . . . you know, it rings a bell, now that you mention it. Yeah, I might know something. Maybe.'

Kanezaki was starting to look decidedly nonplussed. This was the moment I was waiting for.

'Yeah, we might be able to tell you something,' I said. 'But that would be a favor, wouldn't it?'

There was a long silence. Finally, Kanezaki said, 'All right. In return for the favor I did you in getting you the equipment. And then quits.' He smiled a little. 'Until next time, anyway.'

Next time, I thought, *is coming sooner than you expect.*

'How did you know?' I asked. I was pretty sure

I already had the answer, but I wanted confirmation.

Kanezaki shrugged. 'The GPS transmitter. I knew the code, so I just followed it using the mapping software to see where you went. Looks like you spent the night in Wajima. The same night three United Bamboo triad guys were shot to death on the beach there.'

Yeah, that's what I'd been expecting him to say. It was probably true, too.

Dox grinned. 'Hell of a coincidence.'

Kanezaki nodded. 'Yeah, and they were shot with forty-five-caliber rounds. That's a strange coincidence, too. Because those HKs I outfitted you with are forty-fives.'

Dox's grin broadened. 'A drug deal gone bad, would be my guess.'

'Why?' Kanezaki asked. 'Was this just a straight rip-off? Is that what you guys are doing now?'

Dox snorted. 'With the wages you're paying me, son, it's a wonder I don't turn to a life of crime.'

'No, it wasn't a straight rip-off,' I said.

'Then what?' Kanezaki asked. 'You trying to start a war between the yakuza and the triads?'

'What if someone were? Would you object?'

'No. I'd like to see them all snuff each other out, in fact. But I'd want to know about it.'

I thought for a moment. Kanezaki could already place us at Wajima. If he wanted to sell us out to the triads and the yakuza, I supposed he could. I had recognized that potential problem from the moment I first considered going to him for the equipment we needed. It was unfortunate, but unavoidable under the circumstances. You can't get something for nothing. Not anywhere, but especially not in this business.

'I think at this point you can trust me,' Kanezaki added, when I still hadn't responded.

I looked at Dox, who nodded, then back to Kanezaki. 'All right,' I said. 'And you can trust us, too. To hold you responsible if something goes wrong, before or after. After all, no one else could have known. You sure you want that responsibility?'

Kanezaki nodded. 'I'm sure.'

'Then here's the way it'll work. We need a sniper rifle. You provide it. We return it when we're done. At which point we give you a full accounting of what's really going on.'

'And we hold on to the night-vision equipment in the meantime,' Dox added. 'And those HKs, too.' He looked at me. 'Might come in handy.'

A long moment passed. Kanezaki said, 'No.'

Damn, I thought that in the heat of the moment Dox's 'spontaneous' request would slide right past him. Apparently not.

No one said anything for a long time. I waited, thinking Kanezaki might crack.

He didn't. Part of me was impressed. In just a few short years he had really matured. I wondered if it was Tatsu's influence.

Finally I said, 'What do you mean, 'no'?' And even as I said it, I knew that in speaking first I had ceded him the advantage.

216

'I mean, if you want to keep the existing gear and have me outfit you on top of it, you're going to owe me something more than just information in return.'

I looked at him, but he didn't blink. He knew that right now I needed him more than he needed me. It didn't feel good, but there was nothing I could do about it.

I closed my eyes and nodded. 'Deal,' I said.

26

Kanezaki came through with the hardware as promised, handing it off to us in a golf bag the next morning on a moving Yamanote line train. This time I gave him my local mobile number. He already had a decent idea of what we were up to, and, if he learned anything useful, I wanted him to be able to reach us.

Dox and I took the golf bag back to the van. I drove while he sat in back, examining the equipment.

'Hoo-ah, Christmas came early this year,' he said.

'What have you got?'

'The M40A3 I asked for, plus an AN/PVS 10 Day/Night scope, Ops Inc. suppressor, and a hundred rounds of M118LR 7.62 ammunition. Fun for me and doom for the bad guys.'

'Good. Tatsu is putting together a target list for us. Should be ready soon.'

* * *

Tatsu called me that afternoon and I went to see him at the hospital. The bodyguard let me in. Tatsu was alone.

'You've got the list?' I asked him.

'I have it. But I think you'll want to hold off until Saturday.'

Christ, he sounded weak. I almost asked him

218

how he was, but that would have irritated him. Besides, I already knew the answer.

'What's going on?' I said.

'The sumos came in. Yamaoto killed them.'

'Shit.'

'No,' he said, his voice low and raspy, 'it's a good thing. A man called Big Liu, the head of United Bamboo, is coming to Tokyo on Saturday to meet Yamaoto, to try to straighten out the rest of it. Liu is staying at the Grand Hyatt in Roppongi Hills. The meeting is at a club called Whispers in Nishi-Azabu, run by a man called Kuromachi, Kuro, who's as close to a right-hand man as Yamaoto permits.'

'You got this from the informer?' I asked.

He nodded.

'If you've got such a solid insider, why haven't you used him to set up Yamaoto before?'

'I haven't had you to turn to, for one thing. For another, the informant is more afraid of Yamaoto than he is of me. There's always a delicate balance in these matters. If I push too hard, I could lose him entirely. And I'm pushing very hard right now.'

'All right. You're saying if we hit the yakuza before the meeting . . . '

'It could cause the meeting to be canceled. We would lose an unexpected opportunity to remove Yamaoto directly.'

I thought for a minute. 'What do you know about this club? Can I get to Yamaoto there?'

'I don't know. I don't know the layout, and my informant is being difficult. He suspects that I used his information about the delivery in

219

Wajima to set up the hit on the Chinese and the sumos. Yamaoto believes that was an inside job, and wants to find the man responsible. The informer is afraid. I don't know how much more I can get from him about the meeting.'

I considered. We might be able to get Dox positioned on a rooftop, or maybe in the van. Maybe we could drop Yamaoto with the M40A3 as he moved from his car into the club, or on his way out.

But that was nothing to count on. If Yamaoto was as paranoid now as Tatsu claimed, I expected the car would pull right up to the entrance and Yamaoto would be exposed too briefly, if at all, for Dox to take a reliable shot. We could set it up, of course, but if it failed we would need a way in.

'Can you get me a floor plan for the club?' I asked. 'I assume they're filed with the department of public safety, the fire department, something like that.'

'Of course.'

'What about electricity? Do you have people who could shut the power down on the club's block at the right moment?'

'Yes.'

It was a good start. But I realized we would need more than just the plans. A floor plan couldn't tell us where the principals were seated, whether there were bodyguards nearby, or a dozen other things we'd have to know in advance. For all that, we'd need a man inside.

'Tell me everything you know about the club,' I said. 'I assume it's a high-class place?'

'Very. As you know, most of the really high-end clubs are in Ginza and Akasaka, where the hostesses are Japanese girls not available on a cash basis.'

'Right.'

'Then there are the lower-end establishments, more likely to be found in Ikebukuro and Shinjuku, which are staffed by women from China, the Philippines, and other such foreign locales, who can be rented for a nightly or even hourly fee.'

'Yes, I've heard.'

Tatsu smiled. 'Kuro's place is, to a certain way of thinking, the best of both worlds. Its hostesses are from all over the world: Japan, elsewhere in Asia, the Middle East, Africa, Europe, the Americas. They're all beautiful, and all available.'

'How is Kuro able to . . . '

'By making the system profitable enough so that everyone wants to play. The rules are simple. When a customer comes in, the girls discreetly signal the Mama-san their price for a night with that customer. If the man is young and attractive, the price might be low — say, five hundred thousand yen. But if the customer is decrepit and repulsive, the price might be two million yen, or more.'

If the yen equivalent of upwards of four thousand dollars was 'low,' and some customers were spending four or five times that for a single night's pleasure, Kuro must have found a way to appeal to an awfully well-heeled clientele.

'If a customer sees a girl he likes,' Tatsu went on, 'he can ask what it would cost to leave the

221

club with her. If he is willing to pay her price, she's his for the evening. If not, he can ask about someone else.'

'How much do the girls get to keep?'

'Whatever they charge.'

'If they keep what they charge, where's Kuro's profit?'

'There's a fifty-million-yen joining fee and five million yen a year membership fees after that.'

'Fifty *million*?' I asked. That was well over four hundred thousand dollars.

'Yes.'

'Well, that ought to keep out the hoi polloi.'

He shrugged. 'Luxury has gone mass market. The super-rich have to find ways to distinguish themselves. I read about a new sports car that just came out, the Bugatti Veyron. It costs over a million dollars.'

'Yeah, I just put in my order for two.'

He laughed, but the laugh became a cough. He fitted the oxygen tube under his nose and breathed for a moment, then said, 'There are already several owners in Tokyo, you know, and many more on the waiting list. Men who can afford a car like that aren't put off by outrageous club fees. They welcome them, as a sign of status.'

He took a sip of water. 'But there's an important collateral benefit beyond the direct profit: the deals brokered with the politicians, businessmen, and crime bosses who are entertained there as guests. United Bamboo, for example. Yamaoto and Big Liu closed their methamphetamine arrangement at the club.'

'That's why they're meeting there again? Auspicious location?'

'Apparently Big Liu enjoyed himself greatly. He seems to have a predilection for blondes.'

Blondes. My notion of whom we might turn to as a 'man' inside sharpened. But there was no way Delilah was going to agree to this. And I didn't see how I could ask her.

'If the girl's price doesn't match the customer's,' I said, 'she doesn't have to leave with him. But what about when they're entertaining a guy like Big Liu? They're going to just turn him down?'

'For a big shot like Liu, the girls are expected to provide complimentary services. It doesn't matter how old he is or what he looks like. You're his for the night and he had better wake up with a smile the next morning. Otherwise, the girl is fired.'

'And suddenly cut off from the incredible cash flow she's gotten used to.'

'Precisely.'

Not exactly what I was hoping to hear. Maybe I could gloss over the 'If you help me, you might have to sleep with a repulsive, degenerate gangster' part of the sales pitch.

'Well?' he said, after a moment. 'Is any of this useful?'

'Maybe,' I told him. 'There might be someone I can get inside. I'll let you know. You have any pictures of Big Liu? I want to know what he looks like.'

Tatsu pressed the call button by the bed. The bodyguard came in.

'I'll take that file now, please,' Tatsu told him.

The man wordlessly handed Tatsu a large envelope and returned to his post.

'So this is how you're getting all this work done while you're laid up,' I observed.

He smiled and handed me the envelope. I unsealed it and took out a folder. Inside were several police and surveillance photos of a fat but still dangerous-looking Chinese man with graying hair and pockmarked skin.

'Big for a Chinese,' I commented.

'Hence the name,' Tatsu said, with his trademark 'infinite patience' tone.

'I see you've got Yamaoto in here, too. And who's this guy?'

'That's Kuro. I thought a dossier on the principals might be helpful.'

'Thanks. It is.'

He nodded. 'You don't have much time.'

I looked at him, frail and diminished on the hospital bed, tubes in his arms and up his nose, and realized he wasn't talking about Yamaoto's meeting.

'Are you . . . can I get you anything?' I asked.

He looked at me, his eyes fierce and alive inside his pallid skin.

'Yamaoto,' he said.

27

Delilah was on her way back from a morning workout in her neighborhood in the Marais when her cell phone rang. She stopped walking and looked for it in her bag.

Pedestrians carrying fresh bread and cut flowers and bags of fruit from the open-air market on Rue de Bretagne maneuvered around her on the narrow sidewalk. She ignored them and looked at the phone. The caller ID said *private*.

She'd been feeling delightfully relaxed from two hours of yoga and Pilates, but now her heart was suddenly beating harder. She pressed the receive button and said, '*Allo*.'

'Hi. It's me. John.'

This time it's hi, she thought. *Usually it's hey.* She wasn't sure what that meant.

'Hey,' she said.

'How've you been?'

'Fine. I didn't think I was going to hear from you.' She liked the way that sounded. Calm, not accusatory. Just a statement of fact.

'Why did you think that?'

'Last time we talked, it sounded as though you'd gotten pretty tied up in what took you to New York. And then you were going to Tokyo, and I just thought . . . that was it for us.'

Good, this was really good. Be cool, but get it out in the open. Give him the chance and the inclination to explain, without seeming to ask for that.

'I'm in Tokyo now,' he said. 'And I am tied up. But not the way you think.'

'What is it, then?'

There was a long pause. He said, 'I need your help.'

That wasn't what she'd been expecting. Before she could think it through, she said, 'You know, you call for my help more than you call for my company.'

'You're probably right. And I'm sorry for that. But right now I need both. Can you come to Tokyo?'

'Why?'

'I'll tell you when you get here. Please, Delilah. I wouldn't ask if it weren't important.'

She knew she should say no. But . . . there was something in his voice, something she'd never heard before. Whatever the problem was, he must have been nearly desperate to ask for her help after their last conversation.

Desperate about what, though? The only thing she could think of was that something had gone wrong when he visited Midori. But the woman had been relaxed when Delilah had seen her . . . yes, but she was clueless, she wouldn't have known what was going on in the shadows around her.

What could it have been? Was Rain seen? And if so, was his child in danger? If that were the case . . .

She felt her resolve slipping. But still, it was so damn galling. She wasn't sure what he wanted, but for all she knew its ultimate objective might be a life with Midori and the child.

Still, if something happened to Midori or the child that Delilah could have helped prevent, her own hopes for Rain would be doomed no matter what.

Also, she realized, going to him now might give her a chance to try to correct the mistake she'd made in doing that number on Midori, to provide a cushion against its possible consequences should Rain ever find out.

What if he had found out, though? Could this be a setup?

No, she couldn't believe that.

But you ran your kind of op on him. Why wouldn't he run his kind on you?

That made the choice clear, didn't it? She could give herself over entirely to suspicion and manipulation, which was to say she could give herself over to fear. She'd already sampled that particular dish, when she went to see Midori in New York, and the aftertaste was still vaguely nauseating.

Or she could go with hope.

'When?' she asked.

'Can you be here tomorrow?'

'Probably.'

'Let me give you a number. Call me and let me know.'

When they were done, she headed back to her apartment to check on flights. There was a 1:20 on Air France leaving that afternoon from De Gaulle, arriving in Tokyo at 9:20 the following morning. If she hurried, she could make it.

28

Tatsu called me that night to tell me he had some items I'd requested. He warned me to expect a different bodyguard this time, which was thoughtful of him. If I saw someone unfamiliar outside his door at night, he knew, it would make me jumpy.

I went to the hospital, using a lot of care in my approach. Repeated meetings in the same place was a huge violation of SOP, but right now obviously there wasn't an alternative.

The new guy knocked, then let me in. Tatsu was on his bed, pale and sweating this time. I looked at him for a moment. 'You okay?' I said.

He nodded, grimacing. 'It's okay. Just . . . hurts, sometimes. It'll pass.'

I pulled up a chair and sat with him, feeling helpless while he gritted his teeth and groaned.

'Let me get a nurse,' I said. 'She'll give you something for the pain.'

He shook his head. 'They'll give me morphine. It knocks me out. I can't have that. Not now.'

After a few minutes the groaning stopped and his breathing evened out.

'That was a bad one,' he said. 'They're getting more frequent, too. Fewer and fewer breaks. Hand me that towel, would you?'

There was a damp towel on the bedside stand. I gave it to him and he mopped his face.

'Don't worry,' he said, 'I'm all right. You see,

228

cancer is simply nature's way of making you want to die.'

I couldn't laugh, even though I knew he wanted me to. But I managed a weak smile for him.

I put my hand on his shoulder and we sat quietly for a few minutes. I said, 'What have you got for me?'

He pressed the call button. The bodyguard came in and handed him a backpack, then left.

Tatsu gave the backpack to me. I opened it. Inside were a set of floor plans and assorted commo gear.

I pulled out the plans and unfolded them. 'Whispers?'

He nodded. 'And the communications equipment you asked for. Three pairs.'

I shook my head in admiration. 'How do you get ahold of these things?'

He smiled. 'People who owe me favors. The question is, what are you going to do with it?'

'I'm not sure yet. I need to go over these plans, then get a firsthand look at the club. I'll know better after that.'

'What about your inside man?'

I thought about my talk with Delilah. She had called back to say she was coming, but it was tense.

'That's proceeding,' I said. 'But no guarantee yet.'

29

After leaving Tatsu, I bought a pair of binoculars, two pairs of long underwear, and a hat in Shinjuku. Then I went to reconnoiter Whispers.

The club was located in the elegant, tree-lined Minami Aoyama area between Kotto-dori to the east and Nirekedori to the west, not far from the Nezu art museum. Its immediate neighbors were hip restaurants and chic galleries and exquisite boutiques, sometimes unusual combinations of the three, all bracketed north and south by a pair of nameless streets. The northern one led to the club. The southern one ran behind it along a line of buildings, some of them separated by alleys.

There was a construction site north of the club entrance, which provided a decent vantage point. I watched for a few hours as a group of valets helped people in and out of their expensive cars, but I couldn't see much more than that. Still, it was better to have some firsthand knowledge of the club's environs than none at all. By the time I was done, at two in the morning, I was chilled to the bone.

I went back to the hotel and slept for six hours, then took the train to the airport to meet Delilah. She came through customs looking around, but didn't spot me right away amid the sea of mostly Japanese faces. She was wearing jeans and a black leather jacket, and there was a brown leather carry-on slung over one of her shoulders. Her hair was tied back and she was wearing no makeup that I could see. A little tired, maybe, but otherwise looking radiant as usual.

I watched her unseen for a moment and felt a rush of conflicted emotions. Gratitude that she would do this for me. Guilt that I had asked her. Remorse that I'd fucked up and caused this mess to begin with. And confusion, about who and what I even wanted.

I emerged from behind a cluster of people waiting on friends and family and business interests. She saw me then and nodded.

I stopped in front of her. Every other time I'd seen her after an absence, there had been some kind of embrace. Not today.

'Thanks for coming,' I said.

She nodded. 'Where to?'

'Here, let me take that.' She let me slip the bag off her shoulder and we started navigating through the crowds waiting in the arrivals lounge. She looked around as we walked, and I wondered whether it was operational or more in the way of taking in the unfamiliar sights in a new environment. Probably both.

'I've got a van in the garage,' I said. 'It's about an hour's drive into Tokyo. I'll brief you on the way.'

I glanced over and saw her looking at me, but I couldn't read her expression. 'Have you been here before?' I asked.

She shook her head. 'China once. Never Japan.'

'Maybe I'll get to show you around, then. I know a few places.'

She looked at me. 'But business first. Right?'

I thought she was trying to provoke me. Better not to answer.

On the way into Tokyo I told her everything. Not what had happened with Midori in her apartment, of course, or what I'd felt there — that would have been neither relevant nor useful. But everything else.

She listened quietly while I spoke. When I was done, she said, 'Well, you've certainly been busy since I last saw you.'

'That's one way to put it.'

'Your friend Dox must be pretty loyal to you, to stick with you through this.'

I didn't like the comment. I said, 'That's part of it. We also walked away with a lot of money at Wajima. You can have my share if you want it.'

Let her decide whether she wanted this to be business or personal.

She said, 'You'd have to tell me what you're paying me for first.'

'I think you know.'

'Maybe. You want me to pose as an applicant, reconnoiter this club for you.'

'That's pretty much it.'

'What if I actually get the job? Are you going to mind my sleeping with one of the customers?'

I looked at her. 'Yeah, I'll mind. You're not going to be any good to me if you're not on the premises.'

Her lips started to thin out in anger. Then I smiled and she realized I was teasing her. I shouldn't have done it, maybe, but I had to try something to break the tension.

She shook her head and muttered something in Hebrew. I was glad I couldn't understand what. I went back to driving and an instant later I saw her pivot in her seat, too late to do anything about it. She hit me on the top of the thigh with a thunderous hammer fist and I yelled out, 'Fuck!'

'Don't you make light of me,' she said. 'I am not happy about this.'

'Damn,' I said. 'I was just trying to loosen things up a little.'

'Yeah, well, find another way.'

One or two other smart comments did come insidiously to mind, but I thought better of saying them. We drove in silence for a few minutes. I rubbed my thigh, thinking I was going to have to ice it when I had the chance. She knew what she was doing and had really cracked me.

Seeing how pissed and resentful she was, I wondered for a moment why she was helping me at all. I wasn't suspicious, at least not on a professional level. We'd been through too much together for me to believe she could pose that kind of threat. But I still couldn't fully understand why she had come.

I decided that, if she had asked for my help in like circumstances, I would have offered it. Because it was the right thing to do. Because I cared enough about her. Because I wanted someone who could depend on me. Maybe it was the same for her.

I thought a little more. She hadn't asked me what it was like to see Midori, what it was like between us. I thought I understood why she hadn't, and I had no idea what I would say if she did. Well, we'd have time to talk about all that when Yamaoto was done. Right now it was a distraction.

'I assume I'll need some sort of reference when I go there tonight,' she said. 'Have you thought about that?'

I was ahead of her on this one, and had already worked it out with Tatsu. 'It's taken care of,' I said. 'They had a French woman working there two years ago, Valérie Silbert. She lives in Paris now. You met her at a club, she told you about Whispers. You came by to check it out. If it looks promising and they can help you with the visa, you're ready to give it a try.'

'You want me to go in with that? That's the thinnest cover I've ever heard.'

'It's good enough. My contact in Japanese intelligence got the Paris address, but said he couldn't get a phone number without more digging. If he couldn't get it, no one can.'

'What if they already have the number? They might have stayed in touch.'

'Maybe. But no one's going to try to contact the woman on such short notice, anyway. And even if they did, who's to say she didn't talk to you one night at a club? I doubt she'd remember herself. Look, even if anyone were inclined to contact her, this thing will be done long before. Thirty-six hours from now, give or take, that's it.'

'They'll probably want to see identification. A passport.'

Shit, I hadn't thought of that. Too much had been happening.

'You're not traveling under your own name, are you?'

'No.'

'French passport? French pocket litter?'

'Yes.'

I wanted to ask, *Then why did you bring it up?*

Instead I said, 'We're good to go, then.'

'But you didn't think of it. It makes me wonder what else you're missing.'

I glanced over at her and said, 'You want to tell me what's really bugging you?'

There was another pause. She said, 'This whole situation.'

Yeah, me too, I wanted to say. Instead I asked, 'Have you got a place to stay? Hotel?'

'Not yet. I barely had time to make it to the airport.'

Even cranky as she was, I wanted her to stay with me, but operationally it would be safer for her to stay somewhere else. On the other hand, I didn't want her to think I didn't want her. On the other other hand . . .

Jesus. I couldn't take much more of this.

'I'm at the Hilton, in Shinjuku,' I said. 'It's not La Florida, but it'll do. You're welcome to stay with me, if you like.'

There was a pause. She said, 'I think it's better if I stay somewhere else.'

I might have asked, *Better, Why? Is this*

235

personal, or *operational?* But it seemed better to let it alone.

'Tell me about your cover,' I said, 'and I'll make a reservation for you somewhere appropriate.'

She was quiet for a moment, imagining. Then she said, 'I live in Paris. My philandering husband died recently, leaving me with nothing but debts. I need a way to make money, and I want to get away from everything connected with my old life, do something exciting, have an adventure. When I heard about Whispers, it sounded like exactly what I needed.'

I didn't have to ask her about the details. I'd seen her in action before and knew that soon enough all the lies would be carefully thought through and intricately connected.

'Probably Le Meridien Pacific in Shinagawa, then. Makes sense that you'd choose a French chain, and there are only two in Tokyo. The other's in Odaiba, a little far from the center of things. The one in Shinagawa isn't a bad hotel. Close to where Dox is staying, too.'

'Okay.'

I took out my mobile phone and called information, which connected me to the hotel. I asked them if they had availability tonight and for the next five nights. They told me they did. I said I would call back and clicked off.

'They've got rooms,' I said. 'Just tell them you had a reservation, and they'll think they lost it. No big deal for anyone as long as there's still availability. It would look strange if you showed up without a reservation, or if you made one a

236

half hour before checking in.'

'I know.'

I glanced over. 'One other thing. See if you can rent a mobile phone through the hotel. The one you use in France won't work here. I'd get you one myself, but . . . '

'I know. We need something backstopped.'

Damn, she was touchy. Well, I'd rather irritate her by pointing out the obvious than take a chance on overlooking something important.

'What name will you be using at the hotel?' I asked.

'Laure Kupfer.'

'Kupfer with a K?'

'Yes.'

I told her my mobile number. She wrote it down. I told her where Dox was staying, just a short walk from Le Meridien, and that we should plan to meet in his room at seven o'clock that evening unless I heard from her otherwise.

We drove the rest of the way in silence. When I dropped her off, she said she wanted to sleep for a few hours. That sounded like a good idea. It was around four in the morning in Paris, and if things went well at her audition tonight she might be out late.

'Do you have money?' I asked her.

She shook her head.

I reached into a pocket and pulled out some bills. I counted out ten ten-thousand-yen notes and extended them to her. 'This is about eight hundred dollars,' I said. 'Not sure what that is in Euros — maybe seven, seven-fifty, I think.'

'I'll find an ATM,' she said, making no move to take the money.

'That'll be a waste of time,' I said. 'You can pay me back if you want.'

After a moment, she took the money. 'I'll call you later,' she said, and was gone.

30

I needed to clear my head, so I drove the van into Jingumae and parked, then made my way to a place I liked there called Volontaire. Coffeehouse by day and bar by night, Volontaire opened in 1977, around the time I returned to Tokyo following the late unpleasantness of my mercenary days, and I'd spent some time there while living in the city. Hidden on the second floor of a dilapidated wedge of a building off Meiji-dori, Volontaire is the ultimate neighborhood place, seating fewer than a dozen people on faded red velour-covered stools tucked up against a peeling L-shaped counter, with the space behind the bar given over more to a couple thousand vinyl jazz albums than to bottles of booze, and featuring a bathroom so tiny that its door folds in half so as to avoid banging into the toilet and sink inside.

I navigated up the spiral staircase bolted to the building's façade and went through the tiny exterior door. The place hadn't changed at all, not at all. The mama-san was behind the bar, working the espresso machine. I recognized her from before, and, in keeping with the overall timelessness of the place, she seemed not to have aged: a smart, good-looking woman, probably in her fifties, but who could really say? She called out *irasshaimase* — welcome — without looking up. When she saw me a moment later, she smiled and said, '*Hisashiburi desu ne.*' It's been a long time.

That's the problem with the really great bars. They remember their customers.

'*So da ne,*' I said, offering agreement without inviting conversation, and went in. The door closed behind me and the sounds of traffic outside faded away.

The place was half full — it was lunchtime, not yet coffee hour — and I took a stool along the short end of the bar. Alto sax Lou Donaldson's 'Light Foot' was playing, and the album was displayed face out on one of the shelves for all to see. Volontaire's customers come for the music as much as the atmosphere, and like to know what they're listening to.

I ordered the house blend and a roast beef sandwich, then let the smell of the beans, the assured notes of Donaldson's sax, and that wonderful feeling of being alone in a place with some history and gravitas, open my mind and help me start to think.

I hoped I was doing the right thing. Not just in asking for Delilah's help, but in the entire enterprise. I'd started off hoping to see Midori and my son and now found myself in a war, struggling simply to get back to the status quo antebellum. Every move I made seemed to hold in equal measure the promise of a complete fix and the threat of the worst possible outcome.

And I'd been hiding from that outcome, I'd been refusing to face it. Even when Tatsu had brought it up in the hospital, saying how afraid he was that he might have put my son in danger,

I'd cut him off with some bromide about how we were just going to make everything all right.

But maybe we weren't. Things went wrong in war, they always did. You could manage the influence of luck and chance but never eliminate them as factors. And if my luck turned sour now, or if I did something sloppy like what had happened in Manila not so long ago . . .

Say it, goddamnit. Face it.

Midori and my tiny boy would be slaughtered before I could even try to stop it. And it would be my fault.

A chill swept through me as the reality of the concept settled into my gut, my bones.

For the first time, I was facing a real risk, so much so that suddenly all the risks I'd ever run previously felt like silly games by comparison. Up until now, the only chips I'd ever laid on the table had been my own. This time, if I lost a round, my son's life was the collateral to be foreclosed.

I recognized that in some ways I was making a mistake thinking about it. If you focus on the risks, they'll multiply in your mind and eventually paralyze you. You want to focus on the task, instead, on doing what needs to be done.

So why was I tormenting myself like this? It was counterproductive, it was . . .

You know why.

I sighed. There was an alternative. And I had to face it squarely, choose it or discard it deliberately and consciously. Otherwise I was never going to be able to clear my mind and act decisively.

Saturday night, I could walk right up to Yamaoto and blow my own brains out in front of his eyes. Then we'd be quits. Any motivation he or the Chinese might have to harm Midori or my son would end with their ability to harm me thereby. It would be the closest thing possible to a guarantee of their safety.

I didn't want to do it. If I had to do it, if I knew it was the only way, I would. But how could I, while there was still a chance of succeeding by something less extreme?

My own father died just after I turned eight. I grew up without him, and his loss and subsequent absence were the first and perhaps most significant of the scars that shaped what I became. What would it be like for my own son to grow up without me? Would the lack of a father harm him the way it had me? Or would it even make a difference, if I had never been there to begin with?

It didn't matter. My desire to be part of his life, and to have him as part of mine, had impelled me to risk seeing Midori in the first place. My feelings in that regard were as strong now as ever.

Besides, I could hold suicide in reserve. If at any time I concluded it was my only means of preventing harm to my son, I would do it willingly, gratefully. But not now. Not while there was still a chance of a better way.

I'd talk to Dox, though, make sure he knew how to get my share of what we'd taken at Wajima to Midori and Koichiro. Just in case.

I realized I might have been rationalizing. I

242

didn't care. I wasn't going to offer Yamaoto my life until I'd taken my best shot at ending his.

I felt something closing into place in my mind, the old emotional bulkheads, sealing up everything behind them, enabling me to do what I needed to. A part of me was appalled that I retained the ability even under the current circumstances. But I also knew from long experience that it was the only way to get the job done.

I looked down and saw I hadn't touched my coffee or sandwich. Enough. I fueled up and started thinking about the tools we would need for tomorrow night.

31

That evening, I went to see Dox at the Prince in Shinagawa. I stopped at the incongruous Dean & DeLuca on the way and picked up sandwiches and side dishes for three.

He opened the door when I knocked and looked behind me. 'Where's your lady?'

'Coming soon, as far as I know. Don't call her that.'

I walked in and he closed the door behind me. 'You have a fight?' he asked.

'I don't know what's going on.'

'You must be making her sullen again.'

'I guess so.'

'You keep this up, she's going to defect to me. And you won't be able to blame me when it happens.'

I rubbed my sore thigh. 'You can have her.'

'Sorry, man, that must have been a bad fight you had.'

I started taking the food from the bags and putting it on the desk.

'Mmm, that smells tasty,' Dox said. 'But I guess we ought to wait for your lady.'

I glared at him, only to meet the irrepressible grin.

While we waited for Delilah, I took out the plans and drew a grid over them. Top to bottom, I lettered A through K. Left to right, I numbered one through twenty-four. When I was done, we had a convenient and reliable way of discussing every position in the club.

A few minutes later, there was a knock. Dox looked through the peephole, then opened the door. It was Delilah.

'Well, hello there,' he said. 'Ain't you a sight for sore eyes.'

She was, too. She was wearing a black cocktail dress made of some kind of embroidered lace, with a satin capelet thrown over her shoulders. She had on high-heeled shoes, but not stilettos, which would have been too much, and was carrying a black silk beaded evening bag. Her hair was pulled back, and she had employed just a little smoky gray eye shadow and a hint of gloss on her lips.

'Dox,' she said, smiling. She came in and he closed the door behind her. Then she turned and kissed him on both cheeks, European style. I saw the dress had an exceptionally low-cut, open back. The revealed skin and musculature of her back was gasp-inducing erotic, and the material below hugged her ass exactly right — as though her body, not the dress, was responsible for the arresting effect. The overall impression was sophisticated, confident, and sexy as hell.

I saw Dox blushing from the kiss and could have laughed. She'd had that effect on him the first time he saw her in Phuket, and it had never gone away.

'Honey,' he said, 'if they don't offer you a job on the spot tonight, they are either crazy or blind or both.'

Her smile widened. She looked him over and said, 'You kept the beard off. You look great.'

'Well, someone once told me I have good bones, and that was the end of that.'

She laughed, then turned to me and nodded. I nodded back.

The room was noticeably quiet for a moment. Dox looked at Delilah, then at me. 'I don't mean to pry,' he said, 'but I'm detecting some animosity in the air. Is this little tiff the two of you seem to be having going to make it hard for us to work together?'

Delilah and I looked at each other and said in stereo, 'No.'

Dox nodded. 'Good, I feel reassured already.'

The room was quiet for another moment. To fill the silence, I said to Delilah, 'You look good. You bring that outfit with you?'

She shook her head. 'There are so many French designers in Tokyo, I might as well have been shopping in Paris.'

I passed out sandwiches and we ate sitting on the double beds. Dox did a nice job of keeping the conversation going, asking Delilah what she thought of Tokyo, things like that.

'I like it,' she said. 'I slept for a few hours, then spent the afternoon and evening shopping and riding the trains. For some reason I didn't expect to see so many westerners.'

'Depends on where you are in the city,' I said. 'Where we're going to be operating, you won't look out of place at all. In some of the eastern and outlying areas, you would.'

She nodded. 'I did a walk-through past the

club. Minami Aoyama is what, upscale boutiques and restaurants?'

'That's about right,' I said. 'Classy and cool. Perfect venue for Whispers.'

'Right next to Roppongi, too,' Dox added. 'Which is my favorite part of town.'

Roppongi is one of the city's entertainment districts, the premier place for foreign men chasing Japanese women, and Japanese women who want to be chased.

Delilah looked at him. 'I've heard about Roppongi. I strolled around a bit, but it didn't seem like much.'

Dox grinned. 'It's different at night.'

Delilah smiled. 'I reckon it is,' she said in her best southern drawl.

That broke Dox up. I didn't share his reaction.

'All right, here's the plan,' I said. 'Delilah, you go to the club tonight. You want to get inside and see as much as possible. Ideally, you'll find a way to get invited back for tomorrow night, when Yamaoto will be there with Big Liu. But at a minimum, you can confirm certain critical details just by getting inside tonight.'

'How confident are you that I'm going to be able to just walk in there?' she asked. 'From the way you've described the place, it sounds like they're pretty careful people.'

'There's no way to find out except to try,' I said. 'But I have a feeling it'll be easier than you think. It's not a big cash business, so they're not concerned about getting knocked over. Even if there were a lot of cash, it's a yakuza operation, who's going to rob it? And whatever other trouble they might be looking for and trying to screen out, it doesn't look like you.'

'What about language? I speak about three words of Japanese.'

'English will be fine. Almost all their members will speak at least a little. And even if their English is terrible, it'll make them feel cosmopolitan to use it with you.'

Dox added, 'I've, uh, heard there are plenty of foreign hostesses in Japan who don't speak Japanese. 'Course I don't know for sure. John's really the one to ask about that.'

I shot him a look, then said to Delilah, 'In fact . . . in fact, you should stay with French. It'll make you that much more exotic, and anyone there using English will be more comfortable talking in front of you if they think you can't understand. Yeah, whoever you encounter, try French first, and if they can't understand it, switch to basic, struggling, screwed-up, heavily accented English. Play it right and they might actually start to feel protective, want to take care of you.'

She nodded. 'Okay.'

'Now, assuming you can get in, and I think you can, the things we're most interested in at this point are ways of ingress and egress, whether doors open in or out, presence of emergency lighting systems . . . '

'I know how to case a room.'

Whatever tensions we were dealing with personally, I wasn't going to let them cause us to go about this half-assed.

'I know you do,' I said. 'But can we go through

this anyway? It'll help me feel sure I'm not missing anything.'

She caught the reference to the conversation we'd had on the way from the airport and knew I was being diplomatic to the point of sarcasm. But she also knew I was right. She nodded and said nothing.

I unfolded the floor plans and spread them out on the bed. 'Here's the club,' I said. 'Familiarize yourself with the layout. We need to confirm that these plans are current and otherwise accurate, and to know all the relevant aspects of the local terrain that don't show up here in two dimensions.'

She gave me a slow nod that said, *I'm not stupid, you know.*

'I'm not talking down to you,' I said, trying to rein in my frustration. 'I know you know all this. But it's better to say it out loud and not to assume. You know that, too.'

Dox said, 'He does it to me all the time, too. He's a repressed man, and I've come to realize that micromanagement is one of his few ways of expressing affection. Once you realize that, you'll actually start to like it. I know I do.'

Delilah closed her eyes and laughed. I supposed I should have been grateful to Dox for managing the tension in the room, but it was irritating to see them getting along like old friends while I could hardly find anything to say to her that didn't provoke an angry response.

'Start with the entrance,' I said. 'How do you get in? Do the doors open freely, or does someone need to buzz you in from inside? Is

249

there a camera out front? Security? All I could see when I reconnoitered was a pair of valets.'

I pointed to the plans. 'Now we go inside. This space inside the front entrance — I would guess there's a hostess or hostesses waiting there, probably to check coats and lead customers into the club itself. There might also be security. Maybe an additional set of doors. And here, this small room opposite the entrance doors. Probably a back office. It would be good to know what and who is in there.'

'Got it.'

'Now this big space,' I said. 'Presumably it's the main room. I'm guessing tables, booths . . . Is it cluttered? Spacious? Are there clear fields of fire? If there are obstructions, I want to know where.'

'Okay.'

'These rooms here, off the main room,' I said, pointing to the plans again, 'my guess is that they're for private meetings, like the one Yamaoto is hosting tomorrow night. One is bigger than the other, but we don't know how much of an entourage he's going to have, so I don't know which he's likely to use, if he uses one at all. And this room here, probably a kitchen.'

She looked at the plans. 'No kitchen entrance?'

'Not according to the plans.'

'Where do they take the garbage out?'

'I don't know. My guess is, they take it out the front after hours. But I'll check out the exterior and grounds to make sure.'

She nodded.

I pointed to another area. 'There are two emergency exits — here off the main room, and here in the basement. The exterior basement stairs lead to the same side of the building where the front entrance is located, so Dox can cover both the main entrance and the basement emergency exit simultaneously. But the main room exit goes out the other side of the building. We're going to need to find a way to close it off to make sure anyone who gets past me has to cross Dox's field of fire on the way out. Anything you can tell us about the exit doors would be useful.'

'Okay.'

'Now this staircase leads down to the basement level, which is restrooms, a utility room, and again that emergency exit. See if you can use a bathroom break to get into the utility room. My source tells me that code for this building requires emergency lighting run off a backup generator. I need to know what they're using and whether you can disable it tomorrow night. And regardless, look around for stand-alone battery-operated units, especially in stairwells and above doorways. If they're already required by the building code to have a generator system, I doubt they'd go to the expense of installing stand-alone units, too, but we have to know.'

'Okay.'

'The final thing is cameras. They probably don't have any overt ones, except again possibly one monitoring the front entrance. The place is supposed to be the ultimate in discretion, and obvious security cameras inside would spoil the ambience. But they might have some less obvious ones. Here's something that will help you 'spot them if they do.'

I took out the custom-made, pocket-sized bug detector Harry had made for me before he died, and handed it to Delilah. 'Here. It picks up the horizontal oscillator frequency radiated by video cameras. It's not exactly a divining rod, but it'll give you an idea.'

Delilah hefted it in her hand and looked at it approvingly. 'Nice.'

'I'd like it back, if possible. It's one of a kind. And it has sentimental value.'

Dox started to break out into the grin. 'You? Sentimental?'

I looked at him, thinking of Harry. 'Is there a problem?' I asked.

The grin retreated. 'No problem.'

I looked at Delilah, then Dox. 'Questions? Comments?'

Delilah said, 'So Plan A is for Dox to drop Yamaoto as he leaves his car and enters the club. The rest of this is all Plan B.'

'That's right. But Plan A is nothing to count on here. You've seen the street the club is on. There aren't many places we can position Dox for a shot at the front entrance. There's no parking on the street, so we can't set him up in the van. There's a building site near Aoyama-dori that might work, but even then the angle is such that he'll only have a second to make the shot. Yamaoto travels in an armored Mercedes, and he'll probably have a phalanx of bodyguards. Unless he lingers for a few moments outside the entrance, we won't be able to get to him until he's inside.'

'Yeah,' Dox said. 'Plan B is the new Plan A.'

'Makes sense,' Delilah said.

'You manage to get a phone?' I asked.

She reached into her purse and pulled out a clamshell model in screaming yellow.

'Well, that ought to do,' I said. 'Did you figure out . . .'

'I changed the interface to English,' she said. 'It's fine.'

I nodded. 'Are you armed?'

She smiled. 'What do you think?'

I looked her over. She wasn't wearing much, but if she was carrying, I couldn't see it.

'Not that I can tell,' I said.

Her smile widened. She dropped her right hand, hooked her thumb under the edge of the dress, and reached up along her inner thigh. An instant later her hand reappeared, her fingers curled into a fist. A wicked-looking two-inch blade protruded like a talon from between her first and second knuckles.

'Goddamn,' Dox said. 'What is that pretty little thing?'

'FS Hideaway,' Delilah said. She opened her hand, slid the knife from around her first two fingers, and handed it hilt first to Dox.

'Yeah, I've been reading about these, but haven't gotten my own yet,' he said. He tried to slip it on, but the grip was too small to fit over his fingers. 'You like it?'

'I love it,' she said. 'This one's actually a knockoff that our tech people make. It's composite, not steel. Not as tough as you'd like, but it's razor sharp and, best of all, doesn't set off metal detectors. I carried it from Paris on the plane.'

I saw that, instead of a handle, the knife was gripped through a capsule shaped hole. The whole thing was tiny, but when she had it deployed, she looked like a damned velociraptor.

'What have you got down there?' Dox said, looking at her thigh.

She raised an eyebrow.

He blushed. 'I mean . . . ' he started to say.

She smiled. 'Kydex sheath.'

'Well, now I know what to ask for for Christmas,' Dox said, handing the knife back to her. She reached under her dress and returned it to its hiding place.

I pulled the commo gear out of a bag and handed her a transmitter and an earpiece. 'This is the same kind of equipment we used in Hong Kong,' I said. 'We ought to do a dry run tonight. But with your hair up . . . '

'I'll hold the earpiece,' she said, fixing the transmitter just below the neckline of the dress. 'When I get alone for a minute, I'll put it in place. We'll make sure it all works.'

I nodded. 'We could wire you up so Dox and I can hear what's going on around you, not just you talking into your dress.'

She shook her head. 'Not in this outfit. I wouldn't be able to hide the battery bulge. And I don't know what this club is like. People might be free with their hands.'

I nodded again. 'Yeah, you're right. Well, as long as we can hear you, we should be okay.'

She looked at her watch, then at Dox and me. She smiled, and I realized that some part of her enjoyed the rush of an op.

'Okay, boys,' she said. 'Time for me to get into character.'

32

Delilah did a surveillance detection route on foot to ensure she was alone, then caught a taxi to Minami Aoyama. She doubted the driver would ever have heard of Whispers, but he understood the words Aoyama-dori and Kotto-dori well enough, and from that main intersection she could walk. She was glad she'd taken the time to reconnoiter earlier that day. It would be good to have a few things that felt familiar. Certainly everything else about this city and these circumstances was disorienting.

She didn't want things to be so tense with Rain, but damn it, she was just so frustrated with him. None of this needed to be happening. He had rushed off to see his child, and then he'd screwed up, just as she had feared in Barcelona. And now she was getting sucked into the aftermath.

Ordinarily, she felt she had a lot of clarity in her life, especially given the shifting, ambiguous world she lived in, but this time her feelings were a mess. She was pissed at Rain for creating the situation that had caused her to do such an ugly thing as visit Midori in New York. And she was simultaneously appalled at what she had done, remorseful for it, and afraid that Rain was going to find out. She wanted to do something to make amends, and was furious with herself for putting herself in a position where she felt *she* needed to make things up with *him*. And underlying all of it was the fact that she still wanted him, and she was angry at him for that, too.

She closed her eyes, exhaled deeply, and told herself to let it go. She could figure it all out later. Right now, she was on her way to a job interview. She reviewed all the particulars of the role she was playing, why she was here, the job she wanted, her hopes and fears. By the time the cab let her off at the corner of Aoyama-dori and Kotto-dori, she had submerged herself and was fully in character.

She walked south down Kotto-dori, cold in the capelet and skimpy dress, past an intriguing mix of restaurants, boutiques, office buildings, and residences. Cars and small trucks and motor scooters navigated up and down the street, their engines whining and revving at discordant pitches and resounding off the walls of buildings to either side. An occasional horn honked, but never aggressively. A few bicyclists maneuvered around her on the sidewalk. A number of older women were out walking squirrel-sized dogs, some of the animals in tiny wool sweaters. The women and their overly precious canines you saw everywhere in Paris. But here, she noted, looking down, the custom was to clean up after the pets.

She liked the city. Tokyo seemed to have little in the way of zoning ordinances, something that would have horrified the overseers of Paris. But the planning that worked there would have suffocated the eclectic charm that she sensed was what made Tokyo tick.

She turned left on one of the narrow, nameless side streets running east off Kotto-dori. Fifty meters ahead, she saw two men standing purposefully and sensed they worked for the club. When she had walked by earlier that day, there had been no one around, and, if she hadn't known at the time what she was looking for, she would have gone right past without even knowing. There was no sign or any other announcement, just a slate path leading away from the street, now flanked by these two.

They watched her as she approached. They were wearing identical dark suits, fully buttoned, and each had the same metrosexually refined eyebrows and carefully coiffed hair. They were way too soft-looking to be security, and she made them as the valets Rain had mentioned. That made sense — the place was more than upscale enough, and there seemed to be no parking nearby. They bowed as she approached and she nodded to them, catching sight of the wired earpiece each was wearing.

She turned onto the path, head swiveling as she walked, as though impressed by the design of the place. And it was impressive: to either side of the path were dark rectangular pools of water and lush ferns, all of it illuminated softly from below. A pair of clean-cut concrete walls rose out of the ground and increased in height as the path got closer to the building, eventually reaching about three meters and creating a sense of privacy that grew as she walked. There was a faint smell of incense, and the sound of water moving over stones. It was as though the club was gradually taking her in from the noisy, public city outside.

The effect increased as the path turned right. Suddenly everything was quiet: nothing but her footfalls and that calming sound of water trickling in the pools. She walked up a short riser of concrete steps and into a large vestibule discreetly lit with wall sconces. A small square of glass was embedded in the wall to the right of a pair of large wooden doors, surrounded by a metal plate. *Camera*, she thought. She felt the detector Rain had given her buzz in her purse, and was glad to know it was working. Next to the camera was a button. Below it, an embedded plastic unit she recognized as a magnetic card reader. There was no keypad, just the reader itself, and she guessed that the valets carried swipe keys. That meant the door would be kept locked and, valets and other employees excepted, controlled from inside.

She looked around again, just an out-of-town girl taking it all in, and noted no other surveillance equipment. She pulled on both doors, then pushed. They were indeed locked. Okay.

She looked at the button next to the camera as though noticing it for the first time, then pressed it. A moment later, she heard the distinct *clack* of an electronic lock, then the door to her left was swinging outward, guided by another man in a dark suit. Unlike the two out front, this guy had security written all over him. His hair was crew-cut — functional, not stylish — and something in his eyes suggested that if anyone

259

ever tried to metrosexually reshape his brows they'd be hospitalized for their troubles. He held open the door and bowed his head in welcome.

The way he had immediately welcomed her, without checking to see whether she was alone, confirmed that she had been watched via the camera before she pressed the buzzer. The man had opened the door already knowing, or having been told, exactly what was outside.

She nodded and walked in. Soft techno music played from unseen speakers and the air smelled faintly of cigar smoke. She checked the drape of the security guy's suit as she went by. She saw no telltale bulges, but his right side was facing away from her and she couldn't be sure. She'd try for another look later.

This was the small room she'd seen in the floor plans. The design was minimalist, just dark, wood-paneled walls, a leather-wrapped island in the center, and a leather-covered bench to one side. To the left was a pair of large swinging doors, which from the plans she knew led to the main room. Behind the island was another door, the one that led to what they had guessed was an office. To the right, the stairs down to the restrooms and, presumably, the utility room.

Two more men stood off to the right. One was another serious-looking guy she made as security, and there it was, yes, the bulge that was no cell phone at his hip under the jacket. The other guy was as soft-looking as the two out front. *Probably another valet*, she thought. *When a member is ready to leave, this guy runs out for the car, and one of the two outside comes in.*

They rotate. No one's kept waiting.

Two quite stunning Japanese women stood behind the island. Both were dressed exquisitely in gold lamé gowns. Their makeup was perfect, and their long, lustrous hair was set in elaborate chignons. They looked classy, sophisticated, and very, very sexy.

Delilah walked up and smiled a little uncertainly. '*Pardonnez-moi,*' she said. '*Parlez-vous français?*'

The women looked at each other, then back to Delilah. No, they didn't speak French.

'Ah, this is Whispers, yes?' she asked in heavily accented English.

The hostesses nodded. One of them said, with a Japanese accent, 'Whispers, yes.'

Okay, their English didn't seem too much better than their French. Delilah said, 'I am here for . . . a job. Working here.'

The woman who had spoken a moment earlier said, 'Mmm, one minute, please.' She picked up a phone and spoke a few words of Japanese, then hung up. 'Please,' she said, gesturing to the bench. 'Just a minute.'

Delilah thanked her and sat. She glanced again at the first security guy, but his right side was still facing away from her. Well, the other guy was carrying, it was safe to assume they both were.

While she waited, she heard a soft buzzer. She watched the women behind the island. They looked down, presumably at a video screen, then nodded to the first security guy, who nodded back and opened the door. Two fiftyish Japanese men wearing cashmere overcoats walked in. The

261

women came out from behind the island and bowed in welcome. One of the women took the coats and brought them into the room behind the island; the other escorted the men into the main area. A few moments later the women had reassembled in their original positions.

So the security guy didn't have visual access to the vestibule outside. The hostesses took care of that, and he took his cues from them. Okay.

A minute later, another Japanese woman came through the door on the other side of the island. This one was older — late forties or fifties. She was a handsome woman, and looked at home in a black Chanel suit that, while certainly elegant, served to identify her, along with her age and bearing, as management rather than talent.

Delilah stood as the woman approached. 'May I help you?' the woman asked in English.

'Yes,' Delilah said, laying on the Parisian accent. 'I would like to apply for a job.'

The woman nodded and looked Delilah up and down. Delilah could tell the woman approved of what she saw.

'How did you hear about us?' the woman asked.

'Hear . . .'

'About Whispers. This club. How did you learn about us?'

Delilah paused as though to translate the words, then said, 'Ah, I met a nice woman in Paris. Valérie. She . . . tells me about Whispers.'

The woman smiled and nodded. 'Ah, Val. She was very popular here. How is she?'

'She is very well, I think.'

'Do you live in Paris? Or . . . '

'Yes, Paris.'

'Then you're just visiting Tokyo.'

'*Oui*. Yes, visiting.'

The woman nodded again as though considering. Then she said, 'Our membership is exclusive. Men of unusual wealth and taste. Powerful men. Do you think you could entertain such men? Know how to . . . please them?'

Delilah paused again as though having difficulty with the English, then said, 'I like men.'

The woman laughed. 'And I expect they like you. But, forgive me, your English is not very good, is it?'

Delilah smiled a little sheepishly, as though the woman had just exposed a secret. '*Non*, but I am fast learning . . . '

The woman laughed again. 'You'll have to, and some Japanese, too. But first things first. Mr Kuro is the person you need to speak with, and he's not here tonight. But he will be tomorrow. Can you come back then?'

Because it was consistent with her role, Delilah permitted herself a moment of satisfaction. 'Come back tomorrow?' she asked.

'Yes.'

'Yes. What time?'

'The same time as now. I don't know when he'll be free, and you might have to wait for a while.'

'I can wait.'

'Good. And what is your name?'

'I am called Laure.'

'Well, Laure, it's very good to meet you. You

can call me Kyoko.'

'*Enchantée*,' Delilah said, shaking the woman's hand. Then she added, 'Would it be all right to . . . may I see? The club?'

Kyoko smiled and looked her over again. 'I don't see any problem with that. You'll certainly look right at home.'

She took Delilah by the arm and escorted her through the swinging doors. Delilah noted that they swung in both directions, no knobs, no locks.

The room beyond was a large rectangle built on three levels. At the lowest level, in the center, was a freestanding bar. One step up, surrounding the bar and facing it, were four long rows of built-in leather-covered benches. The backs of the benches rose to the floor of the room's third level, where Delilah now stood. A dozen men in suits and twice that number of drop-dead women in equally drop-dead clothes were seated along the rows around the bar, and the techno music Delilah heard earlier now mingled with the sounds of laughter and conversation. Several of the men looked up at Delilah, and she realized this was part of the purpose of the layout, to let the club's members leisurely appraise its hostesses. In fact, she noticed that the lighting, too, was designed for the pleasure of the patrons: the seating areas were illuminated only indirectly, and were therefore private, while this level, which was open to foot traffic, was lit by a series of elegant hanging lights.

Along the wall opposite the doors they had just come through were a half dozen booths.

These, too, were softly lit and had the feel of alcoves. A few of them were occupied, again by prosperous-looking men and gorgeous women of various ethnicities. Several Japanese women, attractive in their own right but less fabulously attired than the hostesses, moved about the room, bringing snacks, freshening drinks, and otherwise ensuring that the members were well provided for.

At one end of the booths was a door. Over it, a lighted green sign signifying that this was one of the two emergency exits. She would have liked a closer look, but sensed that would be overstaying her welcome.

'It's beautiful,' Delilah said.

Kyoko looked at her. 'You think you would like it here?'

Delilah nodded. '*Certainement*. I'm sure I would.'

Kyoko smiled and walked her back to the foyer. They stopped outside the front doors.

'Then we'll see you at the same time tomorrow night?' Kyoko asked.

Delilah nodded. 'Yes. And thank you.'

Kyoko bowed in acknowledgment and went back to her office.

Delilah turned to the women behind the island. 'Ah . . . the ladies' room?' she said.

One of the women gestured to the stairs. Delilah thanked her, noting that, from their position behind the island, the women wouldn't be able to see the restroom doors or that of the utility room. She headed down, opening her purse, taking out an innocent-looking leather key

265

case, and detaching the head from one of the keys on the way. Inside the body of the key, attached to the head, was a lock rake. She palmed the rake, dropped the keys back in her purse, and took out an exceptionally thin steel nail file that always doubled nicely as a torsion wrench.

When she reached the bottom of the stairs, Rain's detector buzzed. She looked up and saw a ceiling camera aimed at the emergency door, presumably to catch an intruder trying to come in the back way. She wondered why the club hadn't invested a trivial amount more for an additional camera covering the interior, then realized it was probably out of deference to the patrons' privacy concerns. It didn't really matter. With the electricity cut and the lights out, the camera would be irrelevant.

She hadn't seen anyone heading toward the restrooms in the last few minutes, and suspected they were empty now. Still, best to check. The men's room first, an embarrassed apology ready in case she had erred. But it was unoccupied, the three stall doors all slightly ajar. Likewise the ladies' room. Okay.

She paused in front of the emergency exit door, behind the camera's ambit, and looked it over. It opened out, with a metal push bar across its center. She wanted to try it, but the camera would have caught that. Also, there was a sticker running along the length of the bar in red Japanese characters, with an exclamation point at the end. Probably a warning that an alarm would sound if the door were opened. She took out her cell phone and snapped a picture. Rain could read it later to confirm.

She walked over to the utility room. Steel door, hinges on the outside, likely a five-pin tumbler in the knob. She tried the knob and was unsurprised to find it locked. Doubtful there could be anyone in there, but you never know, so she knocked, ready to seem extremely clueless about what down here was a restroom and what was a utility room in the unlikely event someone answered. But no one did.

She glanced at the stairs, then slid the file into the lock and turned it slightly, taking up the slack. Then she inserted the rake and ran it back and forth over the tumblers. A moment later the knob turned and she was in.

The room was dark, but she found a wall switch and flipped it on. She saw it instantly: a backup generator, bolted next to the exterior wall. She walked over and looked more closely. Diesel unit, digital control panel, she could shut it down anytime. If there was a problem with the controls, she could simply pull the leads. No worries about after-the-fact signs of tampering on this job.

She looked around, hoping to see a fuse box, which would give them other options. But there was none. Probably in the office upstairs. And therefore, for their purposes, inaccessible.

She turned off the light and walked out, checking to make sure the door was locked behind her. Then she ducked into one of the ladies' room stalls, hid the rake again, and took out the earpiece. She put it in and tilted her head down.

'It's me,' she said. 'Is the reception okay?'

'Loud and clear,' Rain answered promptly.

'Roger that,' Dox added.

'Okay. Leaving now.' She dropped the earpiece back in her purse and flushed the toilet. She walked out of the stall and checked herself in the mirror, already in character again. Then she headed back up the stairs.

The women were out in front of the island, helping a Japanese man and one of the hostesses with their coats. It looked like someone had managed to agree on a price tonight. One of the women buzzed Delilah out. The security guy bowed and held the door for her again.

As she reached the end of the walkway outside, one of the valets went running past her in the direction of the club. She turned around and got back to the turn in the path in time to see him pull a magnetic key from inside his suit jacket and wave it in front of the reader. He slipped it back inside the jacket, and she realized he kept it on a lanyard around his neck. The door started to open and Delilah moved out of its line of sight.

The other valet was in front, holding open the passenger door of a blue Bentley Continental GTC. The engine was idling at a low purr.

Nice ride, she thought. She smiled at the valet and walked off.

33

We reconvened in Dox's hotel room a half hour after Delilah had checked in from the club. She briefed us on everything: entrance and exit layout and procedures; security personnel and protocols; the backup generator. She hadn't missed a thing, and recollected exactly the right details. I wasn't surprised.

'The layout is good,' she said, when Dox and I had exhausted our questions. 'We can control it. The only thing I couldn't confirm was the emergency exit door off the main room, on the ground floor. It's there, but I didn't get to try it. The one in the basement, though, opens outward with a horizontal push bar. But there was a camera in front of it, and something written across it. I think that an alarm would sound if it's opened, so I didn't try. Here.'

She took out her phone and worked the keys for a moment, then handed the unit to me. 'What do you think?'

I had to squint a bit, but it was readable. 'Yeah,' I said. 'It's what you thought. Nice going.'

I considered for a moment, then said, 'I think it's safe to assume that the other door works the same way. Emergency doors in public buildings are installed to code. They always open out with a push bar. So we ought to be able to jam them from outside with nothing more than a steel

269

rod. I'll check on that tomorrow when I recon the exterior.'

'It's an impressive place,' she said. 'Very high-end, smooth operation. And the women are stunning. All of them.'

'It occurs to me,' Dox said. 'Maybe I should reconnoiter this establishment myself. Couldn't hurt to have a second set of eyes, you know.'

I looked at him.

He shrugged and said, 'No need to get irritable about it. Nothing wrong with a man enjoying his work.'

Delilah reached into her purse and took out Harry's bug detector. 'Here,' she said. 'Don't want to forget.'

'You might want it tomorrow night . . . ' I started to say.

'No, it's served its purpose. And nicely. Worked in the vestibule and for the camera watching the basement emergency exit, quiet the rest of the time. I can see why it's sentimental.'

I took it and shook my head. 'That's a story for another time.'

She nodded and rubbed her eyes. 'I should get some sleep.'

'You're right,' I said. 'We can finish planning tomorrow. Why don't you sleep in if you can, and call us whenever you get up.'

'That sounds good,' she said, standing up.

I stood, too. 'I'll walk you back to your hotel.'

She shook her head. 'Better to stay apart for now.'

Once again, I didn't know what was the real motivation there, personal or professional, but this wasn't the time or place to discuss it. 'Okay,' I said.

Dox stood, too. He extended his hand, and Delilah shook it. 'It's great they invited you back for tomorrow, and no surprise, either,' he said. 'You did really well tonight, on unfamiliar terrain and without a lot of preparation, and that's a fact.'

She gave him a nice smile. 'Thank you, Dox.'

'Our glorious leader thinks so, too,' he added. 'Just, like I said before, he's not very expressive about these things.'

Delilah's smile faded and she offered a tentative nod that said, *Let's not go there now, okay?* I was more direct, shooting him a *Stop that shit* look. But he plunged ahead.

'Yeah,' he said, 'the first time I gave him a hug you should have seen him, he was so tense I thought he would pass out. The second time he tolerated it better. Shoot, by the fourth or fifth time, damned if he hadn't started to like it. Now if a few days go by and I forget to throw an arm around him, he actually starts to mope.'

Delilah covered her mouth and looked down. She stood like that for a moment, very still, and then she started laughing. I looked at Dox, half incredulous, half enraged at the shit he was constantly pulling, but he didn't even notice because he was laughing, too.

There was nothing I could do but stand there while their laughter fed on itself and grew. Dox was wiping his eyes and saying, 'I'm sorry, I'm sorry,' while Delilah just stood shaking with her arms crossed and her head down.

After an unpleasantly long time, it subsided. Delilah breathed in and out deeply a few times, then said to me, 'I'll call you tomorrow?'

I nodded and said, 'Yeah. Sure.'

'Good night,' Dox said, and I could tell he was struggling to hold it in.

She made it out without either of them losing it again, but I had a feeling she laughed all the way to the elevator.

I looked at Dox.

'I'm sorry, man, I'm sorry,' he said. 'There's just something about you that brings it out in me!'

'I think that's known as blaming the victim.'

'Go ahead, make fun of me for hitting on Tiara the tranny, it'll make you feel better.'

'No, it would make *you* feel better. That's why I won't do it.'

'Ah, you're a hard man, John Rain, a hard man,' he said, and this time I couldn't help it, I started laughing with him.

34

The next morning, I took a quick run past Whispers, just a local guy out for his morning jog in his shoes and tracksuit, a hat pulled low against the chill air.

I followed one of the alleys to the back of the club. Given their business hours, I doubted anyone would be about this early, but if I were seen, a jogger looking for a place to take a leak wasn't about to raise anyone's hackles.

In keeping with that possible cover story, I paused and started undoing the snaps on the pants of the nylon tracksuit while I scanned the perimeter for cameras. I saw none, just a windowless concrete façade with an emergency exit door on the left, plain steel with no handle or other hardware. A cement path ran the length of the building.

I resnapped the pants and walked over to the door. As I had expected, the hinges were on the outside. A one-meter steel bar jammed in tight at a low angle, with the bottom in one of the expansion joints in the path, would seal it.

I repeated the procedure on the west side of the building, where the basement exit was located at the bottom of a utilitarian concrete stairwell. This door was identical to the first one. Okay.

I continued on my morning run, stopping at Aoyama Park to call Tatsu at the hospital. The phone rang several times, then I heard his voice, almost a groan: '*Hai*.'

'It's me,' I said. God, he sounded terrible. 'I'm sorry to bother you.'

He said nothing for a moment, and I could tell he was trying to catch his breath. 'Bother me?' he rasped, finally. 'These calls are all I look forward to. And visits from my grandson.'

'Any further word on tonight's meeting?'

'Yes, the informant just confirmed. No wonder I'm in pain, no one will let me get any sleep. The meeting is at ten o'clock.'

'Good. We're done with the initial pass. And I'm going to have that man inside tonight, after all.'

'What else do you need from me?'

'Like I told you last time, someone positioned to take out the place's power on my signal.'

'You want the lights out.'

'Yes.'

'What about the backup . . . '

'It's taken care of.'

'I have a man who can help with this. But . . . you're going to have to work fast.'

'What do you mean?'

'From the substation my man can access, he can't shut down power to individual buildings, only to entire blocks. And if the power goes out on an entire Tokyo block for more than two minutes, city regulations require an investigation.'

'Can't you just . . . '

'*City* regulations. I'm federal. Trust me, we don't want an investigation. It would jeopardize good people. Can you do what you have to do in under two minutes?'

I thought for a minute.

'I guess I'll have to,' I said.

'Good. I'll have someone standing by tonight with clear instructions.'

'I'll need his mobile number. I want to talk to him directly, make sure he understands the plan. And I'll need to be able to signal him when I'm ready to go in tonight, too.'

'I'll have him call you.'

'All right. Good.'

We were quiet for a moment. I said, 'You holding on?'

There was a pause. He said, 'Finish it tonight.'

I nodded, feeling grim.

'I will,' I said.

35

Delilah called later that morning. We all headed back to Dox's hotel room. I brought in another Dean & DeLuca meal.

'Here's what I've got in mind,' I told them while we ate. 'We'll be wired up the way we were last night. But this time, Delilah will wear her hair down and keep the earpiece in. There's a construction site just north of the club entrance. Dox, have you checked it out?'

He nodded. 'Last night, like we discussed. I can get in fine, and there's good cover and concealment. The problem is the angle. I'll be a hundred yards out but only ten feet up. That means the possibility of unanticipated, moving obstructions becomes significant.'

'You mean other people,' Delilah said.

Dox shrugged. 'Could be people, could be a car. Hard to say. I do know it won't be like shooting from the top of the University of Texas tower. But that path in from the street runs about fifteen feet before turning right behind a wall. That'll give me time, if nothing's in the way.'

'What about body armor?' Delilah asked. 'You've said Yamaoto is paranoid. You sure he won't be wearing it?'

Dox shook his head. 'Most concealable armor won't stop a high-velocity rifle slug. There are a few that do, but they weigh close to twenty pounds and they're still bulky. Not something you'd want to strap on under a suit.'

'All right,' I said. 'If the shot is there when Yamaoto arrives, Dox takes it and we can all go have a beer. If the shot isn't there, Dox remains as backup, in case Yamaoto manages to make it out of the club despite my best efforts inside. And Delilah, if you get a chance, look Yamaoto over and if you think he's wearing armor under his clothes, you let us know. Questions or comments so far?'

They both shook their heads.

'Delilah, you arrive before ten. We want you there before Yamaoto so you can see where he goes when he gets inside . . . '

'If he gets inside,' Dox added.

I nodded. 'If he gets inside. But the main thing is, I need to know where Yamaoto is inside the club. Who he's with would also be useful. And so would confirmation on the numbers and positions of club security and any bodyguards. With just a little luck, you'll see Yamaoto and Kuro when they arrive, and you'll be able to watch them to see wherever they go. Don't wait. As soon as you have Yamaoto's position, let me know, and go take out the generator. Or, better yet . . . '

'Take it out before Yamaoto arrives,' she said.

I nodded. 'Yeah, that's good thinking. It's not as though anyone's going to notice until afterward. And it'll be one less thing for us to worry about once he's there.'

'But how do we take out the main power?'

'My contact here will have a man in the

appropriate electrical substation. But there's a catch. He can only give us less than two minutes of darkness. More than that, and there'll be some sort of investigation by the city authorities, which my source doesn't want.'

'Two minutes . . . ' Delilah said.

'It should be enough. Because before I call our man and the lights go out, you'll already be next to the emergency exit to let me in. In fact, you'll have to be.'

'Because once the power is cut, the front door will be inoperable. It's got an electronic lock.'

'Exactly. And at the same time, we can't use the emergency door before the power's out — otherwise, the exit alarms would give us away.'

She nodded. 'And the camera pointing at the exit door . . . '

'It'll already be dead when you let me in. I don't know if the video feed gets recorded, but with the power out, it won't make a difference.'

'But what about inside the club? Even after you cut the lights, it won't be totally dark. People will have lighters, cell phones . . . '

'That's perfect,' I said. 'We want just enough light so that people don't panic and start moving around. A little bit of light will keep them calm and in place for a couple minutes while they wait for the power to come back on. With lighters and cell phones and before their eyes have adjusted, they're not going to be able to see more than a few feet in front of them regardless. I'll be moving through in night-vision goggles with a suppressed HK. I'll be in and out in less than two minutes. No one will even know what

278

happened until the lights are back on and we're gone.'

Delilah nodded. We were quiet while she digested it.

'You checked into a new hotel?' I asked.

She was using the same name at Le Meridien and at Whispers, just in case anyone at the club thought to check up on her. Obviously, after tonight, that arrangement would no longer be tenable.

She nodded. 'The New Otani. Near Akasaka Mitsuke subway station. Under Aimée Ackers.'

'Good, then we're set. Now listen. If something goes wrong, if you need me in there for any reason, you just say, 'It's hot in here,' and I'll come running.'

'How would you get in?' she asked.

'I think the HK will be persuasive in a pinch.'

She laughed.

'I'll come, too,' Dox said, 'but I'll be farther away and it'll take me longer.'

Delilah smiled. 'I doubt we'll need the cavalry.'

I looked at her. 'I doubt it, too. And I know you're used to operating without backup, but tonight you have it. 'It's hot in here.' Use it if you need it.'

She nodded, but I could tell it was more to placate me than out of any real conviction. Well, there wasn't much I could do other than to let her know the backup was there. She was probably right, anyway. We probably wouldn't need it.

36

Delilah got to the club at nine-thirty that night. She was wearing a crimson satin halter-top dress she'd bought that afternoon. She'd noticed a lot of black on the hostesses the night before, and thought it would be good to stand out a little. Well, the red satin would be perfect for that, it would catch the club's subtle lighting just the right way. The accessories were right, too: black patent leather heels with a closed toe; an antique silver mesh evening bag; a silver ruched silk stole, to add some texture. On her left wrist she wore a single diamond bangle to catch the light; on her ears, small diamond studs, selected for the opposite reason. No earrings at all wouldn't have been right with this outfit, but she didn't want something that would draw unnecessary attention to her ears, either, given the earpiece she was wearing in one of them. The earpiece was small and fleshcolored and her hair was down, so she would probably be fine regardless, but why take chances?

As she turned onto the club's street, she dipped her head slightly and said, 'Everyone in position?'

'I'm here,' Rain said. He was in an alley south of the club, near where they'd parked the van.

'Roger that,' Dox said. 'I see you clear as day. And honey, you are a vision of loveliness.'

She smiled. If she hadn't seen Dox in action in

Hong Kong, she might have thought he was too much of a joker to trust on an op. But she'd never seen anyone cooler than he'd been that night. Rain had told her Dox was like that, always fooling around until the moment he was about to drop someone from behind that scope. When he was sniping, Rain had said, Dox was as quiet and still as you could imagine. If you talked to him he would answer, but it was almost as though he wasn't there. Or rather, he was so there that at that particular moment you were no longer what was real to him.

'Good, here we go,' she said. She walked on, and there they were, the two valets again, standing like a pair of living lawn jockeys. They bowed to her in unison as she turned onto the path. She nodded and kept moving and a moment later she was inside, the same procedure as the day before, the same two security guys. The hostesses behind the island recognized her this time. They bowed, then one of them picked up the phone and spoke briefly in Japanese.

Kyoko appeared from behind the door and walked out around the island. She shook Delilah's hand and looked her over, clearly pleased with what she saw. She had probably mentioned her find to Kuro, and was glad that Laure was going to make the right impression.

'Mr Kuro isn't here yet,' Kyoko said, 'but he will be soon. He has some business tonight and I'm not sure when he'll be free, but he is expecting you and I hope you can wait as we discussed.'

'Certainly,' Delilah said.

281

'Can we offer you something to drink . . . ?'

Delilah nodded and said, 'Tea?'

'Of course. Milk? Lemon?'

Delilah smiled. 'Just tea.'

Kyoko nodded and gestured to the leather bench. 'Please. Make yourself comfortable. And if there's anything else you need, just let one of the girls know.'

Delilah sat and Kyoko returned to the office. So far, so good: in a moment, she would go to take out the generator. Then, if Yamaoto arrived on schedule, she could see where the hostesses seated him and let Rain in. With just a little luck, this could be over very soon.

A Japanese woman, one of the waitresses, brought tea in a fine ceramic pot on a bamboo tray. Delilah thanked her and sat sipping for about five minutes. No one went down the stairs, and no one came up — long enough to be reasonably sure that the bathrooms were empty.

She stood and said to the hostesses, 'Sorry, the ladies' room . . . '

The hostess closest to her smiled and gestured to the stairs. Delilah nodded and started down.

She repeated the procedure from the day before. This time, though, she turned off the generator before leaving the utility room. And, to be sure, she disconnected the electrical leads. When she was done, she went into the ladies' room.

'Generator's out,' she said.

Rain said, 'Good.'

Dox added, 'Way to go, honey.'

She used the toilet, then went back upstairs

282

and sat sipping tea again, feeling just slightly on edge, in that good way you get when the op has begun and things are going smoothly.

Twenty minutes later, she heard Dox in her ear: 'All right, Mr Big Liu just arrived. Along with two bodyguards and an associate of some type, from the look of things. The valets are taking their car right now.'

'Got it,' Delilah said quietly.

'Yamaoto should be coming soon,' Rain said. 'Be ready.'

'Roger that,' Dox said.

A moment later the buzzer sounded. The hostesses nodded to the security guy, who opened the door and bowed. Four men walked in. She recognized Big Liu from the photos Rain had shown her. The next two were younger and in good shape, and at least as tough-looking. She looked them up and down. Both had bulges on their right hips and a right pants leg riding an inch too low. Pistols in hip holsters — bodyguards. The other guy looked a little more put together, more in charge — management. All as Dox had surmised.

The hostesses came out from behind the island and took the men's coats. Big Liu looked around, smiling, then noticed Delilah. The smile broadened, and lingered to the point of lasciviousness. Well, Rain had mentioned that the man liked blondes.

One of the hostesses led them to the main room. As they went through the swinging doors, Big Liu glanced back at Delilah, still smiling.

Two minutes later, the hostess came back. But

283

rather than returning to her post behind the island, she went into the office. Delilah wondered what was happening.

She heard Dox in her ear again: 'Yamaoto's coming in right now. He moved too fast and had bodyguards in the way, I didn't have a shot. You'll see them all in a second, with Kuro, too.'

'Got it,' she said.

'All right,' Rain said. 'We weren't really expecting to be able to drop him yet. We'll get him inside.'

The buzzer sounded a second later. The security guy opened the door and bowed especially low, and four Japanese men in suits walked briskly inside. The first two she recognized from Rain's photos: Yamaoto was the older one, walking in front, his posture erect, projecting the kind of forceful personality you could feel from across a room. His clothes fit beautifully and she could instantly see from the tailored cut of the jacket and the movement of his shoulder blades beneath the material that he wasn't wearing armor. Kuro was softer-looking, with Brylcreemed hair and more the air of a businessman than of a gangster, coming along a half step behind Yamaoto. The other two, muscles bulging inside their suits and eyes darting from side to side as they struggled to keep up with their bosses, were obviously bodyguards. Like their Chinese counterparts, they had telltale bulges under their jackets.

The hostess behind the island came around and started taking coats. The office door opened, and Kyoko came out with the other hostess.

While the younger women helped the men with their jackets, Kyoko discussed something in Japanese with Yamaoto and Kuro. At various points the two men and Kyoko all glanced at Delilah, then went back to talking.

This time Kyoko escorted the men inside herself. Delilah wanted to get up and see where they went in the main room, but that would have drawn too much attention to her. She'd have to wait for another chance.

She whispered, 'No armor.'

'Roger that,' Dox answered immediately.

A minute later, Kyoko returned. She walked over to Delilah and said, 'We have . . . an interesting situation.'

Delilah raised her eyebrows, thinking she might have an idea now what was going on. She wasn't yet sure whether it was an opportunity or a problem. Maybe a bit of both.

'One of our guests,' Kyoko continued, 'is quite taken with you. And uninterested in anyone else tonight.'

'But you tell him . . . I, not a job yet. Interview.' Rain and Dox would be wondering what was going on, but they'd catch on in a minute.

Kyoko nodded. 'That seemed only to add to the attraction.'

'Which guest?'

'The Chinese gentleman. Mr Liu.'

'Mr Liu wants me to hostess him?'

Kyoko laughed. 'That's exactly what he wants. Look, this is an unusual situation. You haven't even been properly interviewed, let alone trained. But Mr Liu is an important guest. And the two members with him, Mr Yamaoto and Mr Kuro, want him to be happy.'

If she said no, it would look strange. An applicant like Laure would jump at the chance to impress a bunch of important people during her interview. If she said yes, she wasn't sure what she'd be getting herself into. She'd know exactly where Yamaoto was and what was going on around him, true, but she wasn't sure how she'd extricate herself when the moment was right. Well, she'd figure something out.

'Kyoko,' she said, 'do you think I should join them?'

Kyoko sighed. 'Mr Kuro will treat it as the interview you came for. And if you make Mr Liu happy, I can't imagine you wouldn't get the job.'

'Then with pleasure I will join all of them. Again, their names are Liu, Kuro, Yamaoto?' If they hadn't understood already, Rain and Dox would get it now.

'That's right. Now, they know you're only an applicant, so they won't expect you to know everything about the club, our procedures, that kind of thing. So no need to be nervous. Come, I'll introduce you.'

Kyoko took Delilah into the main room. It was more crowded than the night before, perhaps because it was later now, perhaps because Saturday was just a busier night. About sixty people, Delilah estimated, two-thirds of them hostesses.

In the far corner, in the booth adjacent to the emergency exit, sat Big Liu, Big Liu's associate,

286

Kuro, and Yamaoto. She was surprised by that — she had expected them to use one of the private rooms. But no, of course, Big Liu was obviously a lecher; he would want to sit wherever he could best drink in the parade of beauty around him. And Yamaoto probably wanted to indulge him, to use Big Liu's own appetites to distract the man from whatever concessions they were trying to wring from him. After all, that's why they were meeting here to begin with.

Two of the bodyguards, one Chinese, one Japanese, sat across from each other in the outer seats of the adjacent booth. They were watching the room carefully, and each other as well. Understandable, under the circumstances. Their organizations were on the brink, and if Yamaoto and Big Liu failed to reach some understanding tonight, the meeting could end in a war. Delilah glanced across the room and saw the other two in the opposite corner, where they would have a different angle on the principals and a clear field of fire.

As Kyoko and Delilah neared the table, Big Liu stood and smiled. Damn, the man was eager.

'Gentlemen,' Kyoko said. 'This is Laure. She came tonight only to interview for a position, but is so flattered by your kind attention that she would be pleased to join you for a drink.'

'Yes, please,' Big Liu said, shaking Delilah's hand a little too vigorously. He turned to his associate and spoke a few words in Chinese. The man slid out, expressionless, and sat down with the adjacent bodyguards. Well, Big Liu's priorities were certainly clear.

287

Big Liu turned his attention back to Delilah. 'I am Liu,' he said, shaking her hand again. 'But please, call me Big Liu.'

'Yes, Big Liu,' Delilah replied, the Parisian accent thick. '*Enchantée.*'

'Ah, you are French,' Big Liu said.

'Yes, French. My English . . . please pardon, I am still learning . . . '

'So am I!' Big Liu exclaimed with a florid wave of his hands, then laughed as though this was the funniest thing in the world.

Delilah turned to Yamaoto and Kuro. They both bowed their heads in welcome. Delilah reached for Yamaoto's hand. 'You are . . . Mr Yamaoto?' she said.

'Yamaoto,' he said, shaking her hand perfunctorily. She sensed he was tolerating her presence simply to indulge Big Liu. And, presumably, to distract him.

Delilah turned to Kuro and extended her hand. 'And you, Mr Kuro?'

'*Hai*,' he said, shaking her hand.

'Thank you, inviting me at your table,' she said, for Rain and Dox's benefit.

'Please, please,' Big Liu said, gesturing to the bench. Delilah slid in, across from Kuro and diagonal to Yamaoto, and Big Liu sat down next to her.

Kyoko bowed and left them. Delilah smiled and thought, *Here we go*.

37

Listening to Delilah's progress inside the club, I was both pleased and concerned. Pleased that things had turned out so that she was in a position to report precisely on Yamaoto's position. But concerned that she was closer than was ideal. Certainly she had lost some freedom of maneuver. Sure, she could excuse herself to use the restroom, but what if something held her up on the way? Or if, when she went to do it, Big Liu decided to tag along so he could speak to her privately, make a pass, whatever? There were a dozen ways this unexpected arrangement could cause problems for us.

In fact, it already had, because she was no longer free to speak and so couldn't give Dox and me the real-time updates I wanted. She'd been doing a nice job of keeping us informed under the guise of talking to the people she was with, true, but that kind of communication had its limits.

Well, she knew where Yamaoto was right now and could tell me soon enough. In the meantime, I wanted to get things rolling.

'Delilah,' I said, 'I'm going to jam the main room emergency exit door now. We'll use the basement exit, per the plan. If that's okay, clear your throat.'

She did.

'Okay,' I said. 'I'm on my way. I'll be in touch

again in a few minutes.'

I picked up one of the steel bars and started moving in. I was wearing a navy suit, deep blue shirt, and a navy tie. Dark, dark, and dark isn't exactly the height of sartorial splendor, in my book, but the outfit served two purposes. Out here, it would reassure anyone who might see me that I was a fine, upstanding citizen, perhaps carrying away some refuse. I'd have to keep my right side away from an onlooker, of course, lest the suppressed HK and thigh rig spoil the effect, but in low light that would be good enough. A black ninja outfit and matching balaclava just wouldn't have conveyed as favorable an impression. And later, inside the club, with the lights out, the outfit would make me that much less visible. The rubber-soled Clarks shoes I was wearing weren't going to threaten Jermyn Street fashion dominance anytime soon, either, but they were as surefooted and quiet as sneakers. Comfortable, too.

At the end of the alley, I stopped to look and listen — all quiet — then crept over to the rear of the building. I put one end of the bar in one of the expansion gaps in the path, then quietly placed the other at about waist level on the nonhinged side of the emergency door. I played with the angle, up and down, left and right, until the fit was snug, then repeatedly shoved down on the bar until it was wedged as tightly as possible into place. I tried to pull it out, but it wouldn't budge. Okay. I headed back to my position.

'The emergency exit off the main room is jammed,' I said into the transmitter. 'So now it's up to you. I'm waiting for your signal. Clear your throat if you copy and I'll stand by.'

38

Delilah sat with Big Liu, Kuro, and Yamaoto as a quick succession of waitresses brought them hot wash towels, a variety of snacks Delilah didn't recognize, and a bottle of Taittinger champagne. Kuro spoke with the waitresses in Japanese. Delilah pretended to understand the men's English only slightly better.

'Well,' Big Liu asked as a waitress poured their champagne, 'what do you think of Whispers?'

'Whispering?' Delilah asked, with a confused smile. If she played it right, they would think her not only English-incapable, but a bit dim, as well, and it was always good to be underestimated by the people you were manipulating.

'The club,' Big Liu responded, gesturing to their surroundings and smiling indulgently.

'Ah, of course! The club . . . very beautiful, yes.'

The waitress placed the champagne bottle in a silver ice bucket on the table, bowed, and moved off. Yamaoto raised his glass and said, 'Well. To good business.'

They all touched glasses and drank.

She heard Rain in her ear, telling her the door was jammed now, that she should clear her throat if she heard him. She did so.

She glanced around the room. Their toast and apparent bonhomie seemed not to have relaxed the nearby bodyguards, who still looked as though they were on a hair trigger. Rain wanted her to proceed right away, but she thought that, with the way the bodyguards were wired, if the lights went out now they might spring into some kind of action. It would be better if a little time passed and they settled down before something out of the ordinary occurred. She decided to wait just a little. When the atmosphere was more relaxed, she would excuse herself to use the restroom, give Rain the word that she was on the way, and let him in when his man cut the power.

For a few minutes, the men, led by Big Liu, tried to engage her in some polite conversation about how she liked Tokyo, but in short order tired of her struggles with English. They began talking among themselves, their references to business matters initially guarded, but then increasingly transparent as they drank more champagne and became accustomed to talking in front of her. She wasn't surprised. It wasn't as though she could understand, anyway.

At one point Rain, obviously concerned about why she hadn't yet given him a go sign, asked her to say something or at least clear her throat if she was all right. His timing was good — Big Liu had just drained his glass. She said, 'More champagne?' and gave everyone a refill. Rain said all right, he wouldn't bother her, but let's finish this soon.

'As I mentioned on the phone,' Yamaoto was saying, 'I'm convinced that my men were blameless. But certainly someone betrayed us, someone who knew where and when the transaction was to occur and what it was to consist of. We need to list the people on both sides who had access to that information and start there.'

Delilah glanced at Kuro. The man's face seemed a bit too set to her. Maybe his English was limited, and he was uncomfortable not being able to participate.

'Don't know all details,' Big Liu said. He leaned forward and began chopping the air to emphasize his sentences. 'But having man make list. Then ask people on list. Ask hard.'

Yamaoto nodded. 'And I'll do the same.' He turned and spoke in Japanese to Kuro, whose sole response consisted of the word *hai*, repeated crisply several times and always accompanied by a stiff bow of the head.

'One other thing I meant to mention,' Yamaoto said. 'Your man Chan in New York. He hasn't checked in with me in over a week. We had this problem once before and you told me it wouldn't happen again. I'm afraid he's now disrespecting both of us.'

Delilah thought, *Ah, merde*. Rain had briefed her on all this on the way from the airport. It wasn't going to be helpful for Yamaoto and Big Liu to discuss it now.

'Mmm, Chan,' Big Liu said. 'Have . . . problem there. Have to replace.'

'I'm sorry?' Yamaoto said with a frown.

'Chan have bad blood with soldier Wong. Wong hothead. Kill Chan, then disappear.'

Yamaoto's frown deepened. 'When did this happen?'

'Happen one week ago. Big Liu men look for

294

Wong now. Find Wong, he very sorry.'

'You've found Wong or you're looking for him?'

'No find,' Big Liu said, chopping the air again. 'Look. Try to find. Will find. But . . . Wong was man watching woman for Yamaoto. So no report now. Need good replacement.'

'Wait just a moment,' Yamaoto said, leaning forward. 'Are you saying the man who was watching Kawamura Midori disappeared a week ago, after killing his own boss?'

Yamaoto was becoming increasingly direct, even aggressive, in his tone and posture, and Delilah realized she was seeing some sort of default persona come to the surface. It was considerably less polished than the one he'd been displaying until now.

Big Liu nodded. 'Wong bad man. Unreliable.'

Yamaoto shook his head as though he couldn't believe it. 'Killed him how? How do you know?'

'Kill with knife. Find Chan, he very stabbed.'

'Why didn't you tell me this before?'

'Big Liu . . . embarrass by unreliable man. Find replacement first, then tell Yamaoto, better I think.'

'Yes, but don't you see? Chan was killed and Wong 'disappeared' just before the ambush in Wajima! You think that's a coincidence?'

Merde, Delilah thought again. She should have left earlier. And getting up now, in the midst of Yamaoto's agitation, might precipitate a connection in his mind that she needed to avoid. She would have to ride this out.

Big Liu looked at Kuro, plainly at a loss. Kuro

started to translate, but Yamaoto cut him off.

'My men told me they were ambushed by two men at Wajima. Right after your problem in New York. I don't believe in coincidences. This is the work of John Rain. The man you were supposed to be watching for.'

At the mention of his name, Delilah realized that everything Rain had hoped to accomplish was about to fall apart. Yamaoto had just infected Big Liu with suspicion. For the moment, Big Liu seemed disinclined to agree with Yamaoto's theory, but if Yamaoto died this very night, Big Liu's views would surely change. He would realize that Rain had killed no fewer than five of Liu's people. And his men had been watching Midori in New York. They knew where she, and the child, lived. They could get to them, either as retribution or to bring Rain out in the open, it didn't matter.

There was only one way to prevent that. None of the three men could leave here tonight. She had to tell Rain and Dox, but couldn't until she could excuse herself.

Big Liu was frowning, either at Yamaoto's tone or because he didn't understand, Delilah wasn't sure. Yamaoto barked a few curt words in Japanese to Kuro, who translated.

The men were focused on each other now. They seemed to have forgotten her entirely. But she was aware of exactly how that could change. And how quickly.

Big Liu was quiet for a moment, then said, 'New York and Wajima . . . far apart. Seem . . . '

'They're not far apart at all. Rain must have

gone to New York to see the woman and the child, as we had hoped. He spotted your surveillance and eliminated it, either by accident or design. And then Wajima . . . '

He paused there, then sat back in his chair and was quiet, his head tilted forward, his hand rubbing his chin. Delilah knew he was just a thought or two short of a dangerous epiphany. He would either hit it, or skip right over it, she judged it fifty-fifty.

'You see,' he said, to no one in particular, 'Rain must have had access to someone who had information about Wajima. And . . . ' He looked at Delilah, as though noticing her for the first time. 'There are people who knew about Wajima who also know about this very meeting. Tonight.'

Big Liu started to say something, but Yamaoto stopped him with a raised hand and continued looking at Delilah.

'You came to the club just last night, is that right . . . Laure? And tonight you came back to interview with Mr Kuro, yes?'

She knew he knew, or almost knew. But she gave no sign of it. She thought, *It's hot in here*, but wanted to be sure before she said it.

'That's really a remarkable coincidence,' he went on, with a chilling smile.

The extra comment suggested to Delilah that he wasn't quite certain of himself. He was probing, trying to get her to react and confirm his suspicions. She sensed she could bluff her way through.

She smiled and dipped her head as though pausing to digest his words, then said, as though her substandard English hadn't been adequate to the task, 'Thank you. It's very nice to be here.'

Yamaoto nodded and started to turn back to Big Liu. Then, without warning, he lunged across the table and grabbed the front of her dress. He yanked it hard toward him and the straps gave way, exposing her breasts and belly. Delilah, not expecting the move, gasped. Before she could react, Yamaoto had grabbed her hair and slammed her face into the table. She saw a flash of white light, then felt Yamaoto's fingers digging into her ears. She twisted her head and jerked back, but too late. Yamaoto pulled out the earpiece and shoved her away from him.

'What the hell?' Big Liu shouted. 'What the hell?'

Yamaoto held the earpiece up so Big Liu could see it. 'She's wired!' he said.

The bodyguards had all come to their feet and were looking around wildly for the source of the threat. Their hands were inside their jackets, on the verge of bringing out hardware.

Delilah swept the front of her dress back up and held it against herself. A natural enough reaction, under the circumstances, but she wasn't thinking about her exposed body. The microphone was attached to the halter top, and it wasn't going to pick anything up if it wasn't close to her mouth.

'It's hot in here,' she said.

39

Delilah had been in there for almost a half-hour, and I was getting antsy. I could hear her talking periodically, and from what I could tell she was still at the table. She must have had a good reason for the delay, but I couldn't imagine what it was. The generator was out, she knew exactly where Yamaoto was, all she had to do was get up and give me the word and we could finish this damn thing.

Several times, I considered pushing her, but always decided against it. I didn't want to distract her, for one thing. She had a lot on her hands and needed to focus, to stay in the role. Also, she had a tendency to get prickly when she thought I was telling her how to do her job, and, although I wouldn't have admitted it, Dox's comments about 'micro-management' had stung a little. Anyway, there was nothing I could tell her that she didn't already know.

I cracked my neck and bounced on my toes to stay limber. I'd been out here longer than I'd first expected, and it was cold.

In my ear Delilah said, 'It's hot in here.'

My heart froze. I felt blood draining away from the skin on my face and hands.

'Fuck!' I said. 'I'm on my way.' I sprinted along the west side of the building, the night-vision goggles dancing around my neck.

Dox said, 'I'm coming, too.'

'No, stay put! Cover me at the entrance, I'm going in the front.'

'But . . . '

'Don't argue with me, just do it!'

There was no time to think, but I was aware on some level of just how much danger she must have been in to call for help. Danger I had put her in. And the comforting, back-of-my-mind notion I'd been carrying around, that at least if I died here it would end the threat to Midori and my son, was useless now. Killing myself in front of Yamaoto would do nothing to save Delilah.

I cut right onto the street that led to the front path. The two valets were standing there as Delilah had described in her briefing, watching me approach.

'Drop the valets,' I said. 'Now.'

If there had been another way, I would have used it. But I wasn't going to waste one second getting to Delilah. And I couldn't take a chance on these two using their lapel transmitters to warn anyone of what was coming.

The near valet's head erupted and he slid to the ground. The other guy didn't even have time to register surprise before he was down, too.

I pulled out the Benchmade Dox had given me and thumbed it open without slowing down at all. I leaned over one of the bodies, cut the cord around his neck, and took his magnetic keycard.

I put the knife back in my pocket. My mind was screaming for me to get inside, but I needed just one more second. My hand shaking, I pulled out my cell phone and hit the speed dial I had created for Tatsu's man in the substation.

He answered on the first ring. '*Hai*.'

'You ready to cut the power?' I asked, in Japanese.

'Yes, I'm ready.'

'Do it exactly thirty seconds from now. Got it?'

'I'm looking at my watch,' he said. 'Twenty-nine, twenty-eight . . . '

I closed the phone and dropped it back in my pocket. I took two deep breaths, in and out, in and out, and moved up the path toward the front entrance.

40

Yamaoto seized Delilah by the wrist and stood, pulling her halfway out of her seat and across the table. His grip was hellishly strong. He brandished the earpiece and shouted, 'What's this? What's this?'

'*C'est un appareil!*' she screamed. 'A hearing aid, you pig!'

'Why did you say, 'It's hot in here'? Why did you say that?'

Big Liu and Kuro seemed horrified by Yamaoto's behavior. *Maybe it was a hearing aid,* they might be thinking, *see, that explains her conversational difficulties, it wasn't just a language problem . . .*

Yamaoto grabbed the halter top again and pulled. Delilah got her hand over the transmitter and pulled back — too hard. The fabric tore, and the transmitter detached. She heard it fall to the ground.

Yamaoto shouted, 'Where's Rain? Tell me, you whore, where is he!'

Delilah, staying in character, used her free hand to hold up what was left of the dress and screamed, '*Aidez-moi!* Somebody help me, please!'

The bodyguards had all surrounded the table. Their guns were out now, but they were confused. They didn't know whether to focus on the table, on somewhere else in the club, or on one another.

Delilah looked around. Everyone in the club was watching, trying to see what was going on. About half of them were out of their seats.

Big Liu stood. 'Yamaoto . . . ' he started to say.

'Shut up!' Yamaoto yelled. Then he looked around, too, and seemed for the first time to understand the commotion he was causing. He turned to Kuro and barked something in Japanese. Delilah had a feeling she knew what it was: he wanted to take her somewhere he could control better, where he could get rough and get the information he wanted without frightening the patrons.

She made no move for the knife on her thigh. She was boxed in now and it wouldn't do her any good. When they tried to take her somewhere else, though, there would be an opening, and she was going to cut right through it.

Yamaoto still had her by the wrist. He said to Big Liu, 'Get out of the way.'

Big Liu made no move to comply. He said, 'Bad business you do. This is nice girl. You very rude man.' He called to his associate, who got up and ran over.

More of the patrons and hostesses were getting nervously to their feet. A few had started backing toward the swinging doors. Delilah thought she heard a woman scream from near the front entrance, but the sound was faint and she wasn't sure.

Yamaoto, obviously making an effort to calm himself, said, 'This nice girl is a danger, as you'll see in a moment. Now, if you'll just . . . '

And then the lights went out.

41

I followed the path along its right turn and headed straight to the doors, the keycard in my right hand, night-vision goggles in my left, the HK in the thigh rig. I imagined the hostesses were watching me now through the wall camera, trying to figure out, Who's this guy in the suit? Why don't we recognize him? The security guy would be standing by the entrance, his alertness level low as long as the door was closed.

I strode up the stairs, my heart hammering. I moved directly to the magnetic card reader and swiped the card in front of it. There was a clack inside the door as the lock disengaged. I slipped the card into my jacket pocket and took out the HK. I held the gun behind my back as the door swung open.

The security guy was right there, just inside the entrance. He frowned when he saw me — obviously, when the door had opened in the absence of the buzzer, he'd been expecting one of the valets. As I stepped past him he said, '*Oi!*' Hey!

I glanced left, absurdly aware of some sort of techno music playing in the background. There, the other security guy. I tracked right. The hostesses were staring open-mouthed, trying to figure out what the hell was going on. There was another guy behind them, a valet, from his appearance, just as Delilah had described in her briefing.

The first security guy said, '*Oi!*' again and started coming toward me. Clearly he had misunderstood the nature of the threat. He must have thought he was dealing with a party crasher or something, someone who would be intimidated by a tough-guy stare and a little woofing. Then he noticed my hand behind my back. His eyes widened and he reached inside his jacket.

I brought up the HK and put two rounds in his chest and another in his head. Everything was quiet: just three *pffft*s, then the sound of his body hitting the floor.

I tracked to the second security guy. His eyes were bugging out and he was groping under his jacket. I dropped him with a single head shot.

I looked around again. The hostesses were frozen, obviously in shock. Likewise the valet.

Then the lights went out. The music stopped. The club was suddenly, eerily silent.

One of the hostesses screamed in the dark. I pulled on the goggles and moved through the swinging doors into the main room.

I didn't know where Delilah was. And I had only two minutes of darkness to find her.

42

The moment the lights went out, Delilah dropped the halter top and reached under her dress. She slid her fingers into the Hideaway grip, pulled the knife free from its sheath, and slashed Yamaoto across the forearm. The razor-sharp blade parted skin and muscle like water and sliced down to the bone. He howled in the darkness and released her wrist.

She shoved Big Liu hard and he spilled out of the booth and into the bodyguards. She felt Yamaoto grabbing for her and slashed him again. There were shouts and cries of confusion from all over the room now, the sounds of people stumbling into one another and cursing in the dark.

She crouched on the bench and walked to the edge of it, then dropped down. She started edging along the wall.

Then someone grabbed her ankle, and she was falling.

43

The scene through the green light of the goggles was like something out of a George Romero movie: scores of people stumbling in all directions, expressions fearful, arms splayed in front of them, bumping into one another and crying out in the dark.

I moved to the right, my head swiveling in sync with the front sight of the gun. The near panic in the room was palpable. Things felt one step away from a stampede.

I kept my back to the wall and kept moving to the right, toward the private rooms. That was my best guess for where Delilah had first joined Yamaoto.

I reached the corner of the room and started moving forward. Here and there small flares of light were appearing as the relatively cool-headed took out lighters and turned on cell phones. *Come on, come on*, I thought. I was running out of time.

I reached the first private room and tried the door. It swung open. Empty.

From somewhere in front of me, I heard a man shout in Japanese, 'The emergency exit is stuck!'

A woman cried out, 'What if there's a fire?'

And that was all it took. Everyone charged, mostly toward the front, but some, disoriented in the dark, went the wrong way and collided with the others. People tripped and fell over one another. The ones on the ground, their faces kicked and fingers stepped on, started screaming, and the screams fed the panic.

I heard Dox in my ear. 'You all right, man? Delilah, can you talk?'

'I'm good, I'm in,' I said, moving. 'Stay put. Cover the entrance.'

'Roger that,' he said. There was nothing from Delilah.

I made it to the second private room. Empty, like the first.

The booths, the booths, I thought. I kept going, as fast as I could while keeping my back to the wall. I knew there were four bodyguards in the room, and I scanned for them constantly, but in the chaos I couldn't spot them.

A man came stumbling toward me, his arms pawing the air in front of him. I shoved him to the side and he spilled to the floor with a wail.

The blocked emergency exit was just ahead, the booths along the wall to its left. I moved closer, still scanning. There, in front of the nearest booth, some kind of pileup on the floor, and . . .

There were the bodyguards, two of them, guns out, facing the room, looking sightlessly for the threat.

I cut left to the nearest row of seating surrounding the bar, avoiding stumbling, howling patrons, scanning as I moved. I hopped down onto one of the benches, wanting some cover in case anyone trained on my muzzle flashes and returned fire. I braced the gun on top of the back of the bench and put the laser on the first bodyguard's head.

Pffft. The man quivered and sank to the ground.

The flash was reduced by the suppressor. The other guy didn't see it, or if he saw it he didn't know what it meant. And the reduced muzzle report was eclipsed by the shouting all around us. The man stood there, still looking around, probably not even realizing his partner was now dead on the floor.

Pffft. I dropped him, too, another head shot.

I scrambled over to the opposite side of the bench, in case anyone else had tracked my muzzle flashes. There were still two bodyguards in the room, plus Yamaoto, Kuro, Big Liu, and Big Liu's associate.

But where? I scanned the room left to right. People were still scrambling in all directions. I wanted to shout, *Delilah, where are you?*

A light flared in front of the corner booth. I looked over. It was Yamaoto, holding up a cell phone, trying to see what was going on.

Son of a bitch. The corners of my mouth crept up. I brought the HK around and put the laser on his forehead.

The green inside the goggles was eclipsed by a huge white flash. I blinked and jerked my head away.

I knew instantly what had happened. The power was back on. The goggles had an automatic high-light cutoff feature that saved me from being blinded, but it still took a moment for my vision to adjust. I dropped behind the bench and tore off the goggles. When I popped back up, the HK pointed over the back of the seat, Yamaoto was gone.

Fuck. I scanned the area.

There he was, moving to my left. I zeroed in on his torso.

Bam! A shot slammed into the back of the bench inches from my head. I tracked to my right and saw one of the bodyguards, kneeling on the floor in front of one of the booths.

Bam! Another shot tore into the back of the bench. I didn't think. I just squeezed the grip, put the front sight on his torso, and pressed the trigger. *Pffft.* The shot caught him in the sternum. He fell backward and I put two more in him before he'd even hit the ground.

I swiveled back to Yamaoto. He was running now, and everyone was running with him, away from the gunfire. I brought the gun around, looking for a shot.

'Down!' I heard Delilah call from behind me. I ducked and a bullet whizzed over my head, the crack of a pistol following a split instant later. I scooted to my right and snuck a peek over the back of the bench. It was the fourth bodyguard. He swung the pistol over to my new position and fired again. I scrambled to the edge of the seat, thinking absurdly, *Well, this is going well, isn't it?*

I brought the HK out alongside the bench. The bodyguard saw me and adjusted again.

There was a *Bam! Bam! Bam!* of pistol fire, but not from him. His body jerked and he slumped to the ground. I glanced over. It was

310

Delilah, holding one of the fallen bodyguards' guns.

I brought out a fresh magazine, dropped the nearly spent one, and slammed the new one into place. I reached for the one I'd dropped and said, 'Dox, Yamaoto's on his way out right now — front door or basement emergency exit, I don't know which.'

'Yeah, lot of people streaming out from both,' he said, his voice with that supernatural calm it got when he was behind the scope. 'I'm looking for him, I'm looking for him.'

I turned to Delilah. Her dress was half torn off and she was naked down to her waist, but she seemed oblivious to it. She had the bodyguard's gun up in a two-handed grip and she was scanning the room for danger.

'You all right?' I called to her.

She kept scanning. 'Go! You have to take out Yamaoto, he knows it was you in New York!'

I spun off the bench without another word and ran toward the swinging doors. I peeked through the crack at the center — one side, then the other. The hostess and the valet were gone. I went through, my head swiveling left and right, the HK tracking with it. Island. Office door. Stairwell.

'Goddamnit!' Dox said. 'I hit him, but I didn't drop him!'

'Where is he?'

'Out the basement exit, heading west! He came up the stairs with a crowd of other people and I only had a second, I didn't have the head shot. Drilled him from the side and he went

311

down, but people were in the way and he got back up before I could put him away.'

I started for the stairs. 'West, toward Kotto-dori?'

'Yeah, he's stumbling, you can still catch him!'

I took the stairs three at a time. As I turned the riser, I heard shots from back in the main room. Delilah's position.

I stopped and looked back. Then I looked down again. Just a few more steps and I'd be at the exit, close on Yamaoto.

I took another step down and stopped again.

Dox said, 'Where are you, man? You've got to hurry or we're going to lose him!'

I took one more step down. I heard myself groan. Then I raced back up the stairs the way I had come.

'Shots from the main room,' I said. 'Delilah's in there.'

'Shit! All right, I'm taking off after Yamaoto, you go to Delilah.'

'On my way,' I said. I raced back across the entrance room, repeated my sneak and peek through the swinging doors, then went in.

I saw Delilah, standing in front of one of the booths. I crept closer, tracking with the HK as I moved. The room was empty.

I moved closer. There was something under the table in the booth.

I came up alongside her and looked. It was Big Liu and his associate, their mouths and eyes open as though in dull surprise, a clean red bullet hole in the center of each man's forehead.

Delilah looked at me. 'Did you see Kuro?'

I shook my head.

'We have to find him,' she said. 'Yamaoto told him you were behind New York and Wajima. I don't think Kuro believed him, but he will now.'

I gestured to Big Liu. 'You mean . . . '

'I couldn't let him leave,' she said. 'Yamaoto told him, and this whole thing would have been proof. The triads would have come after Midori and your son, they wouldn't have had a chance.'

But Yamaoto had made it out. He knew it was me, and I could imagine what he would do next. I had to get out of here and call Midori, tell her to take Koichiro and go, hide. She would never see me again, but at least they'd be safe.

Focus, I told myself. *Deal with the situation at hand, then you can warn Midori. Nothing's going to happen that fast. Use your head.*

I heard Dox from the other side of the room: 'I'm coming in, don't shoot.'

We turned and saw the burly sniper moving toward us, the butt of the M40A3 shouldered, the muzzle pointed downrange. A slight lift of the eyebrows was his only reaction to Delilah's half nakedness.

'Yamaoto's gone,' he said. 'Saw his driver pick him up. Shot out the tires, but they're the run-flat type and they kept going. He's bleeding, though. It's all over the street. I knew I hit him good.'

I heard sirens outside. We all stopped and listened for a second. Dox said, 'I respectfully propose that now would be an appropriate time for us to beat feet.'

'Did Kuro leave?' Delilah asked.

313

'I didn't see him,' Dox said. 'But there were a lot of people and I was looking for Yamaoto. Why, was I supposed to shoot him, too?'

'I'll explain later,' I said. 'Come on, let's go.'

'He might still be here, hiding somewhere,' Delilah said. 'We should . . . '

I shook my head. 'You've done enough, more than enough. We need to go.'

I pulled off my jacket and helped Delilah into it, and the three of us hurried out through the basement exit.

The sirens were close now. We cut along the eastern side of the building and through an alley, emerging on the street that bracketed the club complex to the south. The van was there, where I'd parked it earlier. We got in and drove off, Delilah in the passenger seat, Dox in back. Soon we were heading south on Nireke-dori, the serene streetlights and shuttered boutiques surreal after what we'd just been through.

'What about Yamaoto?' Delilah asked.

Dox told her what had happened. I could tell he felt bad he hadn't gotten a confirmed kill.

'That was a hell of a shot you took,' I said. 'Moving, only a second, all those people running around in a panic . . . '

'Yeah, but . . . '

'Yeah, nothing. You hit him badly, no one could have done better.'

'Not as bad as I'd like, but that was a hollow point round and he's wearing a hell of a hole somewhere on his chest right now. Only thing that got that boy to his car was a bucketful of adrenaline and a shitload of luck. I just hope there aren't any hospitals nearby.'

Hospitals, I thought. *Of course.*

I pulled out the cell phone and called Tatsu.

44

I briefed Tatsu on everything that had just happened. He was weak and groaning in pain, but his mind seemed alert as ever.

When I was done, he said, 'Don't worry about Kuro. He can be handled. It's Yamaoto who's the concern. And from what you just told me, within a very short while he'll either be in a hospital or a morgue. I'll find out which and call you back.'

I clicked off and said to Dox and Delilah, 'My source is having his people check all the area hospitals. If Yamaoto shows up in an emergency room, we'll know about it.'

We drove around for an hour, taking turns filling each other in on our different perspectives of what had happened at the club. Tatsu didn't call.

When we were done, it was past midnight and there was nothing else to do but wait for Tatsu. I drove into Akasaka and dropped Dox off first, near the Akasaka Prince Hotel, where he'd reserved a room earlier. After the kind of op we'd just pulled, it was best for all of us to move. Delilah opened the door and he climbed out over her, then turned back to us.

'The second you hear something, you call me,' he said.

I nodded. 'I will.'

'I'm serious. Don't go running off on your own again, like you did in New York.'

'Okay.'

He looked at me, obviously doubtful, then turned to Delilah. 'Will you talk some sense into the man? He has this lone wolf complex.'

Delilah smiled. 'I'll try.'

He patted her on the knee and looked at her. 'Delilah, I'd trust you to watch my back anytime. And you can count on me to watch yours.'

She smiled again. 'You got to see quite a bit of my back tonight.'

Dox blinked and his cheeks flushed crimson. 'What I meant was . . . '

She leaned over and kissed his cheek. 'I know what you meant. And thank you.'

He looked at me and said, 'I have good bones, you know.' Then he closed the door and was gone.

I drove off. Delilah said, 'There's one thing. I didn't want to say in front of Dox, because I can tell he feels bad he didn't finish Yamaoto.'

'What is it?'

'Yamaoto got ahold of me at one point, and I slashed him twice across the arm with the Hideaway. That might have been part of the blood on the street, I don't know.'

I nodded, feeling grim. 'Well, we'll find out.'

'Yeah.'

I parked on a quiet side street near the New Otani, her new hotel. 'I would walk you,' I said, 'but we still need to be careful about being seen together. Especially now.'

She started to answer, but then one of us or maybe both of us leaned in and we were kissing like a pair of drowning victims getting

317

their first taste of air.

She pulled me into the back of the van, where Dox still had his mattress pad laid out. The jacket I'd thrown over her shoulders came off easily. And the dress was half gone anyway. I hiked what was left of it up to her belly while she kissed me and got my pants open. We were breathing hard and my head was pounding and when I touched her and felt how wet she was it drove everything else from my mind. She pushed me back onto the mattress pad and there was no time to get her panties down her legs so I just pulled, hard, and they were gone. She leaned over and straddled me and then I was inside her and I'd never felt anything so good. I thought, *Fuck, not again, not without a condom,* and it was the most fleeting and inconsequential thought I've ever had in my life.

It was as brief as it was furious. Our hands were everywhere and we never stopped kissing. When she came, she groaned something in Hebrew, groaned it right into my mouth, and I came with her.

I settled back onto the mattress pad, spent. She stayed as she was, looking down at me, hands on my shoulders.

'I like when you do that,' I said, looking into her eyes, gray in the interior gloom of the van.

'What?'

'Talk in Hebrew.'

She nodded. 'You make me.'

I watched her. The last time I'd seen her kill someone, she got the shakes afterward. But that had been her first time. It gets easier after that.

'You all right?' I said.

She nodded. 'I shouldn't be, I guess, but I am.'

I reached up and touched her cheek. 'I can't . . . I don't know how to thank you for what you did tonight. For everything you've done.'

She said nothing.

'I don't know what's going to happen,' I told her. 'I do know I don't want to lose you.'

'That's up to you,' she said, her eyes down. 'It always has been.'

We stayed like that for another minute. I thought about Midori again. I could call her and tell her everything, make her understand how bad it was and convince her to move someplace with Koichiro, at least until I'd settled this.

But that would be it for us. I knew it. Whatever tenuous possibility of rapprochement she had hinted at in New York would be extinguished like a flickering ember under a boot heel.

And Yamaoto was wounded now, wasn't he? Hell, for all I knew he had just finished bleeding out in the back of his limousine. Or he was in emergency surgery somewhere. Any minute now I might get news from Tatsu about where to get to him. Nothing was going to happen to Midori and Koichiro just this moment. I could wait a little while longer, see how the situation with Yamaoto played out. If I learned he'd made it, if it seemed I couldn't finish him, I could warn Midori then.

We pulled on what was left of our clothes. I said, 'A lot of people saw you at the club. With Big Liu dead and Yamaoto wounded, they're all going to be in disarray. But Kuro's still at large.

You have to be careful.'

She smiled. 'I know.'

'Sorry. I just . . . '

'I know,' she said again, and kissed me.

She got out of the van and I watched her until she had turned off the street. Then I drove to find a new hotel.

45

I checked into a business hotel in Shinjuku and took a shower and then a long, hot bath. It didn't do much to relax me. I couldn't stop thinking. The thoughts weren't good.

What if Yamaoto didn't wind up in a hospital? What would it mean? A guy that powerful would have doctors on the payroll, people who could patch a bullet hole without involving the authorities. Maybe one of them was making a house call right now. But from what Dox had said, Yamaoto was going to need a lot more than that. A trauma surgical team, probably, and a lot of blood.

Regardless, what if he lived, and told his people, and Big Liu's, what happened at the club? With all the bad blood, the Chinese might not have believed him, but the bullet hole in his chest might be persuasive of truthfulness. And regardless of what the Chinese thought, Yamaoto's own people would do what he told them. If he got the chance to send them after Midori and Koichiro . . .

I glanced at the phone, perched on the edge of the sink counter within grabbing distance of the tub.

Call her, I thought. *Call her right now.*

Just a little while longer. I can get to him. I can finish this. All I need to know is where.

The phone rang. I half leaped out of the bath

321

to grab it. I looked at the caller ID. Tatsu.

I flipped it open, my heart pounding. 'Yeah.'

'You'll never guess where our friend is.'

'Tell me.'

'Right here at Jikei hospital. In surgery. It took my people some time to find him. There are quite a few hospitals in Tokyo, and Yamaoto is here under a false name.'

I was gripping the phone hard and tried to relax. 'Is he going to make it?'

'The doctors seem optimistic. He was lucky. From what I understand, another centimeter and he would have been past saving.'

'How do I get to him?'

'You can't while he's in the operating room. And he'll be in the ICU afterward for at least twenty-four hours, being monitored constantly. You have to wait until he's in intermediate care.'

'I can't wait that long,' I said. I felt like shouting, putting my fist through the wall, smashing things. 'He could move against Midori.'

'I don't believe so. He's fighting for his life now. That's all he's doing. That's all he can do.'

'What about when he's out of the ICU? Won't he have people guarding him?'

'He already does, quite a few of them. Don't worry. I'm going to take care of it.'

'What about Kuro? What's his status?'

'Leave Kuro to me. You focus on Yamaoto.'

I looked left and right as though I might see a way out. Finally I said, 'Goddamnit, just keep me posted.'

'I'll call you the moment I learn more.'

I clicked off and put the phone back on the sink counter.

I thought again about calling Midori. The thing was, even if I warned her, she might not listen. She hated everything about the life and didn't want any part of it.

I realized I might be rationalizing, but I decided to hold off for just a little while longer.

If I was wrong, though, I knew the opportunity to take my own life would seem in retrospect like a state of grace that had been offered to me and that I had stupidly, perversely refused. I'd have no more options then. I would have used them all up and cashed them in for damnation.

46

I hardly slept at all that night. In the morning, I did an intense hour of bodyweight calisthenics and stretches. I worked through Hindu push-ups, Hindu squats, and neck and stomach exercises. I finished with twenty doorjamb pull-ups, suspended only by my fingertips, and a hundred fingertip push-ups after that. When I was done, I felt a little less anxious than I had the night before.

But the rest of the day wasn't easy. I kept picturing Midori and Koichiro in New York, imagining how easy it would be to get to them outside that Greenwich Village apartment, or at a park, or on the way to a store, or anywhere at all.

Whispers was all over the news. There were rumors of yakuza ownership, and the working theory was that it had been attacked by affiliates of United Bamboo as part of a gang war. Three of the dead were Taiwanese nationals, and one of them, called Big Liu, was a known organized crime member. Police were interviewing various employees. But the nature of the club's business, and its organized crime affiliations, seemed to have the effect of preventing witnesses from clearly recollecting the evening's events.

I briefed Dox and Delilah on what I'd heard from Tatsu, but other than that I stayed away from them. I told them it was operational, that it was better if we didn't get together unless we needed to. But there was more to it than that. I felt like I was on the edge of a precipice. If things went one way, I'd be safely back on firm ground. If they went the other, I'd be plunged into the abyss. Despite what had happened with Delilah in the van, I couldn't share the feeling with anyone else. I had to live with it alone.

That night, three United Bamboo members were shot to death in front of a club they ran in Shinjuku. The media was all over it again, treating the shootings as yet another street battle in an ongoing war between the yakuza and ethnic gangs. Tatsu called me about it. He said, 'You weren't behind this, were you?'

His voice was so weak, it hurt to hear it.

'No,' I said. 'I just learned of it.'

'It's good news, then. It means Yamaoto hasn't gotten the word out that you were behind Whispers. If he had, his people wouldn't be retaliating against the Chinese. I told you, Midori and your son are safe for the moment.'

'Not if Yamaoto lives.'

'He's still in the ICU. But his condition is improving.'

'Wonderful.'

'No, it's good,' he said, responding to my sarcasm. 'They may move him as early as tomorrow.'

'All right. Let me give you a list of the things I'll need.'

I told him. When I was done, he said, 'No problem.'

His voice was getting weaker. I said, 'How are you doing?'

'I'm . . . hanging on.'

I clenched my jaw. 'Don't stop, okay?'

'Okay.'

I wanted to say more. What came out was, 'Why don't you get some sleep? You can call me if you hear anything.'

'Okay,' he said again, and hung up.

47

The next morning, I did another hard workout and again it helped calm me down a little. I showered and shaved, ate a good breakfast at a nearby restaurant, then went out for a walk.

It was a sunny morning, cold and crisp. I walked east from the restaurant, past the caffeinated torrents of humanity flowing through and around Shinjuku Station, and eventually arrived at Shinjuku Gyoen park, where the chrysanthemums were enjoying their brief bloom. I wandered among the stalls and gardens, and for a while was able to lose myself in the small seas of yellows and pinks and purples.

As I was leaving the park, my cell phone rang. It was Tatsu. I flipped it open and said, 'Yeah.'

'They moved him this morning. Intermediate care. He's stable but very sedated. Tell me when you'll be ready.'

'I'm ready right now. How many people are watching him, who are they, and where?'

'There are seven of them. Three outside the room, two at each end of the corridor.'

'The nurses are putting up with that?'

'If you saw his men, you wouldn't argue with them, either.'

I thought for a moment. The layered security was smart. I couldn't get to the guards near the room without first engaging two on one end of the corridor. At a minimum, that would slow me down, giving the ones inside the perimeter time to prepare and the two at the opposite end time to move in as reinforcements.

'Didn't you say you were going to take care of this?' I asked.

'Yes. I'm going to have them all arrested.'

'I thought you couldn't . . . ' I started to say.

'I didn't say I'd be able to hold them for long. And yes, this little stunt will probably cost me my job. If they want to fire me, though, they'll have to hurry.' He laughed, then coughed.

The cough went on for a while. It sounded like he was drinking something, then it stopped.

'How soon can you be ready?' I asked.

'Give me an hour. I need to assemble a sizable unit. Yamaoto's men might be . . . uncooperative.'

'You got hold of those items I asked you about?'

'Of course.'

'Then we're good to go. I'm on my way now.'

48

An hour later, I was positioned in one of the stairwells on the surgical ward of Jikei hospital, one floor above Yamaoto. I was wearing standard-issue hospital scrubs. Nonstandard was the HK, in a hip holster underneath. But the gun was only backup and I didn't expect I'd have to use it. My primary weapon consisted of two syringes in the paper bag I was carrying. The first was filled with one hundred milliequivalents of potassium chloride. The second contained an equal amount of ordinary saline.

Saline is procurable anywhere, but unless you have access to appropriate raw materials and equipment, potassium chloride requires a prescription. Fortunately, despite his illness, Tatsu retained his knack for acquiring prohibited items. I had stopped by his room just a few minutes earlier and, as promised, he had what I'd asked for. He'd been pleased when I explained what I was going to do.

'Will it cause him to suffer?' he asked.

'No,' I told him, sorry to disappoint. 'It's the same stuff they use in lethal injections. It'll cause an instantaneous heart attack. You want suffering, we need more time.'

He nodded.

'I'll just shoot him if I have to,' I added. 'Or break his neck. But a potassium chloride injection is hard to detect. The cells release potassium naturally when they break down postmortem. And I think right now natural is better for us. It'll obscure the involvement of your men, my involvement, everything.'

He raised his eyebrows and said, deadpan, 'If I didn't know better, I'd suspect you'd done this before.'

'I'm just a quick study.'

He gave me a wan smile. 'Go. Let's finish this.'

And now I was waiting for his all-clear signal, telling me his men had hauled away Yamaoto's yakuza guards. I'd said nothing to Dox and Delilah. I could do this alone.

My cell phone buzzed. It was Tatsu.

'Go,' he said, his voice weak but eager. 'They're all cuffed and on the way down in the elevator. I've got two other men interviewing the nurses, away from their station, around the corner from Yamaoto's room. You'll only have a minute. Hurry.'

I was already heading down the stairs. 'I'm on my way,' I said, and clicked off. I pocketed the phone and pulled on a pair of surgical gloves and a surgical mask.

When I reached the landing of Yamaoto's floor, I paused and took a quick peek through the door. All clear, as Tatsu had promised.

I moved out and walked briskly down the corridor. Room 203, Tatsu had told me. And there it was. The door was ajar. I glanced inside. Again, all clear.

I walked in and closed the door behind me. Yamaoto was propped up in bed. He was pale and his eyelids were fluttering. His torso was bandaged from surgery and his chest sprouted two tubes that I imagined were there to keep his lungs expanded. A central IV line ran into his neck, feeding antibiotics and probably morphine directly into his jugular.

I walked to the side of the bed. Just to be safe, I moved the call button out of his reach. Then I took the potassium chloride syringe out of the bag and popped off the safety cap.

Yamaoto's eyes fluttered open. He looked at me, but said nothing. Probably he didn't recognize me behind the surgical mask. Or he was too doped up to even know what was going on. Didn't matter.

I kinked off the distal lines running into the central IV. I didn't want any of the potassium chloride to back up. Better to have it go straight to his heart as a single bolus.

I inserted the syringe into a port on the IV line.

Yamaoto smiled. 'It's not over,' he mumbled.

I looked into his eyes, pleased that he was conscious and understood who I was. 'No, it's over,' I said. 'It's been over since you killed my friend Harry. You just didn't get the memo. Well, here it is.'

I shoved the plunger down on the syringe, sending the potassium chloride rocketing toward his heart. Then I took out the saline syringe and repeated the procedure, flushing the dose forward even faster.

Yamaoto watched me. His smile didn't waver. I dropped the second syringe in the paper bag along with the first and looked up at the EKG monitor.

Within seconds, the pointy spikes that represented the proper functioning of his heart had abruptly been replaced by long, curvy sine waves. The potassium chloride had destroyed the muscle's electrical system and it was no longer contracting.

I looked at him. 'What was it you were saying?' I said. 'About this not being over?'

But his eyes had already lost focus. Now they rolled upward, his smile fading with them. His mouth went slack and his head sagged to the side.

I heard an alarm sounding at the nurses' station, warning them that one of their patients was having a cardiac arrest. I moved to the door and looked out into the corridor. Still all clear. I walked quickly back to the stairwell and paused there on the landing, watching the corridor through a crack in the door. It remained empty.

One of the nurses came running now, checking her monitors to see where the problem was located. She picked up a phone to call in the code, but it was already too late. No matter how fast a team moved, they'd have to know to use a huge dose of antidote to reverse the effects of the elephantine bolus I'd employed. And every second that passed before then brought Yamaoto closer to irreversible brain damage at a minimum, more likely closer to death.

I let the door close behind me and continued down to the lobby level. Yamaoto was finished. But there was still Kuro.

49

I went back to Tatsu's room. When he saw me, he raised his eyebrows expectantly.

'It's done,' I said, pulling up a chair next to his bed.

He took my hand and squeezed it. 'Thank you,' he rasped. 'Thank you.'

'There's one thing though. It might be nothing, but . . . '

'What?'

'Before he lost consciousness, he said to me, 'It's not over.' Maybe it was just bluster, but . . . Kuro's still missing. And Yamaoto told him at the club that I've been behind everything since New York.'

'I told you, you don't have to worry about Kuro.'

'Why not?'

'First, because Yamaoto's grudge against you was just that, a grudge. It doesn't extend to other members of his organization. Without him there to give orders, no one has any interest or incentive to try to harm you. Or your family.'

I nodded, not totally convinced. 'Is there a second reason?'

'Yes. Kuro is my informant.'

I looked at him, and felt a smile spreading across my face. 'Son of a bitch. No wonder your information's been so good.'

'Kuro was very unhappy with me after what

happened at Wajima. He thought Yamaoto would find out where the leak had come from and kill him for it. And he was nearly apoplectic after the shootout at his club. But I expect he'll be mollified now. No one is better positioned than he to take over Yamaoto's operations.'

'His colleagues aren't going to suspect he was behind all this?'

'They might. That fear has always inhibited him from moving against Yamaoto previously, despite my strong encouragement. That, and of course his fear about the consequences if a move against Yamaoto failed. But now we've given him a fait accompli. What else can he do but move aggressively to consolidate power?'

'What about the Chinese?'

'Kuro was always Yamaoto's conduit to the Chinese. If he doesn't tell them you were behind this, they'll have no reason to know. And even if he did tell them, would they believe it? More likely they would think you're a bogeyman he was making up to divert attention from yakuza responsibility for the massacres at Wajima and Whispers. No, I suspect Kuro will find a way to end this war simply by putting as much blame as possible on Yamaoto.'

I nodded, thinking about it. It sounded reasonable. But I expected it would be a while before it completely sank in.

'You see?' he asked. 'You can go to Midori and your son now. There's nothing stopping you.'

'I might do that,' I said. But the truth was, at that moment Midori and Koichiro felt farther away than ever.

'Just be sure to stop by before you leave town. I'd hate to miss you.'

'I'm not going anywhere right away. I'd like to spend some time with you, if that's okay.'

He squeezed my hand. 'It's fine. And I can promise not to keep you long.'

I shook my head. 'Come on, stop that.'

He shook his head. 'I have to. I wouldn't have known it, but this is the way I cope. And you have to admit, it's more becoming than self-pity.'

'Mildly,' I said, provoking a short laugh that degenerated into a cough. I got him his water and he sipped it through the straw.

My cell phone buzzed. I looked down and saw a 212 area code. It took me a second to recognize it and realize who it was.

'It's Midori,' I said, standing up.

He smiled. 'Perhaps this is fate.'

I walked over to the window and flipped open the phone. My heart was beating hard.

'Hi,' I said.

'Jun, two men just threatened me outside a club right before a gig. They had pictures of Koichiro and the nanny at a park, our address, my schedule, everything. They said they would hurt us if I didn't tell them where to find you!'

My stomach flipped and I felt like I was going to vomit. I took a deep breath and said, 'Slow down. Did they say who they were?'

'No. They were Japanese, yakuza from the way they looked and talked. You fuck, what did you do?'

'Take Koichiro. Right now, take him some-where no one would know to look for you. Don't use credit cards, don't use your cell phone . . . '

'I am not going to just pull the two of us out of our life! Because of you!'

'Midori, you have to . . . '

'No!'

I thought for a moment. 'Okay, it's going to be okay. I'm going to come out there, I'm going to take care of this.'

'Don't come out here, stay the hell away from us!'

'That's not going to solve the problem,' I said, surprised at the calm in my voice. 'Let's solve this problem, then you can do anything you want. Did you tell them anything? How to find me?'

'What could I tell them?'

'Okay, I'm going to check on something, then I'm going to call you back in fifteen minutes.'

I clicked off without even waiting for an answer. Tatsu was already pale from what he'd overheard. When I told him what had happened, he went white.

'What the fuck is going on?' I said. 'You just told me . . . '

'I told you, Kuro isn't in control yet. No one even knows yet that Yamaoto is dead.'

'Yeah, but when could Yamaoto have . . . '

'Maybe on the way from the club, in the limousine. Before he got to the hospital. Let me check.'

Tatsu picked up his phone and input a number. He asked questions. Listened. Asked more questions. Listened again. He said, 'Call them off.' He listened more, then swore and clicked off. He looked at me.

'Yes, it seems Yamaoto made the call on the way to the hospital. He sent two soldiers to New York. To pressure Midori and the child to get to you.'

'And if the pressure doesn't work?'

He didn't answer. He didn't need to. I could see it in his eyes.

'You told Kuro to call them off. What did he say?'

'He can't. The two men Yamaoto sent were his Praetorian guard, his personal killers, loyal only to him. Everyone else Kuro can reach. But these two have no connection to Kuro and won't take orders from him. Not even with Yamaoto dead.'

My stomach heaved again. I breathed in and out, in and out, willing my gorge back down.

I called Midori. 'I know what the problem is,' I said. 'And I can solve it. I'm on my way to the airport now. I'm going to catch an evening nonstop. I'll be at JFK' — I looked at my watch — 'tomorrow evening your time. I'll call you the second I land.'

There was a pause. She said, 'I hate you.'

I nodded. 'I know.'

50

I raced back to the hotel to get my passport, calling airlines to check on flights on the way. The next one I could get was a JAL nonstop that left at 7:05 that evening and arrived in New York at five in the evening of the same day. I booked a seat.

I checked out of the hotel and returned the van before catching a train to the airport. I could have asked Dox to take care of it for me, but I felt like if I didn't have a task I might explode.

On the way to the airport, my phone buzzed twice — once Dox, once Delilah. I didn't answer.

I thought about how I would find the two goons who had threatened Midori. I didn't expect it to be difficult. They'd be watching her now, waiting for me to show up. And I would show up. Just not where, when, or how they were expecting.

But then something I'd understood since the moment Midori called finally spoke up in conscious terms. It had been right there, in those three simple words: *I hate you.* But I hadn't wanted to acknowledge it.

No matter how this turned out, Midori would never again indulge my protestations about how I could get out of the life. That part was over. The best I could hope for now was merely to restore the way things had been before.

Everything else I'd fought for, everything else I'd wanted, had just been snatched away.

I had no appetite, but I stopped at a noodle place in the airport departure lounge and forced myself to eat. My body wanted to break into a sprint, but it was still way too early in the race for that. I needed to stay calm. Until it was time to not be calm.

When the plane started boarding, I found a quiet corner away from the lines and called Dox. He answered immediately. 'Hey, man, where've you been? You get my message?'

'I saw that you called. Sorry I wasn't able to get back to you until now.'

'Everything all right?'

'Yamaoto's dead. Heart attack in the hospital earlier today.'

There was a pause. Dox said, 'I knew you were going to go off and do something by yourself. Son, you're incorrigible. But nice work, and congratulations.'

'Yeah.'

'You should have called me, though.'

'I'm sorry. I can't put you at any more risk than I already have.'

'What are you talking about, 'risk'? We're partners, remember?'

'Listen. I can't talk long. My plane's about to leave for New York.'

'New York? What's going on?'

I told him about the call from Midori.

'Goddamnit, man, you didn't call me about this? I'm coming to the airport right now.'

'The plane's leaving now. You won't be able to

make it. Even if you came, by the time you got there it would already be done. One way or the other.'

'Goddamnit, John, you're being stupid! You've got friends, man, people who want to help you.'

'I don't need your help.'

'The hell you don't. You're not thinking clearly, it's obvious. Wait, hold on, I'm here having coffee with Delilah, she wants to talk to you.'

There was a pause, then Delilah said, 'John, what's going on?'

I told her about the call from Midori.

'Oh God,' she said. 'Why didn't you call us?'

The boarding line was getting smaller. 'It's not your fight,' I said.

'Yes, it is.'

I didn't respond. What was the point? *No it isn't, yes it is?*

'Dox told me why you didn't go after Yamaoto when he ran out of the club,' she said. 'You went back for me.'

Again I didn't respond. What happened at the club was already irrelevant.

'John, let us help you. Please.'

'Look, I appreciate it, I really do. But I have to go.'

'You set it up this way. You waited to call until it was too late. What, were you afraid we would persuade you to let us help?'

An announcement blared — last call for my flight. I said, 'My plane is leaving.'

'Wait. There's something I want to tell you

about New York . . . ' she started to say.

'Not now. We'll have another chance.'

'But . . . '

'I promise,' I said, and shut down the phone.

51

The twelve-hour flight to New York was torture.
I couldn't sleep, but I wasn't fully conscious,
either. Mostly I stared out the window into the
darkness and tried not to think. I felt like
Schrödinger's cat, trapped in a steel box, neither
dead nor alive, waiting for the intervention of
some outside event to resolve my ambiguous
state once and for all and deliver me from
purgatory.

I emerged from JFK customs and into the
arrivals lounge, dragging my carry-on behind
me. I scanned the crowds, just a guy coming off
a flight, looking for his ride. *Left, sweep the
middle, right, no problems up front. Now farther
back . . .*

Bam. A punch-permed stocky Japanese guy in
a waistlength black leather jacket, his mouth
twisted in a permanent ugly sneer, watching me
with studied nonchalance. Yakuza central cast-
ing, just as Midori had described.

My eyes didn't even pause on him. From his
perspective, it would seem I hadn't noticed him
at all.

I kept moving forward, looking around with
the same casual air. And there, at the opposite
end of the arrivals area, hanging back behind
some waiting people, another Japanese with a
punch perm, taller and even uglier than his
partner. Some men are built for stealth, others,

for intimidation. These two were obviously of the latter variety.

How did they know to wait for me here? They probably didn't, not for sure. But they knew Midori would contact me right after they threatened her. She told me she didn't tell them anything, but in her fright she might have mentioned Tokyo, just to give them something. From there, they could have figured out what would be the next nonstop from Narita to JFK, and wait outside arrivals. If it wasn't this one, it would be the next.

Then I started thinking, *But why not stay on Midori? That's the sure choke point. Maybe they thought they'd have more of a chance of surprising me here. Or maybe . . .*

Stop. I could figure it out later. What mattered was what was happening now.

I took the escalator down to the departure area, moving in such a way that I created several opportunities to unobtrusively check behind me as I walked. My friends were staying with me. Good.

I didn't think they'd move against me in here. There were too many cameras. But a bathroom? That would be too good an opportunity to miss. Jesus, I hoped that knife was still there.

A minute later, I headed into the restroom where I'd secured the Strider just before Dox and I had departed for Tokyo. I knew what the yakuza were thinking: *He just got off an international flight and has no checked bag, he can't possibly be armed. And there are no cameras in that bathroom, unlike just about everywhere else in the airport. We can do it and be on our way back to Japan before the police even know who they're looking for. Give him a minute to unzip, sit down, whatever, then he'll be maximally helpless. We'll do it then.*

How did I know? Hell, it's what I would do.

I walked in, the swinging door closing behind me. There were six stalls in this restroom. All of them were unoccupied. Except one.

The one where I had secured the knife.

Shit. With barely another thought, I said in the most stentorian tone I could muster, 'Sir, you need to evacuate this facility immediately.'

There was no response. I said, 'You, in the stall, sir. You need to evacuate this restroom immediately. Now.'

A voice came from behind the stall door. 'What?'

'Sir, this is an antiterrorism exercise. If you are not out of that stall and out of this restroom within the next ten seconds, I will have you arrested on the spot. One. Two.'

The toilet flushed on three. And I hadn't even gotten to seven when the guy burst out of the stall, struggling with his belt with one hand and a carry-on bag with the other. 'What the hell is this?' he said as he passed me.

'Classified, sir,' I said, as he reached the door. 'But thank you for your cooperation. And have a safe flight.'

I stepped into the stall, dropped down to my knees, and felt behind the toilet for the knife.

It wasn't there.

Come on, I thought. *Come on, come on . . .*

I knew this was the right stall — third from the door. I could even feel some of the adhesive from the duct tape, where it had come off on the porcelain. But the knife itself was gone.

Maybe someone had found it by accident. Or else airport security periodically swept public areas for contraband. It didn't matter. What mattered was what I was going to do next.

I got up and moved quickly to the handicap stall. It was the last one, farthest from the entrance, and, unlike the other stalls, the door on this one swung out, not in. I closed it behind me, but didn't engage the lock. When I let it go, though, it swung slowly outward.

Fuck. I grabbed some toilet paper, squeezed it into a small ball, and pulled the door closed on it. This time the door held.

I opened my bag and pulled out a pair of shoes and pants. I set the shoes down in front of the toilet and piled the pants on top of them. From outside the stall, at a glance, it would look natural enough.

I heard the swinging door open. Hot adrenaline spread through my chest and gut.

I sat on the toilet, took hold of the handicap railing on both sides, leaned back, and raised my feet in front of me.

In my acute state I heard the distinct sound of a folding blade clicking into place. Then another.

Footsteps, to my left. I breathed quietly through my mouth.

The footsteps came closer. Closer.

The footsteps stopped directly in front of me. I saw a shape through the crack at the edge of

345

the door. The shape started to move lower as the yakuza angled for a better peek.

I bellowed a war cry and shot my feet into the door. It exploded outward and blasted into the yakuza's face. He fell backward and something clattered to the floor.

I sprang out. The other yakuza was on my left, a blade in his right hand. Before he could get over the instant of shock produced by my yell and the sight of his partner going down, I bellowed again and grabbed his wrist with both hands.

I trained in judo at Tokyo's famed Kodokan for a quarter century. A quarter century of daily hours of gripping and twisting the heavy cotton *judogi*. More recently, I'd gotten addicted to Brazilian jujitsu in Rio. And on top of all that were my hand and finger exercises. I can say without any false pride that, when I grab someone's wrist, they might as well be caught in a bear trap.

I squeezed hard and the yakuza howled. His knife clattered to the floor. I stepped in close, grabbed his balls with an undergrip, and squeezed as hard as I could. He shrieked and doubled over.

The other guy was on his knees now, groping for his knife under the sinks. I grabbed him by his leather jacket and hauled him back. He tried to catch me with a donkey kick, but I'd anticipated that and was too far to his side. The kick snapped past me. I scooted toward his head, braced my hands on his back, and shot a knee into his face. He fell back. I dropped down, grabbed the knife, and rolled to my feet.

The other guy was staggering for the door now, still doubled over. I snagged one of his pants legs at the ankle and yanked it back toward me. He went sprawling forward onto his face. I did a knee drop onto his spine, mashed his face into the floor, and brought the knife up under his neck. I dug in, then tore out and away.

There was a wet gurgling noise, half cry, half bubbling liquid. I jumped back to get clear of the blood and turned to his partner. He was on his ass now, scuttling backward. His face was a bloody mess — from the door shot or the knee or both, I didn't know.

He bumped up against the wall and started to struggle to his feet. I kicked him in the balls and he folded forward with a grunt. I stepped behind him, hooked my fingers into his eyes, and hauled his head back. Then I brought the knife around and practically took his head off. Blood sprayed from the gaping wound and I shoved him away from me. He crashed into one of the stall doors and went down.

I looked at myself in the mirror. There was blood all over me. The jacket I was wearing was dark enough to conceal the problem, though, and I zipped it up higher. I rinsed my shaking hands under one of the faucets, closed the knife, and shoved it into a pants pocket. Then I rinsed my face and wet my hair, getting the blood off and changing my appearance at the same time.

The swinging doors opened. I glanced over. A black man in a suit started to walk inside. He froze when he saw the tableau. 'Oh, my God,' he said.

'I was attacked,' I said, in a high, frightened voice, looking at his feet to make it harder for him to see my face. 'Find a policeman. Please.'

He backed out through the door. I really had to hurry now.

I ducked into the handicap stall and shoved my pants and shoes into the carry-on. When I came out I had to jump over the pool of blood spreading on the tiled floor. I wanted to wipe down the surfaces I'd touched, but there just wasn't time. I went out the swinging doors. The area was clear. I kept my head down and headed straight for a taxi stand.

Ten minutes later, I was in the back of a cab, heading into Manhattan. I started to feel giddy. A crazy thought zigged through my mind — *Damn, the things you have to do to get a knife in New York* — and I almost laughed.

It was finally over with Yamaoto. I had just finished my last job. And Midori and Koichiro were safe.

52

I called Midori from the cab to let her know I was coming. But she didn't answer. I used the mobile browser on the phone to check her website. She had a gig at a place called Detour in the East Village. I called the club. The woman I spoke to told me Midori wouldn't be there that night. She had had to cancel.

'Do you know why?' I asked.

'No, I'm sorry. A personal matter, that's all I know.'

I told the driver to take me to Greenwich Village, corner of Seventh Avenue and Bleecker. I would walk to her apartment from there.

By the time the cab dropped me off, the trendy Village dinner scene was in full swing. I watched the laughing, contented hipsters and yuppies walking past me in their distressed leather jackets and Tod's shoes. It was like being on some surreal movie set.

I approached Midori's apartment carefully. Tatsu had said there were only two, but caution is a lifelong reflex for me.

When I was satisfied I wasn't going to run into another welcoming committee, I walked up to the front door. The doorman was there, the same guy as last time.

'I'm here to see Midori Kawamura,' I told him.

'Is she expecting you?'

'She should be.'

He nodded and went inside. I sensed I was supposed to wait, but I followed him in. He didn't protest.

He picked up the phone and input a number. A moment later, he said, 'Hello, Ms Kawamura. You have a visitor here. He says you're expecting him.'

He paused, then looked at me. 'What's your name?'

'Jun,' I said.

He repeated my name into the phone. Then he looked at me again and said, 'She can't come down.'

I snatched the phone out of his hand. He jumped back, startled. I raised the phone to my ear and said, 'Either you come down, or I'm coming up.'

There was a pause, then she said, 'Wait.'

I put the phone back in its cradle. The doorman looked at me, angry, obviously trying to decide what to do.

'Let it go,' I said, giving him a flat stare. 'You don't want to get in the middle of this.'

After a moment, he nodded. I stepped outside again and watched the street.

Two minutes later, Midori came out. She was wearing black jeans and a gray sweatshirt. Koichiro was in her arms, wrapped in the blue fleece blanket.

She was holding him with his back to me, but he twisted around and looked. When he saw my face, he smiled. I felt something crack inside me.

'I don't care how you feel about me,' I said. 'I

just came to tell you it's over. You're both safe.'

Her eyes darted left on the sidewalk, then right. Christ, she was jumpy. It wasn't like her. Well, no wonder.

'Do you understand what I'm saying?' I went on. 'Those men. They're not going to bother you anymore. No one's going to bother you.'

Koichiro said, '*Inu!*' Dog!

She speaks Japanese with him, I thought. It couldn't have been more of a non sequitur.

Damn, there was something about her, it felt like she was going to pop out of her skin.

'You're safe,' I said again.

She looked up and down the street.

'Yamaoto's dead, too,' I said. 'No one's going to . . .'

I looked at her, and all at once I realized. I just knew.

'They're not coming here,' I said, my voice sounding far away to me. 'You can stop looking around. They were already waiting, at the airport.'

She stared at me, saying nothing.

My mind knew it was true, but my heart wouldn't believe it. I tilted my head and looked at her as though seeing her for the first time. As indeed, in an important sense, I was.

'You knew I'd come running if you refused to hide,' I said slowly, almost thinking out loud. 'You knew that would get me on the first flight from Tokyo. And when I did just what you knew I would, when I told you I was on my way, you told them. You told them exactly where to wait.'

I kept looking at her, trying to take it all in.

351

She had set me up like a pro. I was trying to fit this new understanding of what she was capable of into the way I'd always known her, and I couldn't quite manage it.

'Do you know what they were going to do to me?' I asked, thinking, *Maybe she didn't, she couldn't have . . .*

She nodded and finally spoke. 'I know.'

I shook my head, trying to understand. 'Is this about your father?'

'No,' she said, holding Koichiro closer. 'It's about my son.'

I paused, then said, 'But I'd fixed everything. Those two were the last ones, and they're gone now, too. I'm done. I'm out, like I told you.'

She laughed harshly. 'And you accuse me of being in denial? What you do is like fighting a hydra. Everyone you kill, it creates two more. If you can't see that, you're insane.'

I didn't respond. My thoughts were sluggish. I felt dizzy, as though I'd been punched in the head.

Koichiro said, '*Inu!*' again.

I looked away, trying to collect myself.

'You know who showed up here right after you did?' I heard Midori say. 'Some blond bitch who said she knew you. She told me you were a danger to Koichiro and me, and warned me to stop seeing you. And you know what? She was right. She was absolutely right.'

I looked at her. 'She . . . came here?'

She shook her head in disgust. 'Why do you look so surprised? You're trailing a poisonous wake, Jun. And every port you pull into, it

352

washes up behind you.'

I licked my lips and tried to think of something to say. Nothing came out.

'Just go,' she said after a moment. 'Just go and never come back.'

I looked at Koichiro. He was still smiling at me, not understanding.

'What about Koichiro?' I said.

'When he's old enough, I'll tell him you're dead. That's what I was planning to do anyway, after tonight. And you are. You really are.' She turned and took him back inside without another word.

I stood there for a long time, watching the building, thinking maybe she would come out again, and I could explain better, or she could, or maybe in some other way we could make it as though none of this had really happened. I hadn't killed her father, I hadn't continually brought danger onto her and our son, she hadn't betrayed me to men who two hours earlier had tried to gut me in some airport toilet stall.

But she didn't come. And it all did happen.

I'd been ready to do anything to protect them, even suicide. I should have realized Midori would be willing to go at least that far.

I watched the building longer. Eventually I started to shiver. Finally I turned to go. It was strange to think how close my son was, and yet now how impossibly far.

53

I took a train to D.C. and spent a few sleepless hours in a motel there. I was reasonably sure the police in New York would have pictures of me from JFK video cameras. The pictures wouldn't be great, but I didn't want to take chances. New York area airports would be a bit hot for me for a while.

The next morning, I caught a flight to Los Angeles, and from there to Tokyo. I was only going back to see Tatsu. And for the money from Wajima.

By the time the plane took off from LAX, I was exhausted enough to sleep. I stayed down for almost the entire flight. It was much better than facing my wakeful thoughts.

It was getting dark when we landed. It felt like I was beginning to live in perpetual night.

When I was clear of customs at Narita, I turned on the Japanese cell phone. I had three messages waiting. Christ, I was going to need a damn secretary.

The first two were from Dox and Delilah, trying to reach me. The third was Kanezaki. He just said, 'Call me.'

I didn't want to, but it might have been something operational. I input his number.

'Hey,' he said after one ring, recognizing who it was from the caller ID display.

'You called?' I asked.

354

'Yeah. Dox gave me back the equipment. And he briefed me. Nice work.'

'If you're about to tell me I owe you a favor,' I said, my tone dangerously flat, 'you're picking a bad time.'

'It's not that at all. It's about Tatsu.'

My jaw tightened. 'What is it?'

'I went to see him today, like you told me. He's not good.'

'Yeah, no shit.'

He paused, then said, 'You want to tell me what the hell's up your ass?'

His gumption surprised me, and I couldn't help smiling. 'I would, but it would take too long.'

He said, 'Anyway, I was just calling to tell you. I know you probably already know and were probably already going to see him, but I thought I should say something just in case.'

I nodded. 'All right. Thank you.'

'There's something else. You've probably heard.'

'What?'

'Our old friend Yamaoto Toshi just died. Complications in the hospital after being treated for gunshot wounds.'

'Really.'

'Yeah. I couldn't help wondering whether it was actually some kind of assisted suicide.'

'I wouldn't know. He had a lot of enemies.'

He chuckled. 'We should talk,' he said. He paused, then added, 'No obligation.'

Right. 'Soon,' I said. 'But not now.' I clicked off.

I took the Narita Express to Tokyo Station. I

checked into a business hotel, where I showered, shaved, and changed my clothes. I went out to find a liquor store, and then to see Tatsu.

The bodyguard let me in. Tatsu's daughter was there again, holding his grandson, sitting by the bed. So was a nice-looking older woman who must have been Tatsu's wife.

Tatsu was sleeping. The daughter greeted me and introduced me to the older woman — her mother, and indeed, Tatsu's wife.

'He told us to wake him if you came,' the daughter said. 'But now I'm not sure.'

'No, let him sleep,' I said. 'He needs it.'

On cue, Tatsu opened his eyes and looked at us. He said, 'Nobody listens to me anymore.'

I laughed. Devious to the last.

'Can you stay for a bit?' he asked me.

I nodded. 'As long as you can stand me.'

He looked at his wife and daughter. 'Why don't you go home? You've been here all day and I know you're tired. I'm just going to talk to my friend for a little while, and then I think I'll sleep. Okay?'

The women got up. Like the first night I had been here, Tatsu kissed his grandson good-bye and whispered to him before they left. It was much more difficult for him this time, and twice he groaned in pain, but he did it.

When we were alone he said, 'I heard about New York.'

I wondered how he could have heard about Midori, and then realized he was talking about earlier, what had happened at the airport. I said, 'Kuro?'

He nodded. 'He's not unhappy. Those men were useless to him and might even have posed a threat. Kuro has no quarrel with you.'

'Good. I'm tired of quarreling.'

'Did you see Midori and your son?'

I nodded.

'And were you able to explain?'

I nodded again. 'I think so, yeah. I think it's going to be all right. It'll take a little time, but yeah.'

He smiled. It was a measure of how beaten and exhausted he was from his battle with the disease that my lie could slip past him.

'I brought you something,' I said, taking out the bottle I had picked up at the liquor store.

I handed it to him, but he was so weak I had to help him hold it. 'A Lagavulin sixteen-year-old,' he said, looking at the bottle. 'Oh, I've missed good whiskey.'

'You want to smell it?'

'Yes. And you have a drink for me, okay?'

'Okay.'

I poured an inch into each of two plastic cups. We touched them together and said, '*Kanpai*.'

I drained mine in one gulp. Tatsu inhaled deeply and smiled. 'It's the little things, isn't it,' he said.

'Yeah. I think that's true.'

'You know, Kanezaki visited me today.'

'Really?'

He nodded. 'You should stay in touch with him. We were . . . working on something together at one point. It might interest you.'

I wondered if this had anything to do with the

'favor' that, sooner or later, Kanezaki was going to extract from me.

'Yeah,' I said. 'I had a feeling you guys were collaborating a little more than either of you ever let on.'

'He's a good man.'

I laughed. 'He just reminds you of yourself.'

He smiled. 'You know, he's the same age my son would have been.'

'You miss him, don't you,' I said.

He nodded. 'Every day. But I'm going to see him soon.'

I argued with him neither about when he was going nor where. Anyone could see he didn't have long. And who was I to tell him what he might find afterward?

We sat quietly for a few minutes. He said, 'Go ahead, have another drink. I'm still working on mine.'

I poured myself another and we toasted again. I drank and he inhaled and we sat a little longer.

'I've got a favor to ask you,' he said.

'Anything.'

'There's a package on the top shelf of that closet. Will you get it for me?'

I got up and brought back the package he had asked for. It was wrapped in brown paper and string. I started to hand it to him, but he shook his head. 'Go ahead, open it,' he said.

I did. Inside was another bottle of potassium chloride and a syringe.

I looked at him and he nodded. '*Onegai shimasu*,' he said. Please.

All at once I realized why he had been asking

358

me if Yamaoto would suffer.

I shook my head. 'Don't ask me to do that. Tatsu, please.'

'With Yamaoto done, I have nothing to concentrate on to get me past the pain. I can't take it anymore. And I don't want to spend my last days in a morphine haze.'

'Tatsu, I can't.'

'This is killing my family, too. My wife sits with me and I hear her crying when she thinks I'm asleep.'

'What about your grandson? You said . . . '

'God help me, it's not enough anymore.'

'But you talk to him. I've seen you, whispering to him.'

'Yes. And tonight I said good-bye. And that I would try to watch out for him.'

I looked around, trying to find an argument. I gestured to his chest. 'Look, they've got you hooked up to the heart monitor. They'll just rush in here and resuscitate you. I don't . . . '

'If you're telling me you have no way around something like this, I'm going to be very disappointed.'

I shook my head and didn't speak.

'Is there a way around it? Rain-san, please.'

I closed my eyes and nodded.

He reached over and took my hand in his. 'Then do it.'

I waited for a long time, looking into his eyes, hoping I would see his resolve slacken. It didn't.

I undid the two top buttons on my shirt, reached over, and took hold of the adhesive pad over his heart. I looked at him. He nodded.

I pulled the pad free and stuck it onto my own chest.

We sat like that for a minute, very still. I looked up at the monitor and watched the tracings of my own heart. It was beating as fast as it was hard.

The nurse stuck her head in. 'Ishikura-san, are you all right?'

Tatsu smiled. 'I'm fine.'

My back was to her. She couldn't see the wire snaking into my shirt.

She nodded. 'There must have been a glitch in one of the machines. Sorry to disturb you.'

Tatsu said, 'That's all right. Could you send my man in, please?'

She nodded and left.

The bodyguard came in a moment later. Tatsu said, 'It's late. Why don't you take the rest of the night off?'

The bodyguard said, 'Sir, my replacement won't be here for another thirty . . . '

'It's fine. My friend here will watch over me until then.'

'Sir . . . '

Tatsu looked at him, and for a moment he seemed his old formidable self. 'Don't make me ask you again,' he said.

The bodyguard nodded crisply and walked out.

Tatsu settled back in his bed and groaned. The effort of momentarily projecting that fierce persona had exhausted him.

'All right,' he said, gesturing to the IV line in his arm.

I filled the syringe and pushed the needle into a distal port on the main line. The tears I'd been fighting welled up in my eyes and spilled over.

'I've always wondered how you go about your work,' he said.

I looked at him. 'I don't usually cry while I'm at it.'

He laughed weakly. 'I won't tell anyone.'

I kinked the main IV line above the port and closed it with the string from the package. We were ready to go. But still I hesitated.

'Rain-san, what are you waiting for?'

I squeezed his hand hard and looked at him. 'You've been a good friend to me,' I said. 'Thank you.'

He smiled. 'And you to me. There's no one else I could ask. You know that, don't you?'

I nodded, but couldn't speak.

'Take care of your family now,' he said. 'There's nothing more important than that. Watch over your boy.'

I nodded again, the tears running harder.

'I've waited a long time to see my son,' he said. 'Please, help me go to him now.'

I squeezed his hand harder and shoved down the plunger.

He was looking at me, and then all at once he was looking somewhere beyond me, someplace I couldn't see. Maybe at someone.

The pressure from his hand diminished, and then was gone.

I withdrew the syringe, put it back in the bag, and unkinked the IV line. I closed his eyes and sat with him, holding his hand, feeling empty and miserable and alone.

After a few minutes, I leaned forward and kissed his forehead. 'Be with your son,' I said.

I took a deep breath, switched the monitor back to his chest, and stood.

The nurse came rushing in a moment later. 'Something's wrong,' I said. 'I don't think he's breathing.'

She raced around the bed so quickly and started checking on him so intently that she didn't even notice when I walked quietly away.

54

I went to a bar I liked, D-Heartman, on one of the backstreets in Ginza. Heartman is an old but elegant place, all mahogany paneling and low light and bartenders in formal pleated shirts and black bow ties. They take their cocktails seriously and have an excellent selection of single malts, and it was just what I needed at the moment.

I called Dox when I got there and told him where he could find me, if he wanted to.

'How did it go in New York?' he asked.

'It went fine. They're all dead.'

Something in my tone must have told him not to inquire further for now. He said, 'You going to call Delilah? She's still here.'

'I don't want to see her. If you want to come, come alone.'

I took the elevator up to the sixth floor and walked inside. The two bartenders bowed when I came in and welcomed me with a low 'Irasshaimase.' I told them I wanted the window seat, and someone walked me over. Heartman does most of its business after midnight, and for the moment I had the place to myself.

I ordered a sixteen-year-old Lagavulin, straight. I sipped and watched the quiet street below. I focused on the taste, the smell, the feeling in my throat. I tried not to think.

Dox showed up forty-five minutes later. I had

just ordered my fourth Lagavulin. My head felt mercifully fuzzy.

He sat down across from me. 'Should I order what you're having, or is it that medicine-tasting stuff?'

'Oh, it's medicine,' I said.

He turned to the waiter. 'I'll just have a double Stoli on ice. Ah, make that a triple. I think I've got some catching up to do.'

I translated, then said, 'I didn't think you'd still be around.'

'Where'd you expect me to go?'

I shrugged. 'I don't know. Where you live. Wherever that is.'

'As it happens, I'm transitioning to a place in Bali I know. I like it there. Our little score at Wajima ought to speed things up for me, too. But I thought I'd spend some time in Roppongi first. Plus I was hoping you'd be back and we'd get to see each other.'

The waiter brought our drinks and moved off.

'Cheers,' Dox said.

We touched glasses. Dox leveled off about two-thirds of his vodka and let out a long, contented sigh. He leaned back in his chair and said, 'You going to tell me what happened in New York?'

I told him all of it. I felt detached as I recounted things, as though I was listening to someone else talking. Must have been the booze.

When I was done, he said, 'Goddamn, man. I'm sorry to hear that. Truly.'

I nodded and drained my glass. Dox did the same and signaled the waiter for two more.

'But you know,' he went on, 'they're safe now. And with Yamaoto dead, so are you.'

'Yeah,' I said. 'They're safe.'

'What I mean is, give it time. You're that boy's father, and nothing can ever change that. Eventually, Midori's going to come to her senses. She's freaked out now, of course she is, but that's not going to last forever. Blood is a powerful thing, partner.'

I laughed without mirth. 'That's funny, she said the same thing.'

The waiter brought us the drinks. He collected our empty glasses and moved on.

Dox took a swallow and said, 'I know what's going on with you and Delilah, man.'

I looked at him. 'What do you know?'

'That you've gotten your signals crossed one too many times.'

'Is that what you call it? You know what she did? She went to New York to try to scare Midori away. And she's so good at what she does, it worked.'

'I know what she did. She told me. She feels awful about it. She tried to tell you when you were leaving for New York, but she says you wouldn't listen.'

'What is there to talk about? She did what she did.'

'She made a mistake, is what she did. And she knows it.'

'Yeah? Well, fuck her.'

'Pardon me for saying so, partner, but is it possible you're being just a tad ungrateful here?'

I took a swallow of the whiskey and glared at him.

He stared right back. 'You know, she flew halfway around the world and risked her life to help you with your problem. She killed one man who was trying to get the drop on you. And she killed two more the moment she realized they would harm your family if they lived.'

'You know why she came out here? She felt guilty over the little op she pulled on Midori behind my back. The one Midori was so freaked out by, it made her set me up to be killed.'

'Who cares why she came? That woman is devoted to you, son, only you're so eager for an excuse to go back to your 'it's me all alone against the world' bullshit that you won't even admit it.'

I looked at him. 'What do you want from me, Dox?'

'I want you not to become the miserable recluse part of you insists on being.'

'You want me to tell you I'm hurt? I feel betrayed? Well, I won't. I don't need your shoulder to cry on.'

'Yes you do, partner. You need someone's.'

'You're wrong.'

'I see what you're doing. You got hurt 'cause you trusted. And now you're telling yourself, 'See? I was right not to trust, this is what happens when you trust. Well, I'll just never trust again, that's what I'll do.''

'Are you coming up with this shit yourself, or have you been talking to Delilah?'

'She sees it, too. But that doesn't mean much.

366

You're so damn obvious.'

'You know, the two of you understand each other so well, why don't you just take her. You've been spending enough time with her, from the sound of it.'

'Oh, this is the part where you make the outrageous accusations to insult your friend so he leaves and spares you the burden of having to admit that you're the asshole who pushed him away.'

I put my elbows on the table and rested my face in my hands.

'It ain't like that between Delilah and me,' he said, 'and you know it. But it is like that between the two of you. And if you walk away from that now, you are the biggest fool I've ever known.'

I looked at him. 'She sent you here to plead her case, is that it?'

'No, dumbass, you told me not to invite her, remember? She doesn't even know you're back in Tokyo, and she's worried about you, too. I'll call her and tell her, otherwise I'll be complicit in your childish nonsense. But if you were smart you'd call her first.'

I finished my whiskey and stood up. 'Do whatever you want,' I said, throwing some bills on the table. 'I just came back to pick up my money.'

55

I went back to Rio. It wasn't home, just where I was living for the moment. But I had nowhere else to go.

I stayed up late and got up late and took a lot of walks. I read some books of the embarrassingly self-help persuasion. None had quite the title I was looking for — *Killer's Ten-Step Conscience Cure*, maybe, or *Your Best Life After Betrayal*, something like that — but I picked up a few insights along the way.

More than anything else, I threw myself into grueling jujitsu workouts. At first, I thought I was having control issues not so different from what drives people with eating disorders. Then I thought maybe it was some kind of age-denial thing, because if you can do two hours of nonstop matwork in an un-air-conditioned room during Rio's December summer, it must mean you're immortal.

But as the workouts grew more intense, resulting in a series of minor injuries, I realized what was really going on. I was trying to punish myself. Because, deep down, I knew everything Dox had said to me at Heartman was true.

Sometimes I think the urge to believe in our own worldview is our most powerful intellectual imperative, the mind's equivalent of feeding, fighting, and fornicating. People will eagerly twist facts into wholly unrecognizable shapes to fit them into existing suppositions. They'll ignore the obvious, select the irrelevant, and spin it all into a tapestry of self-deception, solely to justify an idea, no matter how impoverished or self-destructive.

And that's what I'd been doing. What had Dox called it? My 'it's me all alone against the world bullshit,' that was it. And to support that bullshit, I'd been deluding myself in a variety of areas.

For one thing, I'd been making too much of Midori's memory. Yes, we had chemistry. And the time we'd been pursued by Yamaoto in Tokyo had involved enough friction so that sparks were inevitable. But after our split, I wanted to believe that whatever had been between us was unique, that it could never happen again. Because if it was exceptional, it must be an exception, maybe even the exception that proved the rule. And the rule was that I would always be alone, and could never trust anyone.

But my partnership with Dox didn't fit comfortably with that rule. And my relationship with Delilah suggested that Midori hadn't just been a one-off, either. So now, some wretched part of me was intent on turning Dox and Delilah into exceptions, too, so it could pat itself on the back and proclaim, 'See? I told you so.'

What I was doing, I was sabotaging myself. Well, it was time I stopped.

One day, I called Delilah on her cell phone. When she answered, I asked her, 'How would it be if I came to see you?'

There was a long pause. She said, 'I don't know. How would it be?'

'I'm not sure. But I'd like to find out.'

There was another pause. She said, 'So would I.'

'Where are you? Paris?'

'No, I'm back in Barcelona.'

'Different cover?'

'No. I just need someplace new for a while.'

'How did things turn out at work?'

'The review is over. They told me they were going to give me a formal reprimand. I told them if they did they could kiss my ass and find someone else to do what I do. Now they're rethinking.'

'What are you going to do now?'

'I don't know. I could use someone to talk about it with, though.'

'I'd like that. I could use someone to talk with, too.'

'How soon can you be here?'

I paused, then said, 'I'll be on the next fucking flight, if you'll have me.'

She laughed and said, 'Well, what are you waiting for?'

I smiled. 'Let me go take care of the travel stuff. I'll call you back.'

There was a flight on Iberia, leaving at four o'clock that very day. I booked a seat and told Delilah I was coming. Then I called Dox.

'It's me,' I said. 'John.'

'Yeah? John who?'

I smiled. 'Nice try. Pretty soon you're going to be angling to get me to say my social security number over the phone. But you can only push me so far.'

He laughed. 'How you doing?'

'I'm all right. I've been doing some thinking.'

'Well, that sounds promising.'

'Yeah. I owe you an apology.'

'That's the truth.'

There was a pause. I said, 'Well, I apologize.'

'All right, I accept. Too bad you're not here, I'd give you one of those hugs you crave.'

'Yeah, I'm broken up about that, too.'

We were quiet for a moment. I said, 'You know, you called me a dumbass.'

'Well, you were acting like one. I didn't mean to imply that the condition was permanent. That's up to you. Sounds like maybe you've opted for something better.'

'Maybe 'recovering dumbass.''

He laughed again. 'You talk to Delilah?'

'I'm going to see her later today.'

'Good. You let me know how that works out, all right?'

'I will.'

There was another pause. I said, 'Where are you, Bali?'

'Yeah, I'm building a house out here. You ought to come see it.'

'I'd like that. And if you need a break, why don't you come out to Barcelona?'

'That where you're going to see Delilah?'

'Yeah. You should come out. You know, the three of us never had a chance to celebrate after what we did in Tokyo. And you're rich now, you can afford the flight.'

He laughed. 'That's true. Tell you what, I'll come out today.'

'Uh, maybe you should wait just a few . . . '

He laughed again. 'I'm pulling your leg, man. You two have a lot to talk about and I don't want to be in the way. Plus I reckon you'll need some of the old conjugal time together. So I'll tell you what. You call me in a few days or a week, and if everyone's amenable it'll be my pleasure to come out and pop some of the bubbly.'

I found myself thinking of Tatsu. I said, 'You're a good friend to me, Dox. Thank you.'

'Don't mention it, man. I'll see you soon, here or there.'

I caught a cab to the airport. I watched through the window as the city's famed beaches went by, and was pleased to think that in just a little over half a day I would be walking along their Mediterranean counterpart.

I thought about my son. I wasn't going to have the relationship with him I'd been hoping for. I couldn't be part of his life. But forever? That's a long time. Maybe Dox was right. Blood matters, and not just in the way Midori had suggested. I couldn't be with my son today, but in five years? Ten? I didn't know. The uncertainty wasn't a happy prospect, true, but it was better than accepting that I would never see him at all. It was better than if he had never even existed. It was a hard path ahead, I thought, but on balance, I ought to be grateful for it.

And Tatsu had told me to watch over my boy. I wanted to do that. Not just for the child. And not just for myself, either. But for Tatsu. Fate had denied him a life with his son, and it had been important to him that my fate be different.

I would try to make it so.

Still, I couldn't deny the justice in Midori's urge to keep Koichiro from me. I had told her Yamaoto and the two thugs in New York were the last, that it was over, I was out. But Dox was still in the life, and so, probably, was Delilah, and if either of them ever needed me I'd have to be dead not to come running.

And then there was Kanezaki, and the 'favor' I owed him. I didn't know what it was, but it was a safe bet it would involve more than watering his houseplants while he was out of town.

But why think about all that now, on my way to see Delilah? Barcelona had been an interlude before. It could be one again.

No, that wasn't quite right, I realized. Barcelona hadn't been an interlude. It had been . . . an armistice.

But that was all right, too. An armistice wasn't so bad. It was better than being at war. And if I could find a way to another armistice, and then another, maybe I could string them all together, and one day they'd actually add up to peace.

One day.

Acknowledgments

Once again, I've written a book that has been made much better through the generous contributions of many friends. My thanks to:

My agents, Nat Sobel and Judith Weber of Sobel Weber Associates, and my editor, Dan Conaway (aka Mad Max Perkins) of Penguin, for always steering me toward the truth and never letting me get lazy.

Michael Barson (master of Yubiwaza) of Penguin, for introducing Rain to New York's Ear Inn, and for doing such an amazing job of getting out the word on the books.

Massad Ayoob of the Lethal Force Institute, for sharing his awe-inspiring knowledge of and experience with firearms, tools and tactics, for the great instruction at the LFI I (see you at II, Mas), and for helpful comments on the manuscript.

Tony Blauer, for teaching Rain the SPEAR technique he uses in the combat sequence outside Midori's apartment, and Mike Suyematsu, certified Blauer PDR instructor and a guy who shares Rain's roots, for terrific CQC instruction and for helping me choreograph the SPEAR sequence.

Matt Furey, for again providing some of the Combat Conditioning bodyweight exercises that Rain uses in this book to stay in top shape (and that his author uses, too).

Dan Levin, for sharing his remarkable knowledge of Japanese swords and swordsmanship, and for helpful comments on the manuscript.

Peyton Quinn of Rocky Mountain Combat Applications Training and author of *A Bouncer's Guide to Barroom Brawling and Real Fighting*, for his concept of the previolence 'interview.'

Ernie Tibaldi, a thirty-one-year veteran agent of the FBI, for continuing to generously share his encyclopedic knowledge of law enforcement and personal safety issues, and for helpful comments on the manuscript.

Novelist Marcus Wynne, for sharing his experience with knives (particularly the FS Hideaway), tactics, and the Special Ops community.

Again and always, *sensei* Koichiro Fukasawa of Wasabi Communications, a singular window on everything Japan and Japanese, for years of insight, humor, and friendship, and for helpful comments on the manuscript.

Yukie Kito, for introducing Rain to Shinagawa, a part of Tokyo with which Rain was insufficiently familiar, for keeping an eye out for Dox in the Shinagawa Station Starbucks, and for helpful comments on the manuscript.

Patricia Escalona, Sylvia Fernandez, Carlos Ramos, Blanca Rosa, and everyone else at Roca Editorial, my Spanish publisher, for introducing Rain to the bars of El Born, Torre d'Alta Mar restaurant, La Florida Hotel, and so many other marvelous places in the marvelous city of Barcelona.

Naomi Andrews, for guiding me on all things

French and Parisian, and for helpful comments on the manuscript; Joshua Geller, for sharing his expertise on the New York jazz scene; Lori Kupfer, for continued insights into what sophisticated, sexy women like Delilah wear and how they think, for advice on New York and Paris museums, art, and shopping, and for helpful comments on the manuscript; and Chad and Christi, for making Rain feel so welcome at Milk & Honey.

Roberta Parks, M.D., Owen Rennert, M.D., Evan Rosen, M.D., Ph.D., and Peter Zimetbaum, M.D., for offering no-longer-reluctant expert advice on some of the killing techniques in this book, and for helpful comments on the manuscript.

The extraordinarily eclectic group of philosophers, badasses (mostly retired), and deviants who hang out at Marc 'Animal' MacYoung's and Dianna Gordon's www.nononsenseselfdefense.com, without whose imagination and expertise Rain and Dox could never have prevailed against the sumos. In particular, thanks to Dave Bean, for sharing his encyclopedic knowledge of all things forbidden, including a firebomb sequence that didn't quite make it into the final version of this story; Wim Demeere of the Grinding Shop, for his friendship, great CQC instruction, and enthusiasm for John Rain; Dr Maude Dull, for saving lives when she can and comforting the bereaved when she can't, and for her unusual attempts to get Rain to kill a pig by natural causes (next time, Maude, I promise . . .); Jack 'Spook' Finch, Mr Lawsey, Lawsey himself, veteran of the Vietnam War's Easter Offensive, Operation Just Cause, Operation Desert Storm, and Silver Star awardee, for sharing his experiences with 'the cost of it,' for teaching Dox to carry more blades than a combine, and for helpful comments on the manuscript; Montie Guthrie, for sharing his knowledge and experience with firearms, tools and tactics, for becoming sexually stimulated by the 'love scenes,' and for helpful comments on the manuscript; and Michael 'Mama Duck' Johnson, for helping Rain find a knife in New York. A special thank you to Marc MacYoung and Slugg, experts on criminal behavior, operator mindsets, combat tactics (Delilah's 'finishing move' in Barcelona, for example, is Marc's), and tradecraft, without whose experience, insights, and stern beyond-the-call-of-duty comments on the manuscript John Rain might not have survived this story.

My friends at Café Borrone in Menlo Park, California, for serving the best breakfasts — and especially coffee — that any writer could ask for.

Eve Bridberg, Vivian Brown, Alan Eisler, Judith Eisler, Shari Gersten and David Rosenblatt, Tom Hayes, novelist Joe Konrath, Sarah Landis, Doug Patteson, Matt Powers, Sandy Rennert, Ted Schlein, Hank Shiffman, Pete Wenzel, and Caryn Wiseman, for helpful comments on the manuscript and many valuable suggestions and insights along the way.

Most of all, to my wife, Laura, who helps me conceive and revise these books, and then enjoys them, like no one else. Thanks, babe.

Author's Note

The Barcelona, New York, Tokyo, and Wajima locales that appear in this book are described, as always, as I have found them. I don't know whether Tokyo CIA station stockpiles the kind of hardware that Kanezake provides Rain and Dox. Tokyo's Jikei hospital has no separate cancer ward that I know of, but it did a first-rate job of patching me up after my eighteen-foot fall to the Shibuya concrete in 2001.

We do hope that you have enjoyed reading this large print book.

Did you know that all of our titles are available for purchase?

We publish a wide range of high quality large print books including:
Romances, Mysteries, Classics
General Fiction
Non Fiction and Westerns

Special interest titles available in large print are:
The Little Oxford Dictionary
Music Book
Song Book
Hymn Book
Service Book

Also available from us courtesy of Oxford University Press:
Young Readers' Dictionary
(large print edition)
Young Readers' Thesaurus
(large print edition)

For further information or a free brochure, please contact us at:
Ulverscroft Large Print Books Ltd.,
The Green, Bradgate Road, Anstey,
Leicester, LE7 7FU, England.
Tel: (00 44) **0116 236 4325**
Fax: (00 44) **0116 234 0205**

Other titles published by
The House of Ulverscroft:

ONE LAST KILL

Barry Eisler

Freelance assassin John Rain has a new employer — the Mossad, which wants him to fix a 'problem' in Manila — and a new partner — Dox, the ex-Marine sniper whose laid-back style masks an operator every bit as deadly as Rain himself. But when Rain's conscience causes him to hesitate and botch an assignment, he discovers that he's become the ruthlessly efficient Israeli intelligence agency's next target. And when Delilah, the Mossad agent he once fought, then loved, suddenly reappears in his life, he can't be sure whether she's there to help him — or to finish him off.

CHOKE POINT

Barry Eisler

Ex-government assassin John Rain is trying to leave his violent past behind him . . . But when his former employer, the CIA, tracks him down in Brazil, he is persuaded to take on a high-risk assignment well suited to his particular skills: to end a man's life leaving no trace of murder; to bring death by natural causes . . . This time, it's clear the man deserves to die and Rain sees the job as a shot at redemption. But before he can even get close, he'll need all of his formidable talents simply to survive. Because Rain is not the only killer closing in on the target — and it could be that the entire mission is an elaborate cover for an even more sinister set up.

HIDE

Lisa Gardner

The case had always haunted Bobby Dodge and now, in an underground chamber, the gruesome discovery of six mummified corpses resurrects his nightmare: the return of a killer he thought dead and buried. Bobby's only clue is a locket discovered with one of the dead — engraved with a name . . . Annabelle Granger has always been hiding, never knowing what her family was running from. When the body bearing her locket is unearthed, the danger is inescapable — but this time she won't run. Could it be the dead psychopath's copycat, his protégé — or something more terrifying? Dodge must solve the mystery of Annabelle Granger by teaming up with a woman who may be as dangerous as the new killer — a survivor-turned-avenger, with an eerie link to Annabelle . . .

THE AFGHAN

Frederick Forsyth

When British and American intelligence
discover a major Al Qaeda operation in the
works, they need information about the
attack. What can they do? With no sources in
Al Qaeda, it's impossible to plant someone.
Unless . . . The Afghan is Izmat Khan, a
prisoner of Guantanamo Bay, and a former
commander of the Taliban. The Afghan is also
Colonel Mike Martin, a 25-year veteran of
war zones around the world, born and raised
in Iraq. For the intelligence agencies will
attempt to pass off Martin as the trusted
Khan . . . He'll need extraordinary luck —
nothing can prepare Martin for the dark
world he is about to enter. Or for the terrible
things he will find there . . .